MORE
Than WORDS

MORE

JUDITH MILLER

Than WORDS

DAUGHTERS OF AMANA

BETHANYHOUSE
MINNEAPOLIS, MINNESOTA

Cover design by Lookout Design, Inc.
Cover photography by Aimee Christenson
With special recognition to The Amana Historical Society.

Scripture quotations are from the King James Version of the Bible.

Published by Bethany House Publishers
11400 Hampshire Avenue South
Bloomington, Minnesota 55438

Bethany House Publishers is a division of
Baker Publishing Group, Grand Rapids, Michigan.

Printed in the United States of America

Library of Congress Cataloging-in-Publication Data

Miller, Judith, 1944–
    More than words / Judith Miller.
        p.   cm.
    ISBN 978-0-7642-0643-6 (pbk.)
    1. Amana Society—Fiction. 2. Young women—Fiction. [1. Iowa—History—19th century—Fiction.] I. Title.
    PS3613.C3858M66   2010
    813'.6—dc22

                                                                        2010014685

To Jim
I love you—
more than words

Books by

Judith Miller

FROM BETHANY HOUSE PUBLISHERS

The Carousel Painter

DAUGHTERS OF AMANA
Somewhere to Belong
More Than Words

BELLS OF LOWELL*
Daughter of the Loom
A Fragile Design
These Tangled Threads

LIGHTS OF LOWELL*
A Tapestry of Hope
A Love Woven True
The Pattern of Her Heart

POSTCARDS FROM PULLMAN
In the Company of Secrets
Whispers Along the Rails
An Uncertain Dream

THE BROADMOOR LEGACY*
A Daughter's Inheritance
An Unexpected Love
A Surrendered Heart

*with Tracie Peterson

JUDITH MILLER is an award-winning author whose avid research and love for history are reflected in her novels, many of which have appeared on the CBA bestseller lists. Judy and her husband make their home in Topeka, Kansas.

But the Lord said unto Samuel, Look not on his countenance, or on the height of his stature; because I have refused him: for the Lord seeth not as man seeth; for man looketh on the outward appearance, but the Lord looketh on the heart.

1 Samuel 16:7

CHAPTER 1

April 1885
Homestead Village
Amana Colonies, Iowa

"Come down from that tree, *Oma*!" I'd done my best to sound firm. Taking a sideways step, I shaded my eyes to gain a better view among the bloom-laden branches of the apple tree.

My grandmother peered down at me with a devilish grin, her leather-clad feet wedged into a crook of the tree. "*Nein*, Gretchen! I'm going to get an apple." She pointed a gnarled finger toward a spindly branch bearing a few spring blossoms.

"Don't go any further, Oma. There aren't any apples, and that branch won't hold you."

Ignoring me, she grabbed another limb and hiked her right leg toward a scrawny branch that would surely crack under her weight. The old woman's addled brain might be willing to make the climb, but her aged and fragile body was going to end up on the ground.

After steadying the ladder that Oma had placed against the tree trunk, I lifted my skirt and stepped onto the bottom rung. "Just wait until Stefan gets home!" I issued the muttered warning from between clenched teeth and cautiously began my climb. No matter how often I scolded my brother, Stefan never put anything away. He'd used the ladder to retrieve a ball from the roof yesterday afternoon, and instead of putting it back into the shed, he'd left it sitting outdoors. Out where it created an alluring diversion for Oma, who had somehow managed to drag it across the yard and balance it against the apple tree.

A low-hanging branch snagged my finely knit black cap, and Oma chuckled as she watched my attempts to disentangle the head covering. After finally grabbing the cap and giving it a one-handed shove onto my head, I glanced upward but quickly averted my eyes. "Oma! Put your leg down. I can see your undergarments."

She leaned forward and peeked down, as if she intended to check the truth of my statement. Her body listed sideways, and one foot slipped from the branch. A snowstorm of flowering blossoms showered down on me.

"Hold on, Oma! I'm coming up to help you."

"Don't bring the blackbird," she shrieked. "It will eat the apples."

My frustration mounted as Oma continued the childlike behavior. For all of my life, my mother's mother had lived with us, and we shared a special bond. But when these bouts of dementia took hold, there was no dealing with her. "There are no blackbirds and there are no apples, Oma." I took another step up the ladder and reached for a thick branch. The rough bark dug into my palm as I tightened my hold. If I inched a little closer, I could grab hold of her leg.

"Go away! You're bringing the blackbird with you."

She climbed higher into the tree, and I gasped in fear. Now I couldn't even reach her foot. "There are no birds in the tree, Oma. I've frightened them all away. Come back down to me."

She peered over her shoulder. A flash of terror shone in her dark eyes. Her once-gentle lips twisted in a menacing jagged line. The look would have held a stranger at bay, but I wasn't a stranger, and I wouldn't be deterred.

"There's a blackbird on your head," she cried. "Get it away! Shoo it off before it eats my apples."

Utter defeat shot through me. Would I ever learn to deal with Oma's episodes? If I didn't get her out of the tree within the next few minutes, my father might discover the dilemma. That thought alone propelled me back into action. I yanked the hat from my head. "The blackbird flew away. See, Oma? Look at me!"

Lips curved in a toothy grin, she leaned forward, peered around my shoulder, and cooed, "Pretty boy, come and get me."

"Oma! Please come . . ." I lifted my foot to mount the next rung but was stopped short when two strong hands encircled my waist. I grabbed hold of the ladder and glanced over my shoulder. "Conrad." I exhaled my friend's name along with a silent hallelujah.

"Come down, Gretchen. I'll get her." His hands remained clasped around my waist while I descended to the ground. With one sympathetic gaze, I was enveloped in comfort. He touched a finger to my trembling lips, and warmth spiraled up my spine. "You should have come for me when you first discovered her."

"I know, but I thought she'd listen to me."

He tilted his head toward the ladder. "Did she drag this from the shed by herself?"

"Stefan," I said.

He nodded his understanding. "He's a boy. In a few years he will begin to remember what you tell him."

I thought it would take more than a few years before Stefan remembered anything other than how to have fun, but I didn't say so. "I don't know who creates more problems, Oma or Stefan. Neither one of them will listen to me."

With a chuckle he mounted the ladder and waved to my grandmother. "I've come to rescue you, Sister Helga. Let me help you out of the tree."

I stood below and prayed this wouldn't take long. For a brief moment Oma eyed Conrad with curious suspicion—a strange occurrence, for she usually fancied him her beau when in a delusional state of mind. I immediately feared the worst.

Finally she pointed to a far branch. "First an apple I must pick."

Conrad wagged his finger and shook his head. "Nein. It is too early in the year for apples, Sister Helga, but I promise I will pick you a large red apple come September."

"Ja?" She gave him a toothy grin that creased her aged skin into a thousand wrinkles. "Then I will come down to you, pretty boy."

With skirt and petticoat askew and slowed by an occasional snag to her black stockings, Oma shimmied and slid down the tree until Conrad held her in a firm grasp. He maintained his hold until the old woman's feet were firmly planted on the ground. She turned to face him and jabbed her finger in a tap-tap-tap rhythm on one of his shirt buttons. "Permission from the elders you must have before you marry me."

If Oma's outburst had caused Conrad any unease, his feelings remained well hidden. I couldn't say the same for myself. Heat climbed up my neck in a thousand fingers and splayed across my cheeks. How could Oma recall a marriage requirement of our faith, yet fail to remember that old women don't climb trees or that apples aren't ready for harvest until fall? Those thoughts, along with Oma's behavior, caused my head to ache.

"Thank you for your help, Conrad." I hoped he wouldn't notice my embarrassment. "I apologize for Oma's words."

With the tip of his fingers, he lifted my chin. "What is this with apologies? We have known each other for twenty-two years. We look after each other, ja?" He took a step closer and leaned forward. "I know this is hard for you, Gretchen." His eyebrows dipped low over cobalt blue eyes.

I bobbed my head. "I don't know what I'd do without you." I forced a grin. "But we haven't really known each other for twenty-two years. I think you can only count from the time we reached the age of four. Before that, I remember nothing."

He chuckled. "From now on I will just say I have known you all my life."

Conrad thought he understood my daily plight: the rigors of trying to keep my work completed at the store while attempting to hide Oma's behavior from my father, and striving to keep Stefan on the proper path to manhood. I didn't want to dash Conrad's belief, but he could only partly understand. He wasn't there day and night to see my struggles.

The right side of his mouth lifted in a half grin. "And you don't have to worry about what to do without me, because I will always be here to help. I'm not going anywhere."

Before I could respond, Oma clutched Conrad's arm in a

viselike grip and tugged. "Come on, pretty boy. Come and sit with me."

He winked at me before returning his attention to my grandmother. "I have a better idea. Why don't you come and sit with me in the barbershop, Sister Helga?"

Shaking my head, I mouthed that he didn't need to take charge of Oma.

"It's the least I can do. You need some time alone to complete the ledgers at the store without worry." He shifted his weight and waved me toward the general store. "And if your work is all done, you can write in your journal. You're always taking care of others. Let me look after you some of the time."

Lifting a bony finger, Oma tucked a wisp of white hair behind one ear. Her black cap remained twisted in a loose knot at the back of her head, but I made no attempt to fix it. If she discovered any black fabric in her hair, she'd probably think the imaginary blackbird had built a nest atop her head. Conrad tucked Oma's hand into the crook of his arm, and she smiled up at him as they strolled toward the barbershop. Conrad glanced over his shoulder and waved. "I'll bring her back before time for the noonday meal."

I stared after the two of them for a moment. Oma continued to cling to Conrad's arm. She chattered to him as though she hadn't talked to him in years. And in her muddled thoughts, perhaps she hadn't. Nowadays, my grandmother often confused Conrad with her deceased husband. I found the idea quite odd, because the two men looked nothing alike. At least not according to my memories of *Opa*. My grandfather had died when I was only nine, but I remember him as short, stoop-shouldered, and bald. A stark contrast to Conrad's tall, broad-shouldered build and crop of thick blond hair. But who could know what went on in my grandmother's mind? Certainly not me, and I'd tired of any attempts to figure out when these strange episodes would occur.

The soles of my shoes clacked on the wooden sidewalk that bordered the storefronts of Homestead. A train whistled in the distance, and I instinctively turned toward the station and picked up my pace. If Father returned from the depot and discovered the store unattended, he'd be unhappy with me. Worse yet, I'd need to give a reason for my absence. I didn't want to lie, yet I didn't want to give him any additional reason to discuss the insane asylum in Mount Pleasant. I'd promised Mother on her deathbed that I wouldn't permit him to send Oma to that place, but with these incidents occurring more frequently, it was becoming difficult to defend my position.

I hurried through the front door, scanned the area, and exhaled a whoosh of relief.

"Ah, Gretchen, there you are."

I swiveled around. My shoulders relaxed when I caught sight of my good friend Sister Mina behind a counter stacked with folded ends of calicos and woolens. I lifted up on tiptoe and met her blue-eyed gaze. "I told Stefan not to stack those pieces so high, but does he listen?"

"*Ach!* He is a boy. I'm surprised he listens to you at all."

Mina circled around the display, and I stepped forward to encircle her shoulder. I gave her a quick squeeze and pecked her cheek with a fleeting kiss before releasing my hold. "It's always good to see you, Mina. We need to find time to visit more often. I miss our talks."

She patted my hand. "I miss you, as well, but it seems there is always something that keeps us busy. It's better in winter, when we can get together and quilt with the other women. In spring and summer, the hours are filled to the brim."

"True. And when Stefan doesn't do as he's told, it takes even more of my time."

Mina chuckled. "Boys don't listen to older sisters. I should know. I have four brothers, and not one would listen to me when they were Stefan's age." She wiggled loose several pieces of the dark calico and unfolded one of them. With a shake of her head, she refolded it. "Not enough for even an apron."

"There are some larger pieces over on the other side." I circled around and directed her to one of the far stacks. "I think you might find a piece or two large enough for an apron or even a waist among these." Always eager to keep the deductions from her account to a minimum, Mina would be happy if she could find a fabric remnant that would serve her purpose. "Do you want dark blue or black?" I yanked at a piece of cloth near the bottom of the pile. "Or maybe brown?" I held the piece aloft.

Mina hitched one shoulder. "I care little about the color so long as there is enough to make a new waist. All of mine are beginning to show wear. Never fails. They all wear out at the same time." She looked toward the door that led to our living quarters.

When my parents had first been assigned to operate the store, we'd lived in one of the houses down the street. But then my mother became ill, and my father asked to have a portion of the store converted into living quarters. The elders had first expressed concern over the idea but eventually agreed when Father assured them he would find a way to maintain the same amount of inventory. And he had. By adding some additional shelving, keeping only samples of some merchandise on the shelves and stocking the additional inventory in the large warehouse located behind the store, he'd been successful. The change meant he spent more time in the warehouse, and I was expected to take over more of the store duties. But having our living quarters within the store had proved more of a blessing than a hardship during my mother's illness. And now, with Oma experiencing bouts of dementia, I was even more thankful for the arrangement.

"Sister Helga is taking a nap?"

Mina's question pulled me back to the present. "Nein. Oma is over at the barbershop with Conrad."

Mina arched her brows. "Again? That Conrad is *gut* to help with her, ja? Not like your *Vater*, who has no patience."

"Vater helps when he can, but he has to be out in the warehouse most of the time." I pointed at the side window. "Oma climbed into the apple tree. Conrad helped me get her down."

"It's a wonder she didn't break a bone, but is gut your Vater wasn't here when it happened. For sure he would start talking about Mount Pleasant again. I am thankful your dear *Mutter* isn't here to see how he behaves." She snapped a piece of fabric in the air and placed it across the table. "This looks like it will do. These end pieces are still less costly than the ones on the bolt?" She glanced toward the myriad bolts of fabric that stood at attention on the nearby shelves.

"Ja, of course. Why would you think otherwise?"

Mina looked about the room. "The last time I was in here, your Vater said he was going to tell the elders it made no sense to sell the end pieces for less. I told him he should leave well enough alone, but who can say about your Vater? Ever since your Mutter died, he's been as changeable as the weather." She patted my shoulder. "You are a gut and patient daughter."

I couldn't disagree with Mina's assessment of my father, but I knew I wasn't as good or as patient as my friend thought. Father's moods had been unpredictable for more than two years, ever since Mother had taken ill. And I'd found it increasingly difficult to gauge his reactions and behavior. "He's said nothing to me about changing any prices. Until he does, we will both agree that the end pieces are less expensive."

"As they should be." Mina's curt tone didn't surprise me. It was simply her way. Few women in the Amana villages were as outspoken as Mina. Other women might murmur among themselves or privately state an opinion to their husbands, but Mina spoke her mind no matter who was present. Some of the men thought her a bit brash—my father among them. But whatever her tone of voice, I loved Mina. Even though she was twenty years older than I, she was my best friend. She was the one who had sat at my ailing mother's bedside during her final days on this earth. She was the one who had offered me solace, comfort, and a shoulder to cry on. And she was the one who had given me my very first journal.

There were so many times I longed to be like Mina—to say my feelings out loud. But I knew better. Instead, I wrote in my journal. Though I'd filled the pages of that very first journal long ago, it remained a secret between the two of us. Mina never told me how or where she purchased the journals, but each Christmas she gave me a new one. "I know there are those who think writing for pleasure is a waste of time, but you're a girl who needs to write your heart. I can see it in your eyes," she'd told me that very first Christmas. Ever since then I dreamed of writing beautiful poems or stories that would capture the hearts of readers. I had always loved reading the Psalms in the Bible. Not that I fancied my writing ability akin to David's, but I did find pleasure expressing my thoughts on paper and hoped that one day others might enjoy my writing. I wasn't sure how that could ever happen. Still, I continued to write.

"You going to list this on my ledger sheet, or are you expecting me to do it myself?"

Once again Mina's voice yanked me back to the present. "Just that one piece? You don't need anything else?"

"That's all." She trailed her fingers across the wide array of lace and trims that were displayed to advantage. "Sometimes I think your father keeps more goods on hand to sell to outsiders than he does for those of us who live here."

"Something you need that cannot be found on my shelves, Mina?" I heard the irritation in my father's voice before I saw him enter the store. He closed the distance in a long determined stride and came to a halt beside me.

Mina didn't back down from his hard stare. "Since you ask, I think you could give over more space to dark calicos and woolens, the ones worn by our people."

My father's gaze settled on the small piece of fabric Mina had selected. "The outsiders come here and buy more in one day than you have purchased in the last ten years." He poked at the small piece of cloth. "More of these tiny scraps I should have on my shelves? Is that what you think?"

Mina squared her shoulders. "Is the store for the people who live here or for the visitors who come to stare at us as though we are some curiosity?"

"The store is here for both, but if you are unhappy with how it is being run, maybe you should speak to the *Bruderrat*."

"I have no desire to speak to the elders, but that doesn't change what I think about the goods you stock."

"Ach! Nothing changes what you think, Mina. I have plenty of goods in the warehouse—you need only tell me what you need." He sent a dismissive wave in her direction. "You are as hardheaded as . . . as . . ."

"As a man?" Mina said. Without waiting for my father's reply, she picked up the piece of cloth and marched out the door.

"That woman, she is not a good example for the other women in this town. Her behavior you should not follow." My father peered at the ledger book. "The accounts are finished?"

"Not yet, but I'll have them completed before this evening."

His jaw twitched. "What is it you were doing while I was at the train station?"

I didn't dare tell him I'd spent my time trying to get Oma out of the apple tree. And one look at the ledgers would tell him that Mina had been my only customer.

"That Mina, she complains about the store and keeps you from doing your ledgers. That one, she talks too much."

Though I briefly considered telling my father he was wrong about Mina, I knew she wouldn't mind if I didn't come to her defense. She'd much rather I protect Oma.

CHAPTER 2

My father's parting words as he headed off to a meeting with the elders this morning had been less than pleasant. He'd bristled when he discovered I hadn't completed the ledgers yesterday. Of course he didn't take into account the many interruptions I'd faced for the remainder of the afternoon and last evening, and I couldn't tell him that keeping up with Oma had become an almost full-time job. Besides, he didn't want excuses; he wanted balanced ledgers.

The minute he departed, I opened one of the thick books. I stopped at the page devoted to Mina's account and deducted the cost for the piece of fabric she'd selected yesterday, marveling at her current balance. Like everyone else in the village, Mina received credit at the store to purchase personal items. Unlike some of the town's residents who used their credit before the next allowance was distributed, Mina always carried a sizable balance in her account. My father said she was as tight as a hangman's noose, but I thought otherwise.

Mina was thrifty—about everything. If she could say something in five words instead of ten, she did so. If she could accomplish something in two steps instead of three, she did so. If she could get by with a few inches less fabric instead of a few inches more, she did so. And I, for one, admired her ability to get things done without fuss or furor.

The scent of wild roses drifted through the window on a warm breeze, and I lifted my head to inhale the sweet fragrance before flipping to the next ledger page. When a train whistled in the distance, I glanced toward the clock. No doubt there would be visitors arriving to tour the town and make purchases at the store. I'd become accustomed to the stares and questions and had memorized a speech of sorts that I recited when a large group would enter the store together. It saved me from responding to the same questions time and again. I'd thought the task quite fun when I'd first taken over my mother's position in the store, but it had soon grown wearisome. Though I understood the outsiders' curiosity, it didn't lessen the tedium of answering their numerous inquiries. And now that spring had arrived, the number of visitors increased with each passing day. The thought sent me back to my paper work. If I was going to get the accounts completed, I needed to quit daydreaming.

When three short blasts signaled the train's arrival, I balanced the Metzgers' ledger sheet and closed the book. "Finally," I sighed. After sliding off the stool, I arched my back and stretched my arms. I had hunched over the accounts far too long, but at least I was done for today. And after Conrad had returned with Oma a short while ago, she had remained quiet and out of trouble. In fact, she'd appeared fine when I'd asked her to arrange spices on the shelves at the far side of the store.

"Oma? Have you finished over there?"

I could hear her muttering, but she didn't answer. Still rubbing the small of my back, I walked toward the spice shelves and stopped in my tracks when I caught sight of her.

"Oma, what are you doing?" I stared at the sack of sugar she'd emptied onto the floor.

She sifted a handful of the white crystals through her fingers. "Playing." She sounded like a young child, her tone so meek and innocent. Her clear blue eyes, so much like my own, were clouded by a gauzy veil of confusion. "Want to play?"

"Not now. You need to go and rest for a while. Let me help you up from the floor." I uttered a silent prayer that she would cooperate. Soon customers would be coming in, and I needed to clean up before they arrived.

She grasped my arm and permitted me to help her to her feet. She turned to me, her eyes suddenly clear and bright as she pointed to the floor. "Did Stefan make this mess? Doesn't he know how much sugar costs? We need to get this cleaned up right now. That boy needs to learn to behave. I'm going to have a talk with your father this evening."

I took a deep breath, thankful Oma had returned to her right mind yet wondering if I'd ever adjust to her transformation from normal to abnormal behavior in mere seconds. "I believe it was an accident. The train has arrived, so we'll need to hurry. I'll get the broom." I crossed the room at a near run and grabbed the broom and tin dustpan from the far corner of the store. "Please, dear Lord, let her stay this way until after any customers have come and gone," I whispered.

My grandmother extended her arm and took the broom. In no time she'd brushed the sugar into a heaping pile. I stooped down and held the dustpan in place while she swept the sugar onto it. After resting the broom handle in the crook of her arm, she grabbed the cloth bag and held it open while I dumped in the soiled sugar. I tied the sack and headed toward the back door.

"Nein!" she called and waved me in the other direction. "Put that in the corner so your Vater can see what Stefan has done. Such a bad boy he can be sometimes."

There wasn't time to wage a battle before the customers arrived. I could only hope that Oma would forget about the sugar by the time Stefan or my father returned home.

A fashionably dressed group of ten women and five men entered the store, the women snatching an occasional glance at Oma and me when they thought we weren't looking. Once they'd made their way between the rows, I stepped from behind the counter and near the front entrance.

"My name is Gretchen Kohler. My father, George Kohler, operates the general store here in Homestead, and I will be pleased to answer any questions about the Amana Colonies you may have. I usually give a brief history and explanation of our community to those interested."

The men appeared bored by my invitation, but their wives seemed interested. One woman glanced toward her peers and then stepped forward. "I believe we would all be pleased to hear whatever you can tell us. We like to learn new things, and your strange group is fascinating."

One of the men stood at a distance with a small case. Likely a salesman, but I'd never before seen him. He turned toward the woman, his forehead creased in deep ridges. "Perhaps the

word you meant to use is *unique* rather than *strange*, madam."
He pinned her with a dark-eyed stare that made me catch my
breath.

She coughed into her handkerchief and gave a hesitant nod.
"Yes, unique. That is the word I was searching for." She turned
her attention back to me. "Do tell us about your community,
my dear."

"We are known as the Amana Society or the Community of
True Inspiration. There are seven villages in all, and Homestead
is the only village that existed prior to the time we arrived here
from Buffalo, New York. The other villages are known as Main
Amana, High Amana, East Amana, West Amana, South Amana,
and Middle Amana."

A tall man at the rear of the group chuckled. "Not very
original with the names, are you? I hear tell you folks own more
land in Iowa than anyone else. Is that right?"

"Yes, I believe that is true. Our society owns approximately
twenty-six thousand acres. We are known for the fine calicos
and woolens that are woven in our mills. We produce our own
food as well as most of the items needed within our homes. We
are also known for our sauerkraut, onion sets, and several other
farm products that we ship to other markets when we have an
abundant supply."

"Do you and your family own this store?" a tall, angular
woman asked.

Oma shook her head and frowned. "Nein. This store, the
society owns. The things you see, they are owned by all of us. We
own everything, and we own nothing." She waved a dismissive
hand and turned her back.

An older woman inched forward a few steps and tipped her

head. "I heard from a friend that you're like those Shakers. Men and women don't get married or have children."

The tall woman shook her head. "That's not correct, Frieda. The Shakers remain single, but Amish people marry."

"We're not Amish," I interjected. No matter how often disputed, these constant comparisons had become impossible to dispel. "Our religious beliefs teach that to remain single is the best way to live because a person can then devote one's full attention to God. But marriage is not prohibited. Many people in our villages are married and have children. Unlike the Amish, we are interested in all new inventions and time-saving devices. We view anything that helps us complete our work in a more rapid fashion as a good thing. That way we have more time to worship God."

One of the other women nudged her friend in the side. "You see? I told you she was wrong. They do get married."

The woman spoke as though we were some strange species and as though I weren't within hearing distance. "We take our meals together in communal dining rooms, and if you plan to remain for the rest of the day, you may dine with us. You'll be able to observe a few of our customs at that time."

"And eat some gut food," Oma said.

"We'll come back to the store before we leave. I want to see the rest of the town first," the tall woman said. "Come along, group. We can shop later."

This woman was clearly in charge. Even the men did her bidding. All except the one with the case standing near the east wall. He didn't make any move toward the door. I decided he must be alone. Once the others had departed, I looked his way. "If you need assistance with anything, I'll be pleased to help you."

He picked up his leather bag and strode toward the counter. His eyes twinkled, and one side of his mouth curved in a lopsided grin. "I'm Allen Finley—from Chicago. It's a pleasure to meet you, Miss Kohler. I've been looking around your store, and I notice you have a good selection of lace and trims, but I believe I have some that will fancy up even the plainest of dresses." His gaze settled on my unadorned dark waist and skirt.

"Is this your first visit to the Amana Colonies, Mr. Finley?"

"Yes, but you can be certain it won't be my last." He opened his case and spread forth an assortment of delicate lace.

"These must be quite expensive. I've not seen any quite so lovely."

"Imported. From all over the world. That's why I have such a variety. I'm sure the women would much prefer these to anything else you have to offer."

Oma drew near and lifted a piece of the lace between her arthritic fingers. "Fancy lace our women do not use, but this is very nice."

Mr. Finley twisted around and waved toward the rows of trim. "But you have all—"

"We sell to outsiders who come here to visit. We carry a better supply of lace and trim than the stores in Iowa City or Cedar Rapids, so many ladies from those cities come here to purchase their fabrics and trims."

When the salesman opened his case a little wider, I caught sight of several fashion magazines tucked beneath the lace. Heat warmed my cheeks when he noticed me staring at the periodicals.

"You enjoy magazines, Miss Kohler?"

Oma rushed across the room and waved a finger beneath Mr. Finley's nose. "We read the Bible."

"As do I, my dear lady, but I must keep informed on the latest fashions for my employer. If we see a new type of lace or trim in the magazines, we want to be certain we can supply those to our customers."

My grandmother grunted and headed toward the door to our attached rooms, apparently satisfied with Mr. Finley's response. Once she'd moved out of earshot, I leaned closer to the case and pretended to examine another piece of lace, though my gaze remained fixed upon the magazines.

"My father orders all of the supplies for the store. He should return within the hour if you'd like to speak with him about placing an order."

"I would indeed. And if you'd be so kind as to discard these periodicals for me, I'd be very grateful. I read them on the train, and they take up space in my case." He spoke in a quiet voice as he slid the magazines across the counter to me.

"Yes, of course." I shoved the magazines into a basket beneath the counter and covered them with a dustcloth.

He bent at the waist and rested his arms on the counter. "Feel free to read them before you put them in the trash. I promise I won't tell your grandmother."

I didn't respond, but I had no intention of discarding the magazines. Not now. Probably not ever.

"I'm quite interested in learning more about the Amana Colonies, Miss Kohler."

His comment surprised me. We had many salesmen visit our villages, but they wanted nothing more than to conduct business—either to take orders for items needed in our stores or to place orders for our calicos and woolens. "For what reason, Mr. Finley?"

He leaned further across the counter. "Because I am considering making my home in the colonies."

"You are?" I couldn't hold back a chuckle.

He pushed away from the counter and straightened his shoulders. "Why is that amusing?"

"I apologize, but becoming a member of our society is a little more complicated than simply saying you want to live here."

"I'm sure it is. That's exactly why I said I was hoping you would tell me more. The idea of communal living appeals to me, and I think I have abilities that would be beneficial. I'm certainly willing to work." He hesitated a moment. "That's a big part of it, isn't it? Each person must contribute by doing some sort of meaningful work."

He seemed a genuinely nice man, but for me to explain our way of life in a brief conversation would be impossible. "First and foremost, it is our faith that brings us together, Mr. Finley. We work together so that we will have more free time to spend in worship."

"That sounds like a fine thing."

I arched a brow. "We gather for prayer meetings every evening. In addition, we have Sunday services, and on religious holidays, we attend even more often. Does it still sound like a fine thing to you, Mr. Finley?"

The veins in his neck tightened for a fleeting moment. "I'm not running for the train station just yet, Miss Kohler. I understand this is a religious community, but there is much more I would need to know than your schedule of church meetings, isn't there?"

I folded my arms across my waist. "Yes, of course, but one of the elders could better explain to you the ways of our society."

Several strands of unruly brown hair drooped across Mr. Finley's forehead, giving him the appearance of a young boy. "Then we'll let them explain the rules, and you can tell me about everyday life." His look of expectancy reminded me of my brother on Christmas mornings.

Perching my elbow on the counter, I rested my chin in my palm and leaned forward. "I suppose I could tell you—"

"Gretchen!" My father's voice rumbled through the room like thunder.

I straightened and jumped away from the counter, suddenly realizing the unsuitable picture my father had observed of my leaning on the counter and staring into the eyes of a strange salesman as though he were an old friend.

"This is Mr. Finley, a salesman," I said in a strangled voice. "He has some lovely imported lace that I think will interest you. I'm sure the ladies from Iowa City will buy all that we can stock." My rambling attempt to rectify the situation didn't seem to help. My father's jaw twitched as he crossed the room. "He also has an interest in joining the society, but I told him you or one of the other elders could answer his questions in that regard." My father's jaw relaxed a bit.

"Thank you for your help, Miss Kohler." Mr. Finley gave a slight tip of his head and looked toward the floor behind the counter. "Don't forget the magazines," he whispered.

I stooped down and gathered the magazines into the dustcloth as my father circled the counter.

"Please go and tell Conrad that if he has time, I could use his help in the warehouse this afternoon."

I stopped in my room only long enough to tuck the magazines beneath my mattress, where I hoped they would remain undiscovered until I could find a perfect hiding spot.

CHAPTER 3

Unable to believe my eyes, I stopped in my tracks and stared through the window of the barbershop. There stood my grand-mother, with the lower half of her face covered in sudsy lather and a straight-edged razor in her hand. Afraid any sound might startle her, I edged closer to the door, hoping I could make it inside before she hurt herself—and before anyone else discovered what was happening. Where was Conrad? And why had he left Oma alone in his shop? Had there not been a razor involved, the sight would have been comical.

Please don't let the door creak, I silently prayed. Ever so slowly I pulled back on the door handle until I could fit through the narrow opening. Careful not to let the door slam behind me, I sidestepped toward my grandmother.

She looked up and caught sight of me in the mirror. She

waved the razor overhead. "*Guten Tag*, Maria. Sit down in the chair. Do you want a haircut or a shave?"

"I'm Gretchen, Oma." I took a few steps closer. "Why don't you put that razor on the counter and let me clean your face."

"Ach! You stay back, Maria. I can shave my face better than you."

Any time Oma referred to me by my mother's name, a searing pain shot through me like a hot poker. I understood my grandmother wasn't in her right mind, but it didn't lessen my pain. However, there wasn't time to dwell on my sorrow. I must make her understand that she had to put the razor down before she hurt herself.

"I think I would like to have you give me a shave," I said. "Should I sit in the chair?"

"Ja, of course." Razor in hand, she waved me toward the barber chair. "Come. Sit down." She leaned forward and patted the leather chair.

I circled around and scooted back in the seat, all the while focusing on the razor. She grabbed hold of the leather strop attached to the chair and brandished the razor back and forth, as if she'd sharpened it a thousand times before. "A dull razor is not a gut thing." She flicked the edge against her skin and gave a pleased nod. "Lift your chin like this." She jutted her chin and tightened her lips. How many times had she watched Conrad perform this task?

"Maybe you should wipe the soap from your face before you begin to work on me." I hoped my suggestion would give me an opportunity to grab hold of the razor.

Surprise flickered in Oma's eyes when she turned and looked in the mirror. "Ja, you are right." But instead of laying the razor on the counter, she switched it to her other hand, picked up a towel, and swiped her face. Leaning forward, she once again peered into the mirror. "Gut enough. Now I must shave you. Lift your chin." Remnants of the soapy lather remained on her face, but I knew that wouldn't deter her.

Razor in hand, she leaned toward me.

"Wait! First I need the soap to soften my whiskers."

She stared at me for a moment before recognition dawned. "Ja. The soap we need first." Turning around, she placed the razor on the counter behind her and picked up the mug and brush. "This we can use for your face."

Though she no longer held the razor, I couldn't reach it from my position in the chair. "I think I should have a towel around my neck so you don't get soap on my dress."

For a moment confusion shone in her blue eyes, but she quickly recovered and shoved the mug of soap at me. "Hold this." She grabbed the towel she'd used to wipe the soap from her face and slapped it across the bodice of my dress. "There. That is gut."

Before I could think of another objection, she yanked the mug from my hand and daubed the soapy lather onto my face. If I didn't think of something soon, my grandmother was going to slit my throat. As that thought floated through my mind, the door opened, Oma wheeled around, and I turned toward the front of the shop.

"Miss Kohler? Is that you beneath those suds, or could it be Saint Nicholas?"

Oma pointed a bony finger in his direction. "Sit down. You have to wait your turn, pretty boy."

"Oma, that is Mr. Finley, the salesman who was in our store this morning. Do you remember him?"

"He can have his turn after you." My grandmother waved

him toward the chair, but realization shone in Mr. Finley's eyes as he stepped closer.

"I have a train to catch, and I'm certain Miss Kohler would be willing to let me take her turn in the chair, wouldn't you?"

"Ja. Of course I would. Why don't you shave Mr. Finley first, Oma? That way he won't be late for the train."

Shaving mug in one hand and razor in the other, Oma's eyes shifted back and forth between us. Finally she set the razor on the narrow counter and motioned Mr. Finley toward the chair. "You must get up, Maria."

I quickly pushed up from the chair. The towel fluttered down the front of my dress, and I caught it with one hand. "You may sit here, Mr. Finley."

He tapped his index finger on his cheek. I knew I still had soap on my face, but I was more interested in gaining possession of the razor. Stepping around my grandmother, I reached out and grasped the razor, hid it beneath the towel, and backed away from the chair where Mr. Finley was now perched.

Using her open palm, my grandmother pushed against his chest. "Sit back in the chair, pretty boy."

Mr. Finley opened his mouth to protest but was met by Oma's soapy brush. He sputtered and coughed as the mixture entered his mouth. "A towel." He choked out the words and gestured toward a stack of folded towels on the far ledge.

"What is going on in here?"

Like a well-oiled machine, the three of us turned toward the front door of the shop. Conrad was staring at us as though we'd all lost our minds. I could only imagine what he was thinking. Mr. Finley jumped to his feet and retrieved two towels. Using one towel to wipe the soap from his mouth, he strode toward me and reached out to clear the dried lather from my face. In one quick motion Conrad stepped forward, grabbed the towel from Mr. Finley, and placed it in my hand.

"You should not be touching Gretchen in such a manner." His fiery words flooded my cheeks with a scorching heat.

I took a step forward. "Mr. Finley was trying to help. We have had terrible problems because of what you did."

He jerked as though I'd slapped him. "What did I do? I went to help Brother Heinrich over at the barns, and I come back to find this." He spread his arms to encompass the mess Oma had made in his shop.

"You left your razor out where Oma could get it. She was going to shave herself . . . and me."

"And me," Mr. Finley added.

Oma circled around and stood between Conrad and Mr. Finley. She looped one hand into the crook of Conrad's arm and the other hand into the crook of Mr. Finley's arm. "Two pretty boys. All for me," she cooed.

"They aren't for you, Oma." I sent a pleading look to both men. "Please don't say anything about this to anyone." After prying my grandmother's grip from Conrad's arm, I met his gaze. "I promise I'll give you a full explanation later, but I need to return to the store before my Vater comes looking for me. He asked me to tell you he could use your help at the warehouse this afternoon."

I promised Oma a piece of candy, but she refused to release Mr. Finley's arm.

"I'll escort the two of you back to the store. It will be my pleasure," Mr. Finley said. "If I hope to make this place my home one day, I can't start making myself useful any too soon."

Conrad cocked a brow, but there was no way I could explain at the moment. "Tell your Vater I will do my best to come and help him this afternoon." He hesitated a moment. "We can talk before I go out to the warehouse."

I nodded my agreement as Oma yanked Mr. Finley toward the door. As soon as we were outside the barbershop, I wanted to quiz Mr. Finley about his discussion with my father, for it certainly hadn't lasted long. They couldn't have talked for more than thirty-five minutes, and I doubted that had been long enough for my father to place an order much less explain life in the Amana Colonies.

"Your time with my Vater was brief, Mr. Finley. Did he answer all your questions about life in Amana?" The two of us positioned ourselves on either side of my grandmother, but her short stature permitted me to meet Mr. Finley's gaze without interference.

He chuckled and shook his head. "No, but he did place a large order with me."

I wasn't surprised that my father hadn't given Mr. Finley information about the colonies. He didn't have much time for outsiders, even if they did add money to our ledgers.

"Your father said he had a great deal of work to complete. We planned a meeting for when I return with the order. I'm going to arrange to take several days off work and stay at the hotel. That way I'll have more time and won't interfere with his work—or yours." He tipped his head toward me. "And I'll see if I can bring you some additional reading material. Is there anything you'd particularly like to read?"

"You shouldn't bring me anything, Mr. Finley. It is improper for me to accept a gift from you, and we are to concentrate on reading the Bible."

He grinned. "A very proper answer, Miss Kohler."

I was a little disappointed that he didn't insist on a different answer. I would have told him to bring me a book that would teach me how to compose beautiful prose or lyrical poems. Though I loved to read, my true passion would always be writing.

Once we'd walked the short distance to the store, I glanced over my shoulder. Conrad was standing outside the barbershop staring in our direction, and he didn't appear happy. Perhaps it was just as well Mr. Finley hadn't insisted.

My father was in the back of the store when I returned home with Oma. I was thankful that she willingly went into her room to take a nap, but I waited until she was asleep before I returned to the store. Brother Heinrich and my father were standing at the front counter talking. I stepped to the end of a display shelf and returned the items that visitors had moved from their proper places.

"He thinks he wants to live here, but I am not so sure. There is something about him I do not trust," my father said.

There was little doubt they were discussing Mr. Finley and his request to gather information about the colonies.

"What is not to trust? He asks his questions, you answer them, and if he decides he wants to join us, then he can go before the *Grossebruderrat*, and they can decide. It is not for you or me to decide such matters."

"Ja. This I know. But these outsiders who want to join us are mostly just curious fellows. Once they discover there is more to living here than free meals and a roof over their heads, they lose interest."

"You are suspicious of everyone, George. Maybe the young man wants to lead a simple life. And you said yourself that he is a good salesman. If he comes here to live, maybe his talents would benefit us."

My father turned and removed the mail from Brother

Heinrich's box and handed it to him. "Or maybe he will cause lots of problems."

"Ach! Always you think of the bad instead of the good." Heinrich shuffled through his mail and waved a letter in the air. "From my wife's brother in Germany. She will be pleased to see this."

The men returned to talk of the weather and crops, and there wasn't any further mention of Mr. Finley before Brother Heinrich departed.

"I am going out to the warehouse, Gretchen," my father said. "The ledgers, they are done?"

I sighed. They would have been done if he and Brother Heinrich hadn't been in the way. "Only a few entries left. I'll complete them while you're gone."

He gave me a dismissive gesture. "That's what you always say, but does it happen?"

As the condemning question rang in my ears, my anger began to mount like a threatening storm. Why was he always so unforgiving? Why did he expect so much of me? If he wasn't complaining about the ledgers, he was complaining about the way I stocked the shelves or arranged the furniture in the parlor. Since Mother's death, nothing ever suited him.

I finished the entries, shoved the book under the counter, and retrieved my journal from beneath the yarn in my knitting basket. Rather than poetry or some lovely story, I would write about today's events. I tapped the pencil against my lips while I decided where to begin. Hunching forward, I carefully inscribed the date in the upper right corner. Using my neatest penmanship, I detailed Oma's latest episode, Mr. Finley's arrival in Homestead, and my father's unreasonable temperament.

"So you're a writer as well as a reader."

I jerked to attention. "Mr. Finley. I thought you left on the two-o'clock train." Grabbing the corner of my journal, I slapped it closed. At least, that had been my intent. Instead, I squished two of Mr. Finley's fingers between the pages. He let out a tiny yelp and resituated his hand around my book. I knew he wasn't injured, but I practiced proper manners and apologized all the same. However, when he wouldn't release his hold on my journal and even attempted to open the pages for a closer look, I yanked the book from his grasp, not caring in the least if I injured his hand.

"You're quite a fighter, Miss Kohler," he said with a grudging smile. "It wasn't a contest."

He was absolutely correct. Attempting to read my journal wasn't a game: It was more a matter of life and death to me. Along with poetry and meandering prose, my journals were filled with my deepest thoughts. And though I aspired to one day see some of my writings in print, my personal thoughts weren't meant to be read by anyone.

"I do a bit of writing myself and was hoping you might share something with me."

My stomach roiled, and the acidic taste of the sauerkraut I'd eaten at the noonday meal burned in the back of my throat. "I don't share my writing, Mr. Finley. It is very personal."

"I understand. My actions were rude, and I apologize. But as someone who enjoys writing, I'm always drawn to those who share my passion."

"You write?" I couldn't hide my interest. None of the men I'd ever known enjoyed either reading or writing. Throughout my years in school, it had proved a chore for most of the boys to complete their writing assignments. Nowadays, my brother,

Stefan, would rather sweep the floor of the shop three times over than write an essay for English class.

"You appear astonished. Most poets and authors are men, so why does it surprise you when I reveal I find pleasure in writing?"

"Sister Mina says some of those writers are really women who use men's names so they can be published."

He chuckled. "And who is this Sister Mina?"

"She is a dear friend. And whether you agree or not, I believe what she says." I hadn't meant to sound quite so strident, but his laughter left me somewhat annoyed.

"Once again, my apologies. Though it isn't my intention, I seem to continually offend you, Miss Kohler. Your friend Sister Mina is correct. There are some ladies who write under a pseudonym in order to have their work accepted. I don't think that's fair, but until the world changes a bit, I fear it will be true for some. There are, however, a few publishers willing to set aside the prejudice against women." He bent forward and leaned on the counter until we were eye-to-eye. "If you should happen to glance through those periodicals I left with you, you'll discover there are some stories and poems written by women. I've read some of them, and they are excellent. Unless you have already destroyed them."

His tone carried a hint of amusement as a smile played at the corners of his mouth. There was no doubt Mr. Finley knew I would devour every word of those magazines. And they would remain in my possession for years to come. "I will be certain to look for those pieces."

"I happen to have a poem that I wrote not long ago. I'd be pleased to have you read it and give me your opinion." He opened the lid of his case and ruffled through the contents. "Ah, here it is." He pulled a sheet of paper from his case and slid it toward me. "You may read it once I'm gone. I don't know if I could suffer the embarrassment of watching while you read. I am, after all, an amateur."

I glanced down at the precise handwriting. Much bolder than my own but neat nonetheless. No doubt Mr. Finley had applied himself to his studies. No doubt he'd received an excellent education. And no doubt his writing would put my own to shame. "I'd be honored to read your poetry, Mr. Finley. I shall protect it until you return to Homestead."

He leaned even closer and whispered, "Perhaps once you've learned to trust me, you'll permit me to read something you have written?"

At the sound of footsteps I jerked back. Conrad stood in the doorway staring at us. His dark blue eyes flashed an undeniable warning at the salesman. "If you truly want to learn more about our society, Mr. Finley, you'll need to seek information beyond the limits of the general store."

CHAPTER 4

Conrad accompanied us home after prayer service, and when my father mentioned Mr. Finley's name, Conrad didn't hesitate to voice his opinion. "I don't like that man."

"For any reason other than the fact that he took an interest in my daughter?" My father tamped down the tobacco he'd placed in the bowl of his pipe while Oma took up her knitting and Stefan settled on the floor beside my father's chair.

I dropped to the divan. "Mr. Finley didn't take an interest in me. He expressed his interest in the society and asked me questions about our way of life. His interest seemed genuine."

Conrad shook his head. "I don't trust him. He said he wanted to learn about the society, but he didn't bother to talk to any of the men. Instead, he stood around the store talking to Gretchen."

"That's not true. He talked to Vater." I thought about the poem Mr. Finley had given me to read. The gentle words within the poem had resonated as genuine and kind. A man who could write with such beauty couldn't be untrustworthy.

Oma's knitting needles clacked at a steady rhythm. "Conrad is right. A man who reads ladies' magazines we cannot trust."

I jerked so quickly the cords in my neck cramped, and a sharp pain raced downward into my shoulder. "The magazines are for his business."

"Ja. He must see what the competition has to sell." My father struck a match and held it to the bowl of his pipe.

Still rubbing my neck, I said, "You see? Vater agrees with me. A gut businessman must always keep informed about his competition."

Conrad leaned forward and rested his arms on his thighs. "Thank you for the good advice, Gretchen. I will do my best to keep informed about my competition."

His eyes glimmered in the fading light, but I couldn't be certain if they shone with anger or humor. Conrad hadn't been acting like himself ever since he'd first met Mr. Finley. I'd never before seen him act in such an unkind manner. His compassion for others had been one of the many things that made him such a dear friend.

My father grabbed a tight hold on Stefan's shoulder. "Your sister tells me your math is not so gut. I think this would be a gut time for you to go through your book so you can make some improvement, ja?"

Stefan's dagger-filled look annoyed me. He was to blame for his bad grades and the constant visits from the schoolteacher, yet he didn't want to spend any time studying.

"I wish I could go to school in Iowa City," he said.

"And why is that?" Conrad asked.

"Because they go to school only in the fall and winter. They get to stay home during the summertime and enjoy themselves."

"From what your teacher tells me, you already enjoy yourself far too much." My brother's attitude irritated me. I longed to return to the days when I sat in a classroom and had no other concerns. "If you would use your time to advantage, you could learn a great deal, Stefan. Brother Ulbricht says you show gut skills with the machinery. He says your math could help you work with machines in the future."

Stefan curled his lip. "I don't need math to fix broken equipment. He thinks if he tells you that, you'll make me do my homework."

"That is enough, young man," Vater said. "We will go to the bedroom and work on your numbers." Turning to me, he said, "I will leave Oma here to chaperone the two of you while I oversee Stefan's schoolwork."

My father's interest in my brother's math came as a complete surprise. Since my mother's death, he'd shown little interest in the boy's schoolwork. Perhaps Brother Otto had spoken to the elders. The harried man had made visit upon visit to the general store. Yet each time the schoolteacher appeared at our door, my father sent the complaining man to talk to me—as though I were Stefan's parent.

I didn't complain to my father—only Sister Mina heard my complaints. And occasionally Conrad. But he usually sided with Stefan. "Boyish behavior." That was Conrad's answer to everything concerning my brother. Well, I disagreed. Stefan would soon be a young man, and it was time for him to grow up, whether he liked it or not. When our mother died, I'd had no choice but to grow up. He'd had far more time to adjust. And that's exactly what I'd written in my journal the other day.

47

Setting pen to paper and letting my feelings spill out in my journal helped with most everything. I only wished writing about my problems would make them disappear. How wonderful that would be. And how wonderful if it would make my anger disappear. Though the writing helped, sometimes the anger still rose to the surface. Much like my father's tobacco, it had to be tamped down, forced into the tiny spot deep inside that I reserved for it. I suppose that's the one thing Stefan and I shared: the forced change our mother's death had inflicted upon us. And if I was honest with myself, it had forced terrible change upon Father and Oma, as well. Father had physically and emotionally retreated from Stefan and me, while more and more often Oma retreated into her make-believe world.

"I think your grandmother has fallen asleep." I glanced up to see Conrad smiling at Oma. The yarn remained wrapped around her fingers, but the sweater she'd been knitting had settled in her lap. "It was never my intention to make you angry with my comments about the salesman, Gretchen. But I did not like the way he was acting when he was around you." He tapped his fingers on his cheek. "Touching your face with a towel and leaning across the store counter talking to you in such a familiar manner. Such behavior isn't gut."

"You judge him harshly. He doesn't understand our ways. Until he learns, you can't expect him to react to situations the same way you would." I motioned for him to move to the chair beside me so our conversation wouldn't awaken Oma.

"And you are too trusting. I am a man, and I could see his intentions were not honorable. His interest was in you, not our society."

When I tried to offer an objection, he held up his hand.

"Tell me, how many questions did he ask you about our community?"

I hesitated, trying to remember my conversations with Mr. Finley. I wanted to defend him, but the memory of his hand on my journal kept flitting to the forefront of my mind. "He asked about reading periodicals, and Oma told him we read the Bible. He said he thought that was a gut thing. And . . . and . . . he didn't have any objection to attending prayer service each night."

"That doesn't seem like much for the amount of time he spent with you." Conrad reached for my hand and covered it with his own. "We have been friends since we were children, Gretchen. You know how much I care for you—my feelings run much deeper than friendship. I don't think this Mr. Finley will ever want to live by our rules. And I don't want him to hurt you—or me."

"And you know how much I care for you, as well. Mr. Finley will not hurt either of us. His interest is in living here—not in me."

Conrad leaned over and brushed a fleeting kiss on my cheek.

"The last I knew, kissing was against the rules," I whispered.

Conrad grinned. "But my intentions are honorable."

With a loud cough and a snort, Oma's eyelids opened, and her gaze settled on the clock. "Time it is for bed. Go home, Conrad."

He laughed and shook his head. "I think it is still a little early, but I will not argue with you, Sister Helga."

Oma dropped her knitting into the basket beside her. "Gut, because you would not win. See Conrad to the door and then go to bed, Gretchen."

One minute she was the adult in charge of everyone and the next she was a toddler getting into trouble. It was difficult to know which Oma would appear. While she waited in her rocker, I bid Conrad good-night and then returned to kiss Oma on the cheek. "Rest well, Oma. I love you."

Once in my room, I lit the lamp and prepared for bed. Before slipping beneath the covers, I knelt beside my bed and prayed. The minute I said amen, I slid my hand beneath the mattress and withdrew the magazines. I didn't pause to look at the latest fashions or advertisements for beauty creams or face powder. Instead, I turned to one of the stories Mr. Finley had mentioned. Sure enough, the author was listed as a Miss Emily Wilson. I settled against my pillows and began to read. The time slipped by much too quickly, and it was very late when I finally closed the magazine and turned down the wick of my kerosene lamp.

I fell asleep with thoughts of Mr. Finley and his beautiful poem drifting through my mind.

"Mina! How gut to see you." I stepped forward to accept her embrace. "I'm surprised to see you so early in the day. How did you manage to prepare next week's menu before you've even served the noonday meal?"

She reached into her pocket and withdrew a piece of paper. Every week women from each of the several *Küches* in Homestead brought their grocery lists to the store. Filling the orders was always a task I enjoyed. I could visit with the cooks or kitchen helpers while picking items from the shelves. Besides, when Mina brought her order, it gave me the opportunity to talk about more personal things—the things shared between dear friends.

There were times when I envied the women who worked in the communal kitchens. They had the opportunity to visit with one another while they worked. And though they sometimes bickered or didn't agree, mostly they laughed and told stories while they cooked. Of course, there were times when it wasn't so much fun—when they had to hurry back to the Küche to prepare holiday meals rather than spend time with family, but mostly they liked cooking. And I supposed that was true for most of us. We liked our work, but there were times when we'd rather be doing something else. Still, had I been allowed to choose where I would work, I would have chosen the Küche. Partly because I enjoyed cooking and partly because I wanted to spend more time with Mina.

"Two of the older girls are helping us today—extra training. I put them to gut use so I could get my menu ready." Mina grinned. "Let's begin with the flour and sugar first."

I picked up a basket, handed it to Mina, and picked up another for myself. With the basket on her arm, Mina followed behind me down the aisle.

"You get the flour, and I'll get the sugar." I'd lifted two bags into the large woven basket when Mina tapped me on the shoulder. "You selling used sugar nowadays? This bag, it is open."

I watched in horror as she reached inside the cloth bag and removed a handful of sugar containing flecks of dirt. No doubt Oma had found the bag and placed it back on the shelf. I recounted the incident with the sugar to Mina. "I am thankful it was you that discovered the sugar rather than my father."

"Ja, or one of the other cooks. If they would get dirt in their sugar and ruin a pudding or cake, you can be sure your father would have received a tongue-lashing." She covered her mouth and giggled. "Especially from Sister Marguerite. She finds no humor in anything. Maybe you should empty the bag in your burning pit out back. That way your grandmother can't put it back on the shelf and your father won't discover what has happened."

While Mina continued to fill her basket with items from the shelves, I went outside and dumped the contents of the cloth bag into the brick-lined pit we used for burning trash and then returned inside.

Walking down the aisle, I picked up a tin of cinnamon and placed it in Mina's basket. "Now, let's see if we can fill the rest of your order." I scanned the list and began to place items in my basket.

"Who was the visitor that ate the noonday meal with us yesterday?" Mina asked.

"Mr. Allen Finley. He ate his evening meal with us, as well. Weren't you working during supper?"

Her lips took a downward dive. "That's exactly why I didn't see him. I was working. One of the kitchen girls took ill, and I was washing pots and pans while you were eating supper."

I immediately regretted my comment. I knew Mina wouldn't be absent from work. "I'm sorry. I know you would never shirk your duties." I lifted a tin of baking powder from the shelf and handed it to her. "Mr. Finley is a salesman of fine lace and trims, but he has interest in coming here to live. And he writes poetry."

"The man I saw was dressed in a fine suit and doesn't look like the type who would be interested in living here. And he doesn't look like the type who'd be writing poetry, either. I think he must be telling you a story to try to win your heart, Gretchen. You best be careful around that one."

"You sound like Conrad. Just because a man wears a nice suit doesn't mean he can't be trusted. I know he writes poetry because he gave me one of his poems to read. And it's very good. The meter isn't quite perfect, but he has talent, and he admires reading and writing." I emptied the contents of my basket onto the counter. "Aren't we taught that we should not judge others by their appearance, but rather by what's in their hearts?"

"Ja. But we must also use sound judgment. The two of you became well acquainted while he was here?"

I touched a finger to the string of my cap. "Not well acquainted—just acquainted. Vater was away from the store when Mr. Finley arrived. He showed me his samples of lace and trims. They are all imported. Much finer than anything we currently have in the store. Vater placed a big order. Visitors will buy them for sure."

I had planned to mention the magazines Mr. Finley left with me, but Mina was already wary of him. Even though she didn't object to breaking the rules occasionally, I didn't think she'd approve.

"Did you ask him how he'd come to know about us and why he wanted to leave his current life behind?" She added several pieces of flypaper to her basket. "Already the flies bother us in the Küche."

"And everywhere else," I said. "It's almost May. What else can we expect but flies and mosquitoes?" I handed her a bag of rice and stepped to the other side of the counter to measure out two pounds of raisins, ten pounds of coffee, and seven pounds of tea.

"Maybe a few salesmen and some hobos." Mina placed a packet of needles and a spool of darning cotton on the counter. "Keep those separate and deduct them from my account."

I opened the ledger and slipped the list between the pages. Later I would itemize the list into the ledger, tally up the charges, and make certain the total was delivered to Sister Marguerite, the *Küchebaas*, for her records.

"When is this Mr. Finley returning with his pretty lace?"

I couldn't withhold my smile. "In a month. He's going to stay, too. He is asking for time away from his job so he can visit with the elders and find out more about our way of life and see if he would like to become one of us."

Mina's eyes turned dark. "Don't be fooled by him, Gretchen. He may be a gut man. I cannot say for sure. But be sure you decide with your head and not your heart."

"There is nothing to decide, Mina. I'm not the one who will decide if he is a good candidate to move into our village."

Mina shook her head as she loaded the goods into the baskets. She glanced over her shoulder when she neared the front door. "Just remember my warning."

CHAPTER 5

"The Gypsies are here! The Gypsies are here!" My brother raced into the store the next Monday, his shoes clattering on the wooden floor like thumping drumbeats.

I whirled around, my pulse racing. "Where?" My voice croaked like a strangled frog, proof of the anxiety my brother's announcement unleashed. Using my fingers and thumb, I massaged my throat in an attempt to regain my voice and a measure of composure.

Stefan leaned forward and rested his elbows on the counter while sucking in great gulps of air. His dusty brown hair, a trace darker with perspiration, clung to his forehead.

When I again asked the question, he extended a finger in the air.

"Wait . . . out . . . of breath."

I circled the counter and remained silent until Stefan's breathing slowed to a more normal rate. "Where did you see them?"

He placed his palm on his chest. "Me and Freddie were walking back to school from the barn. Brother Denton was teaching us about cleaning and oiling the thresher."

I waved for him to hurry. "I don't need all the unimportant details. Where did you see Gypsies?"

He shot me an annoyed look. "I'm trying to *tell* you. On the way back from the barn, we saw two Gypsies riding their horses in the distance. One had a big white horse. A real beauty."

With a sigh I brushed a lock of Stefan's damp hair into place. "Just because you saw two riders in the distance does not mean they are camping anywhere nearby."

He swiped my hand away from his head. "But they are. Freddie and me went lookin' after school. There's a whole bunch of 'em camped south of town. We hid in the bushes, but one of the men spotted us. We couldn't outrun him."

I gasped and clutched Stefan's hand. "Did they hurt you?"

He shook his head and yanked his hand away. "No, but you're hurtin' my hand. They were nice to us—even let me pet that big white stallion."

"You are going to be in trouble when Vater finds out what you've been up to. What if those Gypsies had decided to keep you there and never let you return home? Then what? We would have never known what happened to you."

Stefan tightened his lips in a smirk. "You'd probably have the hardest time, 'cause then you wouldn't have anyone to holler at."

"I do not holler at you. Only once in a while do I raise my

voice—and only when it is needed. And I think Vater will do more than raise his voice once he knows what you have done."

"Please don't tell him, Gretchen. You can tell him I saw Gypsies, but don't tell him Freddie and me went down to their camp." He grabbed hold of my hand and looked up at me with pleading eyes. "Ple-e-e-ase. I promise I won't go down there again if you don't tell him."

"For sure? You promise?"

He bobbed his head until his hair tumbled forward. "I do, I do. Thank you, Gretchen." He pecked an unexpected kiss on my cheek.

Before he turned away I caught sight of the heightened color in his cheeks and was glad one of his young friends hadn't stepped inside the store. Poor Stefan would be teased for weeks if his friends thought he got along with his older sister.

He shifted and looked over his shoulder. "Where is Vater?"

"He took a shipment of calicos over to the train depot. He hoped you'd be home to help him after school, but when you didn't come straight home, he went on without you."

Stefan's eyes clouded. "Did he think I was in trouble with Brother Ulbricht and had to stay after school?"

"He didn't say, but I'm sure he will have some questions for you when he comes home."

Stefan shuffled back to the counter. "Still promise you won't tell?"

I met his worried gaze. "I doubt Vater will ask me. His questions will be for you. And remember, it is not proper to tell a lie."

"I know. I know." He turned away and trudged to the far side of the room and began to unload a crate of salves, ointments, and tonics, careful to place each one on the proper shelf. I wasn't certain if he thought his good behavior would erase his earlier misdeed, but I didn't ask. I was pleased to have him do his work without an argument.

The sight of my brother bending over the crates without complaint stopped my Vater in his tracks when he returned to the store a short time later. "Hard at work you are, ja?" He strode to where Stefan was stooped down beside a crate. "Where you were after school? I waited and waited for you. I needed strong young arms to help me with the bolts of calico, and the other men were busy in the warehouse."

Stefan stood and placed several bottles on the shelves. "Freddie asked me to go with him after school. I know I should have come home and asked first. I'm sorry, Vater."

Stefan's back remained turned toward my father while he gave his explanation. I thought he probably was afraid his eyes would give him away. Any time my father thought we were telling a lie, he would make us look at him so he could see if there were any yellow spots in our eyes. Stefan still believed Father could tell if he wasn't being honest. Though Father couldn't really see yellow spots, he could look into our eyes and see if we were telling the truth. Stefan's story today was half true. He had gone with Freddie after school; he hadn't lied, but he hadn't told the whole truth, either.

My father ruffled Stefan's hair. "You are doing a gut job. There are three more crates in the back waiting for you. And from now on I expect you to come straight home after school. If there is not work waiting for you here, you have your school lessons to keep you busy, ja?"

Stefan groaned, but he didn't argue.

"Gretchen, we will be busy tomorrow, so I will need you in the store most of the day. There are orders coming and going on every train arriving and departing this week. You will need to keep a sharp eye, for I hear tell there are Gypsies headed our way. They may already be camped outside of town."

Wide-eyed, my brother turned and looked at me.

"Stefan, you need to hurry or you won't have all those crates emptied by suppertime."

He took my cue and turned back to his work. "Who told you about the Gypsies, Vater?"

"A man on the train. He said he saw two on horseback. Then later he saw a whole caravan of them headed in our direction. If they come into the store, you should be careful they don't take anything, Gretchen. Too many things they stole when they were around here last summer."

"Not all Gypsies steal. Some are gut," Stefan said.

"That may be, but I know they took much from us last year." My father wheeled around to face Stefan. "Is one thing if we choose to give help to those in need, but I do not want them to think they have a right to come and steal from us. Sometimes I think they would rather steal than ask for help."

"I think these Gypsies are nice." Stefan's lips smacked shut, and his eyes widened until they were the size of two giant walnuts.

"And how would you know about these Gypsies?"

Too late he'd realized his error. "I'm . . . I'm n-not sure." He swallowed hard. "But wouldn't that be the same as saying everyone who lives in the Amana Colonies is perfect?" He blinked several times. "Wouldn't it?" His voice was no more than a hoarse whisper.

My father stared at him for a long moment. "Maybe you are right, but still we cannot take chances." He tapped his finger alongside his right eye. "We must keep a good watch over our goods when they are in the store. It is the wise thing to do."

Three days passed with no sign of the Gypsies, and I'd almost forgotten about them when Mina entered the store.

I glanced up from the ledgers. My friend's usual smile had been replaced by a deep frown. "Mina! It's good to see you. I'm surprised you're back so soon. This isn't your regular shopping day." I slipped from the stool and embraced her.

Impatience shone in her eyes. "Ja, well, I did not expect to return so soon, either. Do you have any eggs? All of our eggs and three of our chickens were missing from the henhouse this morning. Sister Marguerite is in a dither. She's sure it is the Gypsies who have taken them. But no matter who has taken them, we need to replace the eggs. I offered to change the menu, but she wouldn't hear of it. The older she gets, the more hardheaded she becomes. I tried to reason with her, but she only became more upset. It's easier to purchase a few eggs than have her in a flurry for the rest of the day."

I followed her toward the back of the store. "You are in luck. I have plenty of eggs from Sister Helen and Sister Wilma."

Basket in hand, Mina marched to the egg crates, picked up an egg, and examined the shell.

"Maybe it was some of the hobos. They've been known to steal eggs from time to time."

One by one Mina examined the eggs before placing them in her basket. "Could be, but ever since word spread that the Gypsies were camped outside of town, Sister Marguerite has blamed them for everything from the lack of rain to bugs on the lettuce."

"Three days have passed, and I haven't seen any of them in town. I thought maybe they had already moved on. Has anyone seen them?"

"I don't think so, but with so many women at the Küche,

there's lots of time for chatter and guesswork. And the Gypsies make for exciting talk." She placed an egg in her basket and picked up another. "You may be right about them. The store is usually the first place they visit. I'm surprised they haven't been in here." After selecting a dozen eggs, Mina covered them with her cloth. "I think that will do. Unless the thieves visit us again tonight." She strolled down the aisle and settled the basket on the counter. "Where have you been rushing off to after prayer service the last few evenings? Each night I think we can visit for a little while, but poof." She gathered her fingers together and opened them in a quick explosive motion. "I look around, and you are gone before I can catch up to you."

I couldn't deny Mina's assessment. After prayer service, I couldn't get away fast enough to return home, closet myself in my bedroom, and pore over the magazines Mr. Finley had left with me. The stories between the pages spoke to me in ways I'd never imagined. And the fact that they'd been written by women made my interest run even deeper. Each evening after I read one of the stories or poems, I would spend another hour writing my own poetry or working on a story. Not only had I found pleasure reading the magazines, they'd given me encouragement to continue with my own writing.

"I've been doing more writing in the evening."

Mina perked to attention. "I would enjoy reading some of your work. You haven't shown me any of your poems for a long time." She glanced toward our attached rooms as if she expected me to go and return with my journal.

"You want to see them now?"

"Why not? Your Vater isn't here, and I have time before I must return to the Küche. And if Sister Marguerite complains, she can send someone else to fetch eggs."

Though I wasn't eager to share my recent work, Mina wouldn't be easily deterred. Once she made up her mind, it would be difficult to change. "I won't be long. If anyone comes into the store, tell them I'll be right back." I hurried from the store but slowed my pace once inside our apartment. After I removed the journal from the drawer at the bottom of my wardrobe, I sat down on the bed and waited for several minutes. With any luck, a customer would be waiting for me when I returned and Mina would need to return to her work at the Küche.

"What took you so long? I was thinking maybe you stopped to take a nap while you were in there."

"I'm sorry I was so slow." I flipped through the pages of the journal and opened to an entry I'd written several weeks earlier.

Without so much as a glance at the page, Mina thumbed to the last entries. "I want to see this writing that keeps you from having time to visit in the evening."

I waited, perspiration beginning to form on my upper lip. I watched her gaze travel back and forth across the lines of writing. Occasionally, she glanced up, but I couldn't determine if I saw admiration or censure in her eyes. She gave a backward flip of the page and read what I'd written the previous nights.

Finally she closed the journal and slid it across the counter. "Your writing has changed. It's different."

"Better?"

"Different. The last pages don't sound like you."

"Maybe they are just a different side of me—one you haven't seen before."

Mina pinned me with a steady stare. "I have known you since you were a little girl, Gretchen. There is no side of you I do not know. Something is different, and I can think of only one thing that has happened to cause this change."

"And what is that?" I wondered if she'd somehow found out Mr. Finley had given me the magazines. If she had, I wanted her to tell me.

"Mr. Finley. You think you're in love with him, don't you?"

My breath caught in my throat. "What? No! Of course not. I spoke to him for only a short time. How could I be in love with him?"

"Nothing else has happened that would change the way you've been acting or would change your writing. I believe I am right."

I hadn't planned to reveal my secret, but I didn't want Mina to think I was in love with Mr. Finley. I certainly admired him. He was a nice man and would be a fine addition to our community, but I barely knew him. How could she believe I cared for him?

"I have something to show you. Wait here." I hurried to my bedroom, removed the magazines from beneath the mattress, and returned to the store. I held the periodicals in front of me. "This is what has created the change in my writing. Mr. Finley gave these to me. I've been coming home each night so I can read them." I pushed one of them toward her and flipped open the pages. "Look at this, Mina. These poems are all written by women. And the stories, too. And they're good, every one of them." I hesitated a moment. "At least the ones I've read so far."

"So now you try to write like these women. This is not gut."

"Why? They are much more talented than I am. If I can write like them—"

"If you can write like them, then what? Why would you want to write like anyone else, Gretchen? So you can get your poem in a magazine? That is not why you write in your journal. Now you are trying to be someone else. These things you have written the last few days, it is not gut like the rest of your journal." She slapped her palm on the magazine and pushed it away. "Better you be yourself. Those magazines are not gut help for you." She picked up the basket of eggs. "It is getting late. I need to return to the Küche."

I gathered the magazines and my journal and shoved them beneath the counter, disappointed at Mina's comments. I thought she'd be pleased that I wanted to learn more about writing; I thought she'd applaud my efforts; I thought she'd tell me to keep on improving my work. I was wrong, and I was startled by the depth of my disappointment. Since my mother's death, Mina had been the one person who lavished me with approval and understanding.

Mina glanced over her shoulder when she neared the front door. "I told you Mr. Finley was trouble."

CHAPTER 6

A group of shoppers from Iowa City arrived on the early train the following day. I smiled my brightest smile, directed them to the most recent calico prints, and told them we'd soon be receiving a shipment of fine imported laces and trims. "The most gorgeous I've ever seen," I told the ladies. They purchased calicos and woolens for their summer and winter wardrobes, along with a variety of threads, and seeds for their flower gardens. They departed with a promise to return within the month to purchase some of the promised frills. "Unless you plan a trip to Chicago, you'll find nothing to compare," I said as I bid them good-bye.

They'd been gone only a few minutes when the door opened. Thinking one of the ladies had forgotten a needed item, I turned around with a broad smile, but my smile immediately disappeared.

"Oma! What are you doing?" I gave her my sternest look while I waved her forward. My stomach churned up enough fear to send bile racing to the back of my throat. Only moments ago she had been sweeping the wooden sidewalk in front of the store. Now she was clinging to the arm of a swarthy dark-eyed Gypsy. I tried to control my mounting fear. "Come over here, Oma. I need to talk to you."

"Pretty boy," Oma cooed, still clutching the man's arm. The Gypsy's shaggy hair, tied with a string at the back of his neck, hung oily and limp. Food and drink stained the front of an un-buttoned once-white shirt that lay in an open V, exposing the man's chest. His calf-high boots displayed mud instead of a shine, and even at a distance, my nose alerted me the man needed a bath. Both his appearance and his odor offended, but I dared not look away and searched my mind for some way to entice Oma away from him.

My grandmother's fingers tightened on the Gypsy's arm, and he swaggered toward me, confidence glistening in his eyes. "She loves me," he said, his eyelids lowered to half-mast. "She wants to come and live with me and travel the country, don't you, Helga?"

Strands of white hair danced in a curious rhythm as she bobbed her head. "Ja. See the country," she repeated.

Anger replaced my fear, and I clenched my jaw. "Turn her loose right now. She is an old woman and sometimes loses touch with the real world."

His smug grin revealed a row of uneven stained teeth. "But she likes me. And I like her, too." He patted Oma's hand, and she batted her eyes like a young woman in love. "You see?"

I stomped my foot and raised my voice. "I want you to leave here right now. Without my grandmother."

"What's all this shouting? You are causing trouble, Zurca?"

I turned toward the door. More of them! Panic seized me in a stranglehold that left me speechless as I watched more Gypsies enter the store. The tall one who had spoken had the same dark eyes and olive complexion. Unlike his friend, this one's ebony hair shone as though freshly washed, and his clothing, though odd, looked clean. Several heavy chains hung around his neck, and he wore a colorful sash at his waist.

"There is no trouble. The grandmother brought me here. She wants to give me a present."

"A present, ja." Oma finally turned loose of the man's arm and ambled toward the shoes and boots. "We will find some special boots for Zurca."

I glared at the man my grandmother referred to as Zurca. "So you have convinced her she should give you a new pair of boots? Well, she is not in charge of this store, and she can't give you anything. You must leave."

Oma shrieked at me as though I'd plunged a knife in her heart. "Not until he marries me."

"You need to take a rest before the marriage, Oma. Let me take you to your room. After your nap, we'll talk about the wedding." Using my body to block any view of Zurca, I gathered my grandmother by the waist and moved her toward our apartment. When we were within earshot of the taller man, I said, "Please don't steal from us while I care for my grandmother."

He gave an indiscernible nod of his head. "You have my word."

Though I remained uncertain whether the Gypsy's word meant anything, I led Oma to her bedroom. To have her safe in her room was more important than the goods in our store, but I knew I couldn't linger until she was asleep. I covered her with a sheet and backed from the room. As I closed the door, I prayed she would soon drift off to sleep. If my father returned and discovered the store filled with Gypsies and me missing, he'd be angry for sure. And if I told him of Oma's antics, he would use it as yet another reason why she would be better off at Mount Pleasant. That thought alone caused me to quicken my step.

I reentered the store, my eyes darting in all directions. The two men had taken up a position near the shoes, and the three women who had followed the taller Gypsy into the store now wandered the aisles. They wore full colorful skirts, and bright scarves covered their loose dark hair. Vater said they sewed big muslin sacks inside their skirts to hold the many things they stole from the shelves and counters. There was no way to be sure that was true, but one look at the billowing skirts made the story easy to believe.

The taller of the Gypsies motioned to me. "My friend needs some new boots. You can help us, please."

With my lips set in a tight line, I strode across the room. "They will not be free. You must pay."

He nudged the one known as Zurca. "Show her your money."

Zurca withdrew a pouch from his pocket and dumped several coins into his dirty palm. "Your grandmother said they would be a gift."

"Hold your tongue, Zurca. You will pay for the boots." The tall Gypsy gave a slight bow. "I am Loyco, the leader of our group. There is no reason to be afraid of us. We mean no harm. We just need a few supplies, and Zurca needs new boots."

"Are the women putting your needed supplies in their pockets while I help you with the boots?"

His rumbling laughter came from deep inside. Sudden creases

formed alongside his dark twinkling eyes. I was certain he was laughing at me, but his laughter didn't answer my question. If my father was correct about the Gypsies and their penchant for stealing, this Loyco could be keeping me occupied while the women filled their pockets with our merchandise. Still, I couldn't be in four or five places at once.

"The women are looking; they do not steal." He hesitated a moment before he grinned. "Unless I give them the signal to help themselves. Would you like to see?"

"No!" My shout caused Loyco to jerk backward. "I'm sorry. I didn't mean to shout. But please don't tell them to take anything unless they intend to pay."

Though he'd assured me they would not steal, I continued to sneak an occasional look in the direction of the women.

"You are not like your brother, are you?"

I snapped around to face Loyco. "What do you mean? How do you know my brother?"

He pointed to a pair of black leather boots. "Try this pair, Zurca." Loyco pulled the boots from the shelf, handed them to Zurca, and turned to me. "The boy Stefan comes to our camp to visit. He said his family was in charge of the store. Did he lie to me?"

"He didn't lie. Stefan is my brother, and you can see that we run the store. But what do you mean I'm not like him? You speak as though you know him."

"Slide your foot forward and pull from the back of the boot, Zurca. You cannot stomp your way into them." Loyco glanced over his shoulder as he leaned down to show Zurca. "Your brother is a trusting soul, but you are suspicious of everyone. Still, I think you may have some of your brother's trust hidden deep inside." He tapped his chest with his fingertips.

I wasn't interested in Loyco's impression of me, but I did want to know more about Stefan's visits to the Gypsy camp. "How many times has my brother visited your camp?"

He shrugged his broad shoulders. "How can I know? I don't keep count. He comes at least once a day. Sometimes twice. He has grown to love my horse and is learning to ride very well."

My heart collided against my chest with heavy thumping beats. I couldn't be certain if my reaction was one of fear or anger. Stefan had promised that he wouldn't return to the Gypsy camp, yet he was going there every day. And now the Gypsies were coming into our store, acting as though he was their friend. Had Stefan been within hearing distance, I would have given him an earful. He'd soon discover his disobedient behavior would no longer remain a secret. Vater needed to know of his rebellion.

Loyco's eyes twinkled, and I could see he was taking great pleasure in my discomfort. "I would be very pleased to have you visit our camp. And if you have enough courage, you could ride my horse, too."

"I will not visit your camp, and I have no interest in your horse. And you will not see my brother in your camp in the future. You can be sure of that."

Once again his laughter filled the room. "We shall see. For now, Zurca will buy these boots. Unless you do not want to take his money."

"Of course I will take his money." I gestured to Zurca to follow me. "You can bring the boots to the counter and pay for them."

Instead of following me, Zurca clapped his hands overhead and shuffled his feet in a bouncing dance step. When he finally stopped dancing, he pointed to his feet. "I will wear the boots. They make my feet happy."

I glanced at Loyco, who shrugged and grinned. "They make his feet happy. That is a good thing."

I thought they'd both taken leave of their senses. No wonder Oma enjoyed their company. Their ideas were as foolish and muddled as hers!

The three women were gathered by the door. I couldn't tell if they'd picked up any of our goods, but I longed to check their skirts and see what I might find in their pockets. I calculated the cost of the boots and handed Zurca his change.

"They will be perfect for the wedding, don't you think?" Zurca said.

My startled reaction pleased him, and he laughed. "This is a serious woman, Loyco. She needs to learn how to laugh, don't you think?"

Loyco grinned and agreed. "She is too worried to laugh. Once we are out of her store, she will be happy. Am I correct, Gretchen?"

Gretchen. How did he know my name?

As if he'd read my thoughts, he bowed his head close. "I used no magic. Your brother told me your name. But if you come to our camp, we will read your future in the Tarot cards."

I shook my head. "I have no desire for your fortune-telling. I do not believe in such things."

He signaled to one of the women by the door, and she scampered across the room. She stood beside Loyco, watching as he grabbed my hand and held it palm up on the counter. "What do you see, Alija?"

I tried to wrench free, but he held my hand tight to the counter. The woman's bright-colored scarf draped over one shoulder. She studied my palm and then lifted her head to look at me, her leathery skin wrinkled with age. "This one keeps secrets. And

71

she has a new man in her life." Her bony fingers trembled as she signaled Loyco to release my hand. "I tell no more unless she pays. Maybe the man is you, eh, Loyco?" She cackled and scuttled back to the other women.

I yanked away as if I'd been burned by a hot flame. "I told you I didn't want—"

"Loyco! I didn't know you were going to come here," Stefan said as he burst through the door, his eyes wide and shining with fear. His eyes darted around the store before momentarily settling on me and then on Loyco.

"Stefan, my little friend. It is good to see you. Zurca needed some new boots, so we bring business to your family."

He obviously expected Stefan to thank him for the gesture. Instead, my brother stared at Zurca's boots, his eyes glimmering with fear. When Zurca finally stuck out his boot and pretended to step on Stefan's toe, my brother finally gained his voice. "They look good. Nice and shiny. A gut fit, ja?"

Zurca nodded. "A very good fit." Once again he broke into dance, and one of the women joined him.

My full attention was focused upon the Gypsies and my brother when Oma reappeared, pushed the Gypsy woman aside, and began to dance with Zurca. My stomach knotted, and I swiped my damp palms down my skirt. Zurca tipped his head back, laughed, and spun in circles with his arms extended overhead. Oma lifted her skirt to her ankles and hopped from foot to foot, trying to keep pace with the Gypsy. Even the three women had joined in, adding to the commotion.

Oma shoved me aside and shrieked in protest when I drew near. I balled my hands into tight fists and spun around to face Loyco. "Tell Zurca to quit his foolish dancing. Can't you see my grandmother is going to fall and hurt herself?"

His voice booming, Loyco shouted the command. Hands still poised above his head, Zurca ceased the clapping and slowly lowered his arms while the women scuttled back to the door. Only Oma failed to obey Loyco's order. She continued to circle around Zurca, hopping from foot to foot and clapping her hands. When Zurca didn't follow suit, she looped arms with him and tried to swing him into motion. His heavy boots remained planted in place, and she nearly tumbled to her nose.

I rushed to help her regain her footing, but Zurca caught her shoulders and set her aright. I turned to give Loyco a see-what-I-mean look, but he shook his head, irritation twitching at his lips. "You're the one who wanted them to stop dancing. The old woman was having no trouble until you insisted they stop."

My grandmother turned and strutted toward Loyco swinging her hips like a young girl. She tipped her head and batted her lashes at him. "Who do you call an old woman?"

He chuckled and pointed at me. "That one. She acts like an old woman. You should teach her how to have fun." He snapped his thumb and forefinger together and glanced in my direction. "Even better, maybe *I* should be the one to teach you how to have fun." He leaned toward me until his lips were close to my ear. "Maybe I will—"

"Gretchen! Is there a problem?" Shoulders squared, Conrad marched into the store with an air of authority I'd seldom seen him exhibit.

My mind whirred with thoughts of what he'd seen as he approached the doorway. My lips felt as though they'd been pasted with glue. Before I could worry overmuch about answering, Oma scurried toward Conrad and pulled on his hand. "Come with me, pretty boy. Here's my pretty boy." A hint of color shadowed

Conrad's high cheekbones, but he walked alongside Oma while she continued to cling to his hand.

Zurca placed his palm on his chest. "You have broken my heart, Helga. Already you have forgotten me and got yourself a new love."

"Not her." Alija pointed her bony finger at me. "It's that one who has a new man in her life." She slapped Zurca's arm. "You never listen, you fool."

Zurca rubbed his arm and shouted a curse in return. Before Alija could respond, Loyco stepped forward. "We will now leave!" With a waving motion, he directed the group toward the door. "Farewell, Stefan!" He saluted my brother, then looked at me and winked. "Farewell, Gretchen."

Unable to believe the man's bold behavior, I stood transfixed until Conrad touched my arm. "Did he wink at you? And what did that Gypsy woman mean? Who is this new man in your life?" His eyes shifted toward the door and then back at me. His look of confusion faded to sudden disbelief. "You are in love with a Gypsy?"

CHAPTER 7

During the two weeks since the Gypsies visited our store, I'd been writing in my journal to relieve my frustrations. There was a page and a half devoted to Conrad and his inability to understand what had occurred that day. How he could have ever thought I'd be in love with a Gypsy—much less one I'd met for the first time that very day—still baffled me. It had taken another page to expound upon my frustration when he'd been unable to understand why I hadn't sent for his assistance the minute the Gypsies arrived. Did he truly think I could leave them alone in the store while I dashed to the barbershop? Was I to leave Oma alone with Zurca? Granted, I could have sent Stefan when he finally returned home from school, but my mind wasn't focused upon seeking his help. Instead, I'd been shocked to learn that my brother had been visiting the Gypsy camp daily. I was more concerned about Stefan's miscreant behavior than in seeking help at the barbershop.

Many days later, after several discussions, Conrad admitted much of his anger had been fired by jealousy. A fact he was slow to admit, but one that left me feeling both embarrassed and treasured. From that point on we pushed aside any annoyance or disappointment with each other. And the fact that the Gypsies hadn't reappeared made it easier to forget the entire incident.

Stefan admitted his wrongdoing, and I agreed to keep his secret. Once again, he promised he wouldn't go to the Gypsy camp, and since he'd been coming home directly after school each day, I was confident he'd been good to his word.

I finished the ledgers and pulled out my journal. Thoughts for a poem had come to mind as I drifted off to sleep the night before, and I wanted to get them on paper this morning to see where they would lead. I'd written only a few lines when the front door opened. Expecting to see one of the neighbors needing a spool of thread or a packet of needles, I didn't immediately look up from my writing. Not until the sound of heavy footfalls drew near did I venture a glance.

My breath caught in my throat. "Mr. Finley. What a surprise. I didn't think you'd return this soon."

He scratched his forehead as though the comment had confused him. "Truly? Then I'm pleased I could surprise you." His eyes twinkled with amusement. "I've checked in to the hotel, and I'm ready to learn all you can teach me about your fine community."

I closed my journal and slipped it beneath the counter. "I think any instruction will be given by one of the elders, Mr. Finley. You can go to the barn and check with Brother Heinrich

Denton. He's an elder and can answer your questions, if he's not too busy at the moment." I met Mr. Finley's intense gaze and immediately looked away. "Have you met Brother Heinrich? He's tall and somewhat sharp-featured."

"A beak of a nose, pronounced cheekbones, a thatch of unruly dark hair, right?"

Mr. Finley had rightfully described Brother Heinrich, but I hesitated to agree with such an unkind depiction of the kind-hearted farm *Baas*. "He does have dark hair and high cheekbones. Were you at the barn earlier today?"

"No, but I rented a carriage from him last time I visited." He twirled the brim of his straw hat between his fingers. "Seemed nice enough, but I believe I'd rather wait until your father returns. Is that a problem?"

I shook my head. "No, of course not. You're welcome to wait here. There's a bench back by the shoes if you'd care to sit down."

He leaned his elbows on the counter and rested his chin in one palm. "I'd rather just stand here and stare at your beautiful face."

I looked away, surprised by his boldness. "We do not speak in such a manner, Mr. Finley."

He chuckled. "You see? I knew you'd be willing to teach me. You just needed a place to begin. Why don't you explain why it's improper to tell a person she possesses pleasant features? One glance in a looking glass is enough to affirm such a statement."

"It could cause a person to become vain, and it is the inner person that is important, Mr. Finley. Beautiful features are nothing when compared to fine character, wouldn't you agree?" He didn't immediately respond, so I continued to explain. "We have no choice about our physical appearance, but we do choose how we will treat others and whether we will live in a godly manner."

For a long moment, he pursed his lips together and appeared to be in deep thought. "But you must agree that a lovely physical appearance isn't a bad thing."

"No, it isn't bad. But it is much less important than inner beauty."

His loud guffaw startled me.

"You find my answer funny?"

He covered his mouth with his palm but continued to laugh. "No offense intended." The muffled words filtered through his fingers. He finally ceased laughing and dropped his hand. "I was picturing the process of looking down someone's throat to view their inner beauty." When I didn't join in his laughter, he chided me. "Come now, surely you can see how humorous that would be."

"I suppose there is a bit of humor to be found in what you've said." In truth, I wondered why any person in his right mind would have such a curious thought. Had my grandmother made the strange remark, I wouldn't have been surprised. She didn't have full control of her mind. But Mr. Finley was an intelligent businessman who didn't appear to have any mental problems. At least none that I'd previously observed. Maybe I just didn't understand the humor of outsiders.

"Tell me, Miss Kohler, what did you think of the magazines I left with you? Did you find any of the articles or poems of interest?"

"Yes. All of them." I blurted out the admission without thinking.

A slow smile curved his lips. "So you didn't destroy them.

I'm pleased to know you're interested in learning and expanding your horizons."

"I read them only because I enjoy writing and wanted to see how I could improve my skills." My excuse was weak, but it was the only defense I could offer. Besides, it held a modicum of truth. I'd studied the poems and stories at length. And despite Mina's assessment, I believed my writings had improved over the past weeks.

He lifted his case to the counter and opened the latches. "My instincts told me you were a young woman with a penchant for learning, so I brought along some books you might enjoy." He pushed the case toward me so I could view the bounty inside. "You may keep them as long as you'd like."

A deep sense of longing washed over me. I'd never before experienced such a strong desire to possess anything in my life. I lifted one of the books from the case and read the title. *Anna Karenina*. My excitement mounted as I flipped through the pages. I picked up the next one and smiled. *The Cambridge Book of Poetry and Song*. "They look like books I would very much enjoy."

He nodded and picked up another. "This is *Lorna Doone* and there's *Tennyson's Poetical Works*. I chose books from my library that I thought you would enjoy. Once you've read those, I'd be happy to share others with you."

To accept the books would be considered unsuitable. I did, after all, have better things to do with my time. Yet to learn was a good thing. I reasoned that reading these books would expand my mind and teach me new writing skills. And the books weren't a gift. I would return them to Mr. Finley once I'd read them. Surely it couldn't be improper to borrow some books. My insides quivered, and I glanced toward the front door. If I was convinced borrowing the books wasn't unacceptable, why was I frightened someone would see me?

I forced the thought aside. "I would be pleased to read these books, Mr. Finley, and I will see to their gut care."

He lifted the books from his case and stacked them on the counter. "And I won't mention that they're in your possession, Miss Kohler."

Apprehension nudged my conscience. The two of us now shared a secret. One that could get me in trouble.

"If you'd like to put the books in a place of safekeeping, I'll watch after the store for you."

He pushed the books several inches closer. Close enough that I cast aside my misgivings and scooped the stack of books into my arms before I changed my mind. Once inside the parlor, I slowed my pace and tiptoed across the striped carpet. Oma was asleep in her rocker. If she should awaken, I could use her mental condition to explain away any comments she might make to others, but I hoped that wouldn't be necessary. Her soft snores continued while I entered my room and carefully tucked the books beneath several quilts in the trunk at the foot of my bed. A giant sigh escaped my lips when I returned to the parlor. Only then did I realize I'd been holding my breath.

After assuring myself Oma remained sound asleep, I returned to the store. Mr. Finley was standing exactly where I'd left him. But it was immediately obvious he'd not been in that spot the entire time, for he was now reading my journal. He glanced up but made no effort to hide what he'd been doing. "You're in luck. No customers," he said, tapping the pages he'd been reading. "You have talent, Miss Kohler. I'm impressed."

I grabbed the journal from his hands and slapped it shut. My anger seethed like a boiling teakettle. "Do you frequently help yourself to things that do not belong to you, Mr. Finley?"

"When I think there's good reason."

His calm demeanor annoyed me even more. "And what good reason do you have for sneaking behind the work counter to remove and read a personal journal that has not been offered to you?"

"I thought you'd be an excellent poet, but your prose is every bit as good. Especially when you feel great passion about an issue." He tipped his head to one side, and his lips curved in an easy grin.

In that very instant I was certain he'd read some of the entries I'd made over the past few weeks. My cheeks burned hot, and I wanted to run from the room, yet his words of praise held me in place. I detested my desire to hear more of what he thought about my writing, but I couldn't deny the truth: I cared what Mr. Finley thought about my talent.

He took a step closer. "I'd be honored if you'd permit me the opportunity to read all of your writings, Miss Kohler. Though I'm no authority on poetry, I am convinced you possess great talent."

Great talent. The words caused a tidal wave of excitement to wash over me. He'd read portions of my journal without asking permission, and I still maintained a modicum of anger for his bold conduct, yet his words of praise pleased me, and I was elated to hear him say I possessed a gift for writing.

I shook my head. "I couldn't ever—"

"Don't speak in haste. At least consider my offer. You have time to decide before I depart."

His final words surprised me. "But I thought you came here with the thought of making your home in Iowa."

"Yes, yes, of course. But if I make that decision, I'll need to return to Chicago to advise my employer. And to gather the rest of my belongings."

"Of course. How silly of me. I wasn't thinking." After making such a ridiculous statement, I longed for some place to hide, but Mr. Finley didn't permit me time to linger over my inane comment.

"Is it true that all of my worldly possessions must be turned over to the society if I decide to move here?"

"If the elders agree to accept you and you make your vow to become a member, your personal belongings remain yours, but you would agree to give your money and any holdings to the society." He appeared somewhat put off by my explanation. "But all of your needs would be met, and you would want for nothing. Here we are furnished a place to live, gut food, money enough to make monthly purchases here at the store. It is a gut life, Mr. Finley."

"And if I'm here for a time and decide I don't like living here?"

"You could leave whenever you want, and you would be reimbursed for what you contributed when you joined. We are not a harsh and unrelenting group. We do not want anyone to remain who is not happy among us, Mr. Finley."

He closed the small hasps on his case and set it on the floor. "Does that include you, Miss Kohler? Can you leave whenever you want?"

"Ja. I can leave. But why would I want to? And where would I go? This is my home, the only life I've ever known. This is where my family is."

"You have no desire to see what's beyond this village? To learn what's out there and to write about what you see?"

His words caused me to smile. "I have never found a lack of things to write about, Mr. Finley. I sometimes wonder about the outside world, but enough visitors come through Homestead to give me an understanding of what lies beyond our colonies. I am not eager to go and visit, though I do enjoy seeing pictures and reading about other places."

Mr. Finley was leaning across the counter, and we were engaged in conversation when I glanced toward the front of the store and saw Conrad standing just inside the door. I didn't know how long he'd been standing there watching us, but from the look on his face, I determined it had been long enough to make him unhappy.

"Conrad! Mr. Finley has returned. Come and join us." I waved him forward and did my best to appear jovial and inviting. He ambled across the room. I didn't fail to notice his clenched fists and the tight lines around his lips. "We were visiting while Mr. Finley waits to speak with Vater."

"Ja, I saw from the door what a nice visit you were having."

My stomach lurched, and I swallowed the lump in my throat. "You remember Mr. Finley?"

"I do not think I could ever forget him."

Mr. Finley extended his hand. "Glad to hear I made such a strong impression on you, Mister . . . uh, Mister . . . You know, I don't believe I recall your last name."

"Wetzler. Conrad Wetzler. I am the barber here in Homestead. You were in my shop with Gretchen and her grandmother."

Mr. Finley bobbed his head. "Indeed, I recall the circumstances of our meeting. It was you, I mean your name, that I didn't recollect."

Conrad tightened his jaw. "There is a saying that people

remember what is important to them. I am sure you did not forget Gretchen's name."

"I've not heard that saying, Mr. Wetzler, but I believe I concur. And you're right. I didn't forget Miss Kohler's name or anything else about her." Mr. Finley's lips twitched. "I find Miss Kohler quite unforgettable."

Conrad placed one fist on the counter, and for a moment I thought he was going to punch Mr. Finley in the nose. "Since you say you wish to learn about becoming a member of our society, Mr. Finley, let me explain that we do not make such comments about the women who live here. It is not proper. In fact, most would be insulted by your bold comment."

Blood pulsed in my temples like a banging hammer. Not only had Conrad corrected Mr. Finley, but he had rebuked me for my behavior, as well. I didn't know whether to direct my anger at Conrad or Mr. Finley. At the moment I longed to rid myself of both of them. But it appeared what I wanted wasn't going to happen.

CHAPTER 8

Just when I thought Mr. Finley and Conrad were going to square off in a bout of fisticuffs, Brother Otto banged open the front door and rushed into the store as though he'd arrived regarding a matter of life and death. The schoolteacher's red face was dotted with perspiration, and he tugged his handkerchief from his pocket. Gasping for breath, he daubed his face and leaned against the counter.

I motioned to Conrad. "Please bring a chair before Brother Otto collapses." The schoolteacher didn't argue but fell to the chair before it was in place and nearly ended up on the floor. "Take a minute to regain your strength while I fetch a cup of water for you."

Brother Otto bobbed his head. His heavy breathing continued

while I dipped from the pail of drinking water and poured the liquid into a tin cup. He gulped down the contents. "Thank you." He panted for several breaths before he continued. "I don't have much time, but I'd like to speak to you." He lowered his spectacles on his nose and looked at the two men. "Alone would be gut."

Conrad and Mr. Finley quickly disappeared. I picked up my chair and moved to the other side of the counter so I could sit down and talk to the schoolteacher eye to eye. And a little more time would likely help both of us. At least, I knew it would help me. I couldn't imagine what Stefan had done to cause this visit, but after spending a half hour in the company of Conrad and Mr. Finley, I doubted the schoolteacher's report could be any more disconcerting.

I situated my chair near Brother Otto and folded my hands in my lap. "Now then, Brother Otto, what brings you to the store in the middle of your day?"

I wondered who was with the schoolchildren but didn't ask. Such a question might imply I didn't trust the teacher's judgment. And nothing could be further from the truth.

He mopped his brow one final time and shoved his handkerchief into his pocket. "Stefan brings me here in the middle of the day, Sister Gretchen. This is the third day he has been absent from school, and I am concerned about his illness. Did you receive my message?" His head pitched forward several inches, and he stared at me with bulging eyes.

My throat constricted, and I wondered if my voice would fail me when I attempted to speak. I opened my mouth, and a weak croak escaped my throat. I coughed. "No, no, I di-di-dn't receive any m-m-message." Fear and anger collided inside my stomach and set it roiling. Where was Stefan? If he hadn't been in school for more than two days, where had he been? My thoughts reeled.

The past two evenings he'd asked me to bring his supper home to him so he could continue working on his school assignments. He'd likely feared Brother Otto would see him at supper and inquire about his absence. And here I had thought he'd turned over a new leaf and was dedicating himself to making good grades. I clenched my hands until they ached.

"I thought as much. Today at recess I pulled Freddie aside and quizzed him. He could not look me in the eye, and when I threatened to talk to his Vater, he said he didn't know if Stefan was sick or not." Brother Otto leaned back in the chair. "So this is why I come here. To learn for sure the truth about Stefan."

How I wished my father would walk through the door and take charge. I didn't want this role of substitute mother. "Stefan is not ill, Brother Otto. I thought he was at school. He left this morning with his books. I have not seen him since then."

"And the last two days? I looked, but I did not see him in the Küche for his supper either night."

I cleared my throat. "He said he had a great deal of school-work to complete. Both evenings he asked if I would carry his supper home to him." Brother Otto peered over the top of his glasses. His stern look took me back to those days when I'd been a student in his classroom. I wiggled in my chair.

"So he has lied to you, to me, and to God."

The pronouncement sounded harsh. I wasn't sure Stefan had discussed the matter with God, but the fact that he'd lied did mean he needed God's forgiveness. "Ja, for sure he lied to you and to me."

"And where do you think young Stefan is spending his days?"

"I can't be sure, Brother Otto, but I will do everything in

my power to find him. Once my Vater returns to the store, I will begin my search."

"And you must tell your Vater everything so that he may deal with Stefan. I understand you are not his Mutter, but you are the next best thing." He tapped his finger against the rim of hair that surrounded his bald head. "Is too bad your Oma isn't so good in the head anymore. Sister Helga could make him mind, for sure." He placed a palm on each knee for leverage and pushed to a stand.

I jumped to my feet. "Thank you for your concern, Brother Otto. You can be sure that Stefan will be in class tomorrow."

"Ja, I will be expecting him. You should walk him to school in the morning to make sure he arrives."

That was the last thing I wanted to do. My mornings were already filled with chores at the store and looking after Oma. Now Brother Otto thought I should walk Stefan to school? I gritted my teeth at the very idea. Just wait until I found my brother.

My thoughts scattered in all directions as I walked to the door with Brother Otto. I bid him good-day, feeling as though I was the one who had been chastised for missing school. Anger took hold and I marched back to the counter. Maybe I should walk Stefan to school and let him suffer a bit of embarrassment. It would serve him right. After all, I'd been required to endure Brother Otto's lecture.

I wasn't certain where to begin my search. I glanced about the store. Conrad would help me—he'd know what to do. Then again, I couldn't leave the store until my father returned.

Brother Otto had been gone only a few minutes when Conrad reappeared at my side. "Problems with Stefan?"

"Ja. He has been missing from school for two days now. I must go and look for him when Vater returns. There is no telling where he might be. I don't know where to begin. Maybe I should talk to Freddie. He might know." I scanned the store. "Did Mr. Finley go back to the hotel?"

Conrad shrugged. "I think he's out by the apple tree, but maybe that would be a gut place for him to wait for your Vater. I don't like him in here all the time talking sweet to you."

"He is not accustomed to our ways. Once he knows better, he will speak in a proper fashion. Besides, he does not talk sweet to me." I felt heat rise in my cheeks.

"Ach!" Conrad slapped his palm on the counter. "What do you call it when he says you are unforgettable? Is that not sweet talk?"

I sighed, not knowing how I should answer without starting an argument. We had mended our last argument over Mr. Finley, and I didn't want another. "First you think I am in love with a Gypsy, and now you say Mr. Finley talks sweet with me. Honestly, Conrad, you try my patience. Right now I must worry about Stefan."

He tapped his chest with his index finger. "I was not the one to mention Mr. Finley's name. You're the one who wanted to know if he had returned to the hotel."

"Could we talk about Stefan?"

With a nod he shifted and rested his hip against the counter. "There's no need to waste time asking Freddie. His loyalty is to Stefan. He will tell us nothing, but I'm certain we can find your brother."

"You know where he is?" My excitement mounted.

"Not for sure, but the first place I would look is at the Gypsy camp."

I shook my head, unwilling to consider the idea. "He would not go there, Conrad. He promised. He gave me his word."

"Ja, but he is a boy, and boys like excitement. These Gypsies and that white horse, they are enough to make him take a risk and break his promise. He probably only intended to go down there for an hour or so before school, but then it was too much fun for him to leave."

A group of visitors entered the store, and I lowered my voice and hissed. "Fun? If he is at that Gypsy camp, it will be a long time before he has any fun again. I must take care of these customers, but as soon as Vater returns, I'm going to that Gypsy camp."

"Nein. You must not go down there alone. Come to the barbershop when you are ready to go. I'll close the shop and put up my sign that I'll return in an hour."

I grinned at him. "I hope you have your sign in the window right now, or one of the men might be wondering if the barber ever is in his shop."

"You are right. I had better go back, but promise you will come for me. Or better yet, that your Vater would go with me."

"No! Stefan made his agreement with me. I should be the one to go after him, but your company would be welcome."

While Conrad strode toward the front door, I approached the small group of visitors and gave them a shortened version of my speech. With thoughts of Stefan and the Gypsies skittering through my mind, it was impossible to concentrate. Besides, the women were more interested in the lace and fabric than learning about our customs or faith. After pointing them to the items, I returned to my position behind the counter. There were shelves that I could stock, but I pulled out my journal and began to write. Writing would calm me more than sorting and shelving.

I was well into my story about the disappearance of my brother when one of the customers motioned to me. "I could use some help over here." I slipped from my stool and hurried across the room.

The moment I approached, all three ladies decided they needed assistance with their selections. The fact that outsiders requested my help always surprised me. It would seem more logical for them to rely upon the opinions of one another rather than a store clerk wearing a dress of untrimmed dark blue calico. But now that I'd had an opportunity to look through the ladies' magazines Mr. Finley had left in my possession, I believed I could lend a bit more expertise. When one of the customers pulled a bolt of beige, red, and navy plaid, I dug through the trims for red braided cording and held it up for her inspection.

"Oh, that is absolutely perfect," the woman cooed. "Look at this, Rose. Isn't it an ideal match?"

The woman known as Rose nodded her head and signaled me to join her. She pointed to another piece of fabric. "Find me something even better to go with this," she whispered. "I don't want Jean attending club meeting in a dress that will gain more attention than mine."

Though I didn't understand such silliness, I searched through the trims and laces until I found a length of crocheted lace with a thread of pale pink woven into the design. When I held it aloft for her inspection, she leaped to my side and grabbed my arm.

"Put it down. I don't want the others to see what I'm choosing." A slight blush colored her cheeks. "This may sound strange to you, but I don't like others to copy what I wear." She tipped her head close. "And given the slightest opportunity, Rose is prone to imitate my clothing. Rather childish of her and highly annoying."

I didn't respond, for I thought she was behaving in a childish manner, too. "If you'd like, I'll take these to the front so I can measure and cut them for you."

The woman instructed me to cut ten yards of fabric, but before I could move, she grasped my arm. "Could you hide the bolt of fabric under your skirt so my friend won't see it when you return to the counter?"

My jaw dropped a notch. "No. I don't think that will be possible." I hesitated a moment. "Do you still want the fabric?"

She huffed a discouraged sigh. "Yes, of course I want the fabric *and* the trim. I suppose I can step in front of her and block her view. Let me get into position."

After receiving the woman's signal, I carried the bolt of fabric and trim to the counter, all the while wondering how she had expected me to walk with a bolt of fabric beneath my skirt. I dropped the fabric onto the counter.

I'd measured out the fabric when my father entered through the back door and approached the counter. "Mr. Finley is going to help me unload the wagon, and then we will be leaving so he can visit the other villages. I am depending on you to look after things, Gretchen."

I kept my gaze fastened on the fabric. "I have a few errands I need to complete. When do you plan to return?"

"Hard to tell. I think we will eat the noonday meal in Middle Amana or maybe Main. It will depend upon how many questions Mr. Finley has and what he wants to see. He will meet with the Bruderrat here in Homestead this evening after prayer service. If you must be away from the store, ask Sister Veda to come for a short time and take your place. Your Oma can watch after her baby while Sister Veda assists customers."

"Thank you, Vater. I will check with her." I didn't mention I needed someone to watch after Oma as much as I needed someone to help in the store.

While I cut the fabric and trim for the other customers, I thought about Mr. Finley's offer to have a poet read my work. At first I told myself that having a poet read my poems wouldn't change my desire to write. Whether he thought the poems good or bad shouldn't matter in the least. Still, to have someone with knowledge affirm my ability would be a pleasing thing. *Vanity.* The word crept into my thoughts like an unannounced intruder, and I shoved it aside. Perhaps this poet could write down ways in which I could improve my poetry. The thought excited me. Maybe I *would* send a poem with Mr. Finley. Maybe.

CHAPTER 9

Oma had been quiet for most of the day, and I prayed she'd remain on good behavior. When my mother was alive, we'd seldom needed help in the store, but now Sister Veda occasionally stepped in when needed. During my mother's illness, she'd been assigned to lend a hand when asked. She'd excelled in her ability to work with customers, and she'd quickly learned our system. For residents of the society, she'd write the information on a paper so I could enter and balance their individual ledger sheets later. For other customers she maintained a list of what was purchased and the cost so I could balance the cash box and keep a record of the inventory. After my mother's death, Veda returned to her work in the Küche, but two years ago, she'd given birth to a daughter.

Like all mothers in our villages, Veda had been permitted to remain at home with the baby until she turned three years old. But Veda still took pleasure in helping at the store whenever we needed her. I checked on Oma to make certain she remained asleep, placed a sign in the window, closed the door to the store, and hurried to the home of Veda and her husband. When she appeared at the door, I explained my need for her to watch the store for a short time.

Her little girl grinned at me but clung to her mother's skirts. "I am glad you have come and asked. I'm eager to see a few new faces. I will be there in fifteen minutes. I need just a little time to gather the things I will need for Trudy."

After stooping down to give Trudy a peck on the cheek and a quick hug, I raced toward the barbershop. I skidded to a halt when Brother Bertram stepped across the threshold. "You are in one big hurry, Sister Gretchen. Is not gut to run on a hot day." He patted his cheeks. "Your face is all red from the heat."

"Thank you for your concern, Brother Bertram. I will heed your advice." I circled around him and stepped inside. "Conrad, can you go with me to search for Stefan in fifteen minutes? Sister Veda is coming to watch the store."

"Ja. As soon as I sweep up the floor, I will come. Does your Vater know of this?"

I'd already turned to leave. "He is the one who told me to have Sister Veda come and watch after the store."

"Gut. Is better he knows what we are doing so there is no trouble later."

I stopped short. "He only knows I'll be gone from the store for an errand. He doesn't know about Brother Otto's visit."

"Why did you not tell him? He should know Stefan is missing."

My breath caught in my throat. "Missing? But you said we'd find him at the Gypsy camp."

"Ja, I did. I did. But it's not for certain, and if we do not find him . . ." His voice trailed off on the breeze.

I shuddered at the thought but heightened my resolve. "Then we will find him wherever he is. Come to the store as soon as you finish." I didn't give Conrad further opportunity to tell me what I should have told my father. I already had enough guilt about the secrets I'd been hiding—both Stefan's and my own. If my father knew I'd been concealing the fact that Stefan had already ventured into the Gypsy camp, or if he learned of the books and magazines hidden in my trunk, he would be sorely disappointed. I forced such thoughts from my mind. Right now, I needed to return to the store.

The Closed sign had been removed from the window, and the front door of the store was open wide. I could feel a tremor rising in my throat. I swiped my sweaty palms down the front of my skirt before I walked inside. Oma was standing behind the counter with a pen and paper in her hand. Mr. and Mrs. Wilson, who farmed property adjacent to our landholding, had stacked a pile of supplies on the front counter. I hurried to Oma's side. I met her gaze and could see her eyes were clear—a good sign.

"Let me help you figure the total, Oma." I reached for the pen and paper, but she yanked the pen away and glared at me.

"I have the amount totaled right here." She tapped the pen beside the figure. I leaned sideways to gain a better view and began to recalculate the numbers, but Oma pushed the paper out of my sight. "Do you think I cannot add numbers?" Her blue eyes flashed with anger.

"It's always gut to have a second look, don't you think? This is a large order, Oma."

Mrs. Wilson shook her head. "We don't need you to total our order again, Gretchen. We trust your grandmother's figures."

She nudged her husband's arm. "Give her the money, Herman." Mr. Wilson dug into the pocket of his overalls and withdrew a handful of cash. He peeled off several bills and handed them to Oma and waited while she made change.

She gave me a sideways glance, her lips fixed in a tight frown. As my father would say, she seemed to be in her right mind. He referred to Oma's bouts as being in her right mind or her wrong mind. To make the situation worse, when Oma was in her right mind, she didn't realize she sometimes was in her wrong mind and became angry when anyone questioned her judgment or ability. For me, it was becoming more and more difficult to walk that very fine line. I didn't want Oma angry, but I didn't want to entrust her with matters of importance, for she slipped between her right and wrong mind as quickly as I slipped in and out the front door.

She counted out the change and placed it in Mr. Wilson's hand before she turned toward me. "Did I do that to suit you, Gretchen?"

"Ja, of course. You did it just fine." I gave her a fleeting embrace, pasted on a smile, and stepped around the counter. "Let me help you carry some of these items to your wagon." Helping Mr. and Mrs. Wilson would be preferable to a tongue-lashing from Oma—and I was certain she was prepared to do that very thing the minute we were alone.

Mrs. Wilson and I handed the purchases to Mr. Wilson, who stationed himself in the bed of the wagon and carefully arranged the goods for the journey home. When we had finished, he held one hand to his lower back and straightened with a groan. "That should do it. Now if I can make it home before this pain in my back gets any worse." He motioned to his wife. "Come along, my dear. We have cows that'll soon need tending to."

Mrs. Wilson patted my arm as she scuttled past me and walked to the front of the wagon. "Thanks for your help, Gretchen. You have a fine day. Tell your grandmother to take care, too."

"I will tell her, Mrs. Wilson. And thank you for your business."

Mr. Wilson flicked the reins, and I returned Mrs. Wilson's wave as the wagon rolled down the street. Clouds of dust billowed from beneath the four wheels, evidence we hadn't had rain for far too many days.

When I turned to go back inside, I spotted Sister Veda hiking down the street with Trudy on her hip and a basket slung over her arm. I hurried in her direction and held out my arms to the child. "Let me carry Trudy."

"Thank you." She released the little girl into my arms and wiped the corner of her apron across her forehead. "Each day she seems to get heavier. We could sure use some rain. Terrible hot and dry for this time of year, ja?"

"Ja. I was just thinking the same thing." I slowed my step and touched Sister Veda's arm. "When I returned to the store, Oma seemed to be doing fine. She may question why you have come to help."

A firm nod caused Sister Veda's bonnet to slip forward, and she pushed the brim back from her face. "You should not worry. We will do just fine. She knows you are leaving?"

"Not yet. I was helping load the Wilsons' wagon and was going to tell her when I returned inside."

"You tell her, and I will take over from there. Ja?"

I smiled and bobbed my head. When we entered the store a few moments later, I motioned to my grandmother. "Look who I saw coming down the street, Oma."

My grandmother glanced up from the work pants she was

stacking on a shelf. "Sister Veda. It is gut to see you. And your little Trudy, she is growing as fast as the weeds in my flowers." Oma looked at Sister Veda. "She can have a treat?"

"Sure, sure. A treat is fine," Veda said.

I stood Trudy on the floor and took her hand. The two of us followed after my grandmother, who had headed toward the candy jar. "I have to leave for a short time, Oma."

"Ja. Go on. I can look after the store. It will be quiet. The train won't be here for two more hours. I don't need your help."

"Since it will be quiet," Sister Veda said, "maybe Trudy and I could visit with you and have a cup of tea. I get lonesome for company staying at home all day with Trudy."

My grandmother's eyes twinkled. "That would be very nice. And I think we will open one of these tins of graham wafers to have with our tea." My grandmother waved at me as though flicking a pesky fly. "Go on, Gretchen, go on."

I shot a look of thanks at Sister Veda and strode toward the door. I'd go and meet Conrad at the barbershop. If I waited around, Oma might begin to question exactly where I was going. A sense of relief washed over me once I was out of the store. Sister Veda understood Oma's problems, and for that I was thankful. I knew if Oma suddenly changed from her right mind to her wrong mind, Sister Veda could handle her.

Conrad was placing a sign in the window when I arrived. "Stefan said the Gypsies are camped south of town. Do you think he told me the truth?"

"Ja. They are set up in the elm grove. Lots of shade and water. They always pick a gut spot when they plan to stay for a while. It is closer if we head off this way rather than keep to the road."

Conrad grasped my elbow, and we trudged in silence through the uneven terrain that would lead us to the Gypsies and, I hoped, to my brother. Conrad's legs were longer than mine, but I didn't want to admit it was difficult to keep up. We'd gone only a short distance when my skirt caught between my legs. Had it not been for Conrad's strong hold, I would have toppled to the ground.

He came to a sudden halt. "You should have told me I was walking too fast. I don't want you to fall and injure yourself. Then we would never find Stefan." When his smile didn't quite reach his eyes, I knew his concern for my brother ran deep. Maybe he wasn't as certain about Stefan's whereabouts as he'd boasted.

"I am fine, but we must hurry. If Stefan isn't there, we will need time to look other places." My heart pounded beneath the bodice of my dark calico, and my mouth turned dry with the fear that we might not find him.

"He will be there, Gretchen. God is with us, and God is with Stefan. To pray would be a gut thing."

I hunched forward and pressed on. "There isn't time to pray. We must keep moving."

"There is always time for prayer." He touched the tip of his finger to his straw hat. "Pray in your head while we walk."

I did as he said, my thoughts running through my mind like a herd of galloping horses. No matter how hard I tried, I was unable to tame my thoughts any more than I could have tamed a wild horse. *Please let Stefan be there, Lord. Please let him be unharmed. Please don't let me lose my temper when I see him. Please make the Gypsies cooperate.* One after another, the pleas tumbled through my mind. I could only hope God was listening and could decipher my jumbled prayer.

"Over here," Conrad said. He took hold of my hand and circled to the right.

"Are we sneaking up on them?" I'd intended to whisper, but my question was more of a croak.

"No. I'm sure they already know we are—"

Before he had finished his sentence, the sound of horses' hooves pounded on the ground behind us. We twisted around to see Loyco charging toward us on the giant white stallion with Stefan bouncing behind him. I clasped my hand across my mouth to keep from screaming. Shirt unbuttoned and flapping in the breeze, he circled the horse around us. Reaching behind, he grabbed Stefan around the waist and lowered him to the ground.

"You have come looking for my young friend, I see." Loyco's broad smile revealed a row of even white teeth made brighter by his dark complexion. "He is safe and sound. Even better, he is learning how to become an excellent horseman."

"He is supposed to be in school learning to read and write." I yanked Stefan by the arm and pulled him to my side. "You promised, Stefan. Brother Ulbricht came to the store this morning worried about your illness."

Loyco tipped back his head and laughed. "The boy has horse sickness. He longs to ride and be free, Gretchen. That is not such a bad thing. You should try it sometime. I would be pleased to let you ride with me, and then you will know why Stefan comes to the camp each day."

"He will not be coming here anymore, and if he does, you are to send him home. Do not let him ride that horse again." I stomped my foot in the grass. "Do you understand?"

Loyco swung down from the horse and moved toward me, but Conrad stepped between us. The Gypsy looked from Conrad to me, then gestured back and forth with his index finger. "The two of you, you are husband and wife?"

I squeezed Stefan's shoulder to make certain he didn't move toward Loyco. "Of course not! I am not married."

He eyed Conrad. "And you?"

"I am not married, but I don't know why that matters."

The Gypsy shrugged. "It matters to me." He took a step closer. "Maybe you would like the adventurous life of a Gypsy, riding around the country enjoying your freedom. What do you think, Gretchen?"

I gasped and stared at him, dumbfounded by his disrespectful conduct, but Conrad took a giant step and met Loyco eye to eye. "Do not ever again speak to Gretchen in this way." Conrad's jaw twitched, but he didn't look away or flinch when Loyco raised his hand.

A scream locked in my throat, but Loyco's hand came down on Conrad's head with a light touch and roughed Conrad's hair. "You are in love with Gretchen, yes?"

Conrad bobbed away from Loyco. "That is not a question for you to ask."

Loyco rocked back on his heels with a hearty laugh. Lines creased his face, and he slapped Conrad's shoulder while he hooted. "You are a brave man to defend your woman. I think you are a man worthy of Gretchen, but Gypsy men do not give up so easy. The best man will win her heart in the end." He winked at me, and my face warmed at his ongoing show of improper conduct.

"We have come here to find my brother, not for this silly talk." I grasped Stefan's arm and turned away. "Come, Stefan. You have many questions to answer." Fearing my brother might race toward Loyco for protection, I held fast to his arm. "What were you thinking," I hissed when we were a short distance away.

His eyes gleamed with wonderment when he looked up at me. "Did you see the horse? Isn't he the most beautiful animal you've ever seen?"

I pinched his arm. "You must quit thinking about that silly horse. He belongs to the Gypsies. Then again, maybe they stole the horse. Who can say about such people. Theirs is not a life you should imitate, Stefan. And what about school and all the lies you've told?"

The gleam in my brother's eyes disappeared, and his hopeful smile turned to a frown as we trudged through the thick prairie grass. With each step toward home, the realization that he must face both our father and Brother Otto appeared to weigh heavy on my brother's chest. I steeled myself against the feelings of pity rising in my heart. "I don't know what Brother Ulbricht has in mind for your punishment, but you won't have any free time to enjoy the outdoors once you come home from school. After you finish the schoolwork Brother Ulbricht sends home for you, I will have enough work at the store to keep you busy—sweeping floors, dusting, stocking shelves, and unpacking crates—until bedtime each evening." Though he didn't argue, I knew my brother would do all within his power to escape any extra chores, but this time, I could not relent. Stefan must learn to turn away from such wayward behavior.

CHAPTER 10

When we neared the barbershop, I thanked Conrad for his help. I didn't miss the look of regret he and my brother exchanged. Conrad likely remembered going through similar situations when he'd been Stefan's age. Still, it would make my job all the more difficult if Stefan thought he could make an ally of Conrad.

I grabbed Stefan's hand and tugged him forward. "Come along, Stefan. We need to get back home. Sister Veda agreed to help at the store while I was gone."

"Where is Vater?"

I heard the tremor in my brother's voice. There was little doubt he feared meeting with Father. "He is taking a visitor to see the villages and meet with some of the elders. A salesman who thinks he might like to join the society."

"Mr. Finley?"

I arched my brows. "How do you know about Mr. Finley?"

"Conrad."

"Conrad?" I could hardly believe my ears. "What did Conrad have to say about Mr. Finley?"

Stefan hitched his right shoulder in a shrug. "He said he didn't think Mr. Finley really wanted to come and live in Homestead."

"What else?"

"He thinks Mr. Finley is sweet on you and you're too trusting."

"Trusting? Is that what he said?" I yanked on Stefan's shirt-sleeve.

He bobbed his head and strands of soft brown hair fell across his forehead. "Ja. He said you believe everything the salesman tells you, and you are smitten by him. I asked him what smitten means, but he told me I wouldn't understand."

Stefan took a forward step, but I pulled him back. "What started this conversation? Did Conrad ask if you'd met Mr. Finley?"

He sighed. "No. I asked Conrad if he'd ever heard of anyone named Allen Finley."

I stared at my brother, trying to understand. "You were in school when Mr. Finley was in the store. How did you know about him?"

My brother cocked his head to the side. "Because it's written in those books he gave you."

Heat from the sun's rays beat down on my dark calico, and I swayed toward Stefan. Swallowing hard, I grabbed his arm, fearful I might faint. "Let's get to some shade." I leaned on his shoulder until we were beneath an elm tree that bordered the far end of the limestone store. "This is a little better." I pulled my bonnet from my head and fanned it in front of my face, thankful for the artificial breeze.

"You sick?" Stefan's dark brown eyes reflected his confusion.

I stared at him, unable to believe he'd openly admitted to being in my room and going through my things. "How often do you go through my belongings, Stefan?" He looked up at the low-hanging branches and shuffled his feet. I thought he probably wished he could fly up there and hide from me.

"Not often."

"Not often? So you admit this isn't the first time?"

After some prodding he admitted that he'd checked my room last Christmas to see if his presents were hidden in my trunk or wardrobe. "I didn't find anything."

"That's because they were not in there. And if Vater had known you did such a thing, you wouldn't get any more Christmas gifts."

Stefan pulled a twig from one of the branches. "But you won't tell him, because then I might tell him about all those magazines, ja?"

The comment was enough to make me woozy. Now Stefan was going to use the periodicals as a weapon against me. There was no denying that Mr. Finley had given the magazines to me, or that I was hiding them, or that I knew I shouldn't be reading them, or that I didn't want my father to know anything about them. And my brother had likely concluded all the same things. I wanted to throttle him, but right now I needed to get back to the store. I also needed to think about how to handle this entire matter.

Holding my temper in check, I pushed away from the tree. "I'm certain Sister Veda is eager to return home and put Trudy down for her nap. We'd better go inside." It took every ounce of composure I could muster to maintain a civil tone, especially when I noticed my brother's smug grin.

Veda waved when she spotted us coming down an aisle. I didn't see Oma or Trudy until I neared the front counter. The two of them were sitting on the floor rolling a cloth ball back and forth.

Veda wiped her hands on her apron as she approached. Her brows dipped when she noticed Stefan at my side. "No school today, Stefan?"

"Ja, but I am not going until later."

Before she could question him any further, I said, "I hope there were no problems here at the store."

"Nein. Only one customer while you were gone—a farmer from over near Iowa City and his two boys. Everything is written down for you."

"Thank you. Help yourself to something you would like as payment for your time here. Or I can add to your credit if there's nothing you need."

"Ach! You owe me nothing. It is my pleasure to help out once in a while. You know I enjoy working here." She tapped a finger to the side of her head. "Your grandmother is having some trouble again, but she and Trudy have had great fun playing ball. They stacked the tins of crackers and cookies for a while, but Trudy soon became restless." She glanced toward the south wall of shelves. "I hope I have them back in proper order for you."

"I'm sure they are perfect."

Sister Veda stooped down and gently touched Oma's arm. "I must take Trudy home for a nap, Sister Helga. Will that be all right with you?" Oma looked up, her eyes clouded with confusion, and grabbed the ball tight to her chest. Sister Veda scooped

Trudy into her arms. "We're not going to take the ball, Sister Helga. You keep it here, ja?"

As Oma nodded, wispy strands of white hair floated around her head like the soft white tufts from cottonwood trees. "Mine." I leaned forward and helped Oma to her feet. She continued to clutch the ball until Veda and Trudy were gone.

"Look after the store, Stefan. I'm going to take Oma into her room and see if she'll rest for a while."

Any other day, Stefan would have argued, but today he quickly agreed, a sure sign he knew he was on thin ice. Not only with me but also with Father. Yet I worried about his threat. What if he told about the magazines? Guilt stabbed me like a sharp knife. Why was it so easy to see Stefan's faults and overlook my own? I expected him to give up going to the Gypsy camp, but I didn't want to give up my magazines. *But what Stefan does is dangerous. Reading holds no peril.* The words seemed to justify my actions.

Once Oma had settled in her rocker with her knitting basket, I reentered the store. "I think you should return to school, Stefan. The longer you are away, the more lessons you'll miss. If Brother Ulbricht has any questions about your punishment, you should tell him Vater has not returned from Homestead." Stefan's eyes pooled with tears and I touched his arm. "I think you should tell Vater about all of this, Stefan. It is better if it comes from you rather than from me or Brother Ulbricht, don't you think?"

"It would be best if no one told him. If I promise to never—"

"Stefan! You made that promise before, remember? The matter is out of my hands. Now Brother Ulbricht is involved. If you and I don't tell Vater, you can be sure there will be another visit from your teacher, and it will go even worse for you."

"Ja. I know you are right, but I don't think what I did was so terrible. We shouldn't have to go to school the whole year. I think we should have time away from school in the summer. And Gypsies don't ever worry about school. They learn from one another. I think that would be even better."

"When you are an elder and help to make rules for the village, then you can suggest such a change. Until then, you must go to school." I brushed the dust from his shirt and pushed his unruly hair into place. "And when you become a man, I doubt you will think the rules should be changed. Just wait and see." Gently I turned him toward the front of the store and walked beside him to the door. "Go on, now. And make certain you go to the school and nowhere else."

Late in the afternoon while I was finishing the ledgers, my father strode through the door. I stretched to look over his shoulder. "Mr. Finley is not with me," he said. "He went back to the hotel and said he'd join me at supper." My father tipped his head to the side. "Has Stefan completed his chores?"

"Ja. He swept the floors, and now he is running an errand for Conrad." My father started toward the back of the store, but I signaled for him to stop. "Wait. I have something I must tell you."

He scanned the store. "The Gypsies have been here stealing from us?"

"No. They haven't returned." Before I could say anything more, he interrupted.

"Your grandmother is causing more trouble? Because if she is, we must talk."

"Oma is fine. I need to talk to you about me—something I have done." I bowed my head and inhaled a deep breath. "I have books in my room that Mr. Finley loaned to me," I said, exhaling the words in a giant whoosh. "I know I should not have accepted them, and I have no excuse except that I wanted to read them." I took in another deep breath. I raised my head and was surprised to see no anger reflected in my father's eyes.

"What kind of books?"

I didn't mention the fashion magazines that Stefan had seen. Instead, I gave my father a quick description of the books Mr. Finley had given to me. "I am sorry for my deceit, Vater, and I will return the books to Mr. Finley this evening after prayer service."

"Nein. If they are gut books, is not such a bad thing, so long as you do not neglect your Bible reading. I see no reason to return the books until you have read them."

"No reason? Is it not against the rules?"

"Ja, but even the Bruderrat agrees the rule against reading books is too strict. That rule has not been enforced with the same strictness as in the past. There are plenty in the villages who have books." He grinned. "For sure, I think they read them. Do you think all the people who order books from the catalog are buying them for relatives who live somewhere else?"

I shrugged, but in fact, that's exactly what I had thought. "Thank you, Vater. I promise the books will not interfere with my work in the store or my Bible time."

"Gut." He gave my shoulder an unexpected squeeze. "You work hard and deserve some time to enjoy yourself. If a book is what makes you happy, then read your books."

My father's words of praise didn't come often, so I appreciated his compliments when they finally came my way. To hear him approve my work in the store had been as surprising as his permission to continue reading Mr. Finley's books. For the remainder of the afternoon, a smile tugged at my lips while I stocked shelves and completed the ledgers. As the time drew near for Stefan to return home, I wondered if his confession would receive the same calm acceptance. I had strong doubts.

I heard Stefan's shoes clattering on the walkway a moment before he poked his head around the doorjamb. "Is he here?"

I crooked my finger, and my brother scurried toward me. "Yes. He's putting up some hooks in the back to hang some of the leather straps and belting." I scooted to the edge of the high stool I used at the counter. "Just so you know, I didn't tell him anything about Brother Ulbricht's visit or finding you at the Gypsy camp, but I did tell him about the books I have in my room." He squeezed his lips into a tight seam. "It's up to you what happens now, but one of us must tell him."

"I will." He said and trudged to the rear of the store.

For a short time there was no more than a quiet murmuring, but moments later my father's voice thundered through the room. I looked up at the sound of his heavy boots clomping down the aisle. My stomach churned as he stomped toward me, his complexion a strange shade of purplish red. He was holding the top of Stefan's ear between his thumb and finger. My brother was dancing alongside him on tiptoe, his eyes wide with fear, his lips twisted in pain.

"Vater! You are hurting Stefan." Never before had I questioned my father's words or deeds, but never before had I seen him so enraged. "Please turn loose his ear." My father dropped his hold on Stefan's ear but immediately grabbed hold of him by the scruff of his neck. Father's large hand encircled Stefan's scrawny neck and held him in place like a farmer holding a chicken in readiness for the chopping block.

"How long have you known about all of this, Gretchen?"

"Only since Brother Otto came to the store this morning.

Stefan wanted to tell you himself, so I remained silent until he could do so."

"You went to the Gypsy camp and brought him home?"

"Conrad went with me. I wanted to speak to you before you left with Mr. Finley, but there wasn't time. I knew Conrad would be willing to help."

"Ja, but still it was my place to go after Stefan. The Gypsies caused you trouble?"

Stefan wrested around, his dark eyes revealing deep determination. "I told you they do not cause trouble or hurt anyone. Loyco was kind to Gretchen."

My father waved a dismissive gesture. "Ach! What has happened in my house when my son would rather lay about in a Gypsy camp than study his lessons? For missing school you will be punished by Brother Ulbricht with extra schoolwork. I will speak to him myself. And for going to that Gypsy camp, you will be punished with extra work here at the store. I will see to that myself. And I will walk you to your school each morning. You will once again be like the little children who can't find their way to school on their own."

I couldn't be certain if Stefan's face was burning red with anger or embarrassment. He didn't argue or question his punishment. He knew it would do him no good. But I wondered if any consequence would keep him away from Loyco and that white stallion in the camp of Gypsies.

After returning from prayer services, Father and I sat in the parlor while I darned a pair of my stockings and he studied the latest catalog for new items he might want to order for the store. I was eager to hear about his time with Mr. Finley.

"What do you think about Mr. Finley, Vater? Is he sincere in his desire to live among us?"

After placing a finger between the pages, he glanced up. "Ja, he talks like he would be happy here. He asks lots of questions. All the time we were gone he was talking, talking, talking. My ears, they were starting to hurt by the time we got back home."

I giggled and drew the thread tight before once again poking the needle beneath the hole in the lisle stocking. "But it is gut he asks lots of questions before he decides, ja?"

"Ja, but it will be a decision for the Grossebruderrat. They must be certain of his faith and his reasons for wanting to join us. There is no one to vouch for him, so they will not be so quick to embrace him into the society. Would be different if he had a relative who could speak for him."

I knotted and snipped my thread. "You could speak for him after you know him better."

"It is not the same. He can come here and say anything. I have no way to prove the right or wrong of it. He seems like a nice man. He has gut manners and asked questions about our faith and our history, but that does not mean he would be happy living here or that we would be happy to have him once he has joined us. I can look into his eyes, but I cannot see his heart."

After a little prodding and a lot of questions, my father told me Mr. Finley had worked as a salesman for seven years. "He says he enjoys his work, but he doesn't like the importance the world places on possessions and making money. He says he longs for a life of simplicity."

"Well, I do not think of our life as being simple here in the colonies." I didn't know if I should be offended by such a remark or not. After all, we were a people of invention and foresight who worked hard and produced much. I did not think of our people as living simple lives.

"We have not lived in Mr. Finley's world, Gretchen. I am sure that the way we live appears simple to him because it is different—more stable and dependable."

"Maybe you are right. I don't want to misjudge him, but I don't want him to misjudge us, either."

My father flipped the page of the catalog. "Do not worry about that. Before he is approved, the elders will be sure he understands all he must know about us."

I hoped we would know all we should know about Mr. Finley, as well. Except for detailing his love of poetry, he'd avoided most of my questions about his life or family. He was, it seemed, much better at asking questions than providing answers.

CHAPTER 11

The following day I was surprised to see Mr. Finley enter the store. I was certain my father said he was going to take him to Middle Amana to see the printshop and bookbindery, where the school textbooks, hymnbooks, and other religious books used by the community were printed. He removed his hat and strode toward me with purpose in his step.

"My Vater is gone to the train depot, but he should return in a short time. You are going to Middle Amana today, ja?"

He nodded. "That was our plan, but I received a telegraph requesting my immediate return to Chicago. My aunt Lucille is ill and in need of assistance. Uncle Frederick must leave the country on business, and there is no one else to look after her."

I attempted to hide my surprise. "You did not mention you

have family in Chicago. They will surely miss you if you decide to move here."

"They can arrange for live-in help." His offhand comment reminded me of Father when he spoke of sending Oma to Mount Pleasant.

"But that's not the same as family."

"Next best thing, I suppose. We can't always expect to have family around to take care of us, but my uncle's business is a concern." His attention settled on the telephone behind me. "I need to use your telephone to call Chicago." He dipped his hand into his pocket and removed several coins. "I'm willing to pay, of course."

When I shook my head, he reached into his pocket for more money. I waved aside the gesture. "You can't reach Chicago on this phone. These telephones connect to our villages but nowhere else."

He stared at me as though I'd spoken another language. "I don't understand."

I motioned to Brother Kruger, who had just entered the store. "Could you explain about our telephones to Mr. Finley? He wants to call Chicago from here. I told him that isn't possible, but I don't understand well enough to explain."

The tall, angular man gave a firm nod. "With these telephones you can call the train depot, the doctor, the pharmacy, or the general store, but not outside the Amana communities. We use a ground telephone system with an overhead wire that runs to each telephone in the villages. The telephones are grounded to the earth, which acts as a conductor."

"In other words, there is no telephone that I can use."

Brother Kruger's eyebrows dipped in a frown. "That's what I just explained. To contact someone in Chicago, you must send a telegraph from the train depot." He pointed across the store before turning his attention back toward me. "I need a new pair of suspenders. You will deduct them from my account?"

I hurried to the rack, removed a pair of black suspenders, and handed them to Brother Kruger. After assuring him I would charge his account, I returned to the counter.

"I don't think he liked me."

"Don't be foolish. He doesn't know you. The telephone system confuses most visitors." I opened the ledger to Brother Kruger's page. "So you will depart on the late morning train?"

"Yes. I think that will be best. If my uncle leaves early tomorrow, I'll need time to discuss business matters, and Aunt Martha may need my help."

I tipped my head to one side. "I thought it was your aunt Lucille who was ill."

Beads of perspiration formed along Mr. Finley's forehead. "Of course—Aunt Lucille. My aunt Martha is her sister. I'm always mixing up their names." He traced his index finger beneath his shirt collar. "It's terribly warm today, don't you think?"

I shrugged. "Not particularly. There seems to be a nice breeze. Does your aunt Martha live in Chicago, too?"

He removed his handkerchief from his pocket and swiped his forehead. "No. Aunt Martha lives in New York. Otherwise, she could stay with Aunt Lucille." He leaned his forearms across the counter. "I was wondering if you'd given any more thought to my suggestion."

"Suggestion?"

"About having my friend read one of your poems. And I would be delighted if you would permit me the opportunity to read more of your writing. Perhaps you would allow me to take one of your journals to read on the train?"

The very thought of Mr. Finley reading my personal entries caused my stomach to rage like a summer storm. I clasped a hand to my midsection. "Never. There are many personal reflections in my journal that I would never wish to share with anyone."

"Have you read any of the poetry in the magazines I gave you?"

"Ja, of course."

"Did you notice how those that speak of personal longing and desires of the heart are written with the most eloquence?"

I tried to remember the poems I'd liked the most. None of them were about desire or longing. "I was impressed with the ones that described beautiful scenery, the rain, and snow: the ones that spoke of God's creation."

"Yes, of course. Those are lovely, as well. But the point I wish to make is that people who read poetry don't necessarily believe the poem is about the author's life or inner thoughts. They simply believe it's an artistic expression. Much like an artist who paints a portrait. Those who view his painting don't necessarily believe it is a picture of the artist." His brows arched high on his forehead. "You see what I mean?"

"I do, but I still won't give you my journal."

He slapped his palm to his forehead. "It's my hope to help you, Gretchen. Don't you want to improve your writing?"

"Ja, but—"

He held up a hand to silence me. "What if you cut out several pages? Those that have poems you're willing to let me and my friend read? I'll purchase a new journal for you in which you can write only the things you are willing to share with others."

"I think I could do that, but don't purchase a journal for me. Accepting a gift from a man would be unsuitable." I pointed to a stack of tablets similar to the ones used by the schoolchildren. I'll use one of those."

He glanced at the mound of writing pads. "One of those will be acceptable. You'll be able to easily remove the pages you want to send with me."

The sparkle returned to his eyes. I was happy that my suggestion satisfied Mr. Finley, although I wasn't certain why I wanted to please him. "When will you return?" The question was personal and bold, and I wanted to take it back as soon as I'd spoken, but he didn't appear to take offense. Instead he gave me a broad smile.

"Can I assume you will miss me and want me to return?"

His question caused warmth to rise in my cheeks, and I turned my focus back to the ledgers. "If you desire to make your home among us, you will be most welcome to return. As for missing you, I don't believe I have known you long enough to miss you." That wasn't exactly true, for if he never returned I would always wonder if he could have helped me to improve my writing.

"I don't anticipate my uncle will be gone for too long. I promise to write and keep you informed of my aunt's progress." He tapped my journal with his finger. "Were you going to give me those pages? I have some packing to finish at the hotel."

I fumbled to open the journal and flitted through the pages to find poems that might impress Mr. Finley's poet friend yet not reveal too much about my personal thoughts. After retrieving a pair of scissors from the shelf, I snipped out one page and then another. "I believe these will do." I extended the two sheets of paper.

Mr. Finley grasped my hand with his right hand and removed the pages with his left. Still holding my hand, he raised it to his lips. "Thank you for trusting me, Gretchen. I won't disappoint you."

I twisted my hand and broke from his hold. "We do not indulge in familiar contact, Mr. Finley. I am certain my Vater spoke of such things when you were with him yesterday."

"I'm sorry. Please accept my apology. Your father did explain some of the rules pertaining to men and women. I chose to remember only one."

"And what was that?"

He leaned forward. "That men and women can marry so long as they obtain permission from the elders." The train whistle sounded in the distance, and he folded my pages and tucked them into his pocket. "Promise that you will continue your writing. Try some short stories."

"About what?"

"There is a saying that writers should write what they know. Why don't you write some stories about the colonies? Tell about visits from the Gypsies or how the wine is made. Perhaps a story about the division of men and women during mealtime and church services or about work in the kitchens and the food that is served." He hesitated a moment. "Or how you celebrate your holidays. Those are things you can write about with conviction."

There was an urgency to his request. Probably because he feared the train would leave without him. Still, his persistence created a sense of discomfort. "If I have time, I may consider a story or two, but they can wait until I hear from your friend. He may say that I should never again set pen to paper."

"I've seen enough of your talent to know he would never say such a thing. Besides, it would make me feel closer to you if you would send me your stories. I could learn even more about the villages."

His explanation made sense. My stories could help him decide whether or not he wanted to make the colonies his home. "Ja, I suppose what you say is true."

After pulling my journal forward and flipping the pages to the back, he wrote his name and address and slid the book back to me. "You can mail them to me at this address. Use this to pay for the postage." He pulled some money from his pocket and placed it on the counter.

"That is far too much for postage." I tried to push the money back toward him, but he covered my hand and held it in place.

"There is no way to know how many wonderful stories you may send to me. If there is money remaining, you can give it to me when I return."

I withdrew my hand but didn't soon forget the warmth of his palm or the look in his eyes when I lifted my gaze. "Please don't expect much. I keep busy here at the store, and I have all those fine books of yours to read."

"I know you'll find time." He glanced toward the door. "I really must go. Thank you, Gretchen. I am most grateful. I'll write very soon, and I hope that you will do the same."

The moment he departed, guilt assailed me. A part of me wanted to run after him and demand he return the poems. Yet another part bubbled with excitement over what I might discover about my ability. Besides, if I ran after Mr. Finley, people at the train station would question my unseemly behavior. I couldn't possibly create such a scene. I remained frozen in place until the train whistled a final shrill blast and chugged away from the station carrying both Mr. Finley and my poems off to Chicago. Regret plagued me. I shouldn't have done such a brazen thing. Neither my father nor the elders would have approved of my behavior. I was no better at following the rules than Stefan. But who could say—perhaps one day my writing could be used to benefit the colonies. If Mr. Finley's friend thought I had talent, I'd do my best to think of some way I could use my writing in service to our people and the Lord.

Early that afternoon I was at the front of the store and had completed orders for some ladies from Oxford when my father came through. The shipment we had received the previous day had been a large one. There were always more visitors in the spring and summer, and the surrounding farmers looked to our store to supply all their goods. Rather than make the journey to Iowa City, they brought their business to us—and for that we were grateful.

My father glanced over his shoulder. "You have been selling a lot of candy the past week, ja?" He grinned and pointed at the glass jars and baskets that we kept on shelves near the front of the store.

"Nein. Not many children in the store recently. And not many Mutters buying treats, either." I stretched across the counter and peered at the shelves. My jaw dropped at the sight, and I met my father's watchful gaze. "I don't know where it has gone, but a great deal is missing."

My father rubbed his palm across his forehead. "I am thinking it must be the Gypsies."

"But they haven't been in the store, Vater. And if they are coming in here to steal, it seems strange they would take nothing but candy."

"Is true it does not make sense, but maybe we need to check the inventory and make sure there are not other things missing." He trotted down the aisle and lifted a tin of fruit from the shelves. "Until we count, we have no idea how much could be missing. I am expected to keep the records straight and give a correct accounting in my books." He stared at me, his eyes wide and expectant. "We must check the stock."

"Maybe you are right," I said.

"Of course I am right. First I must unpack this shipment, but then we must check our stock against the inventory list."

The mere thought of counting every item in the store left me breathless, but I could not argue with my father. I could only hope that we would arrive at some other solution before the time arrived to begin the daunting task.

I'd been back at my work for only a few minutes when I saw Mina frantically waving me to come to the front door.

After a quick glance over my shoulder, I scurried to meet her. Mina's cheeks were the shade of ripe tomatoes, and perspiration beaded her forehead and upper lip. "What has happened?"

She held her midsection and gasped for breath. "Do you know where your grandmother is right now?" She made her way inside to the counter while I dipped her a cup of water.

"Ja. She is right over there stocking the shelves." Relief flooded Mina's eyes as she gulped the water. "Why did you think she wasn't here?"

Mina lifted the corner of her apron and wiped the perspiration from her face. "I walked past the south grove taking midmorning refreshments to the garden workers. There were several Gypsy children near the path eating candy. I'm certain one little girl was wearing Oma's cap—the one she crocheted with fine black thread and wears on Sundays. When I called to her, all of the children ran into the thicket. I was fearful your grandmother was in the woods with them. I went and looked but didn't see her, and all of the children scattered like mice on a sinking ship. I would have remained, but three of the workers are out sick today."

Mina's breathing returned to a normal rate, and I handed

her a damp cloth to cool her face. "I appreciate your concern for Oma, but I'm glad you didn't use more of your precious time looking for her."

"And I am thankful she is safe and sound." Mina rested against the counter. "I keep saying we need to have an *Älterschule* for the old people, just like we have the *Kinderschule* for the little children. If we had the Älterschule, there would be no worry about your grandmother's wandering off."

For at least six months Mina had been talking of a place where the older people who developed physical and mental infirmities could come together each day and enjoy the company of one another, then return to their families in the evening. I had assisted her by writing out a plan for the Älterschule. Although she'd talked to a few of the elders about the possibility, she'd shied away from going before the Grossebruderrat with her idea. Perhaps seeing the increasing difficulty with Oma would spur her on with the idea.

"Maybe you should talk to the Grossebruderrat about the Älterschule. You know I think it is a wonderful idea." There wasn't time to discuss the possibility right now, but tomorrow I would again try to convince Mina to speak to the elders.

My grandmother approached, her eyes as clear as the summer sky. "You need some help at the kitchen, Mina? I am through stocking the shelves."

"We can always use a pair of extra hands, but I don't want to take you away if Gretchen needs you here." Mina gave me a can-she-come-along look.

"I think it would be a nice change for Oma to help in the kitchen for a few hours," I said. "I'll come and fetch her when Vater comes in from the warehouse at four o'clock."

"Then it is settled." Mina smiled at my grandmother. "I will be glad to have your help, Sister Helga. There are lots of potatoes to pare."

"Ach! There are always lots of potatoes that need a sharp knife."

I leaned forward and gave Oma a fleeting hug. How I wished her mind would remain as clear as it was at this moment.

The comment about my grandmother's cap nagged at me like a pecking hen. There were no customers in the store, and I wanted to lay the question to rest. Never before had I gone through another's belongings, but this was different. If Oma had managed to be gone from the store for an extended period of time without my knowledge, she was even more at risk than I had imagined.

After searching every nook and cranny of Oma's room, my worst fears were confirmed. Her hand-crocheted cap was missing.

I returned to the store and tried to quiet the worrisome thoughts tumbling through my mind. After several failed attempts to journal my concerns, I set aside my pen and took up Oma's job of stocking shelves. I moved through the store, unable to tame my wild imagination and the frightening questions that popped into my mind at every turn. The questions turned to worry, and the worry turned to outright fear. What if Oma had been injured or lost to us forever? How would I have lived with the guilt? She'd protected me throughout my childhood, yet I didn't seem capable of doing the same for her.

After arranging bolts of fabric for more than thirty minutes, I realized I had placed them in the wrong section and all my efforts had been an utter waste of time. If I was going to rid myself of this unrelenting fear, I couldn't depend upon myself. " 'For God hath not given us the spirit of fear; but of power, and of love, and of a sound mind.' " Over and over I repeated the Bible verse from the book of Second Timothy. I took courage in the words and told myself I could protect Oma. I simply needed to take charge.

"Gretchen! I will be back here working."

My father's voice startled me. I glanced at the clock, pleased to see he'd returned from the warehouse much earlier than expected. If I left now, I could retrace Mina's steps and possibly discover if Oma had visited the Gypsy children. If she'd been there, I could secure her cap and even discover the truth of how they'd gotten their candy. One more look at the clock convinced me there would be ample time before I was expected at the kitchen. "Oma is at the Küche with Mina. I'm going to join them, and then I'll walk Oma back home. Will you listen for the bell?"

"Ja. Go on. I can look after things here. No need to return until after dinner. Mina can use the help."

His response surprised me, but I didn't argue. The extra time would be a help. I grabbed my bonnet and hurried from the store without telling Father I was going in search of Gypsy children before I went to the Küche.

I cut between the buildings, and once I was out of sight, I hiked my skirt and ran. Mina would question me if I was late arriving at the Küche, and I didn't want to undergo one of her lengthy inquiries.

Once I neared the thicket, I slowed my pace, but the children were nowhere in sight. Though I knew I should turn around, I continued until I neared the camp. With careful steps I worked my way among the trees and overgrowth. At the sound of voices I crouched low and took a position where I could see the camp yet maintain a good view of the surrounding area, as well. There was little activity, and I wondered if the Gypsies slept until late in the day. Father said they stayed up until the wee hours of the morning and then lay abed all day. Perhaps he was right.

With renewed courage I worked my way through the underbrush and inched closer to the camp. I stopped at the sound of a young girl's laughter. I strained to the side, and that's when I saw her. A little girl of five or six with unkempt hair was singing and picking wild flowers. I held my breath and prayed she would come in my direction.

Stoop and pick, stoop and pick, ever so slowly she continued to gather flowers and walk deeper into the brush. Closer to me. I fixed my gaze on her. With her light-colored hair and fair skin, she didn't look like a Gypsy child. I'd heard stories of how the Gypsies stole babies and young children when they passed through a town. Could this little girl be one of those stolen children? The very idea caused a scream to rise in my throat. I slapped a palm to my mouth and held back the sound, but my foot slipped and I fell backward, striking my arm on a sharp branch. An involuntary yelp escaped my lips, and the little girl turned and saw me. She ran toward me with a handful of our stick candy. Father had been correct. The Gypsies had stolen the candy. They were guilty of theft, and from all appearances they were also guilty of stealing children.

CHAPTER 12

A lingering dampness from the recent rains remained in the undergrowth, and the earthy smell of molding leaves and rich soil assailed me as the girl continued to come toward me without caution. A streak of pain shot through my arm, and blood oozed from the wound the branch had inflicted. I ignored the pain and beckoned to the girl. "Come closer. I'd like to meet you."

She pushed aside a clump of brush and continued toward me.

I held out my hand to her. "What is your name?"

"The white-haired woman from the store calls me Gretchen, but my name is Lalah."

The girl's response startled me. "How do you know my grandmother, Lalah?"

She shrugged her shoulders. "I was in town one day with one of my friends. The old woman came into the yard alongside the store and talked to us. Promise you won't tell anyone. Loyco says we aren't allowed to go into town without one of the men along to protect us."

Her comment surprised me. The Gypsy leader thought they needed protection from us, and we thought we needed protection from the Gypsies. Strange. I wanted to assure her she didn't need to fear anyone in our village, but then I thought of Sister Marguerite. She might take a broom to the children if she saw them in her garden or henhouse.

"I won't tell if you will answer some questions. Would you do that, Lalah?"

She cast a wary look at me. "Maybe. What do you want to know?" Her eyes reminded me of Stefan—dark brown with a touch of gold that shone in the sunlight. But her hair and skin, both so fair she could have passed as my sister.

"First of all, you may be surprised to learn that my name is Gretchen. Sometimes my grandmother gets confused. When that happens, she doesn't remember correctly."

Lalah's eyes opened wide. "I know. She followed us to our camp. Loyco said she could stay with us as long as she wanted." She stooped down beside me. "Loyco is our leader, but he's my father, too. He says the grandmother brings good fortune, and we should always be kind to her."

"Does he? Well, that's good to know, but when she wanders off, I worry about her. If she comes to your camp again, I would be grateful if you would return her to our store. How old are you, Lalah?" The girl's small frame made me think she might be five or six, but she spoke as though much older.

"Gypsies don't worry about age very much, but Loyco says

I'm six or seven. Alija says I'm seven. But in the mind, she says I am fifteen. She says I ask too many questions." The girl grinned and fastened her dark eyes on me. "You thought I was younger, didn't you?"

"Ja, I did. I have a brother who is ten, and he is much bigger than you. Perhaps you met him when he came down here and rode Loyco's horse. His name is Stefan."

"I know him. He likes to come here, but Loyco says you think we are bad people."

Her forthright comment caused as much discomfort as my injured arm. "I didn't say you are bad people. I think some of your people do bad things." I looked directly at the candy in her hand. "Like steal things that don't belong to them."

"Do any of your people do bad things?"

She was a perceptive child for seven years old, especially since she'd likely had little education. "No one is perfect. Occasionally we all do something wrong. But there are some things, like stealing, that we should never do. It isn't right to take things that belong to someone else. Things like eggs or chickens—or candy."

"But if one person has more than another, it does no harm to take some of the extra. Loyco says that if we take excess from someone, we are not stealing. We are teaching them to share."

I couldn't believe my ears. To teach a child that stealing was a good thing angered my sensibilities, yet the fault wasn't with the child. Loyco was to blame for misguiding her—and likely everyone else in his band of followers. Under other conditions, I would have explained the error of what Loyco had taught her, but this was not the time.

"I didn't steal the candy. Your grandmother gave it to us. She likes us and brings gifts, but we don't steal from her or from your store. Loyco has told us it is not permitted." She gave me a sidelong glance. "Maybe he wants to be your man."

I'd been prepared to apologize for accusing her of stealing the candy, but the remark about Loyco caused me to choke. Tears streamed down my cheeks while I continued to cough. After recovering I looked toward Lalah. "I'm sorry. I had something in my throat."

She nodded. "You choked on your own spit. If there's no food in your mouth, then it's spit that causes you to choke." She beamed at me. "That's what Loyco says."

I didn't argue about the suitability of making comments about spit. The girl's teachings were different from ours, and I'd already heaped unwarranted condemnation upon her. "I am sorry I accused you of stealing the candy. Please forgive me."

"I'm used to it. That's what everyone thinks about us. And sometimes we do steal. Especially if we're hungry."

The child's honesty surprised me, but it was her comment about Loyco that remained at the forefront of my mind. Why would she think he wanted me as his woman? Didn't he have a wife? "Tell me about your mother, Lalah."

"She's dead. Loyco said she died when I was a baby and I shouldn't ask about her because it makes him sad."

Lalah's reply held no remorse or sadness. She'd answered with no more feeling than if she'd been reporting a recent change in the weather. "It's hard without a mother, isn't it? My mother died, too," I told her, "and I miss her very much. Maybe some of the other women could tell you about her so that you feel closer to her."

As the girl swung around, her shaggy hair brushed across her neckline. "I already asked, and nobody remembers her. Alija told me I shouldn't try to remember her because it would cause me to have bad dreams. So I try to forget her because I don't like bad dreams."

I clenched my hands into fists. I'd like to tell Alija exactly what I thought of filling a child's head with such frightening thoughts. I didn't doubt for a moment that Lalah trusted the old woman. Alija was enough to strike fear in the heart of anyone. When she'd grabbed my hand in the store and spoken of my future, her words had caused me great distress. I didn't believe Alija was concerned over bad dreams. With each of the girl's revelations, I became more convinced that Lalah wasn't Loyco's child.

She stooped down and plucked a flower from the ground and motioned for me to lean forward. After pushing aside my bonnet, she tucked the flower behind my ear. "There! That looks pretty. Your people are very plain. Gypsies like bright colors, not the browns and blues that all of your people wear."

"Yes, I have noticed that your people are very fond of colorful clothes." I hesitated a moment, then asked, "Have you seen a black crocheted cap? My grandmother lost hers, and I can't find it among her belongings. Maybe she left it in your camp?"

Lalah reached into her skirt pocket. "This one?"

Holding Oma's head covering by the strings, she waved the cap in front of me. "Yes, that's it."

"I didn't steal it. If I was going to steal a hat, I would choose one with flowers and ribbons." She frowned and shoved the hat into my hand. "Your grandmother put it on my head and told me I must wear it. She said it was a blackbird, but I didn't argue with her."

"That was very kind, Lalah. Thank you for keeping her cap."

At the sound of children's voices, Lalah glanced over her shoulder toward the camp. "You better go before someone else sees you. If the grandmother comes again, I'll bring her home to you."

I touched her cheek. "Thank you, Lalah."

After we'd parted ways, I thought of many questions I should have asked her. I silently chastised myself for such shortsightedness. I would make a list so the next time I saw Lalah, I'd be better prepared.

Mina was pleased to see me arrive more than a half hour early, but Oma didn't appear quite so happy. She was sitting on the back porch with several other sisters, shelling peas and chatting.

"We have much work to finish, Gretchen. Come back later," she said when I stepped onto the porch.

Smiling at my grandmother, Mina squeezed my hand. "Don't worry, Sister Helga. I'm not going to let her take you back home yet. Instead, I'm going to take Gretchen inside and put her to work.

"Ja. That's gut. You put her to work, Mina."

While Oma continued shelling peas, I followed Mina inside. I'd barely cleared the threshold when Mina turned on her heel to face me. "I'm surprised to see you here. I can always use help, but if you had extra time, why didn't you stay at the store and write in your journal?"

"I tried, but my thoughts were jumbled. That doesn't make for good writing. And then Vater came back to the store much earlier than I expected. It has been a long time since I have been able to enjoy some time in the Küche."

"And your Vater agreed?"

"Ja. He said it would be gut for me to have time to visit with you and the other women."

Mina arched her brows. "I am glad to hear this. It sounds as though your Vater is beginning to return to the man he was before your Mutter's death." She held her thumb and index finger a few inches apart. "At least for some of the time. I will keep praying that his heart continues to heal."

I reached for her hand and gave a gentle squeeze. "Thank you, Mina. You are a gut friend."

What I said was true. Mina was dear to my heart, and she cared deeply about all of us, especially me. For a moment I considered tossing caution to the wind and telling Mina what I'd done. She'd surely chastise me, for Mina believed in following the rules. All of them. She never veered to the right or the left but remained on a straight and steadfast course.

Whether I'd met with success or not wouldn't be of importance to Mina. The fact that I'd broken the rules and gone to the Gypsy camp would be the issue that would cause Mina to deliver a sound rebuke. With the Küche full of women and Oma sitting on the porch with the paring knife sisters, I knew it would be foolish to confess my wrongdoing. At least for now.

I glanced around the Küche, enjoying the sights and smells. "I do miss being in the Küche with you, Mina." Though the words were true, I hoped the comment would be enough to stop any further scolding.

"Ja. Well, I am thankful for your help, and Oma's, as well." Mina offered a fleeting smile before she pointed to three large containers of potatoes that had been peeled by the paring knife sisters. "You can grate the potatoes for the patties."

It was not my favorite job, but my mouth watered at the thought of fried potato patties with warm applesauce. I picked up the grater and set to work. "It's pleasant to be around the other women and hear their chatter."

Mina nodded. "Ja, until Sister Marguerite scolds them for not working fast enough. And if it's the talking you miss, don't forget that you'll get to help us when the onions are ready to be harvested."

I wrinkled my nose. Onions and onion seed were grown in all of the villages as a cash crop, and come mid-July, when the onions were ready for harvest, nearly everyone was expected to help. To avoid the heat, we would be in the fields before dawn. Only the older schoolchildren, who were released from their studies during this time, looked forward to harvesting the two thousand pounds of onions.

"I hope you will ask for my help in the Küche. I would rather prepare meals than go out and fill burlap bags with onions." I leaned close and squeezed her arm. "Besides, it would give us time to visit alone."

Mina's lips curved in a broad smile as she lifted a large iron griddle onto the stove. "What about all the chatter? You don't miss it so much when it comes to harvesting the onions?"

I giggled and shook my head.

"I'll see if I can convince Sister Marguerite, but when it's time to plant or harvest the onions or the grapes, you know how it is—the farm Baas and *Gartebaas* would have us serve bread and cheese if it meant we could send more workers to the field."

"Ja, I know, but I have confidence you can convince Sister Marguerite." I peeked out to the front porch to make certain Oma was still shelling peas.

"So your grandmother has made friends with this Gypsy girl, ja?"

Mina's question caught me off guard. I thought she'd forgotten about my visit to the Gypsy camp.

I nodded my head. "Her name is Lalah. I don't think she's one of them. I think maybe they stole her. I've heard stories about Gypsies stealing babies when they pass through a town."

Mina touched her finger to her nose. "You need to keep your nose out of their business, Gretchen. If you get involved with them, you'll be asking for more trouble than you can handle. And you need to keep your grandmother away from them, too."

Mina's words stung. Though I admired my friend's ability to speak her mind, today I would have preferred to have her support rather than her admonition. "And that's why you need to speak to the elders about the Älterschule." I did my best to look after my grandmother. Surely Mina realized I couldn't work in the store and keep Oma within my sight every minute of the day. "I used much of my free time to write out your plan in great detail, yet you still haven't asked to speak to the elders."

"Ja, ja. I need to do that, but when is there time for me to meet with them? It would be different if I had a husband to go with me."

Her comment surprised me. Since when had Mina needed a man to do her talking? Perhaps she wasn't as independent as I thought. "You could ask Conrad. He would go with you."

"Ach! Then they would think I am a woman with no courage, that I have so little confidence about an Älterschule that I must have a man with me."

I sighed. There was no answer that would please Mina, at least none that I could give her. Instead, I would pray she'd gain the necessary courage before Oma ended up in Mount Pleasant. No need trying to explain what Lalah had told me about Oma bringing good fortune to the Gypsy camp. Mina would think I'd become senile and needed a guardian even more than my grandmother.

Mina tapped my shoulder. "What happened to the salesman? I thought he was going to move here, but Conrad said he went back to Chicago."

"You and Conrad were discussing Mr. Finley?" A hint of anger rose in my chest.

Mina spooned a dollop of lard onto the griddle. "You need to shape those potatoes into patties so I can begin frying." Using her apron, she grabbed the griddle by one edge and tipped it to spread the melting fat.

I dipped my hands into the bowl and squeezed the shredded potatoes into firm cakes. "Are you going to answer my question?"

One by one Mina dropped the potato cakes into the sizzling fat. "Ja. I talked to Conrad about Mr. Finley. No need to get so upset. I just asked if he'd decided to live here, and Conrad said he went back to Chicago." She stepped closer. "You need to work faster."

"But he's coming back. Did Conrad tell you that?" I pointed for her to take the potato cakes from the tray.

"Nein." She returned to the griddle and carefully dropped more potato cakes into the melted grease. "I am guessing that Conrad is praying that will not happen. From the look on your face, maybe I should join him in that prayer. I hope you are not thinking you care for the salesman in a romantic way. I told you already that I think he is trouble." Using a long-handled turner, Mina checked the potatoes. She shook her head and dropped the potato cake back in place. "They haven't browned enough. So why do you think this Mr. Finley is so special?"

I'd never said he was special. Mina was putting words in my mouth. Now that I knew she and Conrad had been discussing the salesman, I didn't want to tell her I had written a poem to send to him or that I'd been working on a story about life in the Küche for his review. But I didn't see anything wrong with having a professional writer look at my work. Mina would say that to seek the praise of another person was vain. Maybe it was, but I wanted to know if Mr. Finley was correct about my ability. After all, if I had talent, it was a gift from God that should be used to glorify Him. And what better way than to write beautiful poetry and stories that would tell others of Amana and its people? Of course, I was certain Mina wouldn't agree.

Mina flipped the potato cakes and gave an approving grunt. "You going to answer my question about the salesman?"

"I'm interested only because he's someone new, but I don't have a romantic interest in him. Besides, you know Vater would never approve of such a thing."

Mina scooped the potato cakes that were done onto the turner and then slid them onto a white oval platter. "Maybe, but it's not your Vater I'm thinking about. You would break Conrad's heart. You know he hopes to marry you one day."

"Ja, we have talked about marriage, but we have not yet asked the elders for approval."

"Hold the platter while I lift the ones from the back of the griddle." She handed me the plate and leaned across the stove. When she finished, she looked me in the eyes. "Conrad is sure. And I think you were sure until Mr. Finley showed up with all his fancy talk and magazines that set your head to spinning."

"I'll take these to the serving table." I had longed to spend time with Mina, but this wasn't what I'd envisioned. We'd done nothing but disagree since I arrived. And all because of Conrad telling her about Mr. Finley. Why had he been confiding in Mina, anyway? That wasn't a question I needed to ask him, for I already knew the answer: He knew Mina would take up his cause and warn me against Mr. Finley. Instead of being pleased to discover Conrad cared enough to seek Mina's help, I was angry. Angry he'd used my friend to try to influence me.

My thoughts whirled as the bell rang and the men and women entered the dining room and sat down at their separate tables. Mina assigned me to serve the tables where the men were seated. Conrad's eyes shone with surprise when he saw me approach the table, but I looked away. After I placed the milk pitchers on the table, I saw his look had changed to confusion. Let him be confused. Let him wonder what he'd done. Let him ask Mina— she'd be sure to tell him.

CHAPTER 13

Two weeks had passed since I'd sent my poem and writing about the Küche to Mr. Finley. I'd been watching the mail for an acknowledgment from him, but so far there had been nothing. I continued to write stories but made the decision to send nothing further until I received a response. There was no need to continue sending my writings to Mr. Finley's friend if he thought I lacked talent. In truth, I didn't know what I would feel if the man rejected my efforts as trite and amateurish.

I shouldn't have allowed myself to become excited over the prospect of receiving praise for my work. But if praise should come, I would give thanks to the Lord for gifting me with a talent, and I would use it only to honor Him. That's what I told myself when I sorted the mail each day. And today would be no different.

My heart pounded with anticipation when my father walked through the doorway carrying a crate with the mailbag on top. "Leave the bag on the counter. I'll take care of it." Sorting the mail wasn't a task that took long. Most of the residents didn't receive many letters and didn't bother to check until they came to purchase something at the store.

"Why are you so eager to sort the mail?" Resting one edge of the crate on a shelf, he tossed the mailbag onto the front counter. "Always before it could sit and wait, but now I hardly make it to the door before you are asking."

Rather than meeting his questioning eyes, I gave him a half-hearted shrug of one shoulder and focused upon the sack. If he looked into my eyes, he'd know that I was hiding the truth. "If I do it first thing, then I don't forget later in the day." I hoped the simple explanation would be enough to satisfy his curiosity.

"Ja, well, don't forget there are crates of thread and yarn to be sorted and stocked. And be sure to count each item so we get the inventory right."

I sighed. "Yes, Vater, I know."

My attempt to avoid an impatient tone failed, and my father glanced over his shoulder with a frown tugging at his lips. "This is how you were taught to speak to your Vater?"

"No. I'm sorry, Vater. Please forgive me. It's just that I've been counting and stocking the shelves for all these years, and still you remind me of the same things over and over."

He settled the crate on the floor. Using the toe of his boot, he shoved it along the wall. "I accept your apology. To be reminded is a gut thing, Gretchen. Even though you don't think it is needed, an extra reminder hurts nothing and can halt mistakes."

I didn't want to argue. He was probably correct, but it didn't lessen my irritation. In truth, his question about changes in the mail routine is what had set me on edge. The reminder to count the stock had simply added to my annoyance. Once I heard the claw hammer pulling at nails and the creak of a wooden lid being loosened, I unfastened the canvas mail sack and dug to the bottom of the bag. There wasn't much inside, but when I removed the contents, my heart quickened at the sight of my name on one of the envelopes with a Chicago return address.

I glanced around the room to make certain no one was watching before I shoved the letter into my pocket. After slipping the remaining mail into the proper mail slots, I tied the bag and tucked it beneath the counter. Father would take it with him tomorrow morning and exchange it for the incoming mail. How I wished I could rip open the envelope and read the letter right now, but I dared not take a chance. I'd waited this long. A few more hours wouldn't make a difference.

Only minutes after I'd convinced myself I could wait, my father strode to the front of the store. He raked his fingers through his hair and grabbed his straw hat from the hook along the wall. "I forgot that I promised Conrad I would stop by the barbershop this morning." I arched my brows, expecting further explanation, but my father offered nothing more. "Maybe you should finish the crate I was working on before you begin the ones with yarn and thread. Better to finish one task before beginning another."

"Will you return soon?" I thought my question would urge him to tell me why he was going to visit Conrad, but it didn't.

"I cannot be sure. Expect me when you see me. And if those Gypsies come around, keep a good watch over them. No more stealing candy—or anything else."

There wasn't any way I could defend the Gypsies without implicating Oma. And implicating Oma meant telling Father that my grandmother was having more frequent spells of senility.

For now, the Gypsies would have to remain the thieves, at least in my father's mind. A disquieting thought that I forced from my mind. Perhaps one day I could explain and clear them of any wrongdoing.

With my hand resting on the pocket of my skirt, I walked down the aisle to where my father had been unpacking kerosene lamps. I sat down on the low stool beside the crate and removed the letter. Hands trembling, I slid one finger beneath the seal and opened the envelope. I willed my fingers to quit shaking and removed the thick sheets of cream-colored stationery. After carefully pressing open the pages, I scanned the bold script for the words I longed to read. My attention didn't remain upon the portion relating to the weather or his journey to Chicago. I could read that later. For now, I wanted to know if Mr. Finley's friend had read my poems and short story. I turned to the second page and slowed when the paragraph spoke of my writing.

> As promised, I have taken your writings to my friend Mr. Philpott. He tells me you possess immense talent. In addition, he would count it a privilege if you would permit him to read more of your work. He is particularly interested in reading stories about the Amana villages. He says they are filled with a quaint and variant style that is particularly engaging. He will be pleased to read any additional poetry you wish to send, as well.

The letter went on to say I could forward anything I'd completed by return mail. I slowed and once again read the final paragraph.

> I hope to return to Homestead soon. My uncle has been unexpectedly detained in his travels. I will write under separate

cover and explain the circumstances to your father. I am eager
to make my return.

> Your fellow poet and admirer,
> Allen Finley

My cheeks turned warm at his closing words. That he considered me a fellow poet was a compliment of the highest regard,
but I wasn't certain about his use of the word *admirer*. Had he
meant he was an admirer of my writing or of me as a woman?
To admire my writing was one thing, but to consider himself a
personal admirer would be improper and unacceptable. Then
again, maybe this was suitable manners for outsiders. I wouldn't
take offense, but should Conrad or my father ever see what Mr.
Finley had written, I doubted they'd be so generous.

At least the man had enough foresight to realize the importance of writing a separate message to my father. Had he asked
me to explain his delayed return, there would have been many
questions about why the salesman had written to me. Questions
that would be very difficult to answer.

I folded the letter, shoved it back inside the envelope, and
tucked it into my pocket. I'd read it again this evening when I was
alone and could digest each word. For now, I needed to unpack
the lamps, or Father would return and ask what I'd been doing
during his absence. I plunged my hand into the straw packing
and wrapped my fingers around one of the glass chimneys. Lifting with care, I shook the pieces of straw into the crate and then
wiped the chimney with the polishing cloth Father had dropped
atop the crate. My thoughts focused on the letter from Mr. Finley, and my excitement mounted as I considered how many of
my writings I should send. I didn't want to take advantage of

Mr. Finley's friend, yet the letter encouraged me to send several compositions.

After Mr. Finley had returned to Chicago, I had continued to write more stories about life in the colonies, though I doubted such tales would be of interest to anyone. I thought each story more boring than the last. Was that why Mr. Finley's friend referred to my writing as having a "quaint and variant" style? Was that a kind way of saying boring and abnormal? Yet if he wanted to see more, it couldn't be so terrible. I must quit analyzing each word of the letter and stop questioning my own ability. I would place the short stories in the mailbag, and tomorrow they would be on their way to Mr. Finley and his friend.

At the sound of footsteps I looked up from my work. Oma wandered down the aisle, dusting shelves and humming one of the hymns we sang in church.

"Where is your Vater this morning?"

Good! She was still in her right mind. At breakfast she had appeared somewhat confused, and I'd worried this would be one of Oma's bad days. "He went over to the barbershop."

"He goes for a haircut with all this work that needs to be done? Ach! What is he thinking?" She dusted with more fervor. "I will help uncrate when I finish the dusting."

Her impatience with my father's absence brought me to his defense. "I didn't say he went for a haircut, Oma. Conrad wanted to meet with him about something, but he did not tell me anything more."

"Ohhh, I think I know why they are meeting." Oma clasped her fingers across her mouth. I could see the smile beneath her fingers.

What would make her smile about a meeting between my father and Conrad? I doubted she truly knew anything, but I would play her game. "What do you know, Oma? Tell me why Vater went to see Conrad. I promise I won't tell that you told me." I folded my hands in supplication. "Please tell me, Oma. Please."

Her eyes twinkled, and her slight grin widened into a broad smile. She was enjoying the moment. "You will act surprised when your Vater speaks to you?"

"I promise to act very surprised."

"Maybe I should not say." Her eyes turned wary, and she glanced over her shoulder. "I am guessing a little. Your Vater did not tell me, but after prayer service Conrad said he wanted to have a talk about you."

"Me?"

"Ja." She nudged my arm. "I think he wants to know if your Vater would object if he asked the elders about marriage to you." She lowered herself onto a nearby stool. "This makes me very happy. I did not think Conrad was ever going to gain courage to speak with your Vater."

We had spoken of marriage, but I always thought Conrad would tell me before he asked Father for his permission. "I am surprised he didn't tell me first."

She shook her head back and forth. "Nein. That would not be proper. First he must speak to your Vater." She slapped the air with her hand. "And what difference? You and Conrad have been talking of marriage from the time you were little children, ja?" My grandmother stared at me waiting for my reply.

"What happened when the two of us were children playing games isn't important; we didn't understand the true meaning of love or marriage. It's not the same."

"Ach. He loves you; you love him; your Vater will agree; the elders will agree. You should just be glad that you have a gut man like Conrad. Now we must pray the Grossebruderrat will decide he can stay in Homestead until you marry."

I didn't respond, but I knew what Oma meant. Once the Grossebruderrat gave permission for marriage, the man could be sent to another village for a year. During the time of separation, the couple saw each other only on Sunday afternoons or on special occasions. Since members of our faith believed an unmarried person could more easily remain focused upon God, it was a test of commitment prior to marriage. Most people remained steadfast and married, but a few decided to remain single before the year of waiting had ended. If I agreed to marry Conrad, and the Grossebruderrat gave their permission, we would still be required to wait a year, but I thought they would permit Conrad to remain in Homestead. Some of the old rules had been relaxed, but you could never be sure until the elders gave their final decision.

"There isn't time for talk of love and marriage right now. We need to unpack these crates, or Vater will question what we've been doing during his absence." I lifted one of the glass shades from the crate and admired the painted scene. I would have no difficulty selling these lamps.

I had finished unpacking all of the lamps and was working my way through a shipment of teapots when I heard the clomp of boots. Both my father and Conrad entered the store. Blotches of red colored Conrad's cheeks, and his eyes were fixed on the floor. He reminded me of a schoolboy who'd been called before the class to recite his lessons.

My father nudged Conrad's arm. "Go on and tell her. No time like the present."

Conrad raised his chin a notch, but he still didn't look at me. Oma and my father stared at him while he coughed and then struggled to gain his voice. "I have asked your Vater's permission to court you, Gretchen. I hope this meets with your approval."

I didn't miss the question in his quivering voice. Before I could offer a response, Oma gave a single clap of her hands. "Ja, she approves, and so do I. Now, let's get to work on the rest of these crates."

"You and Vater can go on without me, Oma. I would like to speak with Conrad alone. We will go out to the backyard for a few minutes."

Neither of them questioned my statement, nor did Conrad. I could hear his footfalls behind me as I walked to the apple tree. I wanted to be well out of earshot, for I knew my grandmother wouldn't be above standing inside the back door listening. I inhaled a deep breath and gathered my courage before I turned around to face Conrad.

He smiled down at me, his familiar blue eyes searching my own. "Please say you are not angry with me for speaking to your Vater. I wrestled with what I should do first: Should I speak to Brother George before I speak to Gretchen, or should I speak to Gretchen before I speak to Brother George." With his palms toward heaven, he moved his arms up and down as if testing the weight of his options. He did his best to appear confident, but his voice failed him and trembled. He lifted his hand to the side of my face. "Please tell me you are not angry."

It hadn't been so long ago that we'd had to resolve our differences because he'd been discussing Mr. Finley's behavior with Mina. After an hour or more of talking, we'd finally settled the matter, but I could see the concern in his eyes. He feared he'd stepped into trouble again.

"I am not angry, but I am somewhat distressed by your decision. I understand the rules and your obligation to speak to my

Vater, but we have known each other all our lives. I never thought you would go to him before you spoke to me. If we are ever to be married, I want you to make decisions *with* me—not *for* me."

"We would first look to God for help with our decisions, ja?"

I leaned back against the tree. "And is that what you did this time? Did you first ask God and then ask my Vater?"

"I did. But from now on, I will first ask God, and then we will talk. This is gut?"

His answer satisfied me, and I nodded my agreement. The Bible taught, and I believed, a husband should be the head of his household. If we should marry, I would abide by Conrad's decisions, but I wanted assurance he would listen to my opinions. Besides, he still didn't have the agreement of the Grossebruderrat. Without their agreement it didn't matter what any of us decided.

Taking a step closer, he bent forward and brushed a kiss on my cheek. "Maybe I should ask permission from the elders right away so our year of waiting will begin immediately. What do you think?"

Conrad was a good and loyal man, one who had always kept my confidence, and the one I'd repeatedly relied upon in difficult circumstances. "Since you asked my Vater for permission to court me, I think you should first court me, and then we will see if our love runs true."

His head jerked as if I'd slapped him. "After twenty-two years, I would think you would know if your love for me runs true." He touched his finger to the shirt pocket that rested over his heart. "I love you, Gretchen. I have known for all my life that I loved you and wanted you for my wife. I thought you felt the same."

He'd never before said he loved me, and my heart welcomed

the words like rain after a long drought. Not since my Mutter died had anyone spoken of their love for me. My father thought such endearments between family members unnecessary. When I asked Father why he never spoke of love, he'd merely said, "Actions speak louder than words."

I wanted to tell him that actions were nice, but most people longed to hear the words, as well. But I hadn't. Maybe because I feared he'd ask me for proof of my claim, and I had none. I wanted to believe most people were like me, but I couldn't be certain.

"Our love for each other has been tempered by our beliefs. Now that we have Vater's permission, we will have time to explore the depth of our true feelings for each other. I am sure that time will only deepen our love."

His smile faded and disappointment tugged at his lips. "This is not what I hoped to hear, but it is sound thinking. We will wait, and I will court you, but my heart tells me that it will not be long before you ask me to speak to the elders."

I knew Conrad's boast was no more than an attempt to hide his disappointment, so I didn't challenge his comment. Besides, he probably was correct. I grinned and tugged on his sleeve. "We'd better go inside before Oma or Vater comes looking for us."

He grabbed my hand and lifted it to his lips. "So now I can come and visit with you after prayer service each evening, and on Sunday afternoons we can go for picnics and fishing. Maybe I can ask your Vater to arrange for a buggy one Sunday afternoon, and we can take a ride in the country—or to one of the other villages. Your Vater is gut friends with the farm Baas. I think he could convince Brother Heinrich that we would take gut care of the horse and buggy."

"But still we would need a chaperone," I said.

"Ja. Maybe your grandmother would like to go and see friends in one of the villages. She sometimes talks about someone who lives in High."

I nodded. "Sister Margaret Whaley. She died years ago. When Oma's not in her right mind, she forgets some of her friends have already gone to be with the Lord."

Conrad continued to hold my hand in a firm grasp as we strolled toward the back door. "Then we will take her to visit some of her other friends." His eyes shone with delight. "I plan to be with you during all of your free time."

His comment hit me with an unexpected jolt. If I was in Conrad's company for all of my free time, how would I find time to write?

CHAPTER 14

"Help! We need water and a damp cloth, please. Hurry!"

At the sound of the shouted demand, I snapped to attention and rushed to the front of the store. I had neither water nor a damp cloth when I reached the man's side, but after one look at his traveling companion, I grabbed a chair from behind the counter. The well-dressed man was struggling under the weight of a lady, and I shoved the chair behind her.

"Sit her down," I said, returning to the counter to obtain a cloth. I dampened several clean rags with a dipper of water and ignored the excess that dribbled on the floor. It would dry soon enough. I didn't take time to fetch a glass of water. The woman didn't appear able to open her eyes, much less swallow.

Taking giant strides, I returned to the woman's side and applied a cloth to her forehead and daubed her cheeks with another. The man knelt beside her and attempted to fan her with his hand. I pointed to one of the racks. "There are fans on the second shelf. I believe one of those would do more good." Remaining on one knee, he stretched his body until I thought it would break in two. But to my amazement, he reached one of the fans and picked it up without losing his balance. He snapped it open and flapped it in front of the woman's face.

"Winifred! Can you hear me, my dear?" The man glanced in my direction. "She doesn't faint often, but when she does, it can sometimes take a while to bring her around."

"I could obtain some spirits of ammonia if you—"

"No! Absolutely not," he shouted loud enough to alarm anyone within earshot. "Smelling salts cause her to become violently ill."

"Very well," I said in my most soothing voice. "Is there anything else I can do that might help?"

He fixed a hard glare on the front door. "Make sure none of those filthy Gypsies come anywhere within sight."

My stomach lurched. "The Gypsies accosted your wife?" I leaned close, not wanting to miss a word of his story.

"No. Not now. Not this very minute. I mean not since we've been in town." He stumbled over his words like some of the hobos when they'd had too much beer. He sighed. For a moment he ceased fanning his wife and wiped the beads of perspiration from his forehead. "It happened a year ago. Gypsies came to Springfield and stole our daughter. My wife hasn't fully recovered from the incident. The mere sight of Gypsies when we stepped off the train caused her to become lightheaded—and now she's fainted."

I swallowed the yelp that lodged in my throat and inhaled a deep cleansing breath. When the woman stirred, I touched the cloth to her cheek. "I'll fetch a glass of water and refresh this cloth with cooler water."

"I appreciate your help." He looked up at me and then rose to a half stand. "I'm sorry. I haven't introduced myself. I am Emory Lofton." He looked down at the woman. "And this is my wife, Winifred."

"I am pleased to meet you. I am Gretchen Kohler. I help my Vater operate the store for our village." I took a backward step and raised the cloth in the air. "I'll take care of this and be right back."

Oma, obviously roused by all the commotion, tottered into the store. With her attention fixed upon Mrs. Lofton, she leaned close to me and whispered, "What's wrong with that woman?"

"She had a fright and fainted. I'm trying to help her husband bring her around, but we're not having much success." While I explained to Oma, Mr. Lofton continued to urge his wife to open her eyes and speak to him.

"Smelling salts," Oma hissed. "Works every time."

She started for the wooden box where we stored medical supplies, but I grasped her thin wrist and shook my head. "Mr. Lofton says they make his wife very ill. We can't use them."

Oma massaged her forehead. "How long she has been like this?"

I shrugged. "A short time. The damp cloth and fan don't seem to have much effect."

"Wait here." Oma marched to the far side of the room and gathered a piece of oilcloth. She waved a finger in the air. "Bring that glass of water."

I wasn't certain what she planned to do, but she appeared to be in her right mind, so I followed her instruction. She pushed Mr. Lofton aside and, in one sweeping motion, draped the oilcloth over the front of Mrs. Lofton's fancy blue gown. Before I realized what was happening, she snatched the glass of water from my hand and pitched the contents onto Mrs. Lofton's face.

I gasped, Mr. Lofton bellowed, Oma jumped backward, and Mrs. Lofton sputtered and came to life. "Emory! Whatever are you doing throwing water in my face?" As the water-spattered oilcloth slid to the floor, I hastened forward and offered the damp cloth I'd used only a short time ago. Mrs. Lofton frowned. "I believe a dry cloth would prove more beneficial."

After shooting my grandmother an annoyed look, I hurried and grabbed a dry rag from beneath the counter and handed it to Mrs. Lofton. It wasn't until she'd swiped her face that I realized I'd grabbed Oma's dustrag. The woman's face was smudged a murky shade of gray. Without thought to proper manners, I grabbed the rag from her hand and hurried to find a clean one.

Poor Mrs. Lofton appeared completely bewildered when I returned and slapped another rag in her hand. "I do believe this one is better. The other one was, well, it was . . ."

"My dustrag," Oma said. "You got smudges right here." She pointed to Mrs. Lofton's forehead and cheek. When the woman didn't hit the right spot, Oma snatched the cloth from her hand and wiped her face. "There! That is gut. All clean now. And wide awake, too." Oma squared her shoulders and stared down at Mrs. Lofton as though she'd done her a great favor by tossing water in her face.

No apology could erase the distress the poor woman had endured since arriving in town. "I am very sorry, Mrs. Lofton. Your husband explained you couldn't use smelling salts. When my grandmother saw that you weren't regaining consciousness, she wanted to assist. Please forgive her. In her desire to help, she sometimes goes too far."

Mrs. Lofton patted the fringe of damp, curly bangs that now clung to her forehead. "I accept your apology and thank you for coming to my aid. I would have preferred a bit less exuberance from your grandmother. Still, I thank you both."

My face burned with embarrassment, and when I saw Oma returning with another glass of water, I jumped between the two women. However, my movement didn't deter my grandmother. She sidestepped me and extended the glass toward the disheveled woman. "Drink this." Mrs. Lofton accepted the glass and stared at the purple liquid in the glass. Oma pushed the woman's hand closer to her lips. "Drink. It is gut medicine. We make it here in Amana. Drink it down. Like this." Oma pretended to toss back the contents of the glass in one giant gulp, and Mrs. Lofton followed suit.

"That didn't taste so bad," Mrs. Lofton said. "Indeed, it was quite good."

Oma bobbed her head. "Ja, I told you. We make gut wine. You want some more?"

"Wine?" Mr. Lofton grabbed the glass from his wife's hand.

I shuddered when I saw his forehead furrow with concern. He undoubtedly thought Oma had offered his wife a medicinal cure rather than a simple glass of wine.

"My wife isn't accustomed to imbibing strong drink of any sort. Wine will only serve to inhibit her recovery."

My grandmother, who obviously didn't agree with Mr. Lofton's decision, took the glass and turned on her heel. I lightly grasped her wrist. "No more wine, Oma."

She grunted and stalked off. I turned my attention back to Mrs. Lofton. "If you need to rest, I can offer you a more comfortable chair in our parlor." I pointed toward the door leading to our private rooms.

Mr. Lofton patted his wife's shoulder. "If you have no objection, we'll just remain here until Winifred feels strong enough to continue."

The two of them were stationed in the center aisle of the store, but I couldn't ask them to move, not with Mrs. Lofton in a fragile state. "Did you come to take a tour of the villages, or are you here on business, Mr. Lofton?"

"We have friends who visited here, and they suggested we might benefit from the change of scenery. My wife isn't fond of traveling, but she couldn't resist making the journey after hearing of their enjoyment. Unfortunately . . ."

His voice trailed off, but the reminder had been enough to set his wife on edge. She stiffened, and beads of perspiration soon dotted her forehead. Spotting the fan her husband had used to help revive her, Mrs. Lofton plucked it from his hand. With a flick of her wrist, the fan snapped open, and she waved it with a vengeance.

"Those ghastly vagabonds. I hope your people don't encourage them to camp around your towns. They steal children, you know. They took my little—" her voice caught, and she covered her lips with her fingers—"my little Cecile, and we've never been able to find her." She reached for her handkerchief and dabbed her eyes. "Such a beautiful child, isn't she, Emory?" Her words slurred as she tipped her head to look up at her husband.

"Indeed. Just like her mother, sweet and lovely." Once again Mr. Lofton patted his wife on the shoulder. "Perhaps . . ." He glanced back and forth between his wife and me. "Do you think someone could show me where the Gypsies are camped so I could check to see if they have our little Cecile—or know of her whereabouts?"

My thoughts jumbled as I attempted to form the proper

answer. I didn't want to admit I'd been to the camp. Before I could answer, Mrs. Lofton began to weep. "Please don't go there, Emory. What if they kill you? Then I'd be without both you and Cecile. I can't bear the thought."

Mrs. Lofton's head lolled from side to side. I wasn't certain if it was the wine or fear of losing her husband, but I was afraid she might swoon again. "Given your wife's concern, it might be best if you refrained from visiting the Gypsy camp. I may be able to gather some information for you. I'll do my best."

Mr. Lofton nodded his agreement. "Thank you, Miss Kohler. You are most kind."

A group of customers entered the store, but when I noticed my grandmother still holding the wine bottle in one hand, I hurried to her side. "No more wine for Mrs. Lofton. Please go and help the customers. I'll see to Mrs. Lofton."

"Ach! The wine, it helps her. Look at the color in her face." Before she turned and marched away, Oma pointed a spindly finger at Mrs. Lofton's bright pink cheeks.

If my grandmother thought her terse remark or Mrs. Lofton's pink cheeks were proof the swooning woman needed another glass of wine, she was sorely mistaken. The opposite was true, confirming Mr. Lofton's assertion that his wife did not imbibe. I doubted the woman could stand without assistance. Stepping close to Mr. Lofton's side, I quietly said, "I do believe it would be best for your wife to rest in our parlor. Even though a wagon will take you to the villages, a good deal of walking is required."

"I'm fine," Mrs. Lofton said. "Just look." She pushed up from the chair. Her body swayed like a tree branch on a windy day, but she appeared completely unaware of her condition. Had her husband not grabbed her around the waist, she would have dropped to the floor. "What time do we depart?"

Mrs. Lofton's knees buckled, and her husband gathered the woman into his arms. "I believe we will need the use of your parlor, Miss Kohler."

I directed the way and pointed to the divan. "Why don't you let your wife rest there? I'm sure the effects of the wine will wear off soon." At least I hoped so. Mr. Lofton's wife was no more alert than when he'd stepped inside the store. "As I mentioned earlier, my grandmother sometimes is overly zealous in her efforts to help."

"She meant no harm, and who can say? Maybe the wine will help my wife forget she ever saw those Gypsies." When he pinched the bridge of his nose, I wondered if he was thinking of his lost child.

"Do sit down and make yourself comfortable. There is no one here to disturb you." I glanced toward the door leading into the store. "Unless my grandmother decides to come in and check on your wife's progress. However, I'll do my best to keep her busy."

He dropped to a nearby chair. "Do those Gypsies come here each year, Miss Kohler?"

I folded my hands in a tight knot. "Not those particular Gypsies, but we frequently have groups who camp in the area during the summer months. Sometimes they camp near another village, sometimes near ours, but they generally don't stay the entire summer. We never know how long they will remain."

"But you don't try to make them leave?"

"No. We try our best to be hospitable to all people, Gypsies and hobos included. Some make it easier than others. The Gypsies tend to do a little stealing from time to time, and the hobos would rather we didn't require them to chop wood or pull weeds for their food, but the Bible teaches we should share with those in need." I could see the concern in Mr. Lofton's eyes. "This latest group of Gypsies hasn't caused trouble like some who have been here in years past."

He hunched forward to look at his wife. "I know all about the trouble they can cause." Then he looked at me, but his eyes had glazed as if he were in a trance. In a monotone voice, he told me that he and his wife had been on a picnic in a park a short distance from their home when out of nowhere they'd been approached by two Gypsy men and a woman. The men asked for money and the woman stooped down and admired Cecile. He'd given them what money he had in his pocket, but they'd been dissatisfied. Then the Gypsy woman had insisted upon Mrs. Lofton's cameo, but she refused to give it up.

Mr. Lofton rested his chin in his palm, agony twisting his features as he told me the Gypsies warned them they'd be sorry they hadn't cooperated. Even though the Loftons didn't believe anything further would happen, their outing had been ruined, so they decided to pack up their picnic basket and return home. They'd gone only a short distance when Mrs. Lofton remembered they'd left their daughter's doll under the tree where they'd spread their blanket.

Mr. Lofton raised his head, his eyes filled with tears. "I ran back to retrieve the doll, and in those few short minutes, they rushed in and grabbed our beautiful Cecile from my wife." He dropped his face between his hands. "At night I think of how my daughter must cry for us. I know it's wrong of me, but I hate all of those people."

My throat constricted, and I struggled to keep my tears in check. "I can't imagine the pain you and your wife have suffered." *Hate* was a strong word, but I couldn't bring myself to tell Mr. Lofton he shouldn't hate the people who had stolen his daughter. "I doubt this group of Gypsies is in any way connected to those who took your daughter. I know that probably won't ease your wife's misgivings—or yours, for that matter—but the chances of . . ."

He waved me to silence with a firm nod. "I know. But it doesn't change my feelings about the entire group of them. Our little Cecile was only five years old when they took her." His voice cracked with emotion. "It was a year ago this very week. That's one of the reasons I planned this trip. As summer approached, my wife became more despondent." He locked his fingers together in a prayerlike fashion. "She sees children outdoors playing, families on picnics, mothers in the park with their daughters, and it all comes back to haunt her."

The child would now be six years old. *Lalah.* The girl's name popped into my head and wouldn't depart. She'd said she was seven, but she didn't look seven. Though I should have returned to the store, I remained and asked for more details about the Loftons' daughter. Had she a fair complexion? Did she have dark hair or light? What of her eyes? Were they as blue as the sky or dark gray like the fabric of his suit?

He didn't seem to mind my questions. In fact, his eyes shown with delight as he told me Cecile was fair like her mother with light brown hair and eyes the color of walnuts. "If she'd had blue eyes, I don't think she would have appeared so fair. But those large dark eyes—they were beautiful." He trembled, as if shaking himself from a distant dream. "I'm sure you have work that needs your attention. I'll sit here with my wife until she rouses, and then I'll take her to the hotel. We have rooms there."

"If your wife is feeling well enough, there is a tour later this afternoon. If not, there is a restaurant in the hotel or you can join us at our Küche, where we eat our meals. You would be most welcome." I was pleased to know Mr. Lofton had taken a room at the hotel, for I didn't think his wife would be well enough to sit in a bumpy wagon for the remainder of the day. In fact, I wondered if she would awaken before suppertime.

I returned to the store with thoughts of Lalah heavy on my mind. I wanted to see her again. Perhaps with a gentle nudge, she would remember something about her early years. Although I doubted she was the Loftons' child, I didn't believe she belonged to Loyco. And I wanted to know the truth.

CHAPTER 15

Mr. and Mrs. Lofton hadn't joined us for supper. In fact, they'd departed the following morning. Mr. Lofton stopped by the store to thank me for my kindness and to say he thought his wife would fare much better if they returned home. Given her fragile condition, he didn't believe it would be wise to stay any longer. I concurred, for who could say when a group of the Gypsies might appear at the store or in one of the villages.

I had hoped to have an opportunity to speak with Lalah prior to the Loftons' departure. In my heart I was certain the child was not their Cecile, but I'd held a somewhat selfish hope that I could have been the one to reunite the couple with their daughter.

Mr. Lofton had given me his address in case we gathered any information from the Gypsies. And he'd shown me a picture of the three of them, one he carried in the case of his pocket watch.

His daughter had been only two years old at the time of the photograph. He smiled and pointed to her hair. "She has a dark birthmark on her head that makes one patch of her light brown hair appear darker than the rest." As if to seal away the memory, he snapped the metal case together and shoved the watch back into his pocket. I doubted I'd ever see Mr. and Mrs. Lofton again, but I doubted I'd ever forget them, either.

That night after I'd gone into my room, I prayed for Mr. and Mrs. Lofton and Cecile. Perhaps God would reunite this family. If not, I prayed He would grant the child safety and her parents the peace they needed to continue their lives without her.

After completing my prayers, I gathered my writing paper and pen. Ever since Conrad had spoken to my father about courting me, there had been little time for writing. For the past week I'd been delaying going to bed so that I could complete my latest story. Tomorrow I hoped to have two more stories to send Mr. Finley. I'd expected his return before now, but my father had received two letters explaining why he'd been detained. His uncle hadn't yet returned to Chicago, and his aunt had taken another turn for the worse, thereby requiring that he remain in Chicago until she exhibited definite signs of recovery.

Both letters had contained assurances that Mr. Finley remained eager to return and learn more about the colonies. He even asked my father to explain his circumstances to the Bruderrat and express his continuing desire to join the community. When Father read those portions of Mr. Finley's letters to me, my heart had taken wing. To explain my excitement would have been impossible. Conrad had implied on more than one occasion that he thought I was fond of Mr. Finley. Even though I denied such feelings, Conrad couldn't understand my admiration for the man. Now I refrained from speaking of him—at least I did my best.

My lamp burned late into the night while I worked to complete the latest tale. I wanted everyone who read my stories to understand that neither our people nor our ways were so different from those of our ancestors who had come from Germany. Although we lived communally and did our best to live righteous lives, we still held fast to the ways of our ancestors. Like them, we simply wanted to live and worship our Lord without condemnation for our beliefs. We continued to live frugal lives and make good use of everything the Lord entrusted to us—even nature's provisions.

Our grapevines clung to trellis supports on the east, west, and south sides of our homes to help keep them cool in the summer. Like most things in Amana, the grapevines served a dual purpose. In addition to shielding us against the summer heat, they provided fruit for jams, jellies, and a few bottles of wine. Our communal wines were made from the grapes harvested from our vast vineyards. When the grapes were ripe, the winemaker sent word to the village that the harvest would begin the following day. Schools closed down, mills ceased their work, and shops closed. The harvest was hard work but also gave us much pleasure.

I chuckled as I wrote how we fought off the bees and wasps in the vineyards. The insects were determined to have their fill of the juicy ripe grapes and would sting anyone who got between them and the fruit. It took more than one or two swinging bonnets to keep them away from the grapes. Mostly the men and women worked on opposite sides of a row. Last year I worked opposite Conrad. We would snip the clusters and, with a gentle hand, settle them in wicker baskets. With the difference in our height, he saw clusters I would miss, and I would see some that he had missed. The system worked well for us. But with forty thousand pounds of grapes being picked throughout the colonies during a single harvest, many older folks suffered backaches, while the younger members took pleasure in the task and didn't seem to suffer at all.

I turned my sheet of writing paper over and continued. I wanted to tell how the three successive batches of wine were made, so I carefully listed how the first-run wine was made from the first-run juice and how we performed three runs on our grapes with the most robust wine coming from the third run. This wine was the least sweet, the driest, and the darkest in color. From the harvesting of grapes to the final step of storing the vats of wine in the church basement, I'd written out the process. Now I wondered if anyone would truly be interested in this custom of ours. Without further guidance from Mr. Finley, it was difficult to know what kinds of stories I should write. He'd said he wanted to hear about life in the colonies, and winemaking was an important part of our life. We used the wine in our church services, and each family member received a ration of it, with the men receiving the greatest portion. In particularly good seasons, we even sold our wine to outsiders, just as we sold our sauerkraut and onion sets.

I hoped that my story wouldn't read like a boring schoolbook, but the hour was late, and I couldn't take time to ensure my words would prove engaging. I would read the story again in the morning. Right now I needed to sleep.

Morning arrived far too soon, and every movement proved an effort. Had I been able to remain abed an extra half hour and skip breakfast, I would have done so. But Father would have wanted a prolonged explanation, and I wouldn't have gained the extra sleep I desired. I wouldn't remain awake tonight, of that I was certain. I could only hope there would be few customers and no arriving shipments that would require my attention.

Conrad signaled to me from across the dining room. I gave a slight nod in return. If one of the elders took note, his behavior could draw unwanted attention and the elders wouldn't hesitate to question him about his failure to adhere to the rules. Even worse, they might question him about our relationship. He couldn't lie. He'd be required to tell them he'd asked permission to court me. Then Father might have to answer questions. It could become a thorny issue. I would speak to Conrad the next time he came to the store. He should be more careful. There was no need to take such risk when he could walk the short distance from the barbershop and talk to me most any time.

After we'd recited the morning prayer, Oma settled on the bench beside me and passed the bowl of fried potatoes. "Conrad waved to you," she hissed. "You should not ignore him."

"I didn't ignore him, but he needs to be careful or the elders will question his behavior."

"Ach! They have more important things that need their attention." She helped herself to a slice of dark rye bread.

I didn't argue. We weren't supposed to be talking. Of course Oma didn't abide by the rule of silence during meals unless she wanted to—she said being old gave her special privileges. I wasn't sure the elders agreed.

We stood and recited our final prayer before departing the dining room. Oma clung to my arm as we made our way back to the store and said, "My head is hurting a little. I think I should rest for a while."

She'd been doing well of late. There had been no more episodes of senility since she'd been to the Gypsy camp and given Lalah her black cap, and I was hoping there would be no more. "I don't think we will be busy today, so if your head is hurting, you should rest. I can manage without you."

"What about the trims that came in last week? I was going to sort those this morning."

I shook my head. "Those can wait. If I have time, I'll work on them. Ridding yourself of a headache is more important than sorting lace." She readily agreed, a sign the headache was worse than she'd indicated. When we arrived at the store, I walked her to her room and removed her shoes. She refused my offer of headache powders but permitted me to pull back the quilt and cover her with a sheet. "You rest, and I'll come check on you in a little while."

She mumbled her agreement and closed her eyes. In a few minutes she'd be asleep. How I wished I could join her. Instead, I stopped in my room long enough to collect my story. If time permitted, I would read it, make any necessary changes, and then put the most recent stories in the mailbag this morning.

When I returned to the front counter, my father grabbed his hat from a peg near the door. "I am going out back to the warehouse. I don't know if a new shipment will arrive today, but the store is quiet and I need to prepare the boxes we will be shipping out in the morning."

I waved to him as he departed. At the moment, there was little work in the store that required his attention. He'd rather be at the warehouse or the train station, where he could visit with the men. Unless a customer arrived, I would have ample time to read without interruption.

Pen in hand, I read through the story. On several occasions I stopped to make changes from one word to another or to simplify an explanation, but overall I was pleased with what I'd written. I hoped Mr. Finley's friend would agree. Together with a recent poem, I folded the pages of my stories and tucked them into an envelope. With a careful hand, I penned Mr. Finley's name and address. I hoped I would receive a favorable response.

I was sealing the envelope when Sister Marguerite strode into the store, carrying a large wicker basket. Had I confused the days of the week? She waved, and her cheeks plumped like two ripe apples when she smiled.

Before I slipped from the stool, I shoved the envelope beneath a stack of mail to be placed in a mailbag when the next train arrived. "Have you changed your shopping day?"

"Nein, but the Grossebruderrat will be arriving for a meeting and will eat at the Küche tomorrow."

She didn't need to explain further. Having the elders from all of the villages eat in one's kitchen was an honor for any Küchebaas. Such an event was not taken lightly, and only the best meal would do. Sister Marguerite was obviously on a mission to make certain she had every item available to prepare an unforgettable meal.

Most of what she needed for the meal would be items from the garden, chickens from the henhouse, or meat from the butcher. Her food would be seasoned with herbs from the garden, but a few items, ones to make the meal extra special, such as spices or extra sugar, could be purchased only from the store. Once I'd filled her order, I turned back toward the front of the store.

My stomach lurched when I spotted Conrad standing at the counter sorting through the stack of mail. I started toward him. "That is the outgoing mail!" I hadn't meant to shout, but I hoped to stop him before he discovered the letter addressed to Mr. Finley. My eyes darted from his face to the stack of mail and back again. His expression remained fixed—no smile, no frown. A blank slate. Blank enough for me to feel certain he'd seen the envelope. It wasn't until I drew near that I could see the disappointment in his eyes. Or was it pain? If he would give me an opportunity to explain and would act in a reasonable manner, everything would be fine. At least I hoped it would. I must convince him to keep my secret, for Father would not understand.

"I can explain," I whispered as I settled Sister Marguerite's basket on the counter. He didn't respond. While I calculated the cost of Sister Marguerite's merchandise, Conrad strolled through the store as though seeking some special item. I didn't think Sister Marguerite was fooled by his behavior, but she didn't say a word. Any other time, she would have quizzed me, but today she was more intent upon the meal she would prepare tomorrow. The minute I'd added her total and entered it on the ledger sheet maintained for her Küche, she hustled from the store with the basket swinging from her arm.

She'd barely cleared the threshold when Conrad reappeared from the back of the store. I slipped the stack of mail beneath the counter. I decided it best to take the offensive. "You should be more careful in the dining room. One of the elders might see you signal to me. It could cause problems."

"And you should be careful where you place the letters you

are writing to an unmarried man who is not a member of our community." He pointed at the counter. "No need to hide the mail. I have seen the letter."

"You had no business going through the United States mail. Only those who work in the store are permitted to handle the mail."

"Ach! Everyone who lives in Homestead has looked through the unsorted mail from time to time. It is your guilt that causes you to say such silly things."

I wanted to argue that only rarely had I seen anyone sift through the mail, and they had asked permission. But I knew such a comment would only make matters worse. "Would you like to know what is in the envelope?"

"I've already seen that it is a letter to Mr. Finley," he said.

"It isn't a letter. The envelope contains two stories and a poem. Mr. Finley has a friend in Chicago who is a poet, and Mr. Finley offered to have him read some of my writings."

"Strange that he would offer to do this, I think. And strange that he is in our village for only a few days and already he knows about your poems and stories." His lips tightened into a thin line. "You think this is proper, that you contact this man?" He lifted the envelope and waved it in the air. "I do not like this, Gretchen."

"There is no reason for concern. What I am sending is no different than submitting a lesson for a teacher's correction."

"Ja? Then why didn't you give it to Brother Otto? He is a teacher, and I'm sure he could correct your mistakes." He folded his arms across his chest and stared at me.

"It isn't the same. Brother Otto doesn't even like poetry. I want someone to read my work who is a skilled writer. Is that so wrong?"

"I do not know why it matters what someone else thinks of what you write. If he dislikes your work, you will be discouraged."

Although I'd already heard that Mr. Finley liked my stories, I couldn't divulge that information to Conrad—at least not now.

"And what does your Vater think of this? He does not think it foolish?"

"He does not know."

Conrad bowed his head closer. "Did you say he does not know? So you are doing this without his permission?"

"Promise you won't tell him, Conrad. If not because you care for me, then because it is unfair to Mr. Finley. He does not understand our rules. He offered out of kindness and nothing more. If you make an issue of this, I fear it would influence the elders when he returns." I reached across the counter and grasped his sleeve. "It is not fair to punish him because you question my decisions."

"You have sent him other mail?"

"Ja. Nothing personal. Just poems and stories. I will open the envelope and show you if you don't believe me."

"That is not necessary. I will not tell your Vater if you agree this will stop. Even if you are not writing him letters, we both know that for a single woman to keep such contact with an outsider is against our rules."

Relief flooded over me as a local farmer and his wife entered the store with their two young children in tow. For now, further talk would be impossible. "I must help the customers," I whispered.

"Ja, but we will talk more later."

The train whistle sounded, and a short time later my father entered the store. He dropped the mailbag on the counter, and after I had removed the arriving mail, I slipped the stack of letters into the canvas bag—including the envelope addressed to Mr. Finley. Guilt nagged me for the remainder of the day, and when I slipped into bed that night, sleep eluded me. Well into the night, I continued to weigh the consequences of my decision, attempting to overcome my feelings of remorse for what I'd done. As daybreak dawned, I had another thought—a thought that I liked, a thought that told me I'd spent far too much time on my stories to simply tuck them away and forget they'd been written.

When I arose that morning, I promised myself this would be the last of it. I wouldn't send anything else to Mr. Finley.

CHAPTER 16

During the past week I had hoped for an opportunity to go and search for Lalah at the Gypsy camp. Each time I thought I could sneak away, something or someone had interfered. Finally I created my own opportunity. Today the onion harvest would begin, and Mina had requested my assistance in the Küche. To my relief, Sister Marguerite had agreed. I much preferred preparing food rather than harvesting in the fields in the hot sun. Since I would be helping in the Küche now, I was certain I'd be assigned to help dig the onion sets in August—especially if any of the regular kitchen workers complained.

The Gartebaas expected help from all of the women, and my father always offered my assistance in both July and August. After the August digging of the sets came cleaning off the dirt and sorting the sets by size. At least I could sit and visit with the women during the cleaning and sorting. When our task was completed, usually a week later, a portion of the sets would be shipped to seed companies. The rest would be stored in the cellars of the kitchen houses.

But today the July harvest had begun. While Mina worked alongside me in the Küche, I told her about Mr. and Mrs. Lofton and their daughter. She agreed we should pray for the family. "We'll spread the word so that others will pray for the little girl's safe return." She arched her brows. "And what if the elders told each of the prayer-meeting groups, so we'd all be praying for the family? That would be gut, wouldn't it?"

"Ja. I will ask Vater to speak to them." After receiving Mina's compassionate response, I decided it would be safe to tell her about Lalah. She clung to every word as I described my trek into the grove, where I found Grandmother's missing cap in Lalah's possession.

Her mouth agape, Mina dropped the kettle onto the stove with a bang. "You went to the Gypsy camp alone? You know better, Gretchen Kohler!"

Perching a fist on each hip, I met her hard stare with one of my own. "What was I supposed to do?"

She squared her shoulders and pointed at me. "You could have asked Conrad to go with you. Even Stefan would be a better choice than to go alone."

"Stefan wasn't around. Besides, there wasn't time to seek help. I didn't want Vater to know Oma had been to the Gypsy camp. You know how he feels about taking her to Mount Pleasant."

Her shoulders dropped a notch and her gaze softened. "Ja, I know, but I don't think he will really send her away. If your Mutter were alive, he knows she would object. If nothing else, he will think twice because of your Mutter's wishes."

"Maybe, but I can't be certain. He isn't the same as when

Mutter was alive. Now he acts angry most of the time." As I spoke, I recalled his kindness over reading the books and added, "But once in a while I see a glimmer of the man he used to be—his kind heart—but mostly he is unhappy or provoked."

"If he speaks of Mount Pleasant, you should remind him of your Mutter's wishes. Even if it makes him angry, it will cause him to think." She tapped her finger to the side of her head. "And he needs to think before he does something foolish. Your grandmother belongs in Homestead with her family."

Mina didn't need to preach at me. I already agreed with her. It was my father who needed to be convinced. "I will remind him, but I hope you will move ahead with the idea for the Älterschule." Though I agreed to tell my father, I wasn't sure I could carry through. To dispute Vater when he was annoyed usually made matters worse rather than better.

Mina didn't comment on the Älterschule. From her frown, I could see she didn't want yet another reminder from me. She grabbed a knife and pointed to the ham. "I'll slice the ham. You slice the bread. We need to make sandwiches." After we both set to work, she said, "Now, tell me what happened when you got to the grove near the Gypsy camp."

Hoping to justify my actions further, I told her that I hadn't gone into the camp, but that Lalah had come to the grove. "The girl was quite dirty, but from the moment I set eyes on her, I wondered about her parents. She didn't look like a Gypsy."

Over the next few minutes, Mina asked all the questions I had hoped to hear. One by one, I answered them; then I mustered courage for my question. "I need to go speak with Lalah—to see if she has that dark spot on her head. I know she probably isn't the Loftons' child, but I can't quit thinking about the possibility." I touched Mina's sleeve. "And just think what it would mean to them if she is their child. Not only would it restore their lives, but it would give Lalah the opportunity she deserves for a better life."

Mina stared at me as though she hadn't understood a word I'd said. Finally she took a backward step. "Are you saying that you want to go back to the Gypsy camp?" When I nodded, she hesitated for only a moment. "Now? You want to go there now?"

"After we take the food to the workers, I could go to the grove, and you could return to the Küche."

"And what am I to tell Sister Marguerite when she asks why you've disappeared from the Küche?"

Mina wouldn't lie, so I would have to find a solution. I thought for several minutes and then turned to her. "Before we leave for the field, I'll tell Sister Marguerite that I need to stop by the store on our return so that I can check on Oma and make certain Vater doesn't need my help."

I saw the disbelief in Mina's eyes. "You would lie?"

"It won't be a lie. I'll stop by the store after I go to the Gypsy camp. Then I will return to the Küche." I could see the hesitation in Mina's eyes, but I was pleased with the plan.

She slapped a piece of ham between two slices of bread. "I'm not so sure this is gut. I don't like you going to that camp alone. What if something should happen to you? Maybe if Conrad went with you, I wouldn't worry so much."

Asking Conrad wasn't a part of my plan. Besides, since the incident over the mail to Mr. Finley, Conrad wasn't easily influenced. He would likely tell me the idea was foolish and I should stay away from the Gypsies.

I handed Mina several more slices of bread. "It would take far too long. My way is best."

"That's what you always think, but I'm not so sure."

Instead of arguing, I remained silent. There wasn't anything more I could say that would influence her. Both she and Conrad often remained stuck in their thinking, unwilling to step to the right or the left of a straight line. But I didn't believe they had a clear understanding of everything. Sometimes a step to the left or the right could be a good thing—at least that's what I wanted to believe. I could only hope Mina would think about the little girl and agree to help me. When we'd finished packing the baskets that would feed the workers from our kitchen, I glanced at her. "Should I speak to Sister Marguerite?"

She inhaled a deep breath and closed her eyes. "Ja, you can tell her, but you'd better be careful. If anything happens to you, I won't be able to forgive myself."

"Thank you, Mina." I pulled her into a quick embrace. "You're doing the right thing."

"We will see," she said.

I should have known that Mina's agreement didn't mean she would remain silent on our journey to the field. While we sat in the back of the wagon with women from the other kitchen houses, she whispered her stern warnings. On the return it was the same. We both jumped down from the wagon at the edge of town. I was glad when the other women decided to ride until they were closer to their own kitchen houses.

I nudged Mina toward our kitchen. "Go on. I'll be fine. I should be back within an hour."

"If you haven't returned by two-thirty, I will go and fetch Conrad."

Her warning was enough to send me running toward the grove at breakneck speed. I didn't want Conrad or my father to know what I was doing. Neither would approve. When I drew closer to the grove, I slowed my pace. Better to go slow and be cautious. If

I was to go undetected, I'd need to avoid any undergrowth that might crackle beneath my feet or low-hanging branches that could snag my clothes. I approached the spot where I'd hidden on my earlier visit and crouched beside the tree.

Peering through the brush, I kept a vigilant watch for Lalah, but she was nowhere in sight. The camp appeared deserted except for Alija, who was sitting near a fire stirring some sort of brew in a large iron cauldron. Despite the heat, I shivered. No telling what the old woman had concocted in that kettle.

"Please, Lalah. Where are you?" I whispered, hoping that somehow I could will the girl to make an appearance.

I could wait a little longer, but if she didn't soon appear, I'd need to return. In all my planning, I hadn't considered that I'd have difficulty locating her. Where had all of them gone? I hadn't seen any sign of them when we traveled through town on our way to the fields, but that didn't mean they couldn't be there now. I didn't worry overmuch about the store. If there was any trouble, Vater would shoo all of them outside.

A southerly breeze caused smoke from Alija's fire to drift toward me. I lifted a corner of my apron and pressed it to my nose and mouth. Though the cloth covering offered a little relief, my eyes watered, and I lifted my shoulder and swiped one eye and then the other. If I was going to gain any real relief, I'd need to change positions.

After watching the direction of the smoke, I decided upon a clump of trees and bushes that would provide shelter from Alija's fire as well as hide me from view. Careful to keep low and avoid the brush and limbs, I crept into a spot near a large oak. A short time later, I heard Alija speaking to someone, and I trained my eyes on the cauldron. My view wasn't as clear here as at my earlier hiding place, so I inched forward, hunkered down low, and craned my neck for a better look. My spirits plummeted when I saw it was another older woman talking to Alija.

I'd lifted an inch or two to scoot back into position beside the tree when an arm circled my waist and lifted me off the ground.

My scream was drowned out by a booming voice. "What are you doing?"

I twisted my neck and stared directly into dark angry eyes. *Loyco!* Fear seized me, and I squirmed to free myself, but he held fast. I felt like a chicken being carried to the chopping block. "Put me down." I had intended an authoritative command, but my dry mouth and tight throat permitted no more than a strangled plea.

His harsh laughter filled me with a mounting sense of panic. I kicked and swung until he finally set me on my feet, but he didn't release his tight hold around my arm. "Why are you hiding back here spying on us? What do you want?"

My bonnet had tipped sideways, and I used my free hand to set it aright while I attempted to gain my senses. "I don't want anything." I squared my shoulders in an effort to appear brave, but my body trembled beneath his grasp.

"If you did not want anything, you wouldn't be here. Either you tell me now, or I will take you to Alija, and she will find a way to make you talk."

I didn't know if he was speaking the truth, but I didn't want to go anywhere near Alija. She'd probably boil me in her cauldron. The woman frightened me even more than Loyco. "I wanted to speak with Lalah."

"Lalah?" For a moment his grip weakened, and I attempted to pull free. But just as quickly, he grabbed hold with a vengeance, causing me to yelp in pain. "What do you want with my daughter?" His eyes flashed with anger or perhaps disbelief, I couldn't be certain which.

"Please loosen your hold. I will tell you, but you are hurting me."

He pushed me backward. "Stand against the tree and I will release you." I did as he commanded and he let go. But with a hand on either side of the tree, he pinned me in place. The mustiness of his clothing and the smoky odor that clung to his hair assailed me. "I am waiting to hear what you have to say."

I explained that I'd met Lalah when I'd been looking for my grandmother's cap weeks earlier. "She doesn't look like you."

He tipped his head to the side and gazed into my eyes. "She is not supposed to look like me. She is a girl."

"That's not what I mean. Her hair is light in color, and her complexion is fair, like mine."

"And?"

"And I wondered if she was truly your child, or if . . . if . . ."

He leaned closer. "If what?"

I hated that he was going to make me say the words, but it was too late to change the path I'd taken. "If she belongs to someone else."

He dropped his arms to his sides and took a backward step. "You think she is stolen?"

"I didn't say she was stolen, but if she is, I—"

"She is not stolen!" His words thundered through the grove, and Alija jumped to her feet. Loyco hollered for her to remain in the camp, and she dropped back onto the log where she'd been sitting. "You think because she is fair-skinned and because you hear stories of Gypsies stealing children that she is not my daughter?"

"She said she doesn't remember her mother." My defense was

meager and timid, but if this girl was Cecile Lofton, she'd likely been threatened with her life if she told anyone the truth about what had happened. Either that or her memory had been wiped away by the tragic event she'd endured.

He ran his fingers through his long hair. "That's because her mother died when she was a small child. Her mother wasn't a Gypsy—she was as fair as you."

I wasn't certain whether I could believe him. Even more, I didn't want to believe him. I wanted Lalah to be the Loftons' little girl. "There was a couple who came to town for a visit. They told me of their daughter, who had been stolen by Gypsies."

His jaw twitched while I continued my rambling story about the Loftons' child. "So you come here to look at Lalah's head. To see if she has this dark spot you are looking for, and you won't be satisfied until you see for yourself. Is that what you are saying to me?"

"Ja," I whispered. I should have told him I didn't need to look at Lalah's scalp, that I believed every word he'd told me. But I couldn't—not until I saw for myself.

He shouted Lalah's name, and the child poked her head out of a wagon not far from Alija. "Come to me." She jumped down and raced to him, her hair flying in the breeze, a smile on her childish lips.

She came to a halt beside us. "Oma is here with you?" She peeked around the tree and glanced toward a clump of bushes. "She is hiding?"

"No. She is at the store today."

Loyco pointed to Lalah. "Go ahead and look for yourself."

I asked the girl's permission to look at her hair. "I want to push it aside a little if you don't mind too much."

She shrugged. "You can look, but there are no bugs in there."

I pushed her hair first one way and then the other. "I didn't think there were, Lalah. I'm not looking for bugs, just a dark spot on your scalp." My disappointment swelled when I'd completed my examination. "Thank you for letting me look. The next time you come into the store, you may select something special for yourself—a gift from me."

Loyco sliced his arm through the air like a swinging sword. "No! She takes nothing from you. Go back to the camp, Lalah." Confusion clouded the girl's eyes before she bid me good-bye and scampered away like a frightened rabbit. A branch crackled beneath Loyco's foot. "When we came to your store, I liked you very much. I thought you might be different from the rest, who are always so quick to judge us, but you're not. My child will not be in your store, and I will not be there, either." He leaned a little closer. "Go home and don't come back here."

He didn't have to tell me twice. I ran until pain cut through my chest like a sharp knife and I could no longer draw enough air to continue. I doubled over a short distance later and gasped until air filled my lungs. After a glance over my shoulder to ensure I wasn't being followed, I forced myself to slow down and inhale long, deep breaths while I offered a silent prayer of thanks for my safety.

CHAPTER 17

I'd almost given up hope of hearing from Mr. Finley when he reappeared like an unexpected cold breeze on a hot day. He bounded toward the front counter with a smile splitting his face. I noticed the sales case dangling from his hand, and my pleasure at seeing him dissipated. Apparently he wasn't here to stay.

He slid the case onto the counter. "You are a sight for sore eyes, Miss Kohler."

His intense stare caused me to glance away. Heat crept up my neck and spread across my face like hot flames. "Thank you. I am pleased to see you, as well." I lifted my eyelids only far enough to gain a brief look at him. "I was beginning to think you had completely forgotten the Amana Colonies and your desire to move here."

"Never. How could I forget one as lovely as you, Gretchen?"

He'd moved from addressing me as Miss Kohler to Gretchen in short order, but he'd not mentioned a word about returning here to live. Of course, he'd only just arrived. He'd hardly blurt everything he had to say immediately upon his return. "And how does your aunt fare?"

His forehead creased with wrinkles, but he soon regained his smile. "She's doing some better. Thank you for asking."

"What ailed her? You never said in your letter to my Vater."

"Some sort of palsy, but my uncle never fully explained. Upon my return, she decided it would be better to have a woman come in to assist with her care. Still, I was needed to take charge of business matters."

"And your uncle is now at home and can manage his own affairs?"

"Not entirely. That's what I've come to explain to you—and your father. I do believe my ability to move to the colonies is going to be delayed yet again. Depending on my uncle's schedule, I'll be able to return from time to time. But until my aunt is much stronger and able to attend to everything while Uncle Frederick is away, I'll be needed in Chicago." He snapped open his case and looked around the store. "I know your father is at the train depot, but is anyone else within earshot?"

"Oma is resting in her room, but there's no one else in the store," I said.

"Good. I'm eager to give you some good news." He lifted a magazine from his case and flipped open the pages. He tapped his finger near the center of one page. "Look at this!"

I quickly scanned the first few lines before my jaw went slack. I couldn't believe my eyes. "That's my poem. *And my name.*" My voice cracked at the reality of seeing my words printed in the magazine. I traced my finger beneath the letters. My stomach roiled, and fear raced up my spine like a bolt of lightning. What if somebody saw this? I'd be relegated to children's church for sure. The pure embarrassment of having the entire colony know that I'd performed a glaring misdeed—one that would demote me to the confines of children's church—was enough to cause my toes to curl.

He chuckled "I know it's your name. My friend suggested I submit it to a magazine for publication. He says you have a great deal of talent and it should be shared with others. And the editor of the magazine agreed."

"But you didn't ask my permission," I hissed, fearful Oma might make an appearance.

He traced his fingers through his shock of unruly brown hair. "Here I thought you would be pleased. Instead, you're acting as though I've committed some terrible crime." He slapped the pages together and thrust the magazine into his case.

"Give that to me! I might not be pleased that you've had it published without my permission, but I want at least to read it."

He reached into the case and removed the periodical. I didn't miss his sly grin as he shoved it in my direction and pointed to my name beneath the poem. "Your name looks good in print, does it not?"

I clutched my apron in my hand. "Nein! You should not have put my name in the magazine. What if someone should see it? There would be no end of trouble explaining how I permitted this to happen."

"If anyone brought it to the elders' attention, they would have to explain why they were reading a periodical such as this, wouldn't they?" He rested his elbows on the counter and tipped his head to the side. "Even if someone should read this and recognize your name, they won't take it to the elders. You have nothing to worry about." Reaching into his case once again, Mr. Finley withdrew an envelope and handed it to me.

The envelope had been inscribed with nothing more than my name. "What is this?"

He beamed and pointed to my hand. "Open it. You'll see."

After unsealing the envelope, I removed and unfolded the single sheet of paper. It was from the magazine editor. He'd written that he was pleased with the poems provided by Mr. Finley and would like to publish all that had been submitted to him. I continued to read and then looked up at Mr. Finley.

"He says you negotiated to sell him my poems, and that he has paid you for them. I cannot understand why you would not write and request my permission before doing such a thing."

Once again Mr. Finley's smile diminished. "You make it sound as though I've done something terrible when I've actually done something for which most people would be grateful." He withdrew an accounting that reflected the list of poems and payment made for each one. "Your money," he said, sliding the funds across the counter.

I wasn't certain whether I should refuse the money or scoop it up and tuck it into my pocket. Sunlight gleamed across the counter, and the coins winked at me like twinkling stars. Maybe it wouldn't be so bad to take the money just this once. I could put it in my trunk and save it. To explain how I happened to have legal tender in my possession would be impossible, but one day the money might be more important than any required explanation. I gathered the money and shoved it into the pocket of my skirt.

"I must have your word that you will not publish any more of my poetry, Mr. Finley. I did not send it to you with thoughts of such a thing. I had only hoped for a few words of encouragement from your poet friend."

Mr. Finley glanced toward the bulge in my pocket. "If your hope was only for a few words of praise, I think you should be mightily encouraged. Unless you furnish me with additional poetry, I will be unable to submit them for publication." He pushed the magazine close to my hand. "You should keep this. One day you will be pleased to have a memento of your first published poem."

I did my best to appear nonchalant when I gathered the magazine and placed it beneath the counter in a spot where it would be well hidden until I could take it to my room. "Are my other poems in this periodical, as well?"

"No. Some of your other work will be published in a future edition, and I'll do my best to make certain you receive a copy." He flashed a smile. "I do hope that I'm forgiven for my indiscretion. I should have asked your permission or at least refrained from using your name. I can request the editor remove your name or we could give you a pseudonym." He snapped his finger and thumb together. "That's it! We'll make up a name, and no one will be the wiser. Is there a name you think would be appropriate?"

Using a false name would be ideal. Then there would be no embarrassment to the colonies or trouble for me. I did my best to think of something stylish and grand, but nothing came to mind. "I can't think of a suitable name."

Mr. Finley straightened to attention. "I know! What about Gretchen Allen?"

"You want me to use *your* name?"

His shoulders slumped, and he looked like a deflated balloon. "I'm not attempting to take credit for any portion of your writing, but I thought since I'd submitted your work and had acted as an agent of sorts, that it would be fine. If there's some other name you prefer, I am open to your suggestions."

"No, of course not. Gretchen Allen will be fine. No one will associate me with that name, especially since so few people have ever read my poetry."

"And those who have don't read periodicals," he added.

"Except for you."

He grinned and nodded. "My friend has a keen interest in the stories you've been sending, particularly the last few. He hoped you might have one or two more for him to read when I return to Chicago."

I didn't immediately answer his question. Instead, I decided to ask one of my own. "Exactly when will you return to Chicago?"

"I'm sorry to say that I must leave in the morning. I'm here only long enough take orders from your father, and then I must return to help with my uncle's business."

Obviously, Mr. Finley wasn't as interested in learning about our community as I'd first thought. And I found his uncle's traveling obligations less than clear.

"I don't understand why you must return so soon."

He picked up his hat and placed it over his heart. "Dear lady, please tell me you don't believe I am telling you a falsehood, for it would truly break my heart."

His silly playacting caused me to giggle. "I wouldn't want to break your heart, but I would like to hear the truth." I turned more serious. "You have given me cause to be concerned about some of your decisions, Mr. Finley, and I hope there will be no further surprises."

"Ah, but surprises are good for the soul. They keep us young and carefree."

"Or turn us old and troubled before our time. I am far too

young to become old and troubled, Mr. Finley. I hope you will do nothing to speed that process."

He bowed from the waist and swept his hat in a grand gesture. "I would never want that to happen." He straightened and signaled toward our rooms. "You never said whether you have more stories for me. I know my friend is going to be despondent if I return empty-handed."

I'd had time to write only one more story since I'd mailed my others—the ones Conrad had seen on the counter. Between my work in the store, worry over Oma, and spending time with Conrad most every evening, I'd fallen into bed far too weary to think about writing. Even my journal hadn't received proper attention over the past weeks. Besides, I couldn't imagine that my writing was so magnificent that his friend would be disheartened.

"I have only one story, and it isn't quite complete. This is a busy time of year, both in the store and with our farming. We completed the onion harvest while you were gone. It would be gut if you could come and help with the potato harvest. You would then see how we all work together for the common gut."

He shifted his weight and nodded as though he was interested in the harvest. "I would very much like that. I'll do my very best to be here when the potato harvest begins, but why don't you write a story about the onion harvest. I'd feel much more prepared."

"Ja. I suppose I could do that." The minute I'd agreed, I recalled my promise to Conrad. "I think it would be better if I sent any mail to your aunt rather than directly to you. I wouldn't want anyone to think I'm conducting an improper correspondence."

"Well, I suppose that would work. I can explain to her. Let me write her address for you." I handed him a pen and paper.

"While you write out the address, I'll go and fetch the story from my room."

I leaned down and removed the magazine from beneath the counter. I didn't want Stefan to discover I'd received another periodical from Mr. Finley. I hurried through the parlor and into my bedroom. Instead of placing the magazine in my trunk, where Stefan might find it, I opened my wardrobe. A surprising surge of pride swept through me when I took a moment for one final peek at my name in print before I buried the magazine beneath my undergarments. For sure, pride was something I would need to guard against. Using a false name should stifle such feelings— that's what I told myself as I closed the wardrobe door.

I lifted the lid of my trunk and slid my hand deep inside until I could feel the hard edge of my journal. I pulled it from under the quilts and removed the loose pages that lay inside the front cover. I'd not had sufficient time to correct the story or even complete it the way I'd planned.

After reading this tale, Mr. Finley's friend would think that any talent I'd once possessed had evaporated. If that occurred, it would erase any of my worries about becoming prideful. Rolling the pages into a tube, I closed the trunk and hurried back to the store.

Mr. Finley extended his hand to take the pages. "You were gone so long, I thought you weren't coming back." He flashed a quick smile and shoved the pages into his case.

"Please tell him it's not completed, and—"

He snapped the latches on his case. "I know it will be wonderful, but I promise to explain." The scrap of paper he'd written on sat beside his case, and he slid it toward me. "Here is the address where you may send your stories."

I thanked him and folded the paper.

"You owe me no thanks, Gretchen. Knowing someone so

kind and lovely has given me renewed hope in mankind. Your talent and beauty are beacons in a drab world."

I wasn't certain if he meant Homestead was drab, or if he was simply using poetic words to impress me. I was thankful he didn't wait for a response, for I didn't know how to reply to such comments. Secretly I had enjoyed the flattering remark, something for which I should ask forgiveness but probably wouldn't. Seldom did I hear such compliments. My father was slow with praise, and though I didn't doubt Conrad's affection for me, words of fondness did not come easily to his lips. I didn't blame him. Such talk wasn't the way of our people—especially the men.

Oma once told me that idle talk wasn't encouraged because it could lead to gossip, and gossip could lead to misunderstanding; misunderstanding could lead to disruption, and disruption would hamper our ability to serve the Lord. After finishing the explanation, she had chuckled. "Of course, the women don't agree with this idea. We believe our work is made lighter when we can visit with one another." She had gently pinched my cheeks. "So let the men remain silent. The women will talk."

Oma was correct: The women did talk. Whether in the kitchen or the garden, the women took great pleasure in visiting, but praise and admiration weren't a part of those conversations, either—not unless you had peeled more potatoes than any other woman, or you polished the silver or scrubbed the pots and pans with greater speed than the others.

For sure it was nice to be praised for your work, but to hear Mr. Finley say that my talent and beauty were beacons in a drab world was more pleasing than being commended for picking grapes.

He reached forward and placed his fingers atop my hand. "I believe that takes care of everything you'll need before I depart."

I snatched my hand away and took a slight backward step. Such familiarity was unacceptable. Should someone walk into the store and observe our hands clasped together, I would be summoned to answer to the elders—a prospect that held no appeal.

I shoved the paper into my pocket and forced aside my feelings of guilt and self-recrimination.

CHAPTER 18

My hands trembled as I clawed my fingers inside the wooden cash drawer. The divided box sat before me completely empty of bills and coins. Granted, the people who lived in our community didn't need cash to pay for their purchases, but I needed money to make change for the visitors who purchased items in our store—and I was responsible for that cash. At least when I was in charge of the counter.

Each morning my father counted the money and placed it in the proper slots of the cash drawer. Each night he removed it. Today had been no different. When we'd returned to the store after breakfast, Father had placed the money in the drawer. Now it was gone. I tried to recall who had been in the store and when I'd last reached inside the drawer to make change. The money was there when a farmer from Marengo made a cash purchase a few hours ago. Then I remembered the couple who had come in after the farmer. They'd been dressed in shabby clothes. I'd never before seen them. The wife had asked me to show her some dishes in the back of the store while her husband had remained up front. They'd departed without making a single purchase. My mind reeled. Had the man helped himself to the cash while I was showing his wife a set of china? The elders had discussed purchasing one of the new cash registers to replace our wooden cash drawer, but they'd not yet reached a decision.

Father had left only a short time ago to pick up bolts of fabric from the mills in Main Amana. I could lock the door and place the Closed sign in the front window, but that would cause a flurry of questions. And visitors would surely arrive on the next train—visitors who would need change for their purchases. My stomach churned at the thought. What could I do? The thought rolled over and over in my mind. *Conrad!* Perhaps he could help.

I hurried the short distance to the barbershop, disappointed when I caught sight of a visiting salesman sitting in the barber chair. Oma was circling the two men, her broom in continuous motion. If her actions were disturbing Conrad, he gave no indication.

My grandmother had insisted upon leaving with Conrad when he'd stopped by the store earlier. Once again, she'd confused him for my grandfather, and once again Conrad had accepted her overtures. When she'd insisted upon leaving with him, he'd quickly agreed and brushed aside my concerns. "She'll be fine. I'll have her straighten the shelves and sweep the floor." To try to keep her at the store would have caused a scene and drawn my father's attention.

Conrad glanced in my direction as I entered the shop. "You

didn't need to come and check on her so soon. She is doing fine—a big help to me, aren't you, Sister Helga?"

Oma offered Conrad a bright smile and completely ignored me. Probably just as well. When she wasn't in her right mind, she feared other women would try to steal "her man."

"When you finish, I need to speak to you."

He stopped clipping and looked over his shoulder at me. "Something is wrong?"

I nodded. "We need to talk as soon as possible. Could you come to the store? Vater is gone to Main Amana, and I had to put up the Closed sign."

"Ja. You go back to the store. Sister Helga and I will come when we finish here."

Oma was sweeping Conrad's shoes when I left. The barbershop held a certain fascination for her, perhaps because my grandfather had enjoyed his visits to the barber, but there was no way to predict what would fascinate her when she wasn't in her right mind—except that she always was happy to be with Conrad, and he never failed to extend great compassion and kindness where she was concerned.

I couldn't count the number of times I'd been thankful for having him close at hand when help was needed. And fortunately the barbershop wasn't busy all the time. The men tended to fit haircuts into their work schedules, and though most liked their hair neatly trimmed and parted in the middle or on one side, during harvest or planting, the haircuts could always wait. And while most of the men preferred their faces clean-shaven, they performed the task themselves at home each morning. Seldom did the local men have time to enjoy a shave at the barbershop. I counted it a special blessing that Conrad had periods of free time, for more and more I found myself in need of his help.

I unlocked the store, removed the Closed sign from the window, and uttered a quick prayer that no cash-paying customers would arrive. Maybe Conrad had cash in the barbershop that he could loan me until the missing money was returned. The thought provided a glimmer of hope, though I doubted he kept as much on hand as I would need.

I paced the wooden floor until he and Oma arrived a short time later. My grandmother discovered a crate of canned goods and began to stack them in the middle of the floor. I quickly explained about the empty cash drawer and asked Conrad if he'd seen the couple who had last been in the store.

"Nein. And if it is the only time they've been here, there's no hope of locating them. Are you certain they are the ones who took the money?"

"I have no idea. I only know it is missing. I made change for the farmer from Oxford who was in here before them."

"Ja, I remember the farmer. I was here when he came in, but Sister Helga and I left a short time—" He turned to look at Oma. "Do you think your grandmother took the money?"

I shook my head. "Why would she take the money?"

He shrugged. "Why would she climb the apple tree? Who can say how her mind works in recent years?" He walked to the center of the store and stooped down in front of my grandmother. "May I buy one of these cans of food, Sister Helga?"

My grandmother looked up at him, her eyes clouded but a smile on her lips. "Ja, but only one."

He reached into his pocket and removed a folded piece of paper and handed it to my grandmother. "I will need some change."

Conrad followed as my grandmother walked to the cash drawer. She appeared baffled when she discovered the empty slots, but moments later she grasped Conrad's hand. "The money is over here, but don't tell anyone." She pulled him down the aisle, pushed aside the jars of honey, and removed an old sugar sack. After handing Conrad several coins, she returned the sack to the shelf and shoved the jars back into place. She touched her fingers to her lips. "This is our secret, Emil."

"Ja. I won't tell anyone."

I couldn't believe what he'd managed to accomplish in such a short time. And how had she remembered where she'd hidden the money? Conrad was right. Who could say how her mind worked? Conrad glanced over his shoulder, and I mouthed a thank-you. He grinned in return.

"Maybe you should rest, Sister Helga. So much sweeping at the barbershop is a tiring job. A little rest would be good, ja?"

After a few minutes Oma agreed I could take her to her room. When I returned, Conrad had returned the money to the cash drawer. "Thank you, Conrad. I don't know what I would do without you."

"It makes me feel gut to help you, Gretchen. I hope you will always come to me when you are in need." He squeezed my hand. "I better get back to the barbershop, but I will see you later."

The following morning I lifted one hand to my brow and shaded my eyes against the bright August sun. Though Conrad waited for us outside the barbershop each Sunday and accompanied us to meeting, I hadn't expected to see him today. "I am pleased to see you have made a quick recovery from your illness," I told him. "I was worried when Vater told me you weren't feeling well last evening."

"It is gut to know you were worried about me."

When he tipped his hat and smiled, I could see he wasn't as

well as I'd first thought. His complexion had a pasty hue, and his eyes appeared dull and lifeless. But it was his comment that troubled me more than his appearance. There had been an edge to his voice—almost as though he didn't believe me.

Yet why should he question my concern for his health? I grasped Stefan's shoulder and motioned him to walk beside Oma. Though the women and men usually walked separately to meeting, my father didn't object when I quickened my step and moved beside Conrad. I would return to my place beside Oma before we neared the meetinghouse. For now, I wanted to question Conrad.

"You sound as though you don't believe I was concerned." I edged closer to his side. "Why is that?" I lifted my chin to gain a better view of his eyes as he looked down at me.

"Maybe because you appear more interested in Mr. Finley. At least that's what I'm told."

"I don't know what you're talking about," I whispered.

His eyes reflected either disbelief or pain, maybe a mixture of both. "So it wasn't you leaning over the counter nose-to-nose with Mr. Finley two days ago? And it wasn't you slipping notes back and forth to him or holding his hand?"

My stomach churned. Who had been telling Conrad such things? I didn't think there had been anyone in the store that day I'd spoken to Mr. Finley. Only once had I seen someone enter while he was there, an area farmer and his wife—not anyone who lived in Homestead. Not anyone who would have cared that I was talking to Mr. Finley. Not anyone who would have carried such information to Conrad.

Forcing my thoughts backward in time, I tried to recreate all that had happened while Mr. Finley was in the store. There had been any number of customers inside the store later in the morning, but I could not recall anyone who might have seen me speak with Mr. Finley. Someone wanted to stir up trouble, and from the look on Conrad's face, they'd been successful. Jealousy had taken hold of him, and the only thing that would set matters aright would be a full explanation. But there wasn't time right now.

"We should go for a walk this afternoon, and I will explain then—if you're feeling well enough." From his appearance, Conrad needed to be in bed, but I doubted he'd refuse my offer of an explanation.

There wasn't the slightest hesitation before he said, "I will call for you at two o'clock."

If the determined set of Conrad's jaw could be used as any measure, he'd expect a detailed report. And I would give him one. I hoped it would set the matter of Mr. Finley to rest. There was no need for jealousy.

We parted as we neared the meetinghouse. The men entered through their door while I walked with Oma to the women's door, where Mina greeted me. I was pleased and surprised to see her. "You don't have to cook today?"

She shook her head. "Sister Marguerite is taking a turn. About time, I say."

I grinned at her reply. Most of the kitchen bosses took their turn working in the Küche on Sundays, but Sister Marguerite was an exception. She didn't like to miss meeting and seldom took a turn working on Sunday mornings. Since Mina was second in charge, Sister Marguerite assigned her to supervise most every Sunday.

"Why the change of heart?"

Mina glanced over her shoulder. "Because I told her I was going to request a move to another Küche."

I followed Mina across the threshold and into the meeting-house. Sun shone through the curtainless windows and splashed streaks of gold on the wooden floor. The shimmering rays of sunshine emphasized the stark whitewashed walls and rows of narrow benches. I tugged on her sleeve and nodded toward one of the benches.

She turned and shook her head. "I'm not sitting way at the back. You can sit there next Sunday when I'm working."

I followed in silence. No need to argue. I wouldn't win. Besides, Mina was right. She should get to sit where she wanted. After we edged into the row, I sat down with Oma on one side and Mina on the other. But instead of listening to the readings and message from the elder, I worried over my explanation to Conrad and how he would react when he discovered I'd given another story to Mr. Finley.

Would he be so angry he would want to set aside our court-ship? At moments such as these, I longed to have my mother at my side. How I longed to ask for her opinion and advice. Instead, I confided in my journal. Not a suitable replacement, since the journal never offered an opinion or advice. And it was a mother's advice I needed right now. Time hadn't softened the feelings of loss that frequently washed over me. In fact, as I grew older, I longed for her counsel and guidance even more.

Sometimes Mina provided me with the listening ear I needed, but she'd never had children of her own. For Mina, the solution to any problem was to follow the rules. She didn't think any rule should ever be broken, or that a problem could be examined from more than one angle. And in matters of love, Mina could lend no help at all. Of course, that didn't mean she was without an opinion on the subject. She had a very strong belief: If you follow the rules, you won't fall in love, and you'll never be required to understand men and their strange ways.

I leaned forward an inch or two and peered across the aisle. Conrad sat on a bench on the men's side of the meetinghouse. He was staring toward the front of the unadorned room, his gaze fixed upon the elder reading from the *Psalter-Spiel*. I thought his color appeared somewhat improved, but given the distance between us, I could be wrong.

Before I could gain a better view, Mina poked her sharp elbow into my side. One glance at her disapproving stare and I sat up straight. Her stern look didn't cause me to focus upon what was being said, but I kept my eyes trained toward the front of the room for the remainder of the service.

When the final prayers were uttered and we stepped back outdoors, Mina grabbed hold of my arm. "Would do you more gut if you listened to what was being said during meeting." She tapped her finger to her head. "What's being said needs to go in up here and then settle in here." She touched her finger to the bodice of her dress, directly over her heart.

There was no reason to disagree. I did need to listen during meeting. But even Mina's harsh looks hadn't been enough to hold my mind captive this morning. Today my thoughts were on Conrad and our looming conversation. For once, I was glad Mina had to return to her kitchen duties. I had no desire to be lectured at length.

Conrad drew near before we arrived at the Küche. He wasn't quite so pale. "If you have no objection, Stefan mentioned he would like to come along with us. He thought we might go to the river and he could try to catch a fish."

Taking Stefan along hadn't been in my plan, but Conrad and I couldn't go off on our own. I'd anticipated taking Oma with us.

Once settled on a blanket beneath a leafy tree, she'd permit us the privacy to talk. With Stefan, there'd likely be constant interruptions. Then again, I didn't know how my talk would progress with Conrad. I might be thankful for a bit of disruption.

Stefan spotted Conrad outside the parlor window and raced to answer the door before I could object. "We're ready." My irritation mounted when Stefan waved at Oma and me to hurry.

I stepped to my brother's side and nudged his arm. "You may be coming along with us, but Conrad has come to call on me," I whispered. "You are not in charge."

He ignored my comment and jerked away. "Did you bring your fishing pole, Conrad? Freddie Miller said he caught some big fish last week. I'm hoping we'll do even better." Stefan pointed toward the door. "I already got my pole from the shed. It's on the porch."

"I haven't been feeling too gut, so I don't think I'll be doing any fishing. I'm going to count on you to outdo Freddie's catch." Conrad ruffled Stefan's hair. "Besides, I want to talk to your sister."

Stefan shot me an annoyed look before going outside to gather his fishing pole. I stepped to Conrad's side. "I don't think your answer met with his approval."

"He'll get over it once he gets a worm on his hook and begins to fish." He gestured toward the blanket Oma held in her arms. "Let me carry that for you."

My grandmother didn't hesitate to relieve herself of the burden. She patted Conrad's arm. "Thank you, Emil."

I locked eyes with Conrad and then looked toward my father to see if he'd heard my grandmother's mistake, but he had his latest catalog open and was looking to see the new products. Oma clung to Conrad's arm, and I motioned for him to leave.

"We'll be back before time for supper. Try to rest this afternoon, Vater."

He nodded. "You have a nice time, and tell Stefan he is to listen to you and Conrad. I don't want him running off as he pleases. He should stay close by."

"I'll be sure to tell him." It would have been better if my father had spoken directly to Stefan. He'd be more inclined to listen. My instructions were often brushed aside without a second thought. But this wasn't the time to linger. From the way Oma was behaving, she was slipping into one of her bouts of senility, and it would be better if Father didn't know.

It didn't take long to confirm my suspicions. We'd gone only a short distance, and when I attempted to speak to Conrad, Oma moved between us and pinned me with an angry stare. "Emil is a married man. You should find yourself someone who doesn't have a wife." She flicked her wrist as if to shoo me away.

Stefan had run ahead, but the three of us stopped, and I looked into Oma's rheumy eyes. I needed to break through the foggy haze that had overtaken her mind. "Oma, this is Conrad Wetzler, the barber in Homestead. He is courting me." I touched Conrad's arm to reinforce what I was saying. "I am your granddaughter, Gretchen. Your husband, Emil, died many years ago."

She jerked back and pointed a crooked finger beneath my nose. "You pretty girls are all alike. You try to steal any man you want." She clutched Conrad's arm in a viselike grip. "You can't have Emil. He loves me, not you."

Instead of helping, my words had caused her to become frantic. I shot a worried look at Conrad. With a gentle touch, he placed his large hand over Oma's gnarled fingers. "No need to worry. Everything is fine, Sister Helga."

His gentle tone soothed her, and she rested her head on his arm for a brief moment. Sadness swept over me like a tidal wave. She'd gone without one of these bouts for a brief time, and I'd built false hope they were gone for good. Today proved I was wrong, yet it also affirmed Conrad's deep concern for my grandmother. The depth of his kindness never failed to amaze me. Even as a boy Stefan's age, he'd been kind and considerate. He'd never lost those qualities, and his ability to manage Oma didn't surprise me. But sometimes it caused me to feel inadequate. How was it possible I lacked the ability to soothe her, yet only a few words from his lips would calm her?

The fishing spot Stefan and Conrad had chosen wasn't far from where the Gypsies were camped. Had they told me in advance, I would have asked Conrad to choose another spot. But he hadn't asked, and it would be best if I didn't voice my opposition now. I'd already upset Oma. No need to have Stefan angry, as well. And with Conrad along, there should be no problem with the Gypsies.

Conrad spread the blanket in a comfortable spot and assisted Oma to the ground. She leaned heavily upon his arm before finally settling against the trunk of a large oak. I'd filled a basket with her knitting and a tin of crackers from the store, but neither interested her. "Why don't you try to take a little nap, Sister Helga. I'll sit here beside you."

My grandmother smiled at Conrad before she shot a warning look in my direction. "Stay away from him. You hear me?"

"Ja. I will remain here on this side of you, and Conrad will sit on the other side."

"Emil! His name is Emil. You are not so smart." She shook

her head and gave me a pitying look that made me want to laugh for the first time today.

Conrad chuckled and lightly touched her hand. "Gretchen is a little slow, but she's very nice."

Oma snorted and turned her back to me. "She wants to steal you. I know her kind."

While Conrad reassured Oma that she had no need to worry, I wondered if someone had once attempted to steal Opa's affection from my grandmother. Had an incident from decades ago stirred some long-forgotten memory when she slipped into this hazy fog of senility? There was no way to know for sure, but I wanted to believe that something similar had happened in her past, something that would leave me feeling less wounded by her attack upon me. After a short time she dropped off to sleep, and Conrad carefully settled her and moved to my side on the blanket.

"Now we must talk," he said. "I am troubled by the things I have heard about you and Mr. Finley." He placed his palm across his chest. "It hurts me deep inside to think you have affection for this man."

"Then you don't need to hurt any longer, because I do not have any affection for Mr. Finley. I think of him as a friend, but nothing more. You know that I have a desire to write and he—"

"Ja, ja. I know he was giving your writing to a friend in Chicago. But you promised the correspondence would end. Then I discover all of these other things, and what am I to believe?"

I inhaled a deep breath. The only way I could hope to restore Conrad's trust would be to tell him the truth and pray that he would believe me. I would also need his forgiveness for sending the latest story. He listened without interruption while I explained all that had happened since the day he'd been in the store and seen the envelope addressed to Mr. Finley.

"So you took this piece of paper with a new address for what reason? To send him more of your stories even though you told me you wouldn't correspond with him?" Conrad clasped his hands around his bent knee and stared into my eyes.

"The stories are supposed to be sent to Mr. Finley's aunt. I can show you the slip of paper if you don't believe me." I was trying to remain calm, but defending myself proved more difficult than I expected. Perhaps because I didn't want to admit I'd committed any wrongdoing. But my heart told me otherwise. I had broken my word, and even though I was sending the mail to Mr. Finley's aunt, the contents were intended for him.

Conrad's features softened as he looked into my eyes, and I was heartened to see his coloring much improved. "This writing is very important to you, and I do not want to make you unhappy. I am not opposed to the writing, but I think it serves no gut purpose to send these stories or poems to Mr. Finley or to his friend."

"He can send me advice on how to improve my writing. I want to compose beautiful stories and poems. He can help me do this."

He lifted my chin with one finger and looked into my eyes. "I am sorry. I hope you'll forgive me for questioning your involvement with Mr. Finley. After all these years, our trust in each other should run deep." He lifted my hand to his lips and gently kissed my fingers. "I am sorry, Gretchen. I promise to trust you always." He tapped one finger against his chest. "But that Mr. Finley, I do not trust. I think he plans to win your love."

My heart twisted in a knot as I listened to Conrad's apology. I should have told the truth. Now it was going to be even more difficult. But if I waited until later, I might never tell him. "You don't owe me an apology, Conrad." I bowed my head, fearful of the anger or betrayal I might detect in his eyes. "While I want my writing to be an offering to the Lord, I also have taken pleasure in the kind words from Mr. Finley's friend." I wanted to defend my actions and tell him no one else cared about my writing, but that didn't make my behavior acceptable. In truth, pleasing myself had been more important than pleasing God. And though it was difficult, I finally confessed to Conrad.

"I am so sorry," he said.

The sadness in his voice cut to the quick. I had expected him to rail against me, not say he was sorry. Still, those words could mean so many things. Did they mean he no longer wanted to marry me? Did they mean he was sorry I had lied? Did they mean he was sorry I was a prideful woman? When I could bear the silence no longer, I looked at him. "Why are you sorry? You've done nothing wrong."

He bobbed his head. "Ja. I have been wrong because I didn't read your stories and because I didn't show understanding for all you must do each day. That is not gut. Who can say? Maybe one day you will write the words to a song that we will sing in meeting."

"I've already had one of my poems published in a magazine." Bolstered by his kindness, I blurted the admission without proper thought.

The ruddiness that had returned to his cheeks a short time earlier disappeared before my eyes. I'd likely gone too far with my truth-telling.

"Conrad! Come quick! I need help." Stefan's shouts echoed through the woods and delayed the possibility of a rebuke from Conrad.

Oma didn't stir from her sleep, but Conrad and I jumped to our feet and raced toward the river's edge. Fear had taken hold, and by the time we arrived, I was gasping for breath.

With his arms lifted high in the air, Stefan was arching backward, pulling up on the pole to hold his line taut. "I've got a big one and need help."

I leaned over and exhaled a deep sigh while Conrad continued to the riverbank. Rather than take the fishing pole from Stefan, he stood beside the boy and offered firm direction.

"That's it. Pull back. You're doing gut, Stefan." The instruction continued until I could see a fish flopping in the shallow water near the bank. Conrad grabbed a net and walked to the water's edge to scoop up the fish. "A fine big fish you have caught, Stefan." With a broad smile on his lips, Conrad strode toward Stefan and extended the net for the boy to have a better look.

I stepped forward and peeked into the net. The fish was quite large, and Stefan beamed when I praised his ability.

Conrad extended the net toward the boy. "You will need to get the hook out and then clean it, ja?" Stefan looked up at Conrad as if giving the idea considerable thought. "Or you could throw it back in the water and let it swim away. It's up to you, Stefan."

Stefan grinned. "I think I'll put it back and let someone else have the fun of catching it."

I stood at a distance while Conrad helped Stefan remove the hook. Then the two of them released the fish into the river. Conrad clasped Stefan's shoulder. "That was a fine fish, and if anyone doubts how big it was, you tell them to come and ask me. I will tell them it was this big." Stefan laughed as Conrad stretched his arms wide before slowly bringing them closer together.

Stefan baited his hook with a fat worm and cast his line back into the river. "You think that fish is too smart to let me catch him again, Conrad?"

Conrad shrugged his shoulders. "Who can say? I do not know how smart a fish can be, but if you catch him again, we'll know he isn't so clever, ja?"

I hoped Stefan's interruption had softened or erased Conrad's memory of my earlier confession. It had been foolish to speak of the published poem. He'd already forgiven a great deal, and I didn't think he'd look kindly upon a poem being published in a periodical. I remained hopeful as we returned, for his only comments were about Stefan's fine catch.

As we drew near to the tree, I glanced in every direction. My heartbeat quickened, and I clutched Conrad's arm. "Oma's gone!"

CHAPTER 19

Panic wrapped me in its unyielding grip as I scanned the wooded area. Conrad grabbed me by the hand and bid me follow him toward the river. We'd gone only a short distance when I pulled free of him. "We should go in opposite directions. We'll be able to search a larger area."

He nodded. "You're right. But stay close to the river and check there first before you go into the woods. I do not think she would wade into the river, but who can say."

Who indeed! In Oma's condition, there was no way to know where she would go. She could be anywhere. "Once we check the river, we should look near the Gypsy camp. She has a fondness for going there when she's not in her right mind."

We agreed to go a quarter mile along the river in opposite

directions. "Go as far as the high rocks that hang out over the water." I knew that spot well. Many of the older boys liked to jump into the water from those rocks. I didn't believe Oma could have gotten past us while Conrad had been helping Stefan net his fish, but there was always the possibility. When she wasn't in her right mind, Oma had a cunning nature that defied normal behavior. I looked back and forth from the water to the uneven ground in front of me. The fishy scent of the river filled my nostrils, and I wrinkled my nose at the unpleasant odor. I wasn't certain how far I'd walked when I spotted Oma's bonnet floating in the water. Fear struck me with a blow to the midsection.

"Oma! Where are you?" I slipped on a rock and momentarily lost my footing. If I wasn't careful, I'd end up in the river and be of no help to Oma.

Frightening thoughts raced through my mind, each one worse than the last. Bushes slapped at my skirt, and tree branches snagged my bonnet as I hurried along the uneven path. Gritting my teeth, I picked up my pace until I finally caught sight of Oma sitting in the water not far from the bank. Relieved yet saddened by the sight, I waved and called out to her. When she stood, I expected her to move toward dry ground. Instead, she waded into deeper water. Her dark calico ballooned in the water like a giant bedsheet. She giggled and slapped at the fabric floating around her. Once again I called to her. But the louder I shouted, the further in she went.

"You should quit shouting. Can't you see that your squawking is making her go out further?"

I swirled around and was face-to-face with Zurca. I didn't think he had washed or changed his clothes since he'd come into our store when the Gypsies had first set up camp. His hair was still dirty and bound at the nape of the neck with a scruffy piece of cloth.

Straightening my shoulders, I planted a fist on each hip. "Don't tell me what to do. She is my grandmother, and she needs to get out of the water before she drowns."

"Silly woman. Can't you see that the water will soon be over her head? She's trying to get away from you. If you keep screaming and she sinks under the water, you will have no one to blame but yourself."

I stared at him in disbelief. Who did he think he was, telling me what to do! "I am trying to save her."

"If you are trying to save her, then you should do as I say. Shut your mouth and let me take care of this." He tapped the side of his head with his grimy fingers. "She is out of her head, so she will want me—not you."

He spoke with a prideful authority that raised my irritation to new heights. Instead of heeding his warning, I ran to the water's edge. "Oma! Come to me, right now! The water is too deep." I stretched out my arm and waved, hopeful I could entice her to come to me. More than anything, I wanted Oma out of the river before she hurt herself. But I also wanted to show Zurca that he wasn't as smart as he thought—at least not where my grandmother was concerned. I sat down on a rock and unlaced my worn work boots while silently giving thanks I'd chosen to wear them instead of my good shoes that buttoned down the side. Without a buttonhook, it would have been impossible to remove them.

After yanking off the boots, I stepped into the water. "I'm coming, Oma."

"Nein!" Her scream pierced the air like a shrieking crow. I watched in horror as she backed away and suddenly disappeared beneath the water.

Lifting my feet high, I pranced through the shallows, but soon the water weighted down my clothes and slowed my progress. Oma's head bobbed to the surface, and I screamed to her. Using my arms I tried to propel myself forward, but the undercurrent held me in place. Zurca splashed into the water beside me and disappeared beneath the surface in a leaping dive.

Moments later Oma's crown of white hair broke through the dark water. Zurca thrust her heavenward and shook his dark oily mane, causing beads of water to dance in the sunlight. I watched in disbelief, my mind a jumble of horror, disbelief, and astonishment as he swung Oma onto her back. Careful to keep her face out of the water, he held her head in the crook of one arm while he swam toward me using the other. When he neared me, he stood up, guided Oma's body forward, and lifted her into his arms. I splashed along beside him until we reached the river's edge.

"Is she alive?" I hadn't intended to scream, but fear had taken control when I couldn't see any sign of her breathing. I jerked the sleeve of Zurca's wet shirt.

He yanked free of my grasp. "Step away!" Turning away from me, he placed Oma on the ground and rolled her onto her stomach.

I remained frozen in place while he turned her head to one side, but when he straddled her body and began to push on her back, I lunged at him with a fury. "Get off of her! You're going to crush her!"

With a mighty force, Zurca shoved me away and sent me sprawling onto the sandy riverbank. "Get back, woman! I am trying to save her life. She is going to die if you don't let me help her." His nostrils flared, and he pinned me in place with a cold stare.

I paced at a distance watching Zurca's every move, certain

he would crush any life from Oma's tiny frame. My wet clothes clung to my body, and I shivered in spite of the day's warmth. What would my grandmother think if she should return to consciousness with this man perched over her? In all probability, she'd scream and once again lose consciousness. Yet I had no choice but to trust her to this character who looked as though he belonged in a nightmare rather than real life. He was her only link between life and death.

After he pressed on her back several more times, Oma sputtered and groaned. He yanked the filthy scarf from his neck and swiped at Oma's mouth. Damp, stringy strands of hair dropped across his face, but he didn't seem to notice. He spoke to her only once, then lifted up and pushed on her back once more. This time she responded with more gusto. Her coughing and sputtering were soon followed by a squeal, and she twisted to free herself from Zurca's straddled hold.

Only then did he motion me forward. He rested his hand in the sandy bank and pushed to his feet while Oma clutched his scarf in her fist. "She will be weak. I will carry her back to your store."

If Oma was in her right mind, she would fight against Zurca's help. If she was still in her senile condition, she'd probably want to marry him. Either response would be unacceptable. Before I could adequately form a reply, I heard Conrad's shouts and saw him running toward us along the riverbank. With a quick salute, Zurca disappeared into the woods before I could thank him.

Moments later Conrad dropped to his knees near Oma's side. "Is she all right? Did that Gypsy hurt her?" His brow furrowed.

"No." I shook my head. "He saved her life. If he had not come along, she would have drowned in the river."

Conrad snapped around to look at me. Amazement shone in

his eyes, but he didn't ask any more questions. Instead, he leaned close to Oma's face. "Sister Helga, do you think you can sit up if I help you?"

"Ja." Her voice was soft and raspy.

Conrad circled her with his arm and elevated her to a sitting position. "I think you may be too weak to walk home. I may have to carry you."

"Is too far," she croaked.

Her clear response confirmed that she'd returned to her right mind. Though she would have drowned without Zurca's help, it was best he had returned to the Gypsy camp. Had he attempted to carry her back to town, Oma would have fought against him and worsened her condition.

"You weigh very little," Conrad told her. "Besides, it will help to build my muscles."

She nodded and leaned heavily on his arm. "If it will help your muscles, then you should carry me."

I grinned at Conrad as he lifted her into his arms. "I'll fetch Stefan, and we'll meet you on the road." My thoughts raced faster than my feet as I ran along the riverbank. Explaining Oma's wet clothing and recounting the near drowning to my father would be tricky. I didn't know how I'd justify her condition without saying she'd been suffering a bout of senility. Only God's intervention could help.

As we continued on our way, I silently prayed Father wouldn't be at home when we arrived. Perhaps he had gone to visit friends or gone for a walk in the woods—a silly notion, but I needed a thread of hope that I wouldn't be met by his countless questions about Oma. Today had been worrisome enough without the added concern of another discussion about Mount Pleasant.

When we arrive home, Father was sitting in the parlor. Under different circumstances, his delayed reaction as he glanced at us and then startled to attention would have been most amusing. Today, it only caused concern.

I motioned for him to remain seated. "Everything is fine. I'm going to go into the bedroom and help Oma out of her wet clothes."

My grandmother beamed at him. "Such excitement, George. I will return and tell you everything that happened."

"And I shall be eager to hear." My father picked up his small leather pouch of tobacco. Wrapping one hand around the pipe, he tapped a small amount of tobacco into the bowl.

I hurried into the room behind Conrad. Once he'd settled Oma into her wooden rocker, he gave a slight wave and hurried back to the parlor. I wondered if Conrad had lost all feeling in his arms. Several times on the way home, I'd suggested he rest for a spell, but he had refused. No doubt he'd be quite sore come morning.

I stepped forward and leaned over my grandmother. "Let me help you unbutton your dress, Oma."

She didn't argue. In fact, she seemed to enjoy the attention. Once I'd helped her into dry clothing, she was more than happy to let me dry her hair. In order to remove all of the sand and river water, her hair would need a good washing, but she was impatient to return to the parlor and wouldn't agree to doing that now. She obviously hoped to bask in the attention a little longer.

I grasped her hand as she pushed up from the rocking chair. "Exactly what do you plan to tell Vater about what happened this afternoon?"

She looked at me as though I were the one who needed to be committed to Mount Pleasant. "Why, the truth, of course."

She gave her hair a final pat and motioned for me. "Come along. Let's not keep your Vater waiting any longer."

When we returned to the parlor, my father was settled back in his chair. A curl of smoke circled above his head like a translucent crown. Holding his pipe in his hand, he motioned toward the divan. "Sit down, Helga. I want to hear your story. Conrad and Stefan said they were netting a fish, so I didn't learn much from them." He lifted his pipe to his lips and waited.

All signs of Oma's misadventure had disappeared. She scooted to the edge of the divan. "For sure it was an exciting day, George. Let me tell you, I thought I was going home to meet my Maker."

Father squinted through the pipe smoke. "Ja? So tell me how come you were in the river. You think you are now a fish?"

She cackled at his remark. "Nein. I still do not know how to swim, but I saw such pretty flowers on the other side of the river, and I thought I could make it across using rocks I saw in the water." She rubbed her forehead. "Ach! I did not realize my eyes could deceive me so much. Instead of rocks, it was the sun shining on the water. But I was already standing on a rock, and when I turned around to return to the riverbank, my foot slipped, and I fell in the water. Such a pull that water had on me."

Conrad nodded. "Ja. There is a strong undercurrent. It can pull you down in a hurry if you are not a strong swimmer."

I was uncertain how much of Oma's story was true. She hadn't been having any trouble in the water until I attempted to lure her back to shore. But that's not what she remembered, and I wasn't going to contradict her. Neither Oma nor Conrad mentioned Zurca, and I didn't, either. I doubted Oma even remembered Zurca had saved her life. Maybe later she would have some recollection, but for now she remained oblivious.

She beamed at Conrad. "And Conrad carried me all the way home. He is stronger than you would think, George."

If my father noticed any gaps or irregularities in her story, he didn't say so and appeared satisfied. I was most grateful and offered a hurried prayer of thanks. My prayer had been answered. Not in the way I'd expected, but the method God used didn't matter—only the outcome. And I was most pleased with that.

For the remainder of the afternoon and evening, I expected my father to surprise me with some question or comment concerning Oma and our outing. But when bedtime arrived and he bid me good-night, I realized my worry had been in vain. He believed Oma's story.

After preparing for bed, I slipped between the sheets, glad the day had ended. It would be good to return to my regular routine tomorrow. It wasn't until I had completed my prayers and was slipping off to sleep that I remembered Conrad had never revealed the name of my accuser. As my eyes popped open, I once again attempted to recall who might have been in the store when I was speaking to Mr. Finley.

The next afternoon Stefan barreled into the store, his schoolbooks tied by a leather strap that he'd slung over his shoulder. Perspiration dripped from his hair, and he swiped the back of one hand across his forehead before tossing the books onto the front counter. "Loyco's gone, and Lalah is afraid something has happened to him."

"Lalah? So you've been back to the Gypsy camp again even though you've been warned to stay away from there." I wagged my index finger back and forth. "I'm not going to protect you, Stefan. If anyone saw you and tells Vater, you'll need to explain yourself. And I don't think he'll be kind about this." I pushed the books back toward him. "And take these to your room. They don't belong on the counter."

"You don't have to believe me." He stomped across the room and slung his cap onto one of the hooks. "And I wasn't at the Gypsy camp. Lalah was waiting by the edge of the road and called to me when I was coming home from school. She was crying because she misses her Vater. He's been gone for over two weeks now."

"I am sorry to hear this, but I'm sure Loyco will return." From the set of my brother's jaw, I could see my answer didn't satisfy him.

"Can you not remember how we felt when Mutter died? That is how Lalah is feeling right now. She is afraid she will never know what happened to her Vater. I think that would be even worse than to know he is dead." My brother continued to stare at me as if this situation were somehow my fault.

"I don't know what you expect from me, Stefan. I don't know what has happened to Loyco. Zurca or some of the other Gypsies would be more help than I can be."

"She asked for our help. Isn't that what the Bible teaches— that we should help those in need?"

I stared at him in disbelief. "After all the bad behavior I've seen from you over the past weeks, you are going to talk to me about Bible teaching?"

He folded his arms across his chest. "I told Lalah you would come to see her tomorrow. You should at least go and listen to her. There may be something you can do."

"I have no way to help her, Stefan, and you shouldn't have promised I would meet her." I wanted to throttle him. It seemed no one asked permission before taking matters into their own hands. First Mr. Finley had agreed to have my poems printed in the magazine without gaining my agreement, and now my brother had promised Lalah I would come and speak with her.

"Don't you have some pity for her? She has no Mutter, and now her Vater is gone. She didn't ask for anything but a few minutes of your time."

I pointed to the broom. "The floor is waiting to be swept, and there are crates to unload." When he continued to stare at me, I gave a curt nod. "I will try to get away from the store and speak with her, but I cannot say for certain when it will be. Unlike you, I must work all day."

Unexpected resentment crept into my reply, followed by a sharp sense of shame. I shouldn't rail against performing my duties. After all, we all worked for the good of the community. It wasn't as though I was expected to do any more than the other members of our village. But I had been required to leave my position in the kitchen to help with the store. And I had much preferred working alongside the other women over stocking the store shelves and managing the ledgers.

And then there was Oma. Always there was the worry over Oma.

CHAPTER 20

The hot days of August seemed to fly by, and before I knew it the month was drawing to a close. We'd dug the onion sets the previous week, and as expected, I'd been assigned to work in the fields. I wrote in my journal that it was probably a good thing, because I'd been happy to return to work at the store when harvest was over. Conrad surprised me from time to time when he asked me to read one of my stories or poems to him. His comments were always kind. He laughed in the proper places and nodded with agreement at others. When I'd finish reading, he would tell me my writing was perfect without any help from an outsider. Then he would grin and add, "But if it makes you feel better to send them, I will not disagree with your decision."

I was thankful for his praise and that he'd understood my ongoing desire to have my work reviewed by someone considered an expert. My only dissatisfaction arose when I'd receive each day's bag of mail and there would be nothing from Mr. Finley. I had expected to receive comments from his friend by now, but nothing had arrived, not even a message from Mr. Finley regarding his anticipated return to Homestead.

Even my father had mentioned Mr. Finley. The laces and trims he'd sold us had been well received by our customers, and Father wanted to place another order while there were still tourists arriving each day. "What kind of company does business like this? If Mr. Finley can't return, they should send another salesman." Father resorted to filling empty spaces on the shelf with some older trims that hadn't sold well in the past.

My father's annoyed comment provided the perfect opening for me. "Could you write to his company or send a telegram and ask for him to contact you?"

He looked up and his eyes shone with delight. "Ja! That is an excellent idea you have, Gretchen. I will send a telegram right now." He copied the company name and address from one of the boxes of trim. Grasping the scrap of paper between his thumb and forefinger, he waved it overhead and strode toward the door. "I will be back soon."

I hummed while I dusted the shelves, pleased that I'd found a way to resolve my father's problem and even more pleased that his action would help me, as well. Surely a telegram would bring a response from Mr. Finley within the week. I was lost in thought, anticipating what message Mr. Finley might send, when there was a tap on my shoulder. I stifled a scream and spun on my heel.

"Lalah!" I slapped my palm across my chest. "You frightened me. I didn't hear you come into the store."

She pointed to her bare feet. "No shoes."

"What can I do for you? Have you heard from your father?" At Stefan's insistence, I'd gone to meet with the girl and had listened to her fears and concerns, but I'd been unable to provide any genuine help. I had no idea why Loyco had left the band of Gypsies or where he might have gone. There truly was nothing I could tell her.

Her hair brushed across her shoulders as she shook her head. "No, not yet."

She was the first of the Gypsies to enter the store since Loyco's departure, and her appearance surprised me. Her father had given strict orders that they were to stay out of the town, and all of them had. At least as far as I knew. There had been no reports of missing chickens or eggs from Mina or the other kitchen workers, so I assumed all was safe within our borders.

After a wary glance toward the front door, she stepped to my left side, where she'd be shielded from view. "I came to warn you that Alija is going to put a curse on you."

Though I certainly didn't believe in Gypsy curses, the idea of the old woman stirring up a brew and chanting my name caused a momentary ripple of fear to wash over me. It also explained why Lalah was watching the front of the store.

"Do you think Alija followed you?"

"Maybe. She's quiet as a prowling cat, so I can never be sure."

"Why would she do such a thing?"

"She thinks you have made Loyco crazy and he has left us here to die."

231

"To die? Is there illness in your camp?"

"No. That's just the way Alija talks when she wants to scare us. That way everyone will agree with her and do what she wants."

I didn't doubt the old woman could scare most anybody. "And what is it she wants the rest of you to do?"

"She says we should make Zurca our leader, and then we can leave here. She wants to move on to another camp. She says that ever since you talked to Loyco about my mother, he has been acting strange in the head. Now the others are angry with me because I am his daughter." Tears pooled in her large brown eyes.

How could I do anything to help? Alija wouldn't believe anything I said. "I wish I could do something to make this better for you, Lalah. I'm sorry if any of my actions caused these problems for you."

"Maybe it would help if you tell her Loyco sent word to you that he's going to return in a week or two."

I shook my head. "I think telling a lie would only make matters worse. Just think what would happen if I did that and Loyco didn't return by the end of two weeks? Alija would put a double curse on me." Hoping to lighten the girl's spirits, I forced a chuckle, but she didn't smile.

She clasped her thin fingers around my hand. "If they decide to leave before Loyco returns, can I come and stay with you?" Fear shone in her dark eyes as she searched my face. "He won't know where to find me if he comes back and we're gone."

Loyco was a resourceful man, and I was certain he could track his band of Gypsies, but such a response wouldn't quell Lalah's fears. I swallowed hard, not knowing what my father would think of such an idea, but I couldn't deny the girl. And in spite of Alija's threats and curses, I thought the Gypsies would remain loyal to Loyco. "Yes, Lalah. If they decide to leave, you can come here, and we will give you shelter until Loyco returns. You have my word."

She wrapped me in a fleeting embrace. "Thank you. I won't come unless it is necessary. And I will do my best to keep Alija from placing a curse on you."

I thanked her and suggested she go out the back door in case Alija or one of the other Gypsies had followed her. If they thought she'd befriended me, they would make her life even more miscrable. I could only hope that Loyco would return before his band of followers decided to move on without him.

In the afternoon I greeted the latest group of visitors that had arrived on the train. "If you're interested in hearing about our people and how they came to America seeking religious freedom, you may gather near the counter."

It was then that one of the women called out, "You going to tell us about how you attend church every evening and three times on Sunday?"

Her question surprised me. "In truth, we attend only twice on Sundays, though on special holidays we sometimes attend more than twice."

One of the men grinned. "How about making the wine? Do we get to see those upstanding churchgoers who get drunk on the church wine?"

What was wrong with these people? I'd never encountered such a group before. They snickered and laughed through-out my entire speech. On several occasions I wanted to stop and tell them they were behaving worse than undisciplined schoolchildren, but I held my tongue. They were our guests, and I would treat them with hospitality—even if they didn't have any manners.

While I helped one of the ladies with a choice of fabric from the calico factory, her husband drew near. "I'd rather come back and help with the grape harvest. Maybe we could get some of that good wine." He chuckled and nudged his wife before he strolled down the aisle.

"Don't mind him." A pink hue tinged her cheeks. Whether from embarrassment or the heat, I couldn't be sure, but she immediately returned her attention to the fabric.

By the time they boarded a wagon to begin their ride to Main Amana, I was pleased to see them leave. There were few visitors who'd ever caused me such discomfort. Their comments and attitudes had been most puzzling.

My father was at the rear of the store when Brother William bounded across the threshold, panting for air. He bent forward, holding a palm to each side of his oversized belly. After two giant breaths, he waved a piece of paper in my father's direction. "Got your reply, Brother George!" He continued his labored breathing while my father hurried forward. "Not gut news." Brother William shook his bald head back and forth.

Father snatched the telegram from the man's thick fingers and scanned the response. "But this is nonsense. Of course he is employed by their company. He sold us their products. This is a mistake. Confusion of some sort."

I tried to peer at the telegram, but my father wouldn't hold still long enough for me to read it. "What does it say, Vater?"

He handed me the telegram, then raked his fingers through his thick hair. The telegram said the company did not have an employee by the name of Allen Finley. My breath turned shallow, and for a moment I thought I might faint. I agreed with my father: This had to be a mistake. I forced myself to inhale deeply before trying to speak.

"I think you are correct, Vater. This has to be a mistake. Perhaps Mr. Finley is no longer an employee. Maybe he had to quit because of his aunt's illness, and this Mr. Hiram Medlow is new to the company and doesn't know Mr. Finley had been an employee."

"And how do you explain the last part?" My father tapped his finger on the final lines of the telegram. "This says their company has never sent salesmen to Iowa."

I gasped. For sure, something was wrong. "There must be an explanation. Maybe you should send a telegram to Mr. Finley and tell him you have urgent questions."

My father scratched his head. "How can I do such a thing? I have only the address for his company."

Brother William stood between us, his head swinging back and forth like a door on a well-oiled hinge. How I wished he would return to his duties, but I knew that wouldn't happen. He was enjoying the unfolding drama far too much.

Turning away from the men, I scurried behind the counter. "I believe he left his home address with his other account information. Let me see if I can find it, Vater."

"That Gretchen is a godsend, for sure, Brother George. Who could ask for someone to keep better records for you, ja?"

While I searched, I kept a watchful eye on the two men and hoped Brother William would keep my father busy while I retrieved the address from my journal. As they continued to talk, I copied the address onto Mr. Finley's paper work, then called to my father. "Here it is. I've located Mr. Finley's home address."

My father stepped to the counter and turned the ledger for a better look. He squinted and leaned close to the page. "Strange, but I don't remember seeing this address on here when I looked at this earlier today."

Brother William clasped my father's shoulder and chuckled. "You are not getting any younger, my friend." He pointed to his own eyes. "You should think about wearing spectacles."

My father grunted. "Quit talking about my old age and write down this address so you can send the telegram and have it delivered to Mr. Finley."

Brother William made another remark about my father's advancing age before he took up the pen and copied the information. He pushed the paper toward my father. "You should write what the telegram should say." My father jotted his message and handed the paper to the stationmaster. *Urgent. Contact immediately. George Kohler, General Store, Homestead, Amana Colonies.*

The stationmaster hooked a thumb behind one of his stretched-too-thin suspenders and gave the elastic a tug. I took a backward step. If one of those suspenders snapped, I didn't want to be within hitting distance. "That is all you want to say?"

"That is enough." My father's firm tone was enough to discourage further questions from Brother William.

He folded the paper and tucked it into his pocket. "Then I will get back to the station and send your message."

Once the stationmaster was out of sight, my father narrowed his eyes. "I cannot understand Mr. Finley. I thought he was a truthful man with a gut heart, but I may have been wrong. Worried I am that he has deceived me."

Though I didn't say so, I was worried Mr. Finley had deceived more than my father, but I wanted to be wrong. I wanted Mr.

Finley to appear in the doorway and announce he'd been detained because of his aunt's illness. I wanted him to say there had been a misunderstanding about his employment with the lace and trim company. I wanted him to tell us he'd returned to become one of us. Instead, I feared I might never see him again. Even worse, I feared I would never again see the stories or poems I'd sent to him.

There had been no response to the telegram, but two days later a young man appeared with a group of visitors from Chicago. Like the past several groups that had visited the store, this group chuckled and made unpleasant remarks while I gave my talk about the colonies. Each time this occurred, I became more perplexed. Until the past week, I'd never before experienced such unseemly behavior. Now they took great pleasure in making a joke of everything I told them, and I was relieved each time a new group departed the store.

The lad remained at a distance from the others and didn't exit with them. "May I assist you in locating a special item?"

In one hand he held a package wrapped in brown paper. "Miss Gretchen Kohler?"

I tipped my head to gain a better view of him. I didn't think I'd ever seen him before. "Yes. I am Gretchen Kohler. How may I help you?"

He extended his arm and thrust the package toward me. "I was asked to deliver this to you. It is from a Mr. Allen Finley."

As soon as I accepted the package, he turned to leave. "Wait! I have questions about Mr. Finley."

The young man glanced over his shoulder and made a slow

turn. "I don't have any answers for you, miss. I work for a messenger service. I was told you worked in the general store and that I was to personally deliver the package to you. That's all I know."

Not for a second did I believe him. I stepped near and grasped his sleeve. "Please tell me what has happened to Mr. Finley."

He looked down at his arm, and I begrudgingly released my hold. "I have never seen or met Mr. Finley. This package was delivered to our office yesterday by a courier from the *Modern Ladies' Journal,* who provided the delivery instructions. Maybe if you open the package, your questions will be answered." He took a backward step. "If you'll excuse me. I'm going to the train station."

He kept a watchful eye on me, as though I would once again attempt to detain him. Thankful my father wasn't in the store to question me about the delivery, I set the package on the front counter. After the young man left, I untied the cord. My fingers trembled as I peeled back the brown paper. I blinked at the glossy cover of the *Modern Ladies' Journal.* The likeness of a young woman wearing a gauzy white dress embroidered with pink rosebuds adorned the cover. Confused, I lifted the magazine from its brown paper cocoon. It was then I saw an envelope bearing my name.

I ripped open the seal and withdrew the contents. When I unfolded the pages, a bank draft fluttered in the air and landed on the counter. The draft was payable to me, and I had to look twice before I could believe my eyes. Why was Mr. Finley sending me a bank draft for so much money? I'd sent him only two more poems, and even if he'd been successful in having them published, this was far too much money for two poems. And where were the stories I'd sent him? Those were what I'd been waiting to receive from him.

His bold script covered the cream-colored writing paper in firm, even lines.

Dear Miss Kohler,

Please know that it is difficult for me to write this letter. I am not proud of my behavior, but I live in a different world than you. In order to advance in my position with *Modern Ladies' Journal*, it was necessary for me to provide the editor with a unique story for our anniversary edition of the magazine.

Inside the pages of the recently released copy, you'll find the stories you penned about life in the Amana Colonies. Most writers would be pleased to receive such news, but I doubt you will take pleasure in seeing the finished project. Please know that I strongly discouraged use of the cartoons that accompany the stories, but my suggestion was ignored. Your stories have been received with great enthusiasm by our readers, and the magazine is selling in record numbers. Few changes were made to your writings. Unfortunately, my editor insisted upon using your real name.

A knot formed in my stomach. I dropped the letter onto the counter and flipped through the pages of the periodical. Near the center of the magazine, my eyes locked upon a title in large, bold print. ***Visit the Amana Colonies: Where Spirits Are Mixed With Religion***. In the columns below and to the right of the glaring title was my story about growing and harvesting grapes and making wine. To the left was a cartoon of two men and a woman sitting in the meetinghouse basement drinking wine. The woman was perched atop one of the barrels with her cap askew and her skirt hiked above her ankles. The men were portrayed with bulbous noses and eyes at half-mast while they sprawled across the floor. All three were holding wine-filled glasses high in the air.

"How could he!" Fury raged within as I turned the magazine pages and saw more horrid drawings. Mr. Finley had made a mockery of the stories—even more, he'd made a mockery of our people and our faith. Every story I'd written had been published in this special section they had titled "Treat for Travelers." He'd been so eager to gain his promotion that he hadn't even insisted the editor protect my identity. My stomach clenched, and I pressed a fist to my mouth to silence the sobs that threatened to rack my body.

What kind of man would do such a thing? Mr. Finley never had any intention of living in the colonies. He'd simply used me to promote himself with his employer. No wonder the recent visitors had been making rude remarks when they came into the store. And how long would it take before the elders discovered what I'd done and the mockery that had been made of our community. Guilt and shame assaulted me. How could I ever atone for the humiliation our society would suffer because of my reckless behavior?

I slapped the magazine onto the counter. As if to mock me, the bank draft floated in the air before dropping back to the counter. I shoved it into the magazine, then looked at the final page of the letter. It was addressed to my father and detailed how Mr. Finley's appearance had been a complete sham. He explained that a friend who worked at Marshall Field had supplied him with the products and catalogs. If my father wanted to purchase more of the trims, he could make arrangements directly through the company in England. He said he was sorry to have misled members of the community with his falsehoods, but he hoped an increase in visitors and sales would help mitigate any pain caused by his dishonorable behavior.

A silent scream lodged in my throat.

CHAPTER 21

After using the brown paper to cover the magazine, I paced the length of the store. Father had departed earlier in the morning to visit the calico factory in Main Amana. I didn't expect he'd return until shortly before the evening meal. Waiting for him would make for a long day, and there would be no opportunity to discuss Mr. Finley and his misdeeds until after prayer service.

My stomach churned. On the one hand I longed to immediately tell my father the whole truth and clear my conscience as soon as possible. On the other hand I feared his reaction to the disgrace I'd caused him. And I had no doubt he would feel disgrace. His daughter had willingly broken the rules. Then again, Mr. Finley had duped the elders, as well. He'd convinced them that he had a genuine interest in joining the community, but his interest conveniently waned once he'd discovered my stories would supply him with all the information he needed for his magazine.

How could I have been so easily convinced of everything the man said? The answer arrived with the swiftness of a bird taking wing: Mr. Finley had tickled my ears with words I wanted to hear. Even though questions had lurked in the back of my mind, I'd pushed them aside, ignored them because I desired the praise of both Mr. Finley and his friend. I grunted at the thought. Did Mr. Finley even have a friend who had looked at my work? Probably not. His editor had likely been the friend. A magazine editor eager to sell lots of magazines. And what better way to sell his magazines than with those mean-spirited cartoons.

My back was turned toward the door when I heard footsteps behind me and swiveled around. "Conrad!" I slapped one hand to my chest. "You surprised me."

"Ja? I hope it is a gut surprise." A wide grin split his face.

I bobbed my head. "Of course. It is always nice to see you."

He squinted and his forehead wrinkled into fine lines. "Your eyes do not say you are happy I am here. There is something wrong?"

Should I tell him? I weighed my decision for only a moment. I wouldn't accomplish one thing if I had to wait until my father returned before telling someone about the package. And Conrad was the perfect person, the person I could trust, the person who cared about me.

Grasping his sleeve, I tugged him to the far side of the room. After circling around the counter, I lifted the package onto the counter. "I have something to tell you. Something that is terrible." My lip trembled, and I bit down. I didn't want to cry.

"What is it that's made you so sad?" Conrad lifted his gaze from the paper-wrapped package, his eyes now dark with concern.

I lifted the contents from the paper and handed Conrad the letter. His features tightened as he read the missive. He nodded toward the magazine. "And your stories, they are in there?"

"Yes. And the cartoons are in there, as well. They're awful," I whispered, flipping to the center of the periodical and turning it toward him.

He thumbed through the pages, not taking time to read the story, but viewing the cartoons and the offensive captions beneath each one. "This man is even worse than I had imagined. How could he betray our people in this manner? It is gut he didn't come back here, because I wouldn't want to turn the other cheek to him."

Conrad's jaw twitched when he saw the portrayal of the barbershop. The barber had been depicted as a drunken, inept character holding a razor aloft in one hand and a bottle of wine in the other. In the cartoon the customer was staring into a mirror with a look of shock and dismay because half of his head was completely bald.

"I am very sorry, Conrad. I know Vater is going to be angry and disappointed. And the elders will not look kindly upon this, either. I'm sure I'll be sent back to children's church when they hear the part I've played in all of this. I won't be able to hold up my head."

He remained quiet for what seemed an eternity. "I do wish you hadn't trusted him so much, Gretchen. Still, the wrong is Mr. Finley's, not yours. You didn't draw those pictures or ask to have your stories published in this maga—" He stopped short and looked at me. "You didn't ask him to publish the stories, did you?"

245

"Nein! He mentioned he might publish another one of my poems, but not the stories. I never thought he'd publish the stories—not without my permission. And never with those horrible pictures." Tears threatened, and I touched the corner of my apron to my eye.

Conrad placed his arm around my shoulder. "Do not cry, Gretchen. There are worse things than a magazine story." He gave my shoulder a gentle squeeze. "We know what we believe and how we live here in the colonies. It is not as though we are seeking outsiders to come here and live, so what difference if people in Chicago think we get drunk and shave our heads? Let them think what they will. We know the truth. We are gut, hardworking people who have a strong belief in God, but Mr. Finley decided to make us a laughingstock. We cannot change what he has done, but we won't let it change who we are."

"I don't think Vater or the elders will be so generous with their reaction, but I am thankful you don't blame me for all of what has happened."

"We will talk to them together. I will stay by your side and speak on your behalf."

His offer warmed my heart. "Are you certain you want to do that?"

"Ja, of course I do. I love you, Gretchen, and I always want to be the one who will help and protect you."

Though I'd never doubted how much Conrad cared for me, his declaration of love and protection was more than I could have hoped for during such a difficult circumstance. I thought it remarkable that he was willing to stand alongside me and take up my cause—especially since he'd professed his doubts about Mr. Finley from the start.

Placing a finger beneath my chin, he tipped my head back as

he bent forward. My breath caught as our lips melded together in a gentle kiss. I eased into his arms with all thoughts of Mr. Finley, the magazine, and a confrontation with the elders evaporating like an early morning fog in sunlight.

Eyes closed, I rested my head on his shoulder and relished the warmth of his embrace. I don't know how long we'd been standing there when I was stunned by a sharp whack across my backside. I squealed and twisted around.

Oma held a broom in her hands, prepared to launch another attack. "Get away from my Emil! You can't have him, you bad girl." I jumped to one side, and Oma immediately stepped forward to take my place. She stroked Conrad's arm while she glared at me. "Find your own man. Emil is mine."

Conrad wrapped an arm around Oma's shoulder. "Come to the other room with me, Sister Helga." With a calm voice, he urged her along. "Let's put the broom over here, and we'll go into the parlor and visit." She took a few steps but refused to release the broom.

All thoughts of the pleasurable kiss fled from my mind while Conrad continued to cajole my grandmother. They had made little progress when Mina entered the store, her basket slung over her arm and a smile on her lips. Her smile quickly vanished as she surveyed the unfolding scene.

She nodded at my grandmother. "It is gut to see you, Sister Helga. You are feeling well?"

Oma tightened her hold on Conrad's arm. "Stay away from Emil. He is mine." She jabbed the broom handle toward Mina and pinned her with a fierce look.

"Ja, for sure he is yours, Sister Helga. I have no interest in a man." As if to prove her point, Mina took a sideways step away from Conrad and my grandmother. "Maybe you and Emil should go and have a cup of tea in your apartment."

Oma tipped her head to the side and tugged on Conrad's arm. "Ja, we will have some tea." She pointed a crooked finger at Mina. "Without you. You can't come with us." She took several steps. "Come on, Emil. Time for tea." I was certain I'd seen her wink at Conrad. I offered a silent prayer of thanks for his kindness and patience.

Mina clucked her tongue and shook her head. "Poor Sister Helga. She would be so embarrassed to know how she acts when she's having one of her episodes. Have you watched to see what it is that seems to bring them on?"

"I can find no pattern to her behavior," I said. "Maybe if you got your Älterschule started, that is something that could be determined."

"You may be pleased to know that I am to have a meeting with the Grossebruderrat when they are in Homestead next week. I have already presented them with the paper you wrote, and they will speak to me after they eat the noonday meal with us." She patted her stomach. "I am hoping that after they have read your plan and they have had a gut meal, they will be agreeable and not ask too many questions."

News that the Grossebruderrat would be in Homestead next week came as a surprise. They'd been in Homestead two months ago. Normally they didn't visit so often. An unscheduled visit could only mean that a decision affecting all of the colonies was going to be discussed or decided upon. "I wonder why they are returning so soon."

"There is trouble over the fees Mr. Harper plans to charge for his studhorse this year. It seems he has written to say the price will be more than double what he charged last year—a large expense that was not planned. They are meeting in each village and then will decide what must be done. If he had told them at the first of the year, they would have arranged to save for the added cost, but he has waited until there is little opportunity to come up with the additional funds. Sister Marguerite says there is grave concern."

"Did they say why Mr. Harper was doing this?"

"Only that he needed the money to pay extra expenses of his own. But Sister Marguerite says he's doing it because he can, that he's a greedy man who doesn't care about his fellow man."

It was obvious the women in the kitchen had been discussing Mr. Harper's demands at length, but I hadn't heard a word from my father. Of course, he was always slow to pass on news. I'd come to rely upon Mina or one of the other kitchen workers to learn of the latest happenings. Now with such a difficult problem facing the elders, I wondered if Mina should wait to speak to the Grossebruderrat about her idea. If their thoughts were on Mr. Harper and the needed funds, they might immediately reject her suggestion. But since she'd already given them the plan I'd written for the Älterschule, it was too late to alter the meeting.

Mina glanced toward the door leading to our apartment. "Maybe you should go with me. If they have questions, you'd be better able to answer and could use Oma and your family as an example."

My stomach lurched at the idea. Using Oma as an example would be the same as telling my father that she needed added care. If the elders didn't approve the Älterschule, he might force the idea of Mount Pleasant. But I didn't want to refuse Mina. She might change her mind if I didn't agree. And to think only of my own circumstance was unfair. There were others in the colonies who would benefit from Mina's idea. I took her hand. "You are my dearest friend. How can I refuse to help? If you need me, I will be at your side."

My father returned a full hour before time for the supper bell—an unanticipated surprise. Though I'd received Conrad's support, I doubted the outcome would be as agreeable with my father. He remained silent far too long after I'd completed my confession, and he continued to mask his emotions as he read the letter from Mr. Finley. Finally he looked at me. "If you have this magazine, I would like to read what you have written."

Perspiration dampened my palms as I extended the open magazine to him. He grunted a thank-you before ambling to a stool near the back of the store. I doubted he'd thank me once he finished looking at the periodical. A part of me wanted to view his reaction, but the other part wanted to hide behind the shelves piled high with supplies. I wasn't ashamed of what I'd written, but even the thought of those awful drawings still caused me to shiver.

My fingers trembled when I heard the thud of my father's boots on the wooden floor a short time later. He dropped the magazine on the counter and slid it toward me. "I will say that I am very disappointed that you did not see fit to follow the rules, Gretchen. They are in place for a reason." He tapped the front of the magazine. "None of this would have happened if you had simply followed the rules." There was sadness in his eyes.

"I am truly sorry, Vater."

He bobbed his head. "Ja, I know. And I am sorry you don't have your Mutter's guidance to help you when you make decisions. She would have given you gut counsel."

"I know," I whispered.

He cleared his throat and straightened his shoulders. "What

you said about our people was gut. You tell about us in a fine way that is true. If he hadn't let them put those drawings with your writing, I think the elders would overlook what has been printed." He hitched one shoulder. "For sure, they would have said to never again do such a thing without permission—and so would I." Instead of the anger and disdain I'd expected, I heard sadness in his voice. "But the pictures change everything."

"Ja, I know, Vater. I only wish I could take it back."

"But you cannot. Mr. Finley fooled us all. Even the elders liked him." My father pointed to the magazine. "Once outsiders have seen this, our people need to be prepared. We will be treated with scorn. Those drawings, they will speak louder than the words you have written."

"The magazine has already been sold to many people. We've now had some visitors who have commented on our wine drinking. When they made their remarks, I didn't understand. Now that I've seen this magazine, I know they had seen the pictures."

"You will need to come with me and meet with the Grossebruderrat next week when they are here. I will meet with the Bruderrat later this week. No need for you to come to that meeting. They will want the Grossebruderrat to decide, but first I must speak to them as a courtesy."

"Thank you for understanding, Vater. I will willingly take whatever punishment is given without complaint."

Later during evening meeting, I silently prayed. I had accepted Jesus as my Savior many years ago. I understood that His death on the cross provided atonement for my sins, and God would grant forgiveness when I repented of those sins. But this time it seemed too easy. This time my guilt pierced too deep.

When we returned home, I retreated to my room and prepared

for bed. How foolish I had been to trust Mr. Finley. He hadn't cared for our people or our way of life. He'd only cared about making a name for himself with his editor. But hadn't I been as guilty as Mr. Finley? I'd been seeking recognition—not of this sort, of course, not where it got me in trouble. Was Mr. Finley's desire to impress his employer so different from what my own had been?

I sat on the edge of my bed, opened my Bible to the first chapter of Colossians, and traced my finger beneath the words I prayed would give me strength. *Giving thanks unto the Father, which hath made us meet to be partakers of the inheritance of the saints in light: Who hath delivered us from the power of darkness, and hath translated us into the kingdom of his dear Son: In whom we have redemption through his blood, even the forgiveness of sins.*

" 'In whom we have redemption through his blood, even the forgiveness of sins.' " I read the words aloud before I finally closed my Bible. After slipping beneath the sheets, I repeated the comforting words until I fell asleep.

CHAPTER 22

Time passed in slow motion during the weeklong wait for the arrival of the Grossebruderrat. The day before they were scheduled to visit in Homestead, my father and I met with Conrad and Mina. After a lengthy talk we arrived at several conclusions. Since I would be going before the elders to confess my misdeeds with Mr. Finley, we decided Mina's meeting regarding the Älterschule would be better received without me. And since my father planned to attend my session with the elders, Conrad would not be included. My father had thanked Conrad for his kind offer to stand with me, but he'd also reminded us that we'd not yet received permission to court. Conrad's presence could create more problems.

Though my father didn't express an opinion about Mina's

idea for the Älterschule, he did suggest Conrad accompany her. "Would be gut for you to have at least one person stand with you. Conrad says he thinks this Älterschule is a gut plan for us, so he could offer support. There is enough difference in your ages that the Grossebruderrat would know the two of you are not . . . not . . ." He looked back and forth between them.

"Not planning to ask permission to marry," Mina said with a chuckle. "For sure, they would know that!"

She appeared somewhat uncertain until I nudged her arm. "I agree with my Vater. I think having another person along will help to influence them. And Conrad understands the need for such a place."

"Ach!" With a dismissive wave, my father shook his head. "I do not know why the three of you think this Älterschule is such a gut idea. Mount Pleasant is not such a bad place."

"How do you know, Vater? You've never even been there. I heard one of the outsiders say they don't treat people so gut in places like that. Besides, to remain among us is better for everyone." I hadn't meant to react in such a forceful manner, but I wanted him to see that Mount Pleasant wasn't the answer for Oma or any other older person in the colonies.

My father leaned back in his chair and stared at me. "I can see why Mina wanted you to attend the meeting with her."

Mina grinned. "Ja. She has gut ideas, like having the Älterschule near the Kinderschule so the older people can be around the little ones and even help when they are feeling gut."

"And they can help teach the older ones how to knit and crochet," I added. "It would be a gut thing for everyone."

My father leaned forward and rested his arms across his legs. "Ja, you are making gut sense with this idea. I know your grandmother likes to help with children. Maybe this would be a place where she could stay during the daytime."

I nodded. "And then she could come home and be with us in the evening."

His large hands came together in one loud, simple clap. "When she is not in her right mind, we wouldn't have to worry. There would be—" He stopped and looked at Mina. "Who is going to care for them? Did the two of you think of an answer for that question? I am thinking the elders will want to know your plan for that."

The question didn't alarm Mina. We had discussed the matter at length before I'd written out the plan. "There are more than enough women and older girls to help. There are extra women in some of the Küches. And I'm sure there are some, like me, who would rather help care for our older people than work at the Küche every day."

My father arched his brows. "I thought all of you women liked being in the Küche. I know Gretchen misses being there with all of you."

"Ja. The Küche is fine for a while. But I've worked there since I was a young girl, Brother George. It is the only place I have worked. To have something different would be a challenge for me."

My father smacked his palm on his knee. "Well, you have convinced me, so I hope you will do as well with the Grossebruderrat."

The transformation in my father's way of thinking surprised and pleased me. Had we been alone, I would have given him a giant hug, but I knew such behavior would embarrass him in front of company. Instead, I patted his hand. "I am pleased by the change in your thinking. We must pray that the elders will decide this is the Lord's work and what is best for the colonies."

Whenever the Grossebruderrat arrived at a colony for meetings, the Küchebaas and all of her workers made every effort to serve the perfect meal. And today was no exception. The food we were served at the noonday meal outshone even our holiday meals. My appetite had taken flight long before we entered the dining room, but it didn't impair my remembrance of the days when I had helped prepare meals in Sister Marguerite's Küche.

Back then, the Küchebaas had told me that serving exceptional food was a way of thanking the Grossebruderrat. She said these men served our colonies and the Lord in a special way. I didn't disagree with her assessment of the work they performed, but sometimes I wondered if all of the preparation and excellent foods were truly a way of thanking the Grossebruderrat, or if serving a better meal than the other kitchens was more a matter of pride for the Küchebaas. Of course, who was I to worry about the pride of others? I would have my own issues of pride to explain in only a short time.

I chased the food around my plate, not daring to eat. Already a lump that weighed like a heavy stone rested in the pit of my stomach. When we stood for our prayer at the completion of the meal, I was glad to leave the smell of ham and roasted potatoes. My father was standing with the members of the Grossebruderrat when I stepped outside. There was nothing significant about the appearance of the men—they looked like all the other men who lived in the colonies. But this small group had the authority to make a decision that could cause me great pain and embarrassment.

"We are to wait outside the meeting hall," Father said. "We will be called inside when it is our time to speak." He turned to look over his shoulder. "You told Sister Veda we might be gone for most of the afternoon?"

"Ja. She said to take as long as we need." I hadn't told Veda we were meeting with the Grossebruderrat, only that Vater and I both needed to be gone from the store this afternoon. She'd been pleased by my request, and I'd been thankful she didn't ask any questions. There would be enough chatter about the magazine once more outsiders arrived in the colonies. I swiped my sweaty palms down the front of my dress. This could be a long afternoon.

Father and I took up our positions outside the meeting hall. We managed to find a spot beneath one of the trees that provided some shade to protect us from the afternoon sun. Before long, the heat and a full stomach lulled my father to sleep. I envied his ability to push aside all worries and enjoy a time of rest. Then again, the worries were more mine than his. He'd come to take up my cause, but I was the one who would need to speak to the elders.

The Grossebruderrat would first speak with Mina and Conrad. After that, Mr. Harper was scheduled to appear and discuss the changes in his stud fees. So we would be last. I couldn't decide if it was better to be first or last. I hoped they might be weary of all their talking by the end of the day, but I doubted that would happen.

While my father dozed against the tree, I watched the door to the meetinghouse, eager to hear how the elders had received Mina's proposal for the Älterschule. She and Conrad were still inside when Mr. Harper arrived. Instead of a fancy buggy, he sat astride one of his beautiful riding horses. He claimed, and everyone in the area agreed, that his stock was the finest in all of Iowa. We had little way of proving the right or wrong of what he said, but Father said Mr. Harper maintained a ledger of the horses and their owners; his list reflected he spoke the truth. From what my father had explained, Mr. Harper had made lots of money from those fancy horses. And now he was going to make even more.

I nudged my father. "Mr. Harper has arrived. Maybe you should tell the Grossebruderrat before he barges in and interrupts Mina."

"I must have fallen asleep." Father rubbed his eyes and, using the tree trunk for support, struggled to his feet. "You stay here."

He didn't need to tell me to remain. I wasn't eager to go into the meetinghouse anytime soon. In fact, I wasn't eager to go in at all. Mr. Harper tipped his hat at me as he strode toward the men's door of the meetinghouse. I offered a slight wave in return. The lanky, beak-nosed man often came into our store to conduct business. He said we carried the best supplies at the fairest price. Too bad he wasn't willing to maintain fair prices for us, as well.

Moments later Mina exited through the women's door while my father and Conrad stopped for a moment to exchange greetings with Mr. Harper. I jumped to my feet and gestured to Mina, my excitement mounting when I saw her smile.

Unable to contain myself, I hurried to her side. "It is gut news, isn't it?"

"For the most part, it is gut. They liked the idea and said what you had written was very helpful and clear, but they want to have more time for the members to discuss the idea with the Bruderrat in each village."

"Why? They have the final say, and this is a gut thing you have proposed to them."

"They thought the idea was a gut one, for sure, but they don't think we have enough older people to have an Älterschule in each village. If not, they would have them in only a few of the villages. This means some of the older members might need to move away from their families, and there would need to be a home where they would go to spend their evenings."

"Couldn't the entire family move?"

I followed Mina's gaze toward the meetinghouse. Mr. Harper had already entered, but my father and Conrad were standing a short distance from the entrance, deep in conversation.

Mina turned around and adjusted the brim of her bonnet against the sun. "Those are the things that need to be decided. If a skilled worker is important to his village, he can't just pack up his family and move. They don't want all the clockmakers in one colony and all the tinsmiths in another. Think of Oma and your family. Your Vater couldn't leave the store and go to High or Middle and operate the store. Those positions are already filled." She arched her brows and stared at me.

I bobbed my head. "Ja, I see. Still, I had hoped for a definite answer today."

Mina's features relaxed once I replied. Even though I had spent many hours writing out the plan, I hadn't thought about the needs within each village and how they would be met if someone was required to move elsewhere. The ability of the Grossebruderrat to quickly identify such problems impressed me. No wonder these men were charged with finding solutions for the members of our communities.

"Do not be discouraged, Gretchen. If it is God's will, these difficulties will be solved. The elders said they would discuss the idea with each Bruderrat and then bring their ideas together. They will have an answer for me when they next meet, and that is not so far away."

Not so far away unless you were attempting to keep your grandmother from running off to the Gypsy camp or climbing apple trees. "I will try to be patient awhile longer, but I do wish you would have gone to speak to the elders when you first had your idea. What did they think was the best part of the plan?"

Mina tapped her chin and looked as if deep in thought. "For sure they liked the idea of having a place that would be close to the Kinderschule. They thought it was a wise idea to have the old and the young close together. One of the men said the young could learn from the old, and the young would make the old feel young again. I think he is right about that, don't you?"

I had mentioned that fact in the written plan, but I didn't remind Mina. Instead, I gave her a quick nod. "Ja. I know Oma likes to have Sister Veda's little girl come and visit. And she took a real liking to Lalah when she was out of her head down at the Gypsy camp."

Mina slapped one hand to her forehead. "Ach! I hope she hasn't been back there again."

"Nein. At least if she has been there, I didn't find out." I forced a weak grin. "It is hard to keep a constant watch over her."

"And that is why we are here today." She hesitated. "At least part of the reason. I will be praying that your meeting goes as well as mine. Let us hope that Mr. Harper's demands don't displease the Grossebruderrat too much. It would be better if they were still in good humor when you spoke to them."

No doubt Mina hadn't meant for her comment to create more concern, but it did. Unlike Mina, I hadn't considered the possibility that their meeting with Mr. Harper could influence their disposition when they met with me.

Mina pointed toward the meetinghouse. "Look! Already Mr. Harper is leaving. That talk didn't take long."

My stomach lurched when I spotted the gangly horseman stride past my father and Conrad without even a tip of the hat. His earlier friendliness had disappeared. I feared Mina's prediction had come true. After a quick embrace I bid Mina farewell, hiked my skirt, and hurried to my father's side. I didn't want to keep the elders waiting, especially if they were in a bad mood. Conrad waved as I approached.

I greeted him before searching my father's face. "Are they ready for us?"

"I think so. You should go to the women's door. I will signal you when they call for us."

Conrad stepped close and bent his head. "I will be praying for you."

"Thank you, Conrad." At that moment I wanted to wrap my arms around his neck and cling to him, but I pushed the foolish thought from my head. Instead, I ran the short distance to the women's door. After a final wave Conrad strode toward the wooden sidewalk and my father pointed for me to enter the women's door. My heart thumped in my chest, and though I'd eaten hardly anything at mealtime, my stomach clenched until bile rose in my throat. I swallowed hard as I walked to the front of the room with my father by my side.

Before either of us could speak, Brother Stresemann pinned

me with a hard stare. "So you have come to talk to us about the article in the magazine, Sister Gretchen." I glanced at my father. He shrugged one shoulder and gave a slight shake of his head. Apparently he hadn't given the elders prior notice. Seeming to note my surprise, Brother Stresemann waved toward the other men. "We know about the story. I have read it."

"You have?" The words sounded as if they'd been croaked by a frog. I cleared my throat. "How did you happen to see the magazine, Brother Stresemann?" The old man's bushy white eyebrows rose high on his forehead. He obviously considered my question quite bold.

"The wife of a local farmer brought a copy to High. She thought I might be interested in what was being published about the colonies." His eyebrows dropped into a tight line that matched the creases of his forehead. "I open this magazine, and what do I see?" He glanced down the line of brothers who were staring at me. "I see it is written by one of us—by Sister Gretchen Kohler, the daughter of our Homestead storekeeper." He pulled a handkerchief from his pocket and wiped the beads of perspiration from his creased brow. "Imagine my surprise."

"I am certain you were all astonished. Please believe that I was horrified, as well."

Brother Stresemann jerked to attention. "Are you saying you did not write those stories, Sister Gretchen?"

"Nein. I wrote them, but I did not ask for them to be in that magazine. And I did not give my permission, either." I inhaled a deep breath, and while the men sat straight-faced, I explained.

"I received a copy of the magazine from Mr. Finley. That is the first I knew of what he'd done."

Brother Stresemann held up one hand. "You will wait outside while we discuss this matter in private."

"But—"

They shook their heads in unison, and I knew further explanation would not be heard—at least not now.

CHAPTER 23

I paced back and forth until my father pointed to the ground. "Sit down before you wear out your shoes." His lips tipped into a lopsided grin.

"If only they would have let me finish all I had to say. I was going to show them Mr. Finley's letter."

My father dropped down beside me. "I think they heard all they wanted to for right now. Maybe after they talk awhile, they will give you a chance to say more. It has been a long day for them with the traveling and all these meetings."

I understood that, but it had been a long day for me, as well. And I'd had to cope with fear and anxiety during that time. I shoved my hand into my skirt pocket to make certain the envelope remained inside and leaned back against the tree.

There was nothing more to say to my father. Now we must wait.

A short time later Brother Stresemann exited the door. He motioned for us to stay by the tree. After lighting his pipe, he ambled toward us and came to halt a short distance from my father's feet. He took a deep draw on his pipe, and soon the scent of cherry tobacco mingled with the breeze. Moments later the rest of the elders exited the meetinghouse. My heart hammered in my chest. Surely they weren't going to leave without calling me back to speak with them again. I wanted to nudge my father, but Brother Stresemann would likely notice and disapprove. Hoping to prod Father to action, I cleared my throat.

"We need some time to refresh ourselves." Brother Stresemann lowered his eyes and turned toward me. "When you see us returning inside, you may enter the women's door and rejoin us." He glanced at my father. "You are welcome to come inside, as well, Brother George."

Their time of refreshment took longer than I'd expected because Sister Marguerite and Mina appeared with jars of iced lemonade and thick slices of buttery pound cake. While Sister Marguerite served the elders, Mina hurried over to speak with Father and me.

"You have not gone in yet?" She handed my father a jar of the lemonade and a tin cup.

"Ja, but they dismissed me before I finished all of what I had to tell them." My father handed me the cup of lemonade and took another empty cup from Mina. "We will go back inside after they have rested a short time." I shook my head when Mina offered a piece of cake, but my father didn't refuse.

"They showed no reaction to anything you said?"

My father pointed to the basket. "I'll take Gretchen's piece of cake if she doesn't want it, Sister Mina." After she handed him the basket, he wasted no time removing the cake.

"They already knew." I leaned a little closer. "A farmer's wife had given a copy of the magazine to Brother Stresemann."

"I know you don't want to hear this, but I warned you that Mr. Finley was trouble. You should have listened." When I nodded in agreement, her features softened, and she grasped my hand. "I'm sorry, Gretchen. You don't need me waving an I-told-you-so flag in front of you."

"But you're right. I should have listened. I wish I knew how many times I've told myself that, but it changes nothing. Now I can only hope that the Grossebruderrat will listen." One of the elders motioned for Mina to bring more lemonade, and she scuttled away.

I watched the men down their refreshments and chat among themselves. Silently I promised God that no matter what happened when I went before the elders, my gift of writing would be used only to compose poems or prayers of praise to Him and record thoughts about my life in Amana. Never again would I permit an outsider to look at my journal, and never again would I send my writing to anyone without permission from the elders. I made sure I told God I wasn't trying to bargain with Him, for even if the elders severely punished me, I would keep my pledge.

The elders stood and wiped the crumbs from their pant legs. Brother Stresemann glanced in our direction—my cue that I should join them. "I must go back inside, Mina," I said when she returned to my side. "Please continue to pray."

She offered a fleeting embrace. "You know that I will. I am glad your Vater is there to stand alongside you."

Chair legs scraped across the oak floor as the elders took their seats. Father and I stood in front of them and waited while

Brother Stresemann shuffled through papers and withdrew a copy of the periodical along with the plan for the Älterschule. "Before we discuss the magazine, I want to tell you that we were impressed with the plan you wrote for the Älterschule. Sister Mina explained that you provided a great deal of help and that you organized and wrote the material she submitted to us. I trust you didn't send a copy of this to Mr. Finley?"

"Nein. He has nothing else that I have written." I could only imagine the fodder a story about the Älterschule would have provided for a cartoon in the magazine.

Brother Stresemann pushed aside the plans for the Älterschule and withdrew his copy of the periodical. "We have gone over every line of this story." He glanced up at me. "It is very long, Sister Gretchen."

"It was written as a number of stories, but Mr. Finley combined them without—"

He signaled for silence. "I will tell you when I want a response, Sister Gretchen. As I was saying, we have gone through each line of the story. Everything you have written is true, and there is nothing we can find that reflects poorly upon the colonies."

"Except those pictures," one of the elders said. "Those drawings . . ."

Brother Stresemann glanced down the table and silenced the brother. "We find the cartoons offensive in every way. They are intended to make us appear like oafish drunkards and fools." He lowered his head and looked at the men sitting to his right and to his left. "We do not care what others think. It is not as though we have ever attempted to convert outsiders to our beliefs. We want only to please God, and we hope you feel the same way, Sister Gretchen." He lifted a sheet of paper. "We do have some questions."

They'd obviously written out a list. My temples pulsed with sharp stabs of pain as I waited to hear the first question and prayed I'd have an adequate answer.

"Did your father give you permission to write these stories?"

"I did—"

My father touched my arm gently and interrupted me. "I will answer, Gretchen. My daughter has my permission to read books and to write stories as long as it does not interfere with her Bible reading and prayers. Mr. Finley did not gain permission from anyone to print those stories. Not from me and not from Gretchen. He is not the man he pretended to be. He told me he was a salesman. He sold me many varieties of lace and trims for the general store." My father motioned to me. "Show him the letter, Gretchen."

I handed the letter to Brother Stresemann, who said he would read it aloud in the interest of saving time. Once he'd finished, the men murmured their distaste for what Mr. Finley had done.

"But the truth is that none of this would have happened if Sister Gretchen hadn't given him those stories," one of the elders remarked.

Brother Stresemann rubbed his temples with his fingertips. "It has been a long day with many problems and few solutions."

Gathering courage, I stepped forward. "If I may speak, I believe I can solve one problem, Brother Stresemann."

The elder traced his fingers through his gray thatch of hair. "And how can you do that, Sister Gretchen? Are you going to tell us what punishment we should mete out to you?"

I shook my head. "I am going to give you more than enough money to pay for the increased fees Mr. Harper wants to charge you."

Brother Stresemann's hands dropped to the table with a thud, and weariness settled in his eyes. Two of the other elders coughed. I thought they were trying to hide their laughter, but I couldn't be certain. I withdrew the bank draft from my pocket, stepped forward, and placed it on the table near Brother Stresemann's folded hands.

He stared at the draft before lifting it for a closer look. "They paid you *this* for those stories?"

"Ja. Mr. Finley's letter said this was the payment for what they printed in their magazine. At first I was going to return it, but then I heard talk that Mr. Harper planned to raise his fees and decided to wait until my meeting with you."

Brother Stresemann pushed the draft down one side of the table and then the other. For a brief time the men appeared bewildered. "Does not seem possible they would pay such a large amount of money for stories," the elder at the far end of the table said.

His comment was met by several bobbing heads and a chorus of "ja's." Their features molded into a strange mixture of disbelief and delight.

"Mr. Finley's letter proves it is true. If you would like me to return the draft to him, I have no objection."

The man at the end of the table shook his head until I thought his hair would fall from his head. "Nein. We have been praying to God for an answer to Mr. Harper's demand for more money, and God has provided."

Another elder held up his hand. "I am not so sure. This money is tainted."

My father straightened his shoulders. "How is it tainted? My daughter did nothing immoral. She wrote gut stories about our people and how we live."

"Brother Kohler is right. Sister Gretchen did not write the

stories seeking money or fame, and the stories speak well of our people." Brother Stresemann looked at me. "Her error was in trusting an outsider rather than seeking guidance from the elders."

"Still, I am not sure this is money we should accept. It gives Mr. Finley and his magazine the idea that we approve of his dishonest deeds." The elder who'd spoken of the tainted money was determined to make his point.

A man sitting next to Brother Stresemann slapped his hand on the table. "Ach! We pray for a miracle; God answers; but you want to refuse? We are to send it back and tell God, 'No thank you. We don't need your miracle'?"

The objecting elder leaned forward, his chest resting on the table as he faced his opponent. "I did not say we should return God's miracle. You are putting words in my mouth."

"Gut! Then you agree we should keep the money and use it to pay Mr. Harper." The man seated next to Brother Stresemann motioned to the others. "I think we are in agreement, ja?"

Realizing he'd lost control of the meeting, Brother Stresemann pushed to his feet. "We will take a vote."

The vote didn't take long. Brother Stresemann called out the name of each man, who then cast a vote—either ja or nein. I held my breath when he called out the name of the elder who had offered the earlier objections. The man's gaze softened when he looked at me. "Ja."

I sighed with relief. The decision was unanimous.

"This money will save us from a most difficult problem, Sister Gretchen. And since word will soon spread about the magazine story, I believe we should explain to all residents of the colonies that the money from the story will be used to pay Mr. Harper."

"And that she had nothing to do with those drawings," my father said.

Brother Stresemann nodded. "As for any punishment, I think the good has outweighed the bad. What has happened is similar to what happened with Joseph when his brothers sold him into slavery." He looked down the row of men as if to encourage them to think back to the book of Genesis. "What Joseph's brothers intended for evil God meant for good. Ja?" When the baffled stares didn't disappear, he continued. "The people at that magazine intended to make us appear foolish, but God is using what happened to provide us with money to keep us strong and independent."

Their eyes shone with recognition when he finished the explanation, and a chorus of agreement could be heard from both sides of the table.

Relief flooded through me. "Thank you for your kindness in this matter. You have been most fair." Though the meeting had gone much better than expected, I couldn't wait to escape the room and withdraw from the steely-eyed men and their difficult questions.

I had turned to leave when Brother Stresemann's voice cut through the shuffle of feet. "One more thing, Sister Gretchen."

I glanced over my shoulder. "Ja? There is something else to discuss?" Perspiration trickled down my neck.

"While we were eating our refreshments, we were talking about your ability to write, and we are thinking you could put your gift to good use here in Amana."

Turning, I stepped closer to the table. Surely I had misunderstood. "You would have me write the history of our people for all to read?"

He chuckled. "I don't know who you mean by *all*, but we think it would be gut to have a permanent record of our history. Who better to do such a thing than you?"

"I don't know what to say. I would be . . . honored. I'm not certain I possess the ability, but I will do my best."

"Gut. Then it is settled. Later we will discuss how you can accomplish your task, but after seeing the plan you set out for the Älterschule, I doubt you will find it so difficult."

Brother Stresemann gestured toward the door. "Unless you have questions for us, Brother Kohler, you and your daughter may leave. I think we are all ready for another fine meal at Sister Marguerite's Küche."

I wanted to race for the door, but I mustered restraint and walked at a ladylike pace. On my way out I thanked God for the great blessing that He had provided. I still couldn't believe the elders wanted to entrust me with the honor of writing for the community. Once my father appeared at the men's door, I rushed to his side. "I cannot believe they were so kind to me. I'm afraid after they give it more thought, they'll decide that I should at least be remanded back to children's church."

"They are fair-minded men who always do their best to abide by God's Word. They will not change their minds once they have given their word."

"Ja. You are right, but I never expected things to go so well. Can you believe they plan to have me write the history of our people?" I took my father's arm and skipped along beside him.

He pointed to my feet and tipped his head back and laughed aloud, a big belly laugh. I hadn't heard such a laugh from him since before my mother died.

"It has been a long time since I have seen you skip."

I giggled. "It has been a long time since I've heard you laugh."

"It is gut we both can be happy. To have the money for Mr.

Harper was a wonderful thing. Why did you not tell me about the bank draft?"

"I couldn't decide what to do about it. I kept thinking I should send it back. I prayed and prayed but didn't receive an answer. Then when I heard about Mr. Harper and the increase he planned to charge each village, I knew the money could be put to gut use. I was sure that was God's answer to me. I can't wait to tell Conrad."

My father pointed toward the barbershop. "Go on. He is waiting outside for you."

Releasing my father's arm, I ran toward Conrad, eager to tell him all the good news.

CHAPTER 24

A bell sounded somewhere in the distance, and I rolled to my side. It was still dark outside, too early for the breakfast bell. My eyes fluttered open and then closed tight. Once again the bell clanged. This time I heard my father's feet hit the floor with a heavy thud, and I jumped from my bed. The distant yet distinctive clang was the watchman sounding the fire alarm. I yanked the curtain away from the window and peered outside. No sign of fire, but when I lifted the window, the frightening odor of smoke wafted on the nighttime breeze.

I grabbed a lightweight shawl from the foot of my bed and slipped it over my shoulders before cracking open the bedroom door. Father was already in the parlor wiping sleep from his eyes with one hand and lifting a suspender onto his shoulder with the other. He shouted for Stefan to hurry and follow him.

When he caught sight of me, he motioned toward Oma's room. "You stay here and keep your grandmother inside. No telling what we've got out there." He cranked his head toward his bedroom. "Stefan! Now!"

The boy's half-tucked shirt hung like a ruffle along the top of his trousers. One shoe was on, the other in his hand. He stopped only long enough to shove his foot inside before hobbling after our father.

Tightening the knit shawl around my nightgown, I followed them to the door and peeked outside, hoping to catch a glimpse of what had caused the watchman to sound the alarm. Other doors swung open, and men rushed into the street, looking first one direction and then the other, each trying to gain a sense of where he was needed. Conrad appeared from his rooms behind the barbershop and peered down the street. Soon the jumble of men and boys aligned themselves and ran in the direction of the sawmill. Every able-bodied man and boy in the village was considered a member of the firefighting unit.

Though we didn't lack water to fight fires in Homestead, the fear of injury and ruin struck fear in every heart. Many a home or business had been lost to fire, but the Grossebruderrat still refused to insure any of our holdings. "Cheaper to rebuild" was always the answer when an insurance salesman attempted to influence the brethren to purchase coverage for our buildings. Long ago they had declared insurance to be an economic waste. When a home burned to the ground, wood was cut at the sawmill and the men set to work replacing the house and furnishings. The fact that no one owned anything of great financial value and little of sentimental value made the loss of a house less distressing than for outsiders.

Fire at a business was not so easily overlooked. The production that was lost until a business could be rebuilt sometimes created great hardship. But whether insured or not, the business couldn't operate until it was rebuilt. Insurance would cover the cost of rebuilding, but there was no way to insure against the hardship to the community. Even those hardships were lessened by the fact that the other villages would supply whatever was needed until rebuilding had been completed. We took care of one another in times of plenty and in times of need.

As the distinct odor of burning wood grew stronger, I knew this could not be a small blaze. I longed to join the women who had followed after the men to discover what was ablaze, but I wouldn't go against my father's admonition. Stepping back, I closed the door and turned toward Oma's bedroom. Picking up the lamp, I stepped toward her room. Strange that the clanging bell and noise in the street hadn't wakened her.

When there was no response to my tap on her door, I pushed down on the metal latch and peeked inside the room. The lamp flickered as I stepped inside. Her bedcovers were as flat as Sister Marguerite's pancakes. My heart stopped for a second and then jolted into a rapid, disjointed beat that made it difficult to breathe. Not wanting to believe my eyes, I stepped forward and patted the covers. Even while I patted, I chastised myself for such foolish behavior. My grandmother wasn't in the bed. Where could she be? I yanked aside the curtains and sighed with relief when I saw that the window remained closed.

"She has to be somewhere in the house or store," I muttered. After placing the lamp on the bedside table, I dropped to my knees and peered beneath the bed. If Oma had awakened to all the commotion and been out of her right mind, she might be hiding somewhere in the house. At least that was my hope. I didn't see anything under the bed, but I dropped to my stomach, stretched sideways, and patted the floor to be certain. Nothing. My heart plummeted.

Resting my arm on the side of the bed, I pushed to my feet and glanced about the room, trying to imagine where I would be if I were Oma. I looked at the door leading into the store. Maybe she'd heard the noise and gone in there to hide. I held out a glimmer of hope that I'd be correct.

Keeping the lamp shoulder-high, I entered the store. "Oma! Oma, are you in here?" Silence. "Please answer me. It's Gretchen. Everything is fine. Just tell me where you are." I waited, straining to hear the slightest noise. Not even a board creaked in response. I walked each aisle, trying to maintain hope. Once I'd checked every aisle and looked in every nook and cranny where she might fit, I leaned against the counter. An unexpected tear trickled down my cheek. I set the lamp on the counter and swiped my cheek with the back of my hand.

I prepared to return to the parlor but stopped in my tracks when the latch clunked at the back door of the store. My heart hammered in my chest. Had an itinerant hobo or a Gypsy decided to take advantage while the men were off fighting the fire? Surely not. I put out the lamp and reached for the broom. If caught by surprise, perhaps a wallop to the head with the broom handle would stop the culprit. I inhaled a shallow breath and crouched behind a stack of fabric.

My heart pounded with a resounding thud that kept pace with the trespasser's footsteps. Perspiration dampened my palms, and I silently chided myself to remain calm. Unsettled nerves wouldn't help in this situation. Only a few more steps.

"Emil? Where are you, Emil?"

Relief flooded over me, and the broom clattered to the floor as I stepped from behind the stack of fabric. "Oma? It is me, Gretchen. Where have you been?" I stepped toward her, but she held out her arm to ward me off.

"Where is my Emil? I have been looking and looking, and I am very tired."

My heartbeat slowed, and I inhaled a deep breath. "He is out of town, but he is coming back in the morning. He said you should get a gut sleep. Would you like me to show you where you can rest?" Even in the darkened room, I could see the confusion in her eyes. "Come. I will take you to the bedroom." I took a tentative step and extended my arm.

As she drew near and grasped my arm, I detected the odor of smoke in her disheveled hair. "If Emil said I should rest, then I will."

My hands turned clammy. "Where have you been looking for him?"

"At the other part of town." She pointed to the lamp. It sat outlined by only moonlight. "We need light." She shoved a free hand into her pocket, retrieved a match, and thrust it toward me. "Here. You can do it."

My breath caught in my throat as I stared at her hand. Why did she have a match, and why did she smell like smoke? I lit the wick, and with Oma holding one arm, I carried the lamp in the other. I prayed the thoughts swirling in my mind were incorrect, that she couldn't have set a fire, that she would never do such a thing; and that the match in her pocket and the smell of smoke in her hair didn't mean a thing except that she had a match and she'd been outdoors. Any questioning might send her into a frenzy, and right now, what Oma needed more than anything was to go to bed before my father returned home.

She sat down on the edge of the bed and held out her foot for me to remove her right shoe. She inched her heel back and forth until the leather stretched, and after a slight tug, her foot came free. One toe peeked through a hole in her black stocking. "We need to mend that, Oma."

"Ja, or it will grow bigger and bigger until all of my toes are sticking out at you." She cackled and wiggled the free toe up and down. "Could be smelly, too." She clipped her nose between her index finger and thumb and grinned while I removed the other shoe. "No holes in this one."

I shook my head and looked into her eyes. I thought I saw a glimmer of recognition. Maybe she was returning to her right mind. "When did you put your shoes on, Oma? I thought you went to bed a long time ago."

She frowned and a grayish-white eyebrow drooped over each eye. "When I got out of bed this morning, that's when I put them on, you silly girl. Why do you ask questions about my shoes? You can't have them. They're mine."

I silently admonished myself. She still wasn't herself, and now I'd given her cause to become upset once again. "I know they are your shoes. Besides, your shoes are far too small for my big feet. See?" I held up my foot, and she leaned forward to examine the length.

"My Emil likes women with small feet." With a glassy-eyed look, she stared into the distance. "Emil was with me down near the sawmill. He built a fire so we could make coffee, but I couldn't find my coffee." Her head jerked, and she glared at me. "You hid my coffee, didn't you? You want to make coffee for Emil so he'll love you."

"I didn't take your coffee, and I haven't been out of the house all night. Did you and Emil start a big fire or just a small one?"

The corners of her lips took a downward turn as she studied me. "It was a little fire."

I twisted the corner of the shawl I'd wrapped over my nightgown. Should I dare to hope what she said was true? At this particular moment I doubted Oma knew the truth from a falsehood. To her, truth was whatever came to her head at the moment. And right now her head was filled with nothing but thoughts of my grandfather.

I helped her out of her dress and picked up the nightgown she'd neatly folded and placed on top of her pillow. How had she managed to get dressed and leave the house without any of us hearing her? I'd never know the answer to that question, either. She shoved her arms into the nightgown and then twisted toward me.

"The fire got bigger and bigger. I told Emil I didn't need that much fire to make coffee." She grinned like a schoolgirl. "I think he was trying to show off for me. I told him I never saw such a big fire for coffee making." She dropped to the side of the bed. "The fire was going in all directions, and I was afraid. I called for Emil, but he disappeared." Propping herself with one elbow, she leaned back and rested her head on the pillow. "Why does he always do that to me?"

"Do what, Oma?"

"Why does he always disappear? I want him here with me. He comes for a little while, and then he disappears. It's not right." She balled her hand into a fist and raised it toward heaven. "I told him he had to quit leaving me like this, but he never listens." She turned her back and whimpered into the pillow.

While I whispered verses from the Psalms, I rubbed her

shoulders. A short time later I heard her soft snores and tiptoed from the room. Sitting down in the parlor, I considered what Oma had told me and now feared the report I would hear when my father and Stefan returned.

If Oma had started the fire, I worried my father would insist she go to Mount Pleasant. Even the promise of the Älterschule wouldn't change his mind. After all, even if there had been an Älterschule, this would have happened. I dropped to my knees and prayed she wasn't responsible. I hoped God would send an answer, for I didn't want to condemn Oma until I was certain of the truth. Even then, I didn't know if I could step forward and place blame on her.

I don't know how long I prayed, but I was on the sofa in the parlor when my father and Stefan finally returned. My father called to me from the doorway, and I awakened with a start. "The fire is out?"

"Ja. Could you bring me some soap and towels? Stefan and I will go to the washhouse and clean up. I don't want to track soot into the house."

I gathered up the towels and carried them to my father. "Is there much damage?"

"The sawmill." He shook his head. "A lot of lumber we lost in that fire."

For once, Stefan appeared eager for the towel and soap I handed to him. He scurried toward the washhouse. My father looked toward the eastern sky. "Sun will be up soon. No time for sleep." He took the towel and then turned and pulled a bright scarf from his pocket. "I found this in the wooded area beyond the sawmill. I'm thinking those Gypsies may be responsible." He thrust the piece of cloth at me before turning and heading to the rear of the house.

His footsteps echoed in my ears like a pounding drum. I held the piece of fabric at arm's length and stared at the array of colors. Zurca's scarf? The colors winked at me in the breaking light. Did Oma have the scarf with her when she went wandering out of the house last night? Could she have returned it to Lalah or one of the other Gypsies? I didn't want to believe they'd been involved in the fire. Why, after all this time, would they do such a thing? It made no sense.

With halting steps I approached my room. My thoughts swirled in a thousand directions as I tossed the scarf onto the bed and donned my dark calico. I sat down and traced my fingers along the rainbow of colors in the scarf. Once again I prayed. This time I prayed not only for Oma but for Zurça and Loyco and all of the Gypsies. I shoved the scarf into my pocket. Perhaps Father would forget about the scarf and the Gypsies. Maybe if I could speak to Lalah . . .

CHAPTER 25

Oma was in good spirits when she awakened, and if she had any remembrance of leaving the house the night before, it wasn't immediately obvious. She wandered into the parlor and pointed to the sleeve of her dress. "Smells like smoke." As if to prove what she'd said, she raised the sleeve to her nose and inhaled before curling her lip. "Stinks."

"Ja, and no wonder. I am sure everything in the village stinks like smoke. I am surprised you didn't hear the fire bells last night." My father's eyes shone with concern, or perhaps disbelief. "Is gut you were able to sleep through all of the turmoil. We lost the sawmill in last night's fire."

She shook her head, then turned to me. "Ach! This can't be

true. Never in my life have I slept through any of the bells. Your Vater is trying to be funny, ja?"

"He's speaking the truth, Oma." I forced a smile. "Maybe we need to have the doctor take a look into your ears." Instead of dwelling on the fire, I reminded her that she'd had the doctor wash out her ears several years earlier.

"But I can hear every word you are saying to me, so makes no sense that I have a problem with my hearing."

When she was in her right mind, Oma was as sharp as a razor, and it was clear I'd not win this argument. "You're right, Oma. I guess you must have been in a very sound sleep. There doesn't seem to be any other answer." I squeezed her arm. "How are you feeling today? Are you tired?"

She looked at me as though I'd taken leave of my senses. "How could I be tired? I slept like a baby all night long—you told me so just a minute ago, ja?"

I grinned. That's exactly what I'd led her to believe. "I'm the one who is tired, Oma. I can't even remember from one minute to the next." I hoped my flimsy reply would be enough to satisfy her.

The breakfast bell hadn't yet rung, but lines had already begun to form outside the Küche. Like my father and brother, the other men had gone home and cleaned up without taking time to sleep. Chatter about the fire abounded, and so did talk of how it started. I heard the mention of Gypsies several times. Surely no one would jump to conclusions and assume the Gypsies were at fault. We'd had many fires through the years, and Gypsies hadn't been present when we'd suffered those losses. I hoped there would be opportunity for me to say that, but maybe such a comment would be better received from one of the men.

When we departed the dining room after breakfast, I motioned to Conrad. Holding his straw hat in one hand, he jogged toward me. Oma was chatting with one of the other women, and my father had already left for the store. "I heard talk about the Gypsies setting the fire," I told him. "You don't think they will be blamed, do you?" Conrad shaded his face with one hand, and I pointed toward his hat.

He grinned and shoved the hat onto his head. "Why didn't I think of that on my own?" Stepping closer, he grasped my hand and gave it a squeeze. "That is why I need you around. You know what I need before I do."

A rush of heat rose up my neck and spread across my cheeks. His tender words warmed my heart. This was a man I could trust with anything, even my heart. "You should not show affection in public. Someone will see." Though I longed to feel his touch awhile longer, I reluctantly pulled my hand from his.

"Maybe I should go to the Grossebruderrat and ask permission to marry you. Then we would not need to be concerned what others were thinking."

"Maybe you should."

Streaks of sunlight danced across his white shirt. He pushed his hat to the back of his head, his eyes as big as china saucers. "Did I hear you right? You agree I should ask for permission to marry? Is that why you motioned for me to come over?"

I peeked out from beneath the brim of my bonnet. "It was your kind words just now that convinced me, Conrad. I really wanted to ask about blame being placed on the Gypsies."

"Then I have the Gypsies to thank for your change of heart, ja?"

"I didn't have a change of heart. You know my feelings for you have always run deep, but when you first talked of marriage, I thought we shouldn't move too fast." I glanced toward the departing women and observed several looks of disapproval.

"When you have some time, you should come to the store, and we will talk. Right now, I think we should separate before both of us are called before the elders."

He straightened his hat and glanced over his shoulder. "I think Sister Marie is going to confront us. She's headed this way, and the look on her face is sour enough to curdle milk."

I chuckled at his remark. "You go on. I'll talk to her."

He nodded but instead of turning toward the barbershop, he strode toward Sister Marie. From where I stood, I couldn't hear their exchange, but his remarks were enough to send Sister Marie bustling in a different direction. From the set of her shoulders, I wondered if he'd angered her. If that was the case, I was sure it wouldn't take long before word reached me.

Oma waved to one of the sisters before joining me. "Your Vater is probably thinking we are never going to return to help him with the work at the store."

"This isn't a busy day. No shipments are due. I don't think we'll be missed too much."

"Ach! He has convinced you he doesn't need our help, but I know better. He couldn't run that store without us."

I didn't argue. I knew my father needed help with the books, and there was no doubt Oma and I provided capable hands to stock shelves and wait on customers, but I didn't fancy myself irreplaceable. In fact, I hoped one day I would be replaced so that I could return to the kitchen.

My father was sitting at the counter going over the ledgers. Sometimes I wondered why he assigned the job to me. He was always checking the figures and asking me questions about this account or that figure. Had he done them himself, it would have saved time and prevented many of my headaches.

"Did you miss us, George?" Oma removed her sunbonnet

and hung it on one of the hooks near the door leading to the parlor. Touching her fingers to her hair, she straightened her black cap.

My father grunted and motioned me to the counter. "I don't understand why you didn't deduct the coffee and yarn from Brother Heinrich's account."

I bit back my words. I didn't want to say something I'd later regret. My father tapped his pen on the counter while I traced my finger along the line. "I did deduct it. You were looking at the wrong line." I held my finger in place while he bent forward until his nose almost touched the page. "Maybe Brother William is correct. Maybe you do need eyeglasses."

"We are not talking about eyeglasses. We are talking about Brother Heinrich's account." He squinted and took a second look at the page. "Ja, now I see what you are saying, but you don't need to be writing the numbers so small."

I sighed. "If I write any bigger, the numbers will not fit in the space, and it will be sloppy. Then you will complain you cannot read because it is messy. I think you should consider using spectacles when you are looking at the ledgers."

"Well, maybe I will try a pair when I am reading the catalogs or checking the ledgers." His gaze drifted toward the front door. "Conrad. What can I help you with?"

Lifting his straw hat from his head, he crossed the threshold and flashed a warm smile in my direction. "I was hoping I could visit with Gretchen for a short time." He glanced around the store. "If it is better, I can wait until later."

"Nein. Today is not so busy. Maybe when the afternoon train arrives, she will need to be here, but now is gut." My father wiggled his index finger, and Conrad stepped closer. "Maybe you should sit out back. Would not be proper for the two of you to be alone."

"Ja. The backyard is gut. Thank you, Brother George."

I was relieved to be away from my father's questions regarding the ledgers. Perhaps he would tire of going through them while I was outdoors. Directing me toward the far side of the yard, Conrad grasped my hand as I settled on a soft patch of grass beneath the apple tree.

He dropped to my side, his smile as warm as the summer day. "Now tell me, what is all this worry about the Gypsies?"

The sweet scent of lush grass lifted on the breeze as I tried to gather my unorganized thoughts. How much should I trust Conrad? Should I only explain my concern that the Gypsies were being unfairly accused? Should I tell him I was certain Oma had been somehow involved in the fire? Should I ask his advice about going to talk to Lalah? I'd been mulling these questions in my mind since we'd parted ways a short time ago. After hearing and seeing a reflection of his love and concern, I'd received my answer. If I planned to marry Conrad, I must be honest and forthright with him. If I expected those qualities from my husband, I must offer no less.

He listened without interruption while I expressed my concern for the Gypsies and explained my fears regarding Oma's possible connection to the fire.

"I understand you don't want the wrong people blamed for something they didn't do. That would not be gut. I also see the fear in your eyes when you speak about Oma. You worry your Vater will decide it is time for her to go to Mount Pleasant, ja?"

An unexpected tear escaped and trickled down my cheek. Gently, Conrad wiped it away with his thumb. "No need for the tears. We will find an answer."

"What if I go and talk to Lalah? She trusts me." I told him about her visit to the store and her request to remain if the band of Gypsies decided to leave before Loyco's return.

"It would be better if I went with you."

I shook my head. "I don't think she would trust having you there. Besides, how could we go there without someone seeing us? There would be talk that we were together without an escort."

"Ja, that is true." He plucked a thick blade of grass from the ground and tucked it into the corner of his lips.

"I could have Stefan go to the camp and ask Lalah to meet me near the edge of the woods. That would be safe enough, don't you think?"

He withdrew the piece of grass and folded it between his fingers. "For sure it would be safer than for you to go by yourself, but I thought you forbade Stefan to go there again."

That thought hadn't entered my mind. I didn't want to tell Stefan about Oma. I knew he wouldn't intentionally jeopardize Oma, but sometimes he spoke without thinking. "I'll tell him it's a matter that must be kept secret. If I tell him a secret is involved, he'll think it's a special adventure."

"Once you have met with Lalah and learn whether your grand-mother has been back to the Gypsy camp, we can talk again and decide what we must tell your Vater and the elders. Try not to worry." He pushed to his feet and extended his hand to me. "You are light as a feather." He pulled me close, and I felt the rise and fall of his muscular chest against my own.

I should have pushed away. Instead, I leaned against him, enjoying the strength of his arms around me. I looked up, and he lowered his lips to mine in a sweet, tender kiss.

"I love you, Gretchen, and I will be the happiest man alive when you are my wife."

Tipping my head back, I looked into his hooded eyes. "And I love you, Conrad. I think I always have."

He lowered his head and captured my lips in an ardent kiss. My heart pounded like a hammer on iron. I was sure he could hear the jolting thuds as he pulled me closer.

"I will ask your Vater if I can request a special meeting with the Grossebruderrat. I don't want to wait until they return next month."

"A perfect idea," I whispered. The scent of the tiger lilies and horned violets blooming in Oma's small flower garden perfumed the air as we returned inside.

Oma waited until Conrad stepped to the front of the store to speak with my father before she grasped my hand and frowned. "Kissing is not allowed. You and Conrad are breaking the rules."

"You are right, Oma. We should not be kissing."

Her frown faded and she shook her head. "Nein. You should be more careful when you kiss." Cackling, she covered her mouth with a weathered hand.

The afternoon train arrived, and before long visitors were strolling into the store. Soon after publication of my story, I'd discontinued my talks about the history of our settlement. I'd learned that my brief speech opened the door to unkind comments from those who had read the magazine and chose to believe the cartoons rather than the story. Now I simply directed them to the woolens and calicos and remained quiet while they wandered the aisles.

As expected, Stefan had been eager to return to the Gypsy camp. He'd asked several questions, but when I explained the matter was of a secret nature, his questions ceased. I couldn't be sure if it was because a clandestine meeting excited him, or because I promised to fully explain at some time in the future. Either way, I was thankful for his swift agreement.

When he'd completed the task, he'd been delighted to report his success. Now that I was on my way to meet Lalah, my emotions were a mixture of fear and dread. I wanted the girl to tell me Oma had returned Zurca's scarf weeks ago, yet I didn't want the Gypsies involved, either. Zurca had saved Oma's life, and the Gypsies hadn't been in the village since Loyco's departure. Although some of the surrounding farmers continued to mention the loss of chickens and produce, there had been no reports of thievery in Homestead.

Fear prickled my scalp as I stepped off the path and into the woods. There was nothing to fear, yet my nerves were taut and perspiration beaded my forehead. My breathing turned shallow as I scanned the area and strained for the sound of footsteps. Where was she?

A branch crackled to my right, and a hand clapped over my mouth. I strained to turn, but a muscular arm grasped me around the waist. A scream caught in my throat as my back slammed against a chest as rigid as a stone wall. "Do not scream and I will take my hand from your mouth."

After grunting a muffled yes, he slowly released his hand but continued to hold me tight against his chest. When I didn't scream or attempt to wrest myself away from him, my captor loosened his hold, and I turned to face him. "Zurca!"

CHAPTER 26

My emotions swirled as my stomach clenched and released like bellows at the forge. I took a backward step and steadied myself against one of the giant pines, the pungent bark scraping my cotton blouse. I had expected to meet Lalah. Instead, I now was face-to-face with Zurca. He stood before me, legs spread wide, arms akimbo, eyes dark and warning. Gone were any signs of warmth or friendship. He was in command.

"Do not try to run. You cannot outrun me, and you cannot overpower me. If you try to escape before I say you can go, you could be injured. I don't want that to happen, but it will be your choice."

My tongue stuck to the roof of my mouth, and I struggled to swallow. "I won't run," I croaked.

He pointed to the ground. "Sit. We will talk. Who knows you have come here?" Zurca dropped to his knees in front of me and stared into my eyes.

What should I say? Should I tell him my father and Conrad knew my whereabouts and would soon come looking for me? I had planned to tell Conrad, but he hadn't been in the barbershop when I'd left. How I wished I had waited for him.

"You have taken too long with your answer, which tells me that no one knows you are here. It is better if you do not lie to me."

I bowed my head to avoid his militant stare. "I came to meet Lalah, not you. I didn't expect any danger."

Using the tips of his fingers, Zurca raised my chin and forced me to look at him. "What you expect is not always what you get, is it? Over and over my people have learned this lesson. Maybe you should learn it, as well." He released my chin and leaned back on his haunches. "Tell me why you seek Loyco's daughter."

"I wanted to speak with her about the fire at the sawmill."

"You think Lalah set that fire?" His dark brows lowered to a menacing angle.

"No, of course not." I summoned all the courage I could muster and reached into my pocket. "I wanted to ask her about this."

He rocked back on his heels. "That is my scarf. The one—"

"The one you used when you saved my grandmother. I know." I hesitated a moment. "This scarf was discovered at the fire."

"I still do not understand why you want to question Lalah."

"I wanted to ask if my grandmother had returned to your camp since the day you pulled her from the river."

Recognition flashed in his eyes. "I see. You want to say your grandmother returned the scarf to me so that you can blame the fire on me instead of your grandmother." Strands of greasy hair had escaped a colorful tie at the nape of his neck and fallen forward to curtain his face. He shoved an oily lock behind one ear. "You would do this after I saved her life? I am surprised."

A breeze whispered through the grove and slapped the strings of my bonnet against my neck. "No. I wasn't going to blame you. I was seeking the truth."

"Seeking the truth—or hoping to protect your grandmother?" His steely eyes demanded an immediate response.

"Both. It wasn't my intent to cast blame on you, Zurca, but there is already talk that members of your group may have been involved in the fire."

"So what is their plan? To hang us?" He slapped his muscular leg and guffawed. "Let them try." He leaned closer, the odor of his body sour. "Just remember, Alija will be happy to place a hex on your town. I need only say the word."

"We do not believe in your hexes, Zurca. My people have no plan to do anything to you or to anyone else. The only thing we plan to do is rebuild the sawmill."

"Still, you should have said to them, 'Zurca is a good man. He saved my grandmother from the river. He would not set fire to our sawmill.' Eh? Why did you not say those things when they accuse me?"

I tapped my finger on my bonnet. "Because I don't want them to know about Oma being out of her head. It would not be gut if they knew about the river."

His brow furrowed. "Why not? Alija says your grandmother has special powers."

How could I explain that my grandmother's going in and out of bouts of senility was not considered a special power; that it was, instead, a tragic consequence of growing old. Not for all of the aged but for some, and my grandmother was one of the unfortunate.

"Among the gypsies, her condition may be considered a special power, but among my people, it is cause for concern. I don't want my Vater to send her to Mount Pleasant."

Zurca's posture relaxed, and his features softened. "What is this Mount Pleasant?"

"It is like a hospital for people who aren't quite right in their mind. I don't know how to explain it to you."

"The old woman should not be in such a place. She needs to be with you—with her family. It is the right thing for her to stay with family." He jumped to his feet. "You can tell them Zurca started the fire if it will help to keep her at home. I don't care what any of them think. They can believe whatever they want."

"If I let them believe a lie, it will follow you and make life more difficult in the future. It isn't right."

He stooped in front of me. "Protect the old woman. It is your duty."

I wanted to thank him and run back to the store, but guilt nudged me like a hot poker. This wasn't fair; it wasn't right. "I can't. It isn't fair."

"Ha! You think life is fair? Far from it. But believe me when I say that even if you clear the Gypsies of any wrongdoing, it will change nothing. People will continue to believe what they want." He joined his fingers together and formed a ball. "They lump us together and say we are all black-hearted thieves." He laughed. "Some of us are, but we are as different as the people in your village. Some of us are good; some not so good. But all of us are trying to make our way much like we did in the old country." He pointed toward town. "Just like your people. We don't want to be told how we should live. Instead of building a town, we travel in our wagons so we can live the way we want."

A branch cracked behind a clump of bushes, and Zurca leaped from his stooped position like a cat springing for prey. A high-pitched squeal followed.

"Zurca! Put me down." Lalah kicked her feet and flailed her arms until Zurca set her on the ground.

"What are you doing out here? I told you to stay in the camp." His gruff voice didn't alarm her.

She twisted her dress back into place and frowned. "You ripped my dress." She pointed to a ripped seam on the side of the frock. "Look at what you've done."

"Look at what *you've* done." Zurca waved a finger in her face. "I told you to stay in the camp. Little girls who don't follow orders end up with torn dresses."

"And Gypsy men who don't follow Loyco's orders get in big trouble." She shot him a defiant look. "Loyco told you to look after me while he was gone. Instead, you spend your time trying to get the others to break camp, and now you rip my dress. You are the one who will be in trouble. Not me."

They squabbled like little children until I finally clapped my hands and shouted, "Stop!" They both turned and gave me startled looks. "We don't have time for this bickering. Soon I must return to the store or my Vater will come looking for me."

Lalah came to my side. "I am sorry about Zurca. He followed me when I was coming to meet you, and then he took me back to the camp and wouldn't let me come with him. Did he hurt you?"

"No, Lalah. He was very kind to me, and to Oma."

The girl glanced about. "She is here?"

"No, but Zurca is going to take the blame for starting the

fire at the sawmill so that Oma will not get in trouble." I grasped her hands between my own. "I don't want her to be sent to live somewhere away from me."

"But Zurca didn't start the fire and neither did your Oma."

Zurca took a long step and leaned over Lalah. "How do you know this, Lalah? Were you away from camp during the night? How many times must I tell you that no one is to—"

She waved him to silence. "Wait until I explain. You always do that, Zurca."

He folded his arms across his chest. "Do what?"

"You never let me finish what I'm saying. And you never listen."

"I listen, but you—"

Once again I clapped my hands. "Please, stop arguing! How do you know Oma wasn't the one who started the fire, Lalah?"

She shot Zurca a don't-interrupt-me look. "Because I was near the sawmill after supper, and I saw a hobo. He had set up camp there. He used some of the shavings and pieces of wood to start a fire. He had a coffeepot and some pots to cook with. It looked like he was going to spend the night there."

What Lalah said made sense. The hobo must have been the man my grandmother had confused for Opa. She'd spoken of making coffee. "Did you get a good look at him?"

She shook her head. "He was wearing a big floppy hat, but I never saw his face. I didn't want him to see me."

"That was wise of you."

Zurca ground the heel of his boot on a spider that scurried toward my foot. "None of this makes a difference."

Lalah wheeled toward him. "Why not? It's the truth."

"Bah, truth! Who believes the truth when it comes from the

mouth of a Gypsy? You tell them about the hobo or you tell them Zurca started the fire, but do not speak of the old woman."

"She had a match in her pocket," I whispered.

Zurca shrugged. "She probably took it from the hobo just like she took my scarf. Lalah saw the hobo start a fire. He is the one responsible." He leaned against the tree and looked me in the eyes. "Protect the old woman. Isn't that what your Bible says? Take care of the sick and the old ones? Remind your father if he speaks of this Mount Pleasant again."

"How do you know what the Bible says?"

He gave me a sidelong glance. "You would be surprised what a Gypsy will do for a free meal. Even sit under a tent and listen to a preacher read from the Bible. But that was long ago. Maybe your Bible has changed."

"No, Zurca. God doesn't change, and the Bible doesn't change. But sometimes people change." I handed him the scarf, and he tied it around his head.

"Sometimes. Sometimes not." He motioned to Lalah. "Come, girl. We must return to camp."

I watched as they walked through the stand of pines, Zurca's hand resting on Lalah's shoulder, his stringy hair swinging from beneath the multicolored scarf. There was much more to Zurca than I'd imagined. As if he'd read my thoughts, he raised his hand and waved. Tonight I would write about him in my journal.

I raced toward the barbershop, praying Conrad had returned. I sighed in relief when I saw the open door and empty barber chair. Conrad was back, and there were no customers. We would have at least a short time to talk.

"Gretchen!" Conrad jumped to his feet and placed an arm around my shoulder while I panted to breathe. "I've been worried.

Your father said you went to visit with Mina over an hour ago, but Mina said you hadn't been to the Küche."

I inhaled a deep gulp of air and shook my head. "I never said I was going to see Mina. I said I was going out for a while." I gasped for another breath. "Since that's the only place I ever go, he just guessed that's where I was. Did you tell him I wasn't there?"

"Nein, but if you hadn't been back in fifteen more minutes, I was going to tell him we needed to go look for you in the Gypsy camp." We sat down in the two chairs at the front of the shop. "That's where you were, isn't it? You went to see Lalah?"

"Yes, just like we discussed. But instead of Lalah, Zurca was waiting for me. He almost frightened me out of my wits."

Conrad balled his hands into tight fists. "I'm going down there right now and have a talk with him. Who does he think he is!"

"Wait. Before you become angry, let me explain everything that happened. I think you'll change your mind about him."

As I told of my conversation with Zurca and his willingness to accept blame for the fire, Conrad's fists unclenched and his muscles relaxed. He leaned back in the chair and rubbed his jaw. "I'm not so sure what should be done. We cannot speak openly of Zurca saving your grandmother from the river."

"No. Oma doesn't even remember that she was in the river. For us to speak of the incident now would cause her even greater confusion. And if Vater finds out, I'm not certain what he would say or do."

"We have been having some talks, your Vater and I, and he now understands that since your Mutter's death he hasn't been the same man. He tries to hide the pain, but he knows he is short with you and Stefan. And I don't think he means everything he says about your grandmother, either." Conrad reached toward me and clasped my hand. "Men have trouble saying what's in their hearts and how they feel deep inside. Sometimes, instead of accepting our sadness, we become angry."

"He told you that?"

His broad smile caused tiny creases to form at the corner of each eye. "Not those exact words, but it is the heart of what he said."

I felt a pang of sorrow that my father had chosen to share his feelings with Conrad rather than with me, yet I was thankful he realized how much he had changed since my mother's death. After Mother died, he adopted a different outlook. A bitterness and an unforgiving spirit had seeped into his words and deeds. Perhaps he'd reached a turning point the day I went before the Grossebruderrat. After that meeting he'd started acting more like the father of my childhood. The one I could go to with my problems, the one who was quick to help everyone, even hobos and Gypsies, and the one who enjoyed laughter.

"Maybe the time has come for you to speak openly with your Vater. Tell him your feelings and concerns."

"I'm not so sure he is ready for such a talk with me, but if there is an opportunity, I will try." A train whistled in the distance, and I turned toward the sound. "I better get back to the store. Visitors will be coming, and Vater will need my help." Conrad continued to hold my hand as he walked me to the door. "Thank you for understanding, Conrad."

He lifted my hand and brushed a kiss across my fingers. "I am always pleased to help you, Gretchen. You bring great joy to my life."

"And you bring great joy to my life, as well." A rush of heat raced up my neck and seared my cheeks. "I must go." I bent my head and hurried outdoors, hoping Conrad hadn't seen my flaming cheeks. I'd gone only a few steps when he called my name. I wheeled around to face him.

Conrad pointed to his cheek. "Your cheeks are a lovely shade of pink. I like that."

I touched my face. "I'm glad you approve, since I seem to have little control over when they do that."

"Ja. I think I control when they turn pink." His jovial laughter carried on the breeze.

I glanced down the street to see if anyone was nearby, then held a warning finger to my pursed lips.

Hooking his thumb behind one of his suspenders, Conrad stepped off the narrow porch and into the street. "Maybe I should shout my love for you so all can hear. What do you think about that, Gretchen?"

"I think you better go back inside the barbershop before I tell the elders you need to be sent off to Mount Pleasant."

He leaned back and laughed. "You would be heartsick without me."

I didn't reply, but he was right. I would be heartsick without him.

CHAPTER 27

"Gretchen! Hurry! I need you to go fetch Sister Veda." My father rushed toward me the minute I entered the store. "Ask her if she will come and look after the store. I just discovered that your grandmother is missing. Stop at the barbershop. If Conrad doesn't have any customers, ask him to come over here, too." My father shooed me out the door. "Go! Go! There is no time to talk."

I wanted to ask when Father had last seen Oma and if he'd checked under her bed, but he hadn't given me the opportunity. My heart thumped against my chest as I raced back to the barbershop. I skidded to a halt outside the door. "Conrad!"

He ambled to the door, a grin on his face. "You couldn't bear to be away for even five minutes?"

"Oma is missing. Vater needs you at the store. I'm going to

fetch Veda." His smile faded, but before he could reply, I ran down the street. Puffs of dirt danced beneath my shoes as I raced down the middle of the street, my arms pumping in synchronized rhythm. My lungs screamed for air, but I didn't stop. Where could she be?

"Veda!" I tried to shout, but my deflated lungs refused to give more than a whimper. I banged on the door. "Veda! I need you."

Where was she? There was no sign of life when I peeked in the window, but a moment later I heard Trudy squeal. The backyard. I jumped from the porch and ran around the side of the house. Veda was sitting on a blanket with Trudy in her lap. "Veda. Can you please come to the store? Oma is missing, and I need to go look for her."

"Ja, of course. Let me gather a few things, and I will be there in fifteen minutes. Put a sign on the door if you must leave before I arrive."

I shouted my thanks and hurried back around the house and down the street. I hoped my father would still be there when I returned. I needed to know when and where he'd last seen Oma. Conrad was pacing outside the store when I returned. I peered around him, hoping to catch a glimpse of my father inside.

"Your Vater is already gone. He said to tell you that your grandmother had been taking a nap in her room. When he went to the parlor to get his pipe, he saw that her bedroom door was open, but she wasn't in there."

While Conrad was speaking, I took several deep breaths and tried to calm myself. "He looked everywhere? Even under the beds?" I moved to step around him. "She's very small and can fit under the beds. He wouldn't think to look there."

Conrad grasped my arm. "I looked under the beds, beneath

the counter, the empty shipping crates—all the places where she might have hidden in the store or apartment. She's gone, Gretchen. Better we begin looking elsewhere than waste more time here." He shaded his eyes with his hand and looked down the street. "Is Veda coming?"

"Ja. She said to put a note on the door if we need to leave before she gets here." I stepped around Conrad and hurried inside. After scribbling a note that said the store would reopen in fifteen minutes, I poked a hole in each end of the paper, shoved a piece of string through the holes, and tied it on the door latch. "Which way did Vater go?"

"He's going to check at the blacksmith, the barns, and the other outbuildings. You check the shops and Küche. I'll go to the woods and the Gypsy camp."

"No. I'll go to the woods and Gypsy camp. They know me, Conrad. It's better if I go."

He hesitated, then nodded. "You're right. Zurca will be more helpful to you than to me. Just be careful."

"I will." I waved and hurried along the sidewalk, into the street, and away from town. My fears lessened as I neared the wooded area. Even though Oma hadn't been to the Gypsy camp in recent days, I was certain I would find her sitting with Zurca or Alija or walking through the brush and trees with Lalah at her side.

The woods were silent except for the crunch of dead leaves and pine needles beneath my feet and the twittering of birds overhead. Sun filtered through the trees and cast shards of light across my path in zigzag patterns. I could understand why Oma liked to come here. Beneath a canopy of leafy branches, these woods provided a peacefulness and seclusion all their own.

Smoke drifted from a cook fire in the Gypsy camp, and I

hesitated, unsure if I should call out and announce my presence or simply wander in without warning. I tried to decide what the Gypsies might prefer, but I hadn't a clue. If there had been a door, I would have knocked, so it seemed more fitting to call out. I strained to see if I might catch a glimpse of Oma, but there was no sign of her from my vantage point. Alija and several other women were standing near the fire.

I cupped my hands to my mouth. "Gut afternoon, Alija!"

The women startled and looked in my direction before backing toward the wagons. All of them were pointing and chattering, the noise enough to draw the attention of several of the Gypsy men. Thankfully, Zurca was among them. Elbowing his way through the women, he waved me forward.

"What do you want, Gretchen?"

"My grandmother is missing, and I have come looking for her. I hoped I would find her here with you or Lalah."

"I have not seen the old woman." He glanced to his right, and Lalah stepped from behind one of the wagons.

Lalah shook her head. "I haven't seen her, either, but if she comes into the woods, I will bring her back to the store." The girl appeared soulfully sad.

I smiled at her, but she remained unresponsive. "Any word from Loyco?"

Zurca shook his head. "I am beginning to think he has deserted us for good. Either that or he is dead. He never stays away this long."

Zurca had given no thought to the girl's feelings with his gruff retort, but his words had impacted Lalah. She disappeared behind the wagon without a word, and I wished I could snatch back my question. "I will pray for his safety." I raised my voice loud enough for Lalah to hear and hoped my promise would bring her a little comfort.

Alija shook her bony finger at me. "We don't need your prayers. We can take care of Loyco using our own ways."

"Bah!" Shoulders squared, Zurca strode toward her. "Your potions and chants haven't brought Loyco home, Alija. Maybe Gretchen's prayers will help. Either way, we break camp at the next full moon."

I didn't look at Alija before I turned to leave. Her angry eyes would only cause distress and further anxiety. And Zurca's statement that they would leave with or without Loyco hadn't helped, either. That opened the possibility of Lalah coming to live with us, which I hadn't yet discussed with my father.

For now, I couldn't worry about other matters. I climbed the path leading out of the woods, my fear increasing with every step. Where could Oma be hiding? I tried to tamp down my rising panic and told myself that when I returned to the store, she'd be back. I told myself Conrad had likely found her sitting on the porch of the Küche with Mina and the other women, or Father had discovered her in the barn with some of the calves. *Please, Lord, keep Oma safe and bring Loyco back to his people.*

Over and over I sent the prayer winging toward heaven, then held my breath as I stepped inside the store and met Veda's steady gaze. "Have they found her?" I asked.

She shook her head. "I've heard nothing from your father or Conrad."

My shoulders sagged under the weight of her words. "If either of them returns, tell them she wasn't in the woods or at the Gypsy camp, and that I went to the garden shed. Maybe she wanted to see some of the women who work in the garden. If she's not there, I'll go out toward the onion fields and circle back around."

Veda tucked a strand of hair behind her ear. "That's a long walk for an old woman."

"Ja, but not impossible for Oma." When she wasn't in her right mind, I was amazed at the things she accomplished. Who would believe she could climb a tree or walk six miles? Not even Oma would suppose such a thing when she was in her right mind, but her mind overpowered her body when she was having one of her spells.

Veda stepped from behind the counter and clutched my hand. "Do you think we should sound the alarm bell so others can help you look?"

"Not unless Vater tells you to. I don't think he wants anyone else to know about the spells with her mind. He thinks it would embarrass her." I squeezed Veda's hand. "Pray that we find her before suppertime."

"Ja, I will be praying."

Confidence eluded me as I walked to the rear of the store and out the back door. The scent of autumn was in the air, and though some of the flowers in Oma's small garden had died, the blooming mums and zinnias seemed to welcome the changing season. I stopped outside the washhouse. Had anyone looked inside? Better to look than discover she'd been so close all this time. There were several good hiding places in the washhouse, but Oma wasn't in any of them.

My trip to the garden proved fruitless, as well. Except for some gardening tools, the shed was empty. Several of the women stopped their work and waved, but I continued onward. If I stopped, they'd ask questions. Questions I wasn't prepared to answer.

I followed the narrow path that would lead me to the onion fields, all the time watching for Oma's slight figure. If she had tired and lain down somewhere, I'd never find her out here.

My disheartening search continued, with my only sightings the men who worked in the fields. Not one sign of Oma. I prayed as I walked, and when my thoughts wandered from my prayers, I tried to think where she could have gone. For the most part, she returned to the same spots when she was out of her mind. I continued my prayers—this time I also prayed that the Grosse-bruderrat would say yes to the Älterschule. *Please keep Oma safe, Lord. Please bring Loyco back to his people. Please, please, please. Do you hear me, Lord? I'm begging for your grace and mercy.*

The sun had begun its slow descent. Soon the men would return from the fields and the supper bell would clang. I stared into the distance, but Loyco didn't appear on his white horse, and Oma's slight figure didn't emerge from across the field. Assailed by defeat, I entered the far end of town and plodded down the street.

Streaks of deep golden sunlight shone through the meeting-house window. A slight stirring captured my attention. I shaded my eyes and stepped closer, but nothing appeared. Nothing more than dancing rays of sunshine on panes of glass. Still, I felt compelled to remain, to watch. And then I saw it again—movement, a black cap on white hair. My shoes clattered up the wooden steps. I pushed down the latch and opened the door, my heart pounding at a frantic pace.

With her head bowed and hands folded, Oma was sitting on one of the benches. She looked up when I drew near. Her eyes were clear, and she patted the bench. "Sit down, Gretchen. We should talk."

I dropped to the bench beside her, silently thanking God that she was safe. "We were worried about you, Oma. How long have you been here?"

"Who can say?"

I heard the wistful regret in her voice, and I reached for her hand. "Vater and Conrad are worried about you. We should return to the store."

"Nein. We must talk." She set her gaze on the unadorned whitewashed wall at the front of the church. "I know that sometimes my mind doesn't work right and I do foolish things. This I have known for some time. I prayed I would get better." She pulled her hand from my grasp and tucked a wisp of hair behind one ear. "God doesn't hear my prayer. I am no better. Maybe worse, ja?" Her eyes said she knew the truth but hoped to be wrong.

"You have had trouble in the past, Oma. But who can say what the future holds? I am here, and I will take care of you, no matter what happens with your mind. I promise."

"Ja, I know. You are a gut girl, Gretchen. Just like your Mutter." She folded her hands together and rested them in her lap. "But it doesn't change the way I feel. It doesn't remove the fear in my heart. If I am not to get better, then I pray the fear will leave me or that death will come."

"Don't say that, Oma. What would I do without you?"

"You would be just fine. When Emil died, I thought I could not live without him, but I have. You have memories that will help you until we are joined again in heaven." She offered a wistful smile. "There would be some peace in dying. I would be with Emil and your Mutter again, but I wouldn't be with you and Stefan." She pressed her palm to my cheek. "It is very frightening to know your mind is leaving you, Gretchen. You want to pull it back, but you can't."

"I understand, Oma."

"Nein. You do not understand, child." She touched her gnarly fingers to her heart. "In here I feel like a young girl—just like you, yet my brittle bones and gray hair, they tell me I am old and feeble. And if that is not enough, now my mind plays tricks on me."

"If only there were some way we knew when it was going to happen so we could protect you from danger. I'm afraid you're going to get hurt."

Wisps of her gray hair danced in the waning sunlight as she bobbed her head. "I know you worry. I worry, too. Sometimes I know when one of these spells is going to happen. I get a little dizzy and can't gather my thoughts. I try to be calm, but fear always wins. Then other times there are no signs at all. Nothing but a hazy memory that something has happened to me."

I didn't know how to respond. Though I knew my fear wasn't the same as Oma's, it was as deep. "When you know a spell is coming on, does it help if you rest?"

"Sometimes, but sometimes not at all." She pointed first to one side and then to the other. "Sometimes I am half here and half there. Alija brewed a potion for me, but it didn't help."

"You told Alija?"

"Nein. She told me. One day when you were away from the store, she came in and talked to me. She said I had problems with my head, handed me the potion, and said I should drink it."

"I cannot believe you would drink something that woman gave you." There was no telling what Alija might have given Oma. After all, she had professed to thinking Oma had some special ability, hadn't she? Maybe it was Alija's attempt to steal the power she thought Oma possessed by using Gypsy rituals. To say such a thing aloud would sound silly, but who could know what Alija would say or do.

"Ach! If it was going to kill me, I would already be dead. And if it was going to help me, I wouldn't have had a spell this afternoon. Enough about Alija. While I still have my thoughts in the right place, I want to confess something to you."

"You should take your confessions to God, not to me."

"You do not need to teach me about the faith, Gretchen. I know my confession of sins is made to the Lord. But this I need to tell to you, because it is about Conrad. I shouldn't have interfered, but I am your grandmother. That's what we are for—to interfere."

I couldn't imagine how she could have interfered with Conrad or how anything she'd said could have created a problem. Still, my shoulders tensed at what I might hear. "What did you tell him, Oma?"

"That you and that salesman were holding hands and whispering to each other. I told Conrad he must not stand back or that salesman would steal you away from us." She pulled her handkerchief from her pocket and pulled at the hem.

I exhaled a breath and relaxed my shoulders. "We settled that matter some time ago, Oma, but I never did understand how he knew."

"He didn't tell you?"

I laughed. "No. Whenever I asked, he avoided my question. Now I know why."

"That Conrad, he is a gut man. Just like my Emil, he protected me."

My exact memory of that day wasn't particularly clear. I'd been so taken aback by Mr. Finley's behavior and his offer to help me that everything else had become a jumble. "I was certain you were taking a nap when Mr. Finley was in the store."

"Ja. That's what you thought, but I wasn't. I watched the two of you and decided Conrad must be told. He was taking too long to tell you of his love. I could see how he loved you from the time he was a young boy, but he didn't have the courage to claim you. And that Mr. Finley. Ach! He was a *dummkopf.*"

"I don't think so, Oma. Mr. Finley is a very shrewd man. He deceived me and many of the elders, too."

She shrugged. "Maybe, but he didn't fool me. I could see in his eyes he was not honest. I hope he never comes back here. Enough trouble he has caused."

"I don't think you need to worry about that, Oma. Maybe we should go home now?"

She shook her head. "One more thing I must tell you, Gretchen. If your Vater decides to send me to Mount Pleasant, you should not fight with him. Is not gut to have trouble in the family. I will go there if it is best."

"How do you know about Mount Pleasant?"

She pulled on her earlobe. "I hear more than you think. I would not like to go there, but I would rather go than cause a problem between you and your Vater."

"I don't think we need to talk about Mount Pleasant. Mina has asked the elders for permission to open an Älterschule. If they agree, you could go there in the daytime and be with Mina. At night you could come home with us."

The twinkle returned to her eyes as I described the Älterschule and Mina's plan for the building to be located near the Kinderschule.

"I can teach the little ones to knit and crochet. Just like I taught you, ja?"

"Yes, Oma. Just like you taught me." The bell rang in the distance. "We must hurry."

She cackled. "Ja. If your Vater and Conrad miss supper on my account, they will not be happy."

We joined hands as we departed the meetinghouse. For now,

she was herself, and for that I was most thankful. Who could say what the future would hold, but I was certain God would provide the answers we would need.

Later that night after I'd gone into my room, I lifted my journal from the trunk and turned to the next empty page. What exciting stories I'd written since the day I'd met with the Grossebruderrat and made my pledge to God. Though none of my stories would be read by anyone except Mina or Conrad, it hadn't diminished my pleasure in taking pen to paper. Not in the least.

CHAPTER 28

"Lalah!" I tried to maintain a calm appearance, but moisture collected on my palms, and my stomach tensed when I saw the child enter the store the next day. I swiped my hands down the front of my apron as she continued toward me with an uneasy step. "I'm surprised to see you." Had Zurca decided to break camp before the full moon? I hadn't told anyone about my promise to the girl—not even Conrad.

Thinking I might spot Zurca or Alija behind her, I glanced toward the front of the store. Lalah didn't miss the furtive look. "I'm alone." She arched forward and surveyed the store. "What about you? Are you alone?"

"For the moment. I expect my father back any time. He's gone to the train station to ship barrels of sauerkraut."

She wrinkled her nose. "I don't like sauerkraut."

"You would like *our* sauerkraut. It's very good." I knew she hadn't come here to pass the time of day. Perhaps she feared telling me Zurca and the others had departed. I was about to ask when she lifted her head and trained her gaze on me. The golden flecks in her dark eyes shone like sparks of amber light.

"Loyco says you must come to our camp right away."

"Loyco? He has returned?" A sense of relief rushed over me. I would have kept my word to Lalah, but I was relieved to hear that Loyco had come back. I doubted the girl could find happiness in our way of life any more than I could find happiness living as a Gypsy.

"He returned last night. He says it is very important for you to come and I shouldn't leave until you promise."

"Nothing bad has happened to him, has it?"

She shook her head. "He is well, but he must see you. Do you promise?"

Impatience laced her words as she shifted from foot to foot. No doubt she was eager to return to her father. "Yes, I promise, though I'm not sure how soon I can leave the store. I'll try to come later this morning, but if there are a lot of customers, I'll need to be here."

"I'll tell him."

"Would you like a few pieces of candy, Lalah?"

After a quick examination of the candy jars, she pointed to the peppermint and lemon confections. "Maybe one of each?"

I gave her several pieces of the lemon and peppermint. "I won't tell Loyco."

She grinned as she shoved the candy into her pocket. "Come as soon as you can." She waved and scurried out of the store, her uncombed hair bobbing on her shoulders.

I couldn't imagine why Loyco wanted to see me, but I doubted he'd send the girl unless he considered the matter urgent. Yet I wondered why he didn't come himself. He hadn't hesitated to enter the town on other occasions.

While I waited for my father to return, I debated whether I should tell him I was going to the Gypsy camp. If I told him, I doubted he would give his approval. He might forbid me to leave the store. I considered the alternatives. I could tell him I was going to see Mina or Conrad. And I could do that very thing before heading off to the woods. It wouldn't be so much a lie as a half-truth. But what if Mina or Conrad came into the store while I was gone? That wouldn't be so good. My father would know I'd told a lie. Better to tell the truth and hope that he wouldn't object.

Moments later he returned with the mailbag and tossed it onto the counter. "You can put the mail in the boxes for me?"

"Ja. I can do that, but first we must talk."

He gestured toward the door. "First I must unload the new shipment of dishes."

"You ordered more dishes?" I pointed toward the shelf. "We have six full sets of dishes and more in the warehouse. Why did you order more?"

"These are the new style. Two farmers' wives saw them in the catalog and asked me to order them."

I stared at him, dumbfounded by the remark. "But did they say they would purchase them?"

"Not outright, but when they see how beautiful they are, I know they will want them."

I sighed. "Wanting them and having the money to purchase them are two different things. Better had you ordered more lace and embroidery thread. They can better afford the smaller items."

He waved aside my comment and returned to the train station while I sorted the mail. I'd finished placing the envelopes into the proper slots by the time he returned with the crates. He placed the boxes on the floor and, with the claw end of his hammer, set to work. "Wait till you see." The wood slat creaked in protest as he loosened it. "Come. You can help me unwrap the dishes."

I stepped around the counter. "I need to go to the Gypsy camp, Vater."

My father stopped and looked up at me as though I'd slapped him with a wet dishcloth. "What is this you're saying? You cannot go there. Why would you want to do such a thing?"

I quickly told him of Lalah's recent visit. "The girl said it is important or Loyco wouldn't have sent for me. There is nothing to fear, Vater. They will not hurt me, and you will know where I am. If I am gone too long, you and Conrad can come after me, ja?" I didn't tell him I'd been to their camp on several occasions and hadn't been harmed. To reveal that information right now would only delay matters.

Deep creases lined his forehead. "What can the Gypsies want with you? Makes no sense for them to send for you."

"I won't know until I go there, Vater. I think it is important. Please give me your permission to go. I shouldn't be gone very long, and it hasn't been busy in the store this morning. Oma is doing well, and she'll be pleased to help you unpack the dishes."

He glanced over his shoulder. "Where is your grandmother?"

"She went to the parlor to do some mending. Shall I fetch her?"

"Ja, better she is here with me if you are going to be gone from the store. I don't want her to disappear again."

"So I have your permission to go?" I almost clapped my hands. Not because I was overly thrilled about going into the Gypsy camp, but because I'd told the truth and my father hadn't denied my request.

"Ja, you can go, but tell Conrad. Better he knows. If you are gone too long, I won't want to bring your grandmother with me while I search for you, and I can't leave her alone in the store."

I leaned down and pecked a kiss on his cheek. "Thank you, Vater."

Surprise shone in his eyes as he lifted a finger and touched the spot I'd kissed. "Has been a long time since you gave your Vater a kiss."

I smiled. "It has been a long time since you gave your daughter a kiss." I untied my apron and strode toward the door leading to our apartment. "I'll send Oma to help you; then I'll be on my way."

As expected, Oma was delighted to hear she was needed. She scurried around me and pulled a chair beside one of the crates. Lifting one of the plates from the straw packing, she held it at arm's length and uttered an appreciative "Oooh."

My father beamed at her. "Pretty, ja?"

"Ja. They are beautiful, George. You should give these to Gretchen for when she and Conrad are married."

"I do not need a set of dishes, Oma. We eat at home only when we have special guests. If I have company, I can use the dishes that belonged to Mutter." I kissed her cheek. "I am going on an errand, but I'll be back soon." I handed her a cloth to wipe the straw and dust from the dishes as my father unearthed them from the packing.

I waved to my father as Oma set to work wiping the dishes. After a stop at the barbershop to tell Conrad of my plans, I set off for the woods at a near run. Though Conrad hadn't been pleased with the plan, he didn't attempt to overrule my father. However, he planned to come after me if I didn't return in ninety minutes. Though I thought it far too short a time, I didn't argue. And I didn't fail to note he was looking at his pocket watch when I departed. If all went smoothly, I would return before the bell rang for the noonday meal.

My breathing was labored by the time I entered the woods, but I didn't slow my pace until my skirt snagged on the overgrown brush. Thorns pushed through the fabric like sharp tacks intent upon holding me in place. If I didn't take my time, the calico would tear. I was engrossed in getting the last of the tiny barbs from my skirt when I heard the crackle of branches. I turned as Lalah emerged from a group of pines.

She pushed about a pine branch and stopped beside me. "I thought you weren't going to come. What took you so long?"

"Right now, what's taking so long is getting my skirt untangled from this hawthorn bush." I glanced down at her. "I don't think it took me very long to get here. I had to wait until my Vater returned from the train station before I could leave. Then I ran the entire way."

She gave me a look that said she didn't quite accept my explanation. "Loyco thought you would come back with me. He is unhappy."

"Well, I'm sorry he's unhappy, but I can't just walk out of the store the minute Loyco sends word. I have duties. I can't come and go at every whim like a carefree Gypsy." The glimmer in her eyes faded, and I was certain my words had wounded her. "I'm sorry, Lalah. I have only a little time before I'm expected back at the store. I didn't mean to hurt your feelings. Please forgive me."

She shrugged one shoulder. "It doesn't matter." But I knew it did. It mattered a great deal, and I hoped she would forgive me. She removed the final barb from my skirt. When she reached for my hand, I was encouraged and hoped it meant she had forgiven me.

Hand in hand, we approached the camp. Every man, woman, and child turned to stare at us, their dark, piercing eyes boring into my very soul. I had been full of courage when I left the village, but my bravery dissolved as I walked into the camp. Had Lalah not been holding my hand, I would have turned and run. Alija was chanting one of her strange incantations and tossing herbs into the cauldron she seemingly guarded day and night. She pinned me with a dark look.

With every bit of daring I could gather, I willed myself to smile at Alija. Perhaps she wouldn't detect the fear lurking behind my trembling upturned lips. "Loyco asked that I come."

She waved her long-handled wooden spoon in the air. "Bah! Loyco has gone soft in the head. First we think he won't return, and then he appears and is shouting orders to everyone. We should have never come to this place. Nothing but trouble since we arrived."

"Hold your tongue, woman." Shoulders squared, Zurca stood as he confronted her. "You are not in charge of where we go or when we leave."

She pointed her crooked index finger at him. "I might not be in charge, but neither are you." Her cackling laughter echoed through the wooded camp.

Lalah squeezed my hand. "I'll go and get Loyco. He is probably sleeping. He was very tired when he returned."

I clung to her hand. "Be sure you tell him that I must return to the village very soon. If he doesn't want to come and talk to me now, I must return to town."

Her hair brushed her shoulders as she bobbed her head. "I will tell him." She glanced toward the group hovering around the black kettle. "Don't be afraid of them. They know better than to ignore Loyco's warnings."

If that remark had been intended to give me comfort, it missed the mark. In spite of the heat, I shuddered. The minute Lalah dropped my hand and stepped from my side, the angry looks returned. Alija walked toward me, still holding the wooden spoon in one hand. She waved it in front of me. "If trouble comes to us because of you, I will place a terrible spell on your village."

"What have I done that would bring trouble to any of you?"

"You have played with Loyco's mind. That's what you've done. No longer does he act like a king of the Gypsies. Instead, he runs off to do your bidding."

Her angry remarks confused me. "I didn't ask Loyco to do anything. You are mistaken."

"Alija!" Loyco appeared from behind one of the wagons. "Get away from her and tend to your cooking. When I need you to interfere, I will tell you."

She startled like a scared rabbit and scampered back to the fire.

"You. Gretchen." He motioned for me to come. "Follow me."

He waited only until I'd taken a few steps before he turned and strode away. Alija glared as I hurried past her and followed after Loyco, but I looked away. Otherwise, I feared I would lose courage. I didn't want to follow Loyco further into the woods, where Conrad might never find me. "Where are we going?"

He glanced over his shoulder. "No questions. Just follow me."

I silently weighed the consequences of doing what he said, yet I couldn't turn back. Something compelled me to follow his orders. Colorful blankets and clothing were draped across the bushes, and some hung from rope that had been strung between the trees. Though the odor defied such an idea, the sight of scattered hanging clothes and blankets gave me hope that these people occasionally laundered their belongings. Canvas had been used to erect makeshift tents, and Loyco stopped near one of them.

He stooped down and pulled aside the canvas. "In here."

My heart tremored, and I thought I might faint. I didn't want to go inside that tent. What if he followed me in and pinned me to the ground. My stomach lurched and I feared I might lose my breakfast. "Why?" The question stuck in my throat, but he'd read my lips.

I was certain the fear in my eyes matched the anger that shone in Loyco's glistening dark eyes. "Because I want you to go inside. It angers me that you do not trust me, Gretchen." Before I could answer, he sprang from his stooped position and grasped my arm. His fingers pressed into my forearm, and I lurched forward. Once again, he dropped to a crouched position and pulled me down beside him. Using his free hand, he pushed my head down until I was peering directly into the canvas dwelling.

Two eyes shone in the far corner. My fear evaporated as I dropped to my knees and crawled inside.

CHAPTER 29

The girl cowered in the corner of the tent as I crawled toward her. Though the child was dirty and bedraggled, I could see her skin was as fair as my own. I extended my hand. "I am Gretchen. What's your name?"

"CeeCee."

I swiveled on my haunches and looked at Loyco, noticing that Lalah had followed us into the tent. "Is this Cecile Lofton?"

"Check her head and see what you think."

"May I look at your scalp, Cecile?"

"My name is CeeCee. The Gypsies don't let me use my old name."

She lowered her head toward me, which I took as agreement. Her hair was as dirty as her clothes. I carefully parted the hair and, with the sun streaking through the open canvas, discovered the dark birthmark that Mr. Lofton had described to me.

I turned to Loyco. "How? Where did you find her? This isn't possible."

"Of course it is possible. She is sitting in front of you."

"But how did you find her? I don't understand."

"With Gypsies is not so hard. Word travels, and there are many of us who return to the same region each summer. I stopped at a number of camps and gathered information while I was searching for her." He shrugged his broad shoulders. "They didn't want her. They wanted money."

I stared at him, unable to comprehend the extent of his response. "Then why did they take her?"

He spread his arms and rested a palm on each hip. The full sleeves of his shirt caught the air and reminded me of a soaring eagle's wings. "I told you. They wanted money. They said they waited a few days to see if the parents would return to the park, but they feared the police might find their camp, so they finally left the area. They would have returned the girl if they'd known where to take her."

"They could have left her at a police station. Did they ask her if she knew her address?"

He untied his scarf and wiped the perspiration from his face. "I said they didn't want to keep her. I didn't say they were fools. I don't know what they asked her, but they couldn't walk into town with a screaming girl who isn't Gypsy, now could they?" He tapped his finger on the side of his head. "Think what you are asking, Gretchen. They would have been lynched from the nearest tree, or shot, or clubbed to death."

I did recall Mr. Lofton saying they'd been in a park when the girl was taken. After fleeing with Cecile, the Gypsies had likely rushed into the woods, where they wouldn't be spotted—and probably tied something around the girl's mouth to quiet her. The thought caused me to shudder. Perhaps Loyco's explanation made sense to the Gypsies, but it would have been better if they'd turned the girl free in the park. Someone likely would have helped locate her parents. But nothing would change what had happened in the past. The girl had been taken.

"I thought Mr. Lofton said there was a story in the newspaper a day or two after Cecile was taken from them. Didn't the Gypsies see that?"

Loyco rocked back on his heels and laughed. "You think Gypsies read newspapers? If we find old newspapers, we use them to start fires or to wrap our belongings. And you can be sure we never buy them."

I still didn't understand why Loyco had taken it upon himself to go find Cecile Lofton. Though his actions were beyond kind and the Loftons would be forever grateful, I wondered if he'd had some other motive. Questions raced through my mind in rapid succession. Was he expecting a huge reward for his return of the girl?

"You are not happy that I found her?"

"Yes, of course I am very pleased, but I'm worried, as well."

He glowered at me. "Why are you worried? If I bring the girl to you, you can be sure there is no need for fear. I told you those Gypsies did not want her." He leaned closer. "Since the day they took her, she cries all the time." He thumped his chest. "Even when she rode on my stallion, with me to protect her, she cried."

Evidence of tears stained the girl's dirty face, and I didn't doubt she'd been crying. I wouldn't feel safe riding that stallion, either. "All these changes in her life. I wonder if the poor girl will ever be the same."

"Bah! You worry about everything, Gretchen. A sapling can withstand strong winds pushing and pulling at its roots. If the wind does not yank it from the ground, it grows into a strong tree. Children are the same. This girl hasn't yet been yanked from the ground, and she has already braved a strong wind in her life. She will be a strong woman." He glanced at the girl. "Isn't that right, CeeCee?"

Tears trickled down her cheeks. The girl nodded and swiped them away with the sleeve of her raggedy dress. She scooted closer to me. "He said you were going to take me to my mother and father. Do you really know them? The other Gypsies told me they were dead."

"I do know them. We will telegraph them, and they'll come on the train for you." I used my most comforting tone. "And you are allowed to use your given name, Cecile. Nobody here will object, will they, Loyco?"

He sat back and folded his arms across his chest. "She can call herself whatever she likes. Makes me no difference."

He could have spoken in a kinder tone, but I thanked him all the same. "Have you ever ridden on a train, Cecile?"

"Yes. Have you?"

"No, but the train comes through our town every day and brings supplies. Do you think you'd like to go with me? I live in a village not far from here. We can telegraph your parents. I have their address. Your father left it with me."

The girl hesitated, clearly unsure what choice to make. No doubt she'd heard plenty of lies during the past year.

Lalah drew near and touched Cecile's arm. "Gretchen is very nice. You'll be safe with her, and you can believe what she tells you. You should go with her. She'll help you find your mother and father."

While Lalah continued to talk to Cecile, Loyco exited the tent and indicated that I should follow. The voices from around the campfire grew louder, and I wondered if a disagreement had erupted. "You still haven't explained why you went to look for Cecile," I said. "Was it because you felt some sort of guilt over her disappearance?"

"Guilt? Why would I feel guilt over her disappearance?"

"I thought maybe you would feel a sense of responsibility because it was other Gypsies who had taken her."

"I have no control over what other Gypsies say or do. I went to look for Cecile to show that I cared about the missing girl. I know how I would feel if Lalah would disappear. Lalah's mother was white, like you, but Marie ran away from her home because her father mistreated her. We were camped about twenty miles from where Marie lived when she came upon our wagons and asked if she could live with us."

"And you let her? Without checking to see if what she'd told you was true? What if she lied and her parents are still grieving over her disappearance?"

Loyco picked up a branch and cracked it in half. "She had bruises, a cut lip, and a broken tooth to prove what she said was true. That was enough for me to agree she could join us." He stared into the distance. "Later, I took her for my wife. She was a good woman." He tossed the branch to the ground and shifted around as if his movement would shake off the memory. "You will take the girl with you?"

"Yes, of course. And I hope you will be here when her parents come for her. I know they will want to offer their thanks." I was giving him the perfect opportunity to tell me if he expected a reward for returning the girl.

He clenched his hands so tight they quivered under the

pressure. He spewed a scornful laugh. "You think those people will want to thank me? That girl's mother would rather die than come into the presence of a Gypsy."

I could see bitterness in his eyes, resentment that he would always be judged for the wrongdoings of others. Though not to the same depth, I could understand his plight. I had suffered for the wrongdoing of Mr. Finley—but I had been forgiven. I hoped the Loftons would be as forgiving as the elders had been with me. Loyco was returning their beloved daughter. I had no doubt they would extend their thanks.

"I think you are wrong, Loyco."

He tipped his head and laughed. "And I *know* you are wrong."

"If you are so sure, then stay until Cecile's parents arrive and prove me wrong." I motioned to Lalah and Cecile.

He snorted and broke a small branch from a tree. "I give you my word we will stay here if you promise to bring her mother to my camp. Together we will see who is right, but I tell you that she will not come here, and she will not thank me."

Using the tip of the branch, he drew a circle in the dirt and spat in the center. After taking a backward step, he pointed to the circle. "Spit in the circle to seal our agreement."

I stared at him. "I don't spit."

"Is not hard, Gretchen. Just pull your cheeks and lips together and spit." He grasped my cheeks between his fingers and thumb. "Squeeze together like this, and then spit." He dropped his hand to his side and waited.

The girls had joined us, and all three of them were now staring at me. "I don't believe I can, but I give you my word." I could see my refusal annoyed Loyco. "Maybe I could sprinkle some water in the circle. Would that do?"

He arched his brows and looked toward heaven. "No, that will not do."

"Then maybe Lalah would spit for me."

I could see the disbelief in his eyes. "Is not Lalah's promise. Is your promise. I don't need her spit."

I wanted to tell him he didn't need mine, either, but I knew my protest wouldn't succeed. If I didn't come to some resolution, Conrad would soon come looking for me. Cecile shot me a look of sympathy. She'd likely encountered similar situations while living with the Gypsies.

"Like this," Lalah said. She worked her mouth back and forth, then spit with the same ease her father had exhibited only moments ago.

With a great deal of reluctance, I mimicked her actions. I didn't quite hit the circle, but Loyco agreed to accept my somewhat futile attempt as a seal to our agreement. I withdrew a hand-kerchief from my pocket and wiped my lips. "Thank you again for all you did to find Cecile. I can't tell you how . . . how . . ."

"What can't you tell me? You can't tell me how surprised you are that a Gypsy would do something kind?"

"I *am* surprised, Loyco, but my amazement is not because you are a Gypsy. It is because you are a person willing to take time away from your own life to find this girl. I think you are very kind, and it pleases me to know you." I extended my hand to the girl. "Come along, Cecile. We're going to go back to the village and send word to your parents."

Loyco bowed and waved his scarf in a sweeping gesture. "Thank you, Gretchen."

I bit back a grin and circled around him.

"Only time will tell us if the girl's mother is as pleased to know me."

I didn't have time to remain and discuss the possibilities of Mrs. Lofton's reaction. But I would do all in my power to make certain she personally thanked Loyco—and not because I'd spit in that silly circle!

We'd cleared the woods and were walking down the street when I saw Conrad in the distance. He waved his hat overhead and picked up his pace.

Cecile slowed and tugged on my hand. "Who is that man?"

"That is Conrad Wetzler. He's the barber and a very gut friend. You will like him." Her frown indicated she wasn't so sure. "I have a brother, Stefan, who isn't too much older than you. He will be home after school."

"I don't like boys very much. They're usually mean and pull my hair."

I chuckled at her observation. "I promise Stefan will not pull your hair." Conrad came to a skidding halt beside me, and I didn't have time to further ease her concerns.

"I was getting worried about you, Gretchen." He looked at the girl. "And who is this?"

"You will be surprised to learn that this is Cecile Lofton. You remember her parents came for a visit to the colonies not long ago?"

His brows knit together, and he shook his head.

I nudged his arm. "Remember? I told you how Oma revived Mrs. Lofton with a glass of water?"

His eyebrows relaxed, and recognition shone in his eyes. He mimicked the act of tossing water from a glass. "Ja. I do recall you telling me about those visitors. Their daughter was taken from them."

He stopped in his tracks. "You mean those Gypsies have been hiding this poor child in their camp all this time?" He pointed his thumb over his shoulder while the angry words tripped off his tongue.

"No. Loyco went to find her. That's why he's been gone so long." I could see the disbelief in Conrad's eyes. While we continued into town, I told him of Loyco's selfless deed and was pleased to see Conrad's anger evaporate.

He pushed his hat to the back of his head. "Are you going straight to the train station and send a telegraph?"

"No. I must stop and get the Loftons' address back at the store."

He nodded toward Cecile. "Doesn't the girl know her address?"

"Dunlop Street," Cecile said with a bright smile. "I lived on Dunlop Street."

I leaned close to Conrad and kept my voice to a whisper. "She remembers the street, but not the house number, and she said it was a very long street. I don't want to press her at the moment."

Conrad nodded. "I have some gut news I have been saving for you. We can talk after prayer service?"

I turned warm and my heart picked up a beat as he continued to stare at me. "Ja. After prayer service would be very gut."

CHAPTER 30

Though it had been only this morning, it seemed as though days had passed since Conrad promised we would talk. There had been much to tend to since Cecile's arrival, and I'd had little time to myself. Returning home after prayer service, I was pleased to hear Oma offer Cecile a knitting lesson. Although Stefan professed a distinct dislike for knitting, I grinned when he offered to help Cecile with her lesson.

Conrad escorted me through the store and out the back door. "I believe Stefan has taken a real liking to Cecile."

"He usually doesn't have much interest in girls, but I think because Loyco rescued Cecile, he's making a special effort." I glanced back toward the house. "And she is a very sweet little girl. I've enjoyed spending time with her."

"And maybe one day you would like a daughter of your own?" Conrad held my hand as I sat down beneath the apple tree.

I could feel the heat work its way up the back of my neck. "Maybe someday. But someone I know must first get permission to marry before there can be any talk of a child."

He sat down beside me and grinned. "Are you speaking about me?"

I tapped his arm. "Ja, I am talking about you. Have you lost your courage? You say you want to marry me, but do I see you marching off to ask the elders if they will give us approval to marry? No, I do not."

There was a scent of autumn in the early evening breeze. Once the sun fully settled beyond the horizon, the temperature quickly cooled. Conrad scooted closer and put his arm around my shoulder.

"Conrad! Someone could see us."

"Who can see us back here? You think Sister Martha is peeking out her window? She can't see through the hedgerow."

"You can't be certain," I said, but I didn't push his arm away. I liked the warmth and protection of his closeness.

"You want me to go and see if she's cut away some branches to give her a better view of your backyard?"

"No, I do not want you going near her house!" I pictured what a scene that would be: Conrad poking through the bushes and coming nose-to-nose with Sister Martha. The woman would be scared out of her wits. But the next day, she'd be busy telling everyone within earshot that Conrad and I had been without a chaperone in our backyard.

"So what is this news you wanted to tell me that's so important?"

He tightened his hold on my shoulder as if gathering his

courage. "I went before the members of the Grossebruderrat and asked permission to marry you."

"What?" In one quick motion, I shifted to my hip so I could face him. His features were shadowed by the waning light. "Without telling me you were going?"

"What do you mean without telling you? We agreed I would go and ask permission, did we not?"

"Ja, but I thought you would tell me on the day you planned to go, so I could . . . could . . ."

"So you could what? Worry? That's exactly what I didn't want. Better to tell you after than to have you worry."

The kerosene lamps flickered inside the house and cast dancing shards of light into the yard. "No, not worry. So I could pray that they would grant permission." I snuggled closer and looked into his eyes. "Don't keep me waiting any longer. What did they say?"

"They gave their permission, but we must wait the customary year before we can wed."

My palms turned damp, and my stomach tensed as I recalled working in the Küche with Sister Wilda. The Grossebruderrat sent her intended husband, Milton, to High Amana during their year of engagement. She'd been able to see him only on Sunday afternoons. On Saturday there would be great excitement as Wilda anticipated Herman's Sunday visit, but on Monday there would be even greater sadness. On Tuesday she would begin to count the days until she'd see him again.

I forced the question from my lips. "Did they say if you must move from Homestead?"

"I will remain here unless they find someone who can take my place. The other barbers are married, and the Grossebruderrat don't want to move any of their families. That is gut for us."

"But if the others are married, who else would there be?" The knot in my stomach remained. I wanted to hear there was no possibility he would leave before next September.

He shrugged. "It could happen. A barber could join the community, or one of the young men in training might become skilled enough to take over for me. I don't think either of those things will happen, but the elders wanted me to understand all of the possibilities." He tipped my chin. "We will be fine. Even if I must leave for a few months, we can survive." Leaning down, he captured my lips in a lingering kiss. Butterflies replaced the knot in my stomach, and I melted against his chest, enjoying the feel of his lips upon my own. I lifted my hand to his cheek and stroked the soft stubble along his jaw, hoping my touch would keep him close. Ever so slowly he lifted his mouth from mine. "I love you, dear Gretchen. I have loved you since I was a little boy. This is the happiest day of my life." Once again, his lips covered my own in a sweet, tender kiss.

His words tugged at my heart. To think that one year from now we would be man and wife. When we finally parted, the moonlight splayed across his face, and I could see the warmth in his eyes. "I will always love you, Conrad. I could never hope for a man to be more loving and compassionate. You are truly God's gift to me."

With a gentle hand, he stroked small circles on my back with his palm and rested his cheek against the top of my head. "So next September, we will plan to be married, ja?"

"Unless you think you might prefer a wedding nearer to the end of the year, maybe December?" His head jerked up, and he ceased stroking my back. I looked up and giggled when I saw the frown on his face. "I was only teasing, Conrad. I don't want to wait any longer than September, either."

"That's gut, because if you wanted to wait, we would have our first lovers' quarrel."

I wrinkled my nose. "Lovers' quarrel? I don't think I'd like to have one of those."

The back door swung open, and the kerosene lamp outlined Stefan's figure as he stood in the doorway. "Are you two ever going to come back inside? It's really dark out there."

Conrad chuckled. "Don't worry about us, Stefan. We are fine, but if I have any problem, I'll give a holler, and you come running."

Stefan hesitated. "You want me to ask Vater if you should come in, Gretchen?"

"That little nuisance," I whispered. I cupped a hand to my mouth. "I am fine, Stefan. Vater knows where I am, and if he wants me to come inside, I'm sure he'll come and tell me himself." If Sister Martha didn't know we were out in the backyard before, she was sure to know by now.

"He is just a boy doing what boys enjoy the most—teasing girls." Conrad reached for my hand and lifted it to his lips. "Still, he is probably right. We should go inside. I do not want your Vater to think I am taking advantage. He may not give me permission to spend time alone with you in the future."

He pushed to his feet and held out his hand to me. As I stood, he gently pulled me close and wrapped his arms around me. "This is what I want for the rest of my life, Gretchen. To always have you close to me."

CHAPTER 31

Had I been alone in my bedroom, I would have penned every word that Conrad had said to me in the backyard. I would have enjoyed sitting in the lamplight, reliving each moment as I wrote about it in my journal, creating a permanent record of his love and desire to marry me. But writing anything in my journal tonight would be impossible.

The moment I'd returned inside the house, Cecile had become a shadow, unwilling to leave my side. Even Oma hadn't been able to entice the girl back to her knitting lesson. Vater and Stefan had already retreated to their bedrooms when Oma started quizzing me about Conrad's visit. I didn't want to speak at length in front of Cecile, so I simply told her my life would change next September. She grinned and pulled me into a warm embrace. It was so wonderful when Oma remained clearheaded. Maybe she wouldn't have any further spells. This is what I told myself each time she remained in her right mind for a few days. I doubted it would last, but these good times always gave me hope that she wouldn't slip back into her secret world.

Oma gathered her yarn and stuffed it into the basket beside her chair. "Is getting late. We should go to bed, or soon the rooster will be crowing and the breakfast bell will sound."

I kissed her cheek and bid her good-night.

I extended my hand to Cecile and pointed toward my bedroom door with the other. "My room is in here." After helping her into the white cotton nightgown Sister Marguerite had brought to prayer service, Cecile snuggled beneath the sheet. I opened the wardrobe door and stepped behind it to gain a bit of privacy while I changed into my nightclothes.

Once I'd settled in beside the girl, she wiggled close to my side. After several minutes she whispered, "Are you going to marry Conrad?"

"Yes, Cecile. Next September—one year from now."

She twisted around to look at me. "Can I come to your wedding?"

I didn't explain that our wedding wouldn't be like ones she might have attended in Springfield. It seemed unnecessary to give her such details, for I doubted she would even remember me a year from now. "If you and your parents want to attend, you would be welcome." I left it at that. If I told her she couldn't attend the wedding but could come to the festivities following the ceremony, she'd likely feel rejected. "You should try to go to sleep now. You want to be well rested when your parents arrive in the morning."

She tossed and turned, and when sleep didn't come, her

questions began. Why did Oma's fingers have big knots; why did all the women dress the same; why did the men go into a different door and sit at separate tables? Would I come to visit her in Springfield, and would I like to ride a carousel at the park with her? One after another I answered the questions as best I could, but each question gave rise to another. Finally I touched my finger to her lips. "No more questions, Cecile. If you ask anything else, I am not going to answer. Close your eyes and go to sleep."

The girl was a restless sleeper. If she didn't moan and groan, she flailed and kicked. The little sleep I got was fraught with dreams of someone hitting me. Before I donned my dress the next morning, I examined my arms and legs for signs of black-and-blue marks. I wasn't surprised to find a few spots that were beginning to take on a bluish tinge.

Everyone, even the old men, beamed at Cecile as we made our way to the Küche for breakfast the following morning. To them, the girl was evidence of God's mercy—a child safely returned to the loving arms of her mother and father. And Cecile basked in the attention.

Once breakfast was over and we'd returned to the store, I sent Cecile to the parlor with Oma. "My grandmother will tell you stories while I work."

"Ja. I can tell you about how we came from the old country to Buffalo, up in New York. You know about New York?" Cecile shook her head, and Oma extended her gnarly hand. "Come with me to the parlor, and I will tell you." She grinned down at the girl. "But first we must have some lemon drops before we can have a story."

Her words were a reminder of my childhood. How often had she said the very same thing to me before she would sit me down and tell me a story? She had been a wonderful grand-mother—still was, for that matter. If only she didn't suffer from these bouts of forgetfulness. I watched her remove a clean handkerchief from her pocket and pour several of the candies from the jar. Picking up the corners of the hankie, she pulled them together and twirled the fabric until the lemon drops were secured inside. The two of them trotted off to the parlor while I replaced the lid on the candy jar, then leaned down to the lower shelf and lifted the inventory ledger to the top of the counter.

The bills of lading had been stacking up for the past week. While Father didn't mind making entries on the ledgers of the residents when they purchased an item, he was not so good with the rest of the paper work. I ruffled through the stack and placed them in piles according to date before I started the process of matching the bills of lading with the invoices. Then I fastened them together with a straight pin. Each one would be properly itemized under the name of the respective business.

My father strode to the front of the store to move a crate of canning jars to shelves near the back. "Complete the sales ledger so I can report to the elders what products are in most demand." He called out the instruction while he hoisted the crate onto his shoulder.

I didn't argue, but there were few changes between the prod-ucts we offered and what the outside world wanted to purchase. The woolens and calicos always topped the list, but depending on the season of the year, our onions, onion seed, and sauerkraut remained in high demand. And today there were several large shipments going out.

I was in the middle of entering the purchases to Rosenblume and Company when a thought struck me. I would be unable to take the Loftons to the Gypsy camp if Father needed me to work the store, for he no longer trusted Oma to take my place.

I had promised Loyco I would take the couple to the camp, and if they wanted to leave on the afternoon train, there would be little time. I hiked myself forward and leaned across the counter until I could see down the aisle. "Vater? Can you hear me?"

His head and shoulders emerged from behind one of the tall cabinets in the rear of the store. "Ja, I can hear you. What is it you are wanting?"

"Since the Loftons are coming, could I have Veda come and work in the store after the train arrives?"

The question brought him into sight, and the slow, heavy thud of his shoes made me fear his answer. He stopped in front of the counter and settled his thick forearms on the counter. "Why should Veda need to come and work? Can't the girl's parents come on over here to the store and wait in the parlor like they did the last time they were here?" He shifted his shoulders and nodded toward the parlor door. "They can visit with the girl in there and then go eat with us at the Küche. Poking your nose in their business is not gut."

I folded my arms across my waist. "I'm not going to poke my nose in their business, but I think they will want to go thank Loyco for bringing their daughter back to them. Given Mrs. Lofton's fear of Gypsies, I thought it would be better if I went with them."

He rubbed his jaw and looked into my eyes. "If this was your plan, why did you wait until now to speak to me? Do you think this store and my permission are not important when you make these plans?"

"No," I whispered. "But I do think it's very important that

they thank Loyco and that Mrs. Lofton sees that she need not fear all Gypsies."

He paused, obviously weighing his decision. A few moments later, he nodded. "Ja. Is true the girl's parents should go and thank the Gypsy." He tapped the open ledger. "Go ask Sister Veda to come over, and come right back so you can finish the accounts before you leave."

I leaned across the counter and kissed his cheek. "Thank you, Vater."

"Ja, ja. Go on, now." Though he tried to hide it with his brusque words, I could see the pleasure in his eyes. "And don't forget to come straight back here. No time for visiting with Sister Veda."

I removed my apron and waved it overhead before lobbing it onto the hook. "Ja, Vater. I will hurry."

With Trudy hoisted on one hip, Veda entered the store as the first shrill whistle announced a train approaching in the distance. My heart skipped a beat. What if the Loftons weren't on the train? What if Cecile didn't recognize them? What if they didn't want to go to the Gypsy camp? Questions swirled around my head like bees seeking nectar.

Veda touched her thumb to the spot between my eyebrows. "You need to smile. That frown is not becoming."

I forced my lips upward and extended my arms toward Trudy. "Would you like to see Oma and Cecile?"

The little girl had no idea what I was asking her, but she bobbed her head. Veda immediately set to work straightening stock while I carried Trudy into the parlor. She bounced in my arm and leaned toward my grandmother.

"Oma," she cried. I bent forward and shifted her onto my

grandmother's lap. Oma nuzzled the child's neck, and Trudy tipped her head to the side and giggled.

"Mo," Trudy said while pointing to her neck. Once again Oma nuzzled the little girl, and Trudy squealed in delight.

Three short blasts of the train whistle announced that the train would be arriving within minutes. Cecile looked at me, then glanced out the window.

"Why don't you put your knitting in the basket, and we'll go to the train station to meet your parents." I silently prayed they would be on the train. "The train should be pulling into the station about the time we get there."

The girl tucked the yarn and needles into the basket beside Oma's rocker and bid my grandmother and Trudy good-bye. After calling to Veda that we were leaving, I reached for Cecile's hand. She swiped it down the front of her dress before taking hold. She was obviously as nervous as I was.

We didn't say a word until the giant engine rumbled into the station and belched a cloud of dark smoke. Then her lower lip quivered, and she said, "What if they didn't come?"

I gave her my most reassuring smile. "Then you will stay with us until they do." I touched a finger to her lips. "You need not worry."

We continued to the platform and waited near the doorway leading into the station. One traveler after another descended the steps. Cecile tugged on my hand, and I looked down. "What if I don't know them?"

I stooped down beside her. "It has only been one year, Cecile. You have changed much more than your parents have. Besides, I know what they look like, so you don't need to worry about that." I lifted her chin. "Isn't that gut? There's nothing to worry about." I stood and turned a watchful eye toward the disembarking passengers. And then I saw them. Mrs. Lofton was wearing a large straw hat with a wide navy blue band and red trim. Behind her, Mr. Lofton, in a fine suit, carried his hat in one hand while he assisted his wife with the other. I held my breath and waited, eager to see if Cecile would make a move.

Suddenly she squeezed my hand and tugged me forward. "It's them! There they are!" I released her hand and watched her run down the platform into their waiting arms. People stopped and stared for a moment before continuing into the station. I waited at a distance, with tears rolling unchecked down my cheeks as I witnessed their sweet reunion.

I was wiping away my tears when Mr. Lofton finally looked up and scanned the platform. I waved and walked toward them. "She looks perfect, ja?" They both agreed. "I know you won't be in Homestead long, but I told Loyco, the Gypsy who rescued Cecile, that you would want to go to the camp and thank him." I hesitated only a moment. "He said he would welcome your visit."

Mrs. Lofton visibly paled at the suggestion. "We have very little time, and I don't think Cecile would—"

The girl shook her head. "I would like to tell them good-bye, Mama. Loyco was very nice to me, and so was Lalah. She's Loyco's little girl."

Mrs. Lofton spun toward her husband with a please-save-me-from-this look in her eyes. He squared his shoulders and met his wife's silent plea with a determined smile. "I think that is the least we can do. He has given us a gift more valuable than gold."

Mrs. Lofton wilted. I hoped she wouldn't faint once we got to the Gypsy camp, and I hoped Loyco would keep Alija out of sight. One mention of a hex would frighten the daylights out of Mrs. Lofton.

We headed off for the camp before Mrs. Lofton could change her mind. When we neared the edge of the woods, I could see the fear in her eyes, but I did my best to keep the conversation lighthearted. I told her Oma had been teaching Cecile how to knit and suggested they could continue the lessons on the train ride home.

Smoke drifted from the campsite, and the sounds of children playing and women talking drifted through the woods. "Are we almost there?" Mrs. Lofton's voice quivered.

I nodded my head but continued moving. If I stopped, I feared she would turn the other way and never return. "Not much farther." I heard a branch crack and then another.

"Welcome!" Loyco's voice boomed. Arms folded across his chest, the Gypsy leader stepped from behind a tree and stopped only inches from me. Mrs. Lofton gasped. Mr. Lofton murmured for her to remain calm, and Cecile lunged forward and wrapped her arms around his waist. He stroked the girl's hair and surveyed our small group. "So! You have managed to keep your word, Gretchen. I am surprised." He dropped down on his haunches and smiled at Cecile. He pointed to her dark blue calico and neatly arranged hair. "I see Gretchen has you dressed like her people."

Cecile nodded. "Is Lalah here?"

He chuckled. "Yes. You can go and see her. She's near the wagon."

I was thankful Mrs. Lofton's strangled denial wasn't heard by either Loyco or Cecile. The child rushed into the clearing with childish abandon while I made the introductions. Loyco offered one of his deep bows and waved us forward. "Please come into our camp, so we can talk."

He pointed toward the logs that circled the fire. Mrs. Lofton directed an anxious look at me. I dropped to one of the logs and motioned for her to sit. For a moment I thought I might have to pull her down beside me, but Mr. Lofton removed a handkerchief from his pocket, placed it on the log, and nudged his wife.

"There you are, my dear. Do sit." He pressed her shoulder with one hand while guiding her downward with the other. With a plop she landed beside me on the makeshift seat. Mr. Lofton settled on the other side of her. "We wanted to extend our deep appreciation to you, Mr. uh . . . Loyco. You don't know how much it means to me, to us, to have our daughter back. It has been a horrible year. My wife has suffered terribly, and Miss Kohler has told us of your unselfish act."

"Who?" Loyco frowned, and Mr. Lofton leaned forward and pointed at me. "Oh, you mean Gretchen. Yes, she is good with the talking. She nags like a wife." He leaned back and guffawed. Mr. Lofton followed suit with an uncomfortable chuckle of his own.

"I am glad we could meet you in person, because I want to give you this." Mr. Lofton withdrew a thick envelope from his jacket and extended it to Loyco.

Loyco didn't move. With a suspicious eye, he fastened his eyes on the packet, but still he didn't reach for it. "What have you brought to me?"

Mr. Lofton's arm sagged, but he continued to offer the envelope. "It is money. The reward we offered for Cecile's return."

Loyco arched back as if Mr. Lofton had fired a shot at him.

"I didn't do this for your money. Because I am Gypsy, you think that's what I want? Your money?" Fire shone in his dark eyes, and he glared at me. "Did you tell them to pay me for finding the girl?"

Mr. Lofton yanked back the envelope. "This isn't because you are a Gypsy. I would give this to anyone who found Cecile. We placed an ad in the newspaper after she was taken and offered this reward. I want you to have it. If you don't want to keep it for yourself, perhaps you could use it for your daughter." He nodded toward the two girls.

Before Loyco could refuse, Alija darted from behind the wagon and grabbed the envelope. "If he won't take it, I will."

Mrs. Lofton clasped her hand to her chest and strained backward. I feared she might roll off the log. "Please don't faint," I whispered. "She won't hurt you. Take a deep breath." Though her complexion had turned a murky gray, she remained upright. Fortunately, Loyco had been busy retrieving the envelope and shouting at Alija while Mrs. Lofton experienced her near-fainting spell. He placed the envelope on the log beside Mr. Lofton.

"I'm glad you came here so you could see that our people are not so different from yours." He looked at me for a moment. "We dress in different clothes, we eat different food, and my skin is a little darker than yours, but we are all just people. I helped you find your daughter. I hope you would do the same for me if someone took my child." He pinned Mrs. Lofton with a steady look. "I know you are afraid of us, but you need to remember that because one or two Gypsies did something bad does not make us all bad."

Mrs. Lofton sucked in a deep breath and forced a smile. "Yes, I understand."

But I could see that Loyco wasn't sure she did understand. He handed the envelope back to Mr. Lofton. "If my Lalah was taken from me, I would want help to find her. If you want to pay me for finding your daughter, do something kind for someone who needs your help. Money is easy, but to give of yourself—that is a real gift." He grinned at Mrs. Lofton. "Maybe one day you will find someone to help—maybe even a Gypsy—and you can return the favor."

Mrs. Lofton's features softened at the suggestion. I hoped his words had made some small impact upon her, but only time would tell.

CHAPTER 32

One Year Later

As the final hours passed before my wedding, I picked up my journal and read through some of the entries. The past year had been one of much excitement and some disappointment. I didn't linger long on the pages about the magazine article or the exchange with Mr. Finley, but I did take great pleasure reading the entries about the fine foals that had been born this summer and the many words of thanks I'd received for supplying the money to pay Mr. Harper.

I read the pages about Loyco and the Gypsies. What an adventure he, Lalah, Zurca, and Alija had provided. And what a wondrous thing he'd done when he'd gone after Cecile. Mrs. Lofton continued to send me letters, along with notes and an occasional drawing from Cecile. I'd saved each one, pleased that the family remembered me with such fondness. We'd spent little time together, yet I felt a strong tie to them and was pleased when Mrs. Lofton wrote to say they planned to attend the wedding celebration.

On a separate page I'd written that the Gypsies had broken camp the day after the Loftons were reunited with Cecile, and that my father and I were able to go before the Bruderrat and tell the elders that a hobo had started the sawmill fire—not the Gypsies—and that Oma was possibly involved. I had written each word in my journal, for I never wanted to forget Zurca's kindness to Oma. How he'd saved her from the river, and how he'd saved her from Mount Pleasant, as well. I only wished Zurca knew that I'd finally done the right thing.

There were many entries about Oma. Though I had prayed for her spells to go away, they hadn't. Nowadays, she seldom knew me, but I was thankful for the occasional days when she was in her right mind. And I was thankful for Mina and her Älterschule. The Grossebruderrat had approved the idea, and the building had been erected and opened two months after the approval. There had been more of a demand than even Mina had anticipated, and she now had four ladies who worked with her during the daytime as well as some young girls who were in training.

Oma still returned home to us at nighttime, but Father had figured how to fix her windows so they could open high enough to let in a breeze, but not far enough that she could crawl out during the night. He'd even placed removable bells above all of the doors. Each morning he would take them down, and each evening he'd place them back on their hooks. His plan had met with success. Even though the clanging bells had jarred me awake on numerous occasions, I was thankful for my father's plan. Not once had Oma been able to wander off during the night.

My father stopped outside my bedroom door. "Writing in your journal?"

I shook my head. "No. I've been reading about all the things that have happened during the last year."

"Ja? And what were you reading just now?" He stepped inside the room and sat down on the side of my bed.

"About Oma and how you fixed the windows and doors to keep her safe."

He smiled and bowed his head. "I should have done it before she got so bad in the head. And I should never have talked about sending her away to Mount Pleasant, either. I promised your mother I'd take care of her. I gave my word, but I was ready to take the easy path."

"But you didn't."

"She is a gut woman who should be with her family. The Älterschule is a gut thing—is much better that she has a place where she can go and be around her old friends and the children at the Kinderschule."

I giggled. "Ja. Sometimes she acts more like a child than the children, but other times she is busy helping them with their knitting and needlework. The mind is a strange thing. One minute it is working fine and the next it is gone." I reached out and grasped my father's hand. "Conrad said that Oma can come and live with us if it is too hard for you to have her here at night."

"Nein. She will stay in this house. This is what she is used to. The change would be hard for her. Besides, she will sit with you at mealtime and at prayer service. If she gets worse and needs you to help her to get dressed, then we will talk again."

I didn't argue, but when that day arrived, we would move her in with us.

"I was looking for you because I have a surprise." Father folded his hands together. "Trudy is old enough to go to Kinderschule in another month, and Sister Veda is willing to come and work at the store. If you would like to go back to working at the Küche, I will ask the Bruderrat if they agree. But first I wanted to talk to you." He chuckled. "I didn't want you to think I was pushing you out."

His offer left me momentarily speechless. Return to the Küche and no longer work in the store. Isn't that what I'd longed for ever since my mother had died? Yet it didn't sound appealing. Maybe because Mina was no longer there, or maybe because I felt closer to my mother's memory here at the store, or maybe because I'd finally accepted that this was the work I enjoyed. "I hope Veda will not be too disappointed, but I don't want to return to the Küche."

His eyes shone with joy, and he tightened his hand around mine. "Ja? You want to stay and work with me?"

I nodded my head. "Ja. Working here at the store is what I want to do."

He leaned forward and kissed my cheek. "I am very happy."

I saw a tear glisten in his eyes, and he quickly stood up and headed for the door. "I must go and get ready for the wedding, and then go to the train station to meet the Loftons." He glanced over his shoulder. "Maybe you should think about getting ready, too."

I donned my best church dress, navy blue with a tiny dotted design, and my mother's black cap with tatted trim that she had worn on her wedding day. Oma wouldn't remember, but she had made the cap for my mother. When I was a little girl, she'd shown it to me and said it would be mine to wear on my wedding day. I could hear the Loftons visiting with my father in the parlor. I gathered my shawl and opened the bedroom door.

Cecile jumped up and started toward me but stopped mid-step. I could see the disappointment in her eyes. I'd written and explained that I wouldn't be wearing a wedding gown, but I don't think she believed me until now. I extended my arms to her. "I would like a hug from my favorite friend from Springfield."

She smiled and embraced me. "Are you really going to wear that dress to your wedding?"

"Ja. I wrote and told you about our custom. Did you not read my letter?"

"Mama read it to me, but I told her I didn't believe it was true. I thought you were going to surprise me."

"I am sorry you're disappointed, Cecile, but no matter what dress I wear, Conrad will still become my husband." I greeted Mr. and Mrs. Lofton and told them they could wait in the parlor or the Küche, whichever they preferred. "I am sorry you cannot attend the ceremony, but I am pleased you'll be able to join us for the meal and the celebration that will follow."

Mrs. Lofton's cheeks turned pink with embarrassment as she apologized for Cecile's outburst. "I truly did explain to her."

I patted the woman's shoulder. "There is no need to worry. She is young, and it is difficult for her to understand. She'll have a grand time at the party."

Conrad arrived, and we walked to the meetinghouse, my hands damp and my heart racing so hard I was certain he could hear it. Oma held my arm while Stefan and Vater followed behind. For the moment Oma was in her right mind, and I was grateful she would see me marry Conrad.

Once we arrived at the meetinghouse, we entered our separate doors, but soon the elder signaled for Conrad and me to come before him. We stood in front of Brother Stresemann for what we knew would be a brief ceremony. He questioned us about our love for each other and asked if we desired to become man and wife. I could see the reflection of love in Conrad's eyes and knew he could see it in mine. After admonishing us always to place God first in our lives and to always seek God's guidance, grace, and mercy, Brother Stresemann declared our lives joined as husband and wife.

We smiled at each other, and Conrad squeezed my hand. Kissing immediately after the marriage ceremony was forbidden, but I knew that the moment we were outside of the meetinghouse, Conrad and I would enjoy our first kiss as husband and wife. Together we walked to the rear of the meetinghouse, where we received hushed congratulations and good wishes.

After we departed the church, we slowly walked to the Küche, where our celebration would be held. "It is gut to have you as my wife." Conrad leaned down and placed a light kiss on my cheek. "That will have to do until we can find a moment alone."

I bit back a grin. "I trust you will do your best to find that time as soon as possible."

He squeezed my hand. "For sure I will do that."

Friends and neighbors from all of the villages had already arrived for the celebration. Mina and some of the other women had decorated the dining room of the Küche with vases of autumn blooms and potted plants they'd brought from home. Cakes of every shape and size had been baked in the village kitchens and delivered for the party. Pitchers filled with grape and cherry juice were ready to serve to the children, and a barrel of grape wine had been brought up from the cellar for the adults.

Once we'd had a slice of cake and a glass of wine, Conrad took my hand and escorted me outside. In the shade of the kitchen house, he kissed me with unyielding passion. "Welcome to your new life, my dear wife. I promise to love and cherish you forever, and I promise to do my best to make you as happy as you have made me this day."

I smiled up at him, enjoying the feel of his arms circling my waist. Nestling my head on his shoulder, I knew that even with pen and paper, I couldn't possibly express the joy that filled my heart. "You have already made me happy, Conrad. I know the vows you have made this day are more than words. Your promises are a joyful reflection of the man God chose for me. For that, I am truly grateful."

SPECIAL THANKS TO . . .

. . . My editor, Sharon Asmus, for her generous spirit, excellent eye for detail, and amazing ability to keep her eyes upon Jesus through all of life's adversities.

. . . My acquisitions editor, Charlene Patterson, for her enthusiastic encouragement to move forward with this series.

. . . The entire staff of Bethany House Publishers, for their devotion to making each book they publish the best product possible. It is a privilege to work with all of you.

. . . Brandi Jones, Amana Heritage Society, for tirelessly answering my many questions, for private tours, and for reading my manuscript for technical accuracy.

. . . Lanny Haldy, Amana Heritage Society, for meeting with me and taking precious hours away from other tasks to provide information, answer questions, and make recommendations.

. . . Mary Greb-Hall for her ongoing encouragement, expertise, and sharp eye.

. . . Lori Seilstad for her honest critiques.

. . . Mary Kay Woodford, my sister, my prayer warrior, my friend.

. . . Tracie Peterson, friend extraordinaire.

. . . Laurie Toth for providing excellent Chicago materials.

. . . My husband, Jim, my constant encourager, supporter, and advocate, and the love of my life.

. . . Above all, thanks and praise to our Lord Jesus Christ for this miraculous opportunity to live my dream and share the wonder of His love through story.